NO DOUBT

BARBARA SEITH

To My Sister Cindy-
Thanks for all your support
and love!
Best,
Barbara

NO DOUBT

Published by
Barbara Seith Unlimited Inc.
www.BarbaraSeith.com/no-doubt
NoDoubtNovel@gmail.com
Facebook.com/BarbaraSeithAuthor

ISBN (print): 978-1-7379615-0-5
ISBN (ebook): 978-1-7379615-1-2

Book design by Domini Dragoone, www.dominidragoone.com
Cover images: Peshkov (euro) from iStock.com; Pogonici (maze), Silvanoaudis (press), Lekcej (woman), and Lodimup (boat) from 123rf.com

TO MY MOTHER,
WHO I AM BECOMING

JUNE 2002

Mallory stared at the sparkling blue waters of the Straits. They were deceivingly beautiful, as was the nickname of the landmass to the east: The Sunshine Coast. Compared to Vancouver, where it rained eighty percent of the time, the coast was sunny, but not compared to any normal place. Today, however, was an exception: The sky was cloudless and the killer whales that typically haunted the Straits were strangely absent. Gazing at the hamlet of Roberts Creek, just off the bow, Mallory knew this was where she belonged.

She inhaled deeply. The air—clean, unsullied, like the aftershave her father had worn—was fresh, sweet, and only vaguely salty, not like some seaside towns where the fishy smell was overpowering. When Mallory washed her face at night, the washcloth was rarely soiled as it was in the city. Just being here she felt cleansed. She had arrived in the frigid air of January; now, in the height of the summer, she thought this was the most beautiful place on earth and all she needed. She had loved the water ever since she was seven, when her father had taught her to sail, but since her parents' accident two years ago, Mallory's life had been turbulent. Finally, with the wind in her hair, the sun on her face, and Todd piloting her thirty-foot sailboat in the sheltered waters off the British Columbia coast, Mallory felt at peace. Well, peace perhaps was overstating it. Real peace was out of the question. She would always be looking over her shoulder. This would have to do.

Her husband, however, was the picture of real peace. Todd really seemed to enjoy sailing, and Mallory was impressed that he captained the boat as if he had been doing it for years. These waters could be treacherous, but in the last few months, Todd had mastered them. It helped that his teacher, Mallory's grandfather, was an old salt and delighted to have him as a student. Just a week prior, the old man had proclaimed Todd fit to sail on his own. Mallory was the only crew on Todd's maiden voyage as captain.

Looking over at Todd, as *The Barbecue* cut through the glassy water of the sound, Mallory thought: *This is the best it will ever be.*

"Sweetie," Mallory called above the wind, "we need to rename the boat." She focused the Minolta on his face and snapped a photo.

"Why?" Todd asked. "It's a great name. Prepare to come about."

Mallory jumped up and loosened the lines on the mainsail and stood waiting for the boat to come about. Then she realized that she hadn't waited for Todd's instruction, and he had probably figured out by now that Mallory knew more about working a sailboat than she had been letting on. If he had noticed, he didn't comment. But Mallory was fairly sure he had. Todd was observant. Over the year they had been together, Mallory had slowly begun opening up to him. There was much to tell, and not all of it was good. Mallory hoped she would never have to tell him everything. She knew her husband loved her, but she wasn't sure he could bear the whole truth.

"Honey," she said as she snuggled next to him in the stern of the boat. "Really, come on, *The Barbecue*?"

"The name has a story."

She raised an eyebrow.

"A classic Canadian story," Todd said. "Barbecues are very important to us. When we set up a new home, we buy a barbecue before we buy plates."

"I thought that was just you."

"I'm serious. When Rusty moved here, he bought the boat right away. His wife was mad because they had to wait to buy a barbecue. To calm her down he named the boat *The Barbecue* so she could tell people they had one." Todd laughed. "Can't change the name; it's perfect." He scoffed. "You don't understand. You're from the States."

A wave of seasickness made Mallory dive for the side of the boat. When she finally raised her head again, they were almost to shore. She had been trying to wean herself from the seasickness patches she normally wore because of their potential side effects. Mallory could not afford to be hallucinating. She needed her wits about her at all times.

When Todd slipped *The Barbecue* into port, Mallory vaulted to the dock and headed straight for their house and the bathroom. As she splashed cold water on her face, the strawberry blond waves of her hair brushing her cheeks, Mallory cursed herself for not having brought saltine crackers along on their sail. She turned to the full-length mirror and examined her image. She looked paler than usual, maybe a little on the thin side, and she wondered if it was stress. Were her breasts smaller? She pushed out her chest and decided they were not. That would have made her happy; Mallory would love to be able to run without an industrial strength bra.

When she emerged from the bathroom, Todd had a cup of tea waiting in the kitchen. As she sipped, he gently rubbed her shoulders. "Today was pretty calm. Next time you should probably take something, or was it the barbecue talk? Or maybe ... morning sickness?" He could barely contain his excitement.

"Don't think so, babe, I just ran out of patches."

"One can hope!" Todd grinned, and, leaving Mallory with her tea, he practically skipped down to the dock to tie down the sails and clean up the boat. He was talking a lot these days about having a family. Mallory hadn't made any commitments, although she was hiding her birth control pills in the back of the silverware drawer. She wanted a family, too. One day. But only when she knew they were safe.

Feeling a little better, she headed out to work on her gardens. Mallory adored the sound of that: her gardens. It sounded as though she had acres and acres of grounds. In fact, their small two-bedroom cottage was on just one acre of land, most of which was seacoast or woods, but the flowerbeds, which Mallory had painstakingly created in the last few months, surrounded the house.

As she approached the shed Todd had built for her, Mallory noticed the door was ajar. They didn't keep the shed locked, but Mallory was always careful to shut the door and latch it tightly. She was concerned about animals getting in and eating something they shouldn't. She edged the door open and scanned the small space. All the equipment appeared to be there. She examined the dirt floor and discovered footprints that were too large to be hers and too small to be her husband's. She stood up and decided that the intruder had been pacing back and forth in the small space.

She methodically scanned the rest of the shed, and a bit of white in the dirt caught her eye. She bent down and dug out a cigarette butt. There was no brand name printed on it because the cigarette was hand-rolled. The tobacco smelled sweet, and Mallory grimaced. She knew this smell. Her heartbeat quickened as she looked out of the shed, searching the grass for any signs of where the intruder might have gone. She paced the dirt driveway, but there were too many footprints to be of use. She headed for the front gardens. Muttering as she walked, trying to convince herself she was overreacting, Mallory knelt down, in the front bed, moving the vegetation out of the way and, as she had feared, found another large footprint. Whoever put it there had been careful not to crush the flowers.

In the middle of the footprint was a mirror image of the word "Bexley." Mallory knew the French boots well, and the sight of the brand sent a chill up her spine. She also knew the chances that anyone in Roberts Creek owned a pair of Bexleys were very slim. She pawed through the rest of the garden until she found a companion print. She stood and planted her feet in the boot prints and found herself staring into her living room window.

Swearing softly under her breath, Mallory walked to the back of the house to check the telephone connection, examining it for a tap. She found none. As she went into the kitchen, her pulse was racing as though she had just finished her morning run. "Okay, relax," she told herself. She sat down at the table and got right back up again, grabbing the binoculars they kept by the kitchen window. She followed the phone wires down to the dirt road. If there was a tap, it was well concealed. Even so, Mallory was taking no chances. If he had been here, if he was that close, he could have bugged the house. Mallory had to assume he was listening.

She walked next door. It always calmed her to talk to her grandfather, and with her parents gone, she counted on Rusty more and more for love and support.

She found him around back grilling lunch, his mop of white hair blowing in the wind. He was humming in a deep baritone and swaying as if he were dancing. Mallory's grandfather was in his seventies, but was spry, and he had a wicked sense of humor.

Rusty greeted her with a hug. "What a nice surprise! I saw you guys out sailing this morning. Join me for lunch?"

"Not hungry," Mallory said, "thanks. We have a problem. Can you find out if anyone has seen a stranger around town recently?"

"Uh oh. We might have to implement the plan, eh?"

"I hope not, but maybe." Mallory paced the grassy area.

"Easy there, I just got this grass to grow. Told Todd yet?"

Mallory stopped. "Not yet. Can't. Don't know how," she said. "But soon, I may have no choice."

— € —

That night Mallory watched Todd sleep, smiling at his tranquility. Often she would force herself to stay awake longer than he did so that his face would be her last sight before she fell asleep. She cherished this bit of vicarious peace, because she could not find it herself. At this moment Todd looked content, happy. Mallory prayed every night, to whom she wasn't quite sure, that he was dreaming of her. Tonight she was not at all sleepy and in no rush to close her eyes. She tried to forget the afternoon's anxiety. She burrowed into the hollow of her husband's warm neck and kissed him softly. Todd wrapped his long arms around her.

When she heard a small noise downstairs, Mallory shot straight up in bed. She listened for a moment. Nothing but silence. She had almost convinced herself that it was nothing when she heard it again. She swung her bare legs over the bed and grabbed her favorite worn cotton robe. Tightening the belt around her waist, she padded toward the doorway as the soft fabric brushed her legs. Careful to avoid the squeaky spots on the floorboards, which she had memorized the day she moved in, Mallory peeked furtively around the landing of the stairs. A thin flashlight beam was dancing around the living room. Mallory pulled back against the wall with a jerk and felt her pulse quicken. Her first instinct was to call for Todd, but she stopped herself. She had to do this alone. When she peered around the banister again, the flashlight beam was pointed directly at a photograph of Mallory on top of the television. Her mind raced with disturbing possibilities. The light went off. She looked toward the source, and what she saw confirmed the worst.

It had been over a year since Mallory had last seen him, and her plan had been never to see him again. But now he had found her, and someone, she knew, was going to die. The only question was who.

CHAPTER 1

DECEMBER 1998

Snow swirled around the quad, and Mallory wrapped her scarf yet again to cover her face. She trudged through the frigid Syracuse wind to her Computer Security class. This wasn't the worst campus weather Mallory had trudged through, but it was close. She loved cold weather, but even for her this was a little much. Today was a five-layer day, with two pairs of socks inside her Gortex boots.

Mallory had chosen Syracuse University not only for its academic reputation, but because the town had a real winter. Growing up in Fort Lee, New Jersey, there had been snowstorms, but they were rare, and the snow almost always seemed to be gone the next day. Snow days were some of Mallory's favorite childhood memories: her small family hunkered down in front of a roaring fire with sugary mugs of coffee and a 1,000-piece jigsaw puzzle. Mallory had loved looking at the snow outside and having an excuse to stay inside. She had also underestimated the challenge of walking to classes in it.

She opened the door to Hendricks Chapel, grateful to be out of the wind for a moment, and headed down to the basement café for her first morning coffee. Despite the storm, Mallory knew Pete would be there. The campus café manager was proud of the fact that his coffee place was never closed due to weather. The bakery items might not get delivered, but there was always coffee.

"Hey, Mallory," the café manager said, reaching for Mallory's regular extra-large coffee cup. "I see you made it."

"Hey, Pete. We're tough, you and me, huh?"

The manager grinned. "That we are." He handed Mallory her coffee and waved away her money. "On a morning like this, if you make it to me, your coffee is free. Stay warm out there!"

"Thanks, Pete. See you tomorrow."

Mallory was grateful for the coffee as her class was early, and she needed the wake-up. It also warmed her hands for the next leg of the journey. She arrived in the lecture hall ten minutes later. The room held 500 people, but there were only three other students present.

Mallory's Computer Security professor was known as a renegade at the university. His work was controversial and his class assignments always pushed the envelope. This was one of Mallory's favorite classes, and she didn't want to miss it. Clearly her fellow students didn't feel the same.

Mallory settled herself in a seat in the middle of the room and shrugged out of her winter gear. She shook out her thick red curls and ran her fingers through the locks to mitigate her hat head. Her light blue eyes shifted to the young teaching assistant as he hurried into the room. "Attention, attention," the TA called out, as though the room was filled to capacity. And then he paused. "Where is everybody?"

"Been outside?" Mallory asked.

"Right, right," he said, "that's what my announcement is about. Dr. Warnock is unable to get to class today. The roads aren't plowed where he lives. He called and asked me to give those students who showed up for class this morning a head start on your final semester project."

Mallory smiled. She didn't need a head start, but she loved Dr. Warnock's assignments. They were always challenging and, well, fun.

"For your final project," the TA said, "you will attempt to hack into the U.S. government Web site of your choice."

Mallory's ears perked up. Now *this* was interesting.

"You are to keep a diary of the process and spend at least ten hours on the project. Select a single government site and log all the roadblocks and firewalls you encounter in the diary. Indicate how you tried to surmount them and your success level. It's due by end of term."

Mallory's mind was clicking away. Along with jigsaw and crossword puzzles, she loved computer hacking; it was the ultimate puzzle. The TA left the room and Mallory stood, re-layering for the weather. She couldn't wait to get started.

On her way to the computer lab, Mallory stopped back at the chapel café and picked up two more cups of coffee and an everything bagel. This time Pete let her pay, and on her way out, Mallory tossed a generous tip into the empty jar. She headed up the basement steps and braced herself for another trek across the snowy quad. If she'd had the laptop she'd put on her Christmas list, she could go back to her dorm room and work, but Christmas was still a few weeks away.

The computer lab was not Mallory's favorite place. She loved the computing power, but it was a fairly small, windowless room, and Mallory wasn't fond of confined spaces. She hadn't figured out the root of that issue, but that didn't make it any less real. When she was in the lab, Mallory tried to focus on the computer screen and not let her eyes wander. The coffee, bagel, and her beloved *New York Times* crossword puzzle provided additional distraction from the feeling that the walls were closing in on her. An empty lab was even more uncomfortable, but at least she had plenty of privacy.

Mallory forced herself to focus on the task at hand; she found a list of government Web sites and selected the first one on the list, the United States Department of Commerce. Mallory loved to hack, but she rarely hacked into Web sites, because it was illegal. She never hacked destructively, just instructively; even so, most of the time the specter of getting caught quelled her enthusiasm for the activity. But now she had permission. This was a class assignment. It was officially sanctioned hacking.

Mallory set a timer on the computer and got to work. First up: getting through the firewall, or the backdoor of the Web site. There's a backdoor in the DMZ of every Web site. The DMZ, or demilitarized zone, is the industry's nickname for the portion of a Web site that is available to the public. Usually there's a key that opens the door to the insides of the site, including access to email and source code. Once through that door, Mallory had unfettered access to the inner workings of the Web site, including the ability to change its content and how it functions. She could also send emails that looked as if they had come from the site's true owners/managers. Finding the DMZ was the hard part.

Mallory located the hacking routines that she had created to search for the backdoor that all Web designers left just slightly ajar. She had over one hundred routines and started one that searched for any obvious entry points. Then she sat back and picked up *The New York Times*. As usual, Mallory forced herself to scan the front page of each section before she flipped to the crossword puzzle. She felt it was important to know what was going on outside of her own little college world. In the business section, Mallory found a full-page feature on the impending establishment of the euro, the new currency that would replace the franc, the mark, the lira, and many other European currencies. She scanned the article—electronic currency to be initiated this month, actual currency in January 2001—and finally found what she was looking for: The printing facilities for the euro were being set up at secret locations in eleven countries, including France. Mallory set the paper down and sighed. It was the biggest currency project ever, and since the initial announcement, it had been Mallory's dream to be a part of this historic project. Hacking and puzzles were fun, but printing was Mallory's true love. Her major was printing, and she would graduate just as the Euro Project was kicking into high gear. Mallory was fluent in French, her minor, and she thought she would be a perfect job candidate or at least a shoe-in for an internship at one of the French printing facilities.

Her first hacking routine had finished running, and Mallory forced herself to focus once again on her class project. She popped the top on her first cup of coffee and breathed in the rich aroma. She tore a piece from the bagel and popped it into her mouth. Mallory loved Java programming. The language was beautiful, flexible, and succinct. Most programming languages were stagnant and stilted, but Java had concepts with names like threads, semaphores, and rendezvous. It was literate, sensible, and a pleasure to work with. If Mallory were planning to be a programmer she would have used Java. But hacking was a pastime. Mallory was going to be a printer, maybe even revolutionize the industry one day; printing was in her blood. Her mother was one of the country's foremost printing experts and responsible for creating the ink currently used for printing U.S. dollars. Mallory dreamed about carrying on that torch, and the Euro Project seemed to be just the ticket.

The first routine had finished searching at the ten-minute mark. No dice. Mallory tossed the business section on the desk and flipped through the rest of the paper, found what she wanted, and expertly folded the page to compactly display the puzzle. She uncapped her pen and reset the computer timer. She and her second search routine would race.

Mallory finished the puzzle in eight minutes.

It was Tuesday, hardly even a challenge.

The second search routine started beeping four minutes later. She was in! The backdoor had been located in the Frequently Asked Questions or FAQ section of the site. Mallory smiled. Twenty-two minutes to find the backdoor. If all aspects of the hacking project went this quickly, her project diary would be very thin. Mallory paused to log her activity in a word-processing document, and then she sat back and sipped her coffee and finished her bagel as she ran a new routine that monitored activity on the way into the channel, searching for a pattern that would hand her the key to the Web site's inner sanctum. Six minutes later Mallory typed in the key code returned by the routine and was granted access to the U.S. Department of Commerce.

Twenty-eight minutes flat.

The site was encrypted, which would normally stop an amateur hacker, but not Mallory. She leaned back in her chair, wiggled her fingers, cracked her knuckles, and then sat back up and started typing again. Less than an hour later Mallory had gained access into the site's email system and had sent herself an email from William M. Daley, the U.S. Secretary of Commerce.

That was it.

Project complete.

Mallory sighed.

It was almost too easy.

She finished her diary, opened the second cup of coffee and glanced back down at the business section of the *Times.* The Euro Project printing locations were a secret, according to the article. Mallory grinned.

She was always up for a good puzzle.

She pulled up the Bank of France Web site and started up her routines. The tiny computer lab bay wasn't bothering her in the least right now. Caught up in the hunt, she was in a wide-open space in her head. Her second cup of coffee turned tepid.

While the routines chugged on, Mallory opened another window on the computer and pulled up what she referred to as her "stories"—email accounts that she had hacked into for fun and had kept track of because they had intriguing conversational threads. Mallory had harvested her "stories" over the past few years; she followed ten or so email accounts at a time. At one point, she had been "eavesdropping" on fifteen different email accounts, but that got to be too much like work. These days, when Mallory ran across a new storyline she found interesting, she dropped one or two old accounts. Yes, it was illegal, but the hacking was also virtually undetectable. Mallory didn't know these people, and their lives were far more entertaining than television—with a lot more variety. She wasn't going to harm them, so what harm was there in a little eavesdropping?

Mallory liked—no, loved—listening in on these emailers' secret conversations because she didn't have any of her own. These were not *National Enquirer*–type secrets, but intimate secrets that no one else knew. They were her secrets, her stories. Mallory knew she shouldn't live vicariously through these people; that she should live her own life. But "shoulds" made Mallory uncomfortable. She was content with her life. Why shouldn't she do things that made her happy, like puzzles and printing and a little personal hacking now and then? She liked to listen, watch, and learn. Maybe someday she would know enough to participate more, but for now she'd stick to her "stories," where she couldn't get hurt.

Mallory's current favorite eavesdropping opportunity was the email account of a married woman who had three affairs going on at once, including one with another woman. Mallory assumed the email address name "Pandora" was a nod to the mythical character who had released The Fates from a box and anarchy had ensued. Pandora was also Mallory's longest running "story." It was the first one she had found in her tour through Yahoo's voluminous email database three years ago, after hacking into the Internet giant's site. Other stories came and went depending on the drama level, but Pandora had endured. "Let me see what you are up to today," Mallory said, clicking on the first email.

To: Dora [Pandora@yahoo.com]
From: Husband [RobertPayne@yahoo.com]
Sent: Tuesday, December 1, 1998 8:20am
Subject: Trip Extension

Looks like I'm going to have to be in Vegas for two more days. Sorry about that. Need airport pick-up.

To: Husband [RobertPayne@yahoo.com]
From: Dora [Pandora@yahoo.com]
Sent: Tuesday, December 1, 1998 8:30am
Subject: Airport Pick-up

Can't ... take a black car.

She is so mean to him, thought Mallory. *Why does he stay with her?* He had even caught her with a lover once when he'd come home early from a business trip. But he was long-suffering. Or was he? Wait, was that what was happening here? Had Husband finally woken up and smelled the coffee? Was he trying to set a trap for Pandora?

To: Dora [Pandora@yahoo.com]
From: Sam Salant [SammyStud@yahoo.com]
Sent: Tuesday, December 1, 1998 8:45am
Subject: Tomorrow

We still on? I'm holding out for you.

To: Sam Salant [SammyStud@yahoo.com]
From: Dora [Pandora@yahoo.com]
Sent: Tuesday, December 1, 1998 8:30am
Subject: Tomorrow

Of course we are on for tomorrow and you had better perform.

Mallory winced. *Sammy's getting too needy, but good Lord, Dora's a bitch.* Mallory worried about Sammy; he was so young and Dora had a history of bedding and shedding the young ones. He was going to get stomped. The only affair that had lasted since Mallory had started following Pandora was the one with the woman.

To: Josie [JosiePussycat@yahoo.com]
From: Dora [Pandora@yahoo.com]
Sent: Tuesday, December 1, 1998 9:00am
Subject: Lunch

Husband gone for two more days, I'll be here waiting.

Mallory could predict the future: The Husband would arrive and interrupt or perhaps join the two women during their lunch-time liaison. She read on.

To: Dora [Pandora@yahoo.com]
From: Sam Salant [SammyStud@yahoo.com]
Sent: Tuesday, December 1, 1998 9:45am
Subject: Today

Not sure I can wait—maybe we should move it up.

To: Sam Salant [SammyStud@yahoo.com]
From: Dora [Pandora@yahoo.com]
Sent: Tuesday, December 1, 1998 10:05am
Subject: Today

Nice try–The usual, tomorrow. You'll need a B12 shot.

Yup, Mallory thought, *he's toast after tomorrow. She must have someone else in her sights.*

To: Frenchman [OlivierDeChance@yahoo.com]
From: Dora [Pandora@yahoo.com]
Sent: Tuesday, December 1, 1998 10:15am
Subject: Ce soir

Toi, moi, ce soir? 7pm

The Frenchman was Pandora's current favorite. Must be the accent, Mallory thought, because she wasn't picking up all that much excitement from their emails. After years of following her, some things about Dora were still a mystery to Mallory.

The Bank of France routines started beeping. She was in! Mallory said adieu to Pandora and starting searching for the location of their euro printing facilities. This was a manual process and Mallory had to be careful not to trip any alarms. It took her an hour to find out that the main facility was in Chamalières, with storage warehouses in three nearby towns. Mallory grinned and ran her fingers through her hair. She now had information that almost no one else in the world had access to. It made her feel powerful and important.

It was magic.

A siren suddenly sounded on the computer, blaring, and Mallory snapped out of her reverie.

A small red box was flashing ALERT in bold white letters.

Crap, crap, crap, crap, crap.

Mallory grabbed the mouse and frantically started clicking on the red box.

CHAPTER 2

DECEMBER 1998

Mallory's hand was shaking so badly that it took her five clicks to activate the ALERT button she had set up. The final click disconnected all her sessions and she was safe. She took a deep breath as the screen filled with text. *Calm down,* she thought. *Calm down.* She scanned the text until she found the source of the problem. She had been tracked and found by a trace from the Bank of France. The tracer had acquired her IP address. Crap, they would know the hack originated at this university, worse yet, in this room. Mallory's heart raced. She had been busted big-time. *Oh my God. What am I going to do? I could be arrested.* She felt like she was going to faint. *No, no, no, I can't panic; that will make it worse.* She closed her eyes and tried to erase the fear, using her meditation routine. Well, it was more like a meditative attempt. Mallory managed to sit quietly for ten minutes once a week or so. Lately it had been less "once a week" and more "or so," which was probably why it wasn't working now. Mallory silently cursed her lack of discipline and that was enough distraction to focus her brain. She continued to sit with her eyes closed and strip away the panicked thoughts, one by one. She needed to focus on a solution.

What was it the TA had said? A U.S. government Web site. The Bank of France was a quasi-government agency. Maybe she could just have conveniently forgotten about the U.S. part. Maybe she could explain this hacking disaster as innocent final project work, but if that was going to work, she would need to redo her project notes and email Dr. Warnock as soon as possible.

Mallory tried to remember what she had done to hack into the Bank of France site. She went through the site firewall, PGP (Pretty Good Privacy), circuit-level gateway firewall and encryption. She figured ten minutes to get through the firewall, twenty minutes for the PGP, thirty minutes for the circuit firewall, and twenty-five for the encryption. Then she had spent an hour searching for the French printing facilities. She fully documented and saved the saga of her Bank of France infiltration and attached it to an email to Dr. Warnock.

In the email, Mallory explained that she had been working on her final assignment and had been discovered by the bank when she'd entered a secure area. Of course, Mallory knew the bank had discovered her, but she couldn't tell Dr. Warnock that. She needed to look innocent. She proofread the email twice, hit send, and then she called up the trace report from her Alert program. If she had closed out the hack after she'd found the euro warehouse facilities, the bank could not have traced her. But Mallory had lingered and that had been her downfall. *Lesson learned,* Mallory thought. And then she winced. She wasn't looking forward to being called on the carpet by Dr. Warnock. Still, she wasn't sorry she had hacked the Bank of France. She had dreamed of being in that printing facility in Chamalières, making currency printing history, following in her mother's footsteps. Now she worried that her hopes of one day going to work for Bank of France would be dashed. *Hacking is bad for me. I gotta stop.* Mallory nodded in agreement with herself, and logged off the computer.

— € —

The walk back to her dorm took no more than twenty minutes, but when Mallory arrived there was already a phone message on her door, summoning her to Dr. Warnock's office at nine the next morning. She felt her heartbeat accelerate again as she unlocked the door and ran through the bank hack once more in her mind. Convincing Warnock that the TA had just said "a government Web site" and not "a U.S. government Web site," would be tricky. Mallory decided that she would meditate and really focus both tonight and tomorrow morning. She needed to lie convincingly at 9 a.m., and being calm was critical.

— € —

The next morning, Mallory stood in front of Dr. Warnock's office door. Although she had meditated just before leaving her dorm, she took another deep, cleansing breath before she knocked.

"Yup," boomed a voice from the other side of the door.

Mallory cracked the door open and peered inside.

"Ms. Richards," Dr. Warnock said. "Please come in. Have a seat."

Mallory calmly—or what she hoped appeared calm—took a seat in a chair across from her professor.

Dr. Warnock looked at her for an uncomfortably long time and her heartbeat accelerated with each lingering second. Mallory tried to interpret the expression. Was it admiration? Well, that was optimistic. Still, the look was not one of a professor about to reprimand a student. Finally, he let out a long, deep sigh.

"You are one of my most talented students, Ms. Richards," he said. "No doubt."

Mallory's heartbeat began to regulate itself.

"You got in, but—and this is a BIG but—you didn't get out."

Mallory looked at her professor for a minute, trying to determine where he was going with this conversation.

Dr. Warnock raised an eyebrow. "Surely, I've taught you better than that."

Mallory blushed. "I was distracted."

"Multitasking is the scourge of the best hackers," he said. "You must be constantly vigilant."

Mallory nodded obediently.

"I've contacted the Bank of France and reported that you were working on a class project. They were grateful that I reported it immediately and, for now, you're off the hook."

"They know it was me?" Mallory gasped.

"No, I told them it was a student who got a little overzealous. Your identity is safe." Mallory slumped in her chair as a wave of relief spread through her.

"Letting me know right away was the right thing to do," Dr. Warnock said. "Tell me, Ms. Richards, how was it you knew that the bank had traced you?"

Mallory hadn't anticipated this question and she wasn't sure she wanted to answer.

"This is serious business, Ms. Richards," Dr. Warnock said. "It doesn't serve you not to be forthcoming with me."

Mallory was still trying to figure out what to say.

"Dr. Warnock—" she started.

"Call me John."

"Um, John." *That felt weird. Why was he being so casual?*

"May I call you Mallory?"

She nodded. "Will this affect my grade?"

"Fortunately, Mallory, you emailed me and I was able to talk to the Bank of France before they contacted the university concerning your infiltration of their Web site. If that had happened I suspect your grade would be the least of your worries. The university tends to prosecute students who use their equipment to hack."

"But it was a project—"

"You weren't supposed to get caught."

"You weren't supposed to give us an illegal assignment."

"Touchè. As I said, you are very talented. Are you planning a career in technology?"

"No," Mallory said, "I'm going to be a printer."

Dr. Warnock frowned. "Kind of an esoteric profession. In a few years, no one will be printing anything."

"Not in my lifetime," Mallory said, before she realized how impertinent that sounded.

He laughed. "Charming, just charming."

Suddenly uncomfortable, Mallory asked to be excused, mumbling something about being late for her next class, which was, in fact, the truth.

"You can go, but we'll be discussing this again," Dr. Warnock said.

— € —

Mallory's next class was printing, which she loved, but had recently become the bane of her existence. She donned her apron and started unpacking supplies from her locker. She was developing a new ink for printing money. The ingredients included dry pigments in a spectrum of colors, oil for mixing to liquefy, and extenders to thicken the mixture and preserve the color. New standards for currency ink called for the ink to be unusually thick and reactive with the paper, making it harder to counterfeit. This ink project was Mallory's Holy Grail and she had been working on it for two years. She'd had some successes, but they had been fleeting. Mallory knew in her gut it was possible to create this ink, however, and so she had kept at it.

There were only four other students in the printing class; they'd been together for the past two years, and their professor, Dr. Louise Cartman, hadn't been able to bring herself to cancel the class due to insufficient enrollment. Mallory had lobbied hardest to keep the class on the roster, and Lou, as Dr. Cartman liked to be called, had agreed with one provision: If the ink project didn't come to fruition this semester, Mallory would give up.

Mallory had given her promise, but she'd never intended to keep it.

Today, Mallory was putting mica in the ink. Mica had unique reflective qualities and Mallory thought it was worth a shot. She stirred the mica fragments into the green ink, reserving some to sprinkle on the paper at the end, and then she rolled the ink onto the printing plate and let it sit for a minute before spreading the paper over the plate and using a roller to press the paper firmly down onto the plate. She flipped the paper/plate combination over and removed the plate with one quick movement, then rubbed turpentine on the plate to clean it while waiting for the ink to dry. As she walked around the print, Mallory thought she saw a slight change in color, or at least in value.

Maybe it was just wishful seeing.

But she wasn't giving up.

For round two, Mallory immersed the mica in oil and spread it onto the paper. While the ink was drying, Lou stopped by her table. Mallory's instructor picked up the previous print and examined it while rolling it back and forth.

"There's something." Lou squinted and moved the print again. "You're making progress. Remember our deal, though. You've almost run out of time on this project, Mallory. If you don't find what you're looking for this semester, that's it for the printing class. I'm sorry."

Mallory nodded, and her instructor moved on. She was running out of time. She picked up her print and rolled it back and forth. Again, she saw something, but it wasn't a different color. She looked at the clock, closed her eyes, and shook her head.

— € —

A week later, on the final day of the semester, Dr. Warnock summoned Mallory to his office again. "Dr. Warnock?" Mallory said, pushing open the slightly ajar door.

"John," he said. "Come in, Mallory. Please, have a seat." He waited for Mallory to seat herself across from him, and then said, "I know you're anxious to get home for the holidays, so I'll get right to the point. I've been talking to the Bank of France about helping them close the loophole in their security. The one you so blithely slipped through a few weeks ago. And you, my dear, are the key to success in this new assignment."

Mallory cocked her head. "Me?"

"I have your project diary, but I need your programs. Your routines. I need to know how you discovered that you had been traced and tracked."

Mallory swallowed. "No consequences?" She asked.

Her professor smiled. "Perhaps, one. I'm planning to write a case study of this work and you could—you should—be its coauthor."

Mallory thought about this for a moment, then said, "I'll need a laptop; no more computer lab for me."

He nodded.

Mallory continued: "I wrote a program that sends me an alert when I'm being traced. I usually get enough warning that I'm able to get out of the site before the trace finishes." Her fatal mistake was that she had lingered. But she wasn't going to admit this. Well, not WHY she had lingered.

"How much time does the program give you?" Dr. Warnock asked.

"It depends on the trace; they seem to be finding me faster."

"Can you find a way to give yourself more time?"

Mallory thought for a moment and said, "I haven't really considered that, since time hasn't been an issue ... until now."

"Think about it."

"Even if I can, I'd need to test it. And I don't think I have the stomach for hacking anymore."

"Tell you what, you develop the program and we'll test it together, using my network, outside the university. It's routed through thirteen different servers. I don't think there is a chance they could find us."

"Or you could make it part of the deal with the bank."

Dr. Warnock looked at Mallory like a proud papa. "My dear, that is genius. Test the new program against the party who was able to trace the old one. Thank you, I'll do just that. I can start right after Christmas, if you can. We would have three weeks before the spring semester begins."

"Dr. Warnock ... "

"John," he said.

Mallory nodded. "This needs to wait until next semester. I haven't seen my parents since September. I need to spend the break with them."

Her professor nodded. "No problem. Merry Christmas, Mallory."

CHAPTER 3
DECEMBER 1998

On the bus trip home, Mallory took stock of her life. After two years she still hadn't found the key to her ink and she wasn't sure she would get another chance. She HAD found the key to the Bank of France Web site and was now going to be forced to work with Warnock on a hacking project next semester, and she already had no social life. She hadn't had a date since her French teaching assistant had broken up with her last spring. She had realized not long after she and Tom had started dating that they had little in common other than sex and French, and toward the end Mallory had found him mildly annoying. She knew she was not one to connect easily; she was selective about her friendships, so much so that she had no one she really considered a true friend at school right now. Since the breakup, she had declined the date opportunities that had come her way. If she didn't feel a spark at first meeting, she didn't think it was worth the effort.

Mallory sighed.

It would be nice to be home.

– € –

Her mom and dad were there to greet her. Dad gave her a bear hug and mom held out a cup of steaming coffee. Mallory took off her coat, grabbed the coffee and they headed into the living room where a nine-foot tree stood gloriously decorated and twinkling.

Mallory could see the ornaments she had made as a child peppering the tree. Most of Christmas was homemade at Mallory's house, including the gifts; it was one of the things Mallory loved most about the holiday. This year she had decided to bake for her parents: lemon shortbread for her father, and blueberry mistake cake for her mother. The mistake cake recipe had started with Mallory's grandmother. The first time Mallory's mom had made it, she had forgotten to put flour in the streusel topping, and it had been so good that she had made it that way from then on. When Mallory first tried her hand at the cake, they had been out of baking powder, so she'd substituted baking soda and a little lemon juice, and the cake had been even better—each generational mistake made the recipe a little bit better.

— € —

Mallory woke early on Christmas morning. The shortbread for her father had been boxed and wrapped, and she had just put the mistake cake in the oven—they would have it for Christmas breakfast—when her dad came into the kitchen, lured by the rich aroma of coffee.

"Is that cinnamon?" He sniffed.

"Both the cake and the coffee," Mallory said as she poured him a cup.

"Mmmm." He poured a cup of coffee and sat down at the table with his daughter. "Lory, are you happy at school?"

"I like school," she said.

"But are you happy?"

"I'm not unhappy," she said.

"I want you to be happy."

"I'd like that too. I'm not sure what that would take."

"Willing to try something?"

"You mean like blind dates?"

Her father laughed. "I was thinking more like a vacation."

"Vacation, where?"

"Club Med."

"Dad?"

"I know it seems a little out of character, but your mom and I ..."

"Andrew, I thought we were going to have this talk together," her mother said, coming into the kitchen. "Mmm, it smells marvelous in here!"

"Sorry—I couldn't help myself," her father said.

Emma kissed her husband on the top of his head and went over to the counter to pour herself a cup of coffee.

"What's baking? It smells heavenly," Emma said.

"Mistake cake. It's your Christmas present," Mallory said.

Emma came over to the table and gave her daughter a one-armed hug and a kiss on the cheek.

"Mmmmmmm. My favorite gift!" Emma said.

"So tell me about this vacation," Mallory said.

"Well, it's ..." her father said.

"I was talking to Mom," Mallory said.

"Thank you, dear. It's next week. We're sending you to the Bahamas."

"Next week? I thought we were going to spend some time together."

"Honey, your father and I think you should be socializing more with people your own age. Even if you don't find anything long term, you need to have some fun."

"I think doing jigsaw puzzles with my parents is fun."

"That's kind of the point. We don't think you really know anything else. Perhaps we've been a bit selfish," her father said.

"I really don't think I want to go off by myself. I just got home," Mallory said.

"We thought you might object, but honey, the trip is nonrefundable. What's the worst that could happen? You spend a week on a beautiful island with a beach, tennis courts, and warm weather," her mother said. "You love tennis. And the water."

"I suppose," said Mallory. She was starting to think it might not be so bad. She stared down at her fuzzy winter slippers and envisioned flip-flops on her feet instead. She smiled as she stood to take the mistake cake out of the oven. The cinnamon aroma filled the kitchen. She placed the cake on a cooling rack and turned to her eager parents. "Okay, I'll go." Her parents jumped up from the table and pulled her into a group hug.

CHAPTER 4

JANUARY 1999

Mallory was jolted awake when the plane touched down on Nassau Island. She blinked and looked out the small window. It was gray and gloomy outside. She hoped this was a weather aberration and not the norm this time of year. She passed through customs, grabbed her bags, and walked out of the airport, where she was greeted by loud reggae music playing and a bunch of happy people clapping and singing. Mallory couldn't help but smile as she was handed a fruity cocktail and escorted onto the Club Med bus.

Within an hour she was settled in her room. It had a king-sized bed and a great view of the beach, but the weather still wasn't very welcoming. It was warm, but the sky was gray. "I didn't come all this way to sit in a hotel room," Mallory said aloud. She slathered SPF 30 onto her fair skin just in case the sun broke through, grabbed a book and a towel, and headed for the beach.

The ocean actually looked quite lovely, and because of the gray sky, Mallory had the beach to herself. She read, watched the sea, and lazed. No sun was not such a bad thing. She didn't have to worry about limiting her beach time to avoid a burn.

Mallory set down her book, sat up and reached for her water bottle, and that's when she saw him. He ran like a gazelle, with a smooth graceful motion. Mallory couldn't help watching as he got closer and closer. His sun-streaked, light brown hair flopped every time he took a step. She could see each muscle in his bare chest, abs, and arms. There was a flutter inside her. She felt her mouth breaking into a crooked smile. She tried not to be obvious about watching him, but wasn't very successful. The runner stopped in front of her, facing the sea, and bent over for a minute with his hands on his knees, breathing deeply. Nice rear view, too. He straightened, turned around, and walked over to Mallory with a noticeable limp that had not been there when he was running. He smiled and plopped down on the end of her chaise.

"Hey," he said, smiling broadly.

Mallory couldn't help but smile back. "Tough run?"

"Always." He flashed an even broader smile. "You look like a runner, too."

"Not this week, I'm on vacation. I'm here to chaise and laze. Maybe a little tennis."

"Well, I'm not. I work here." He extended his hand. "Todd."

Mallory took his hand; it was more of a caress than a shake. "Mallory." She smiled. "I remember you now, from the arrival conga line."

Todd chuckled. "Not my favorite part of the job, but I just have to let go and have fun. The guests like it."

"It made me smile."

"Then it was well worth the humiliation."

She laughed.

"You're a hardy soul, Mallory. The only guest on the beach."

"I like solitude."

"Is that my cue to leave?"

"Not my intent. I'm at the end of a chapter and you're entertaining."

He grinned. "The conga line and now this. I've earned my pay today."

"Ah, so this conversation is part of your job?"

"Everything here is part of my job, but I don't get paid enough to talk to someone I don't want to for more than three volleys."

"I didn't realize we had a metric, so I wasn't counting. What number are we on?"

"More than three."

"Let's see if I can do better. Why do you limp when you walk and not when you run?"

He shrugged and looked down at his knee. "It's actually pretty common. At least that's what the docs tell me."

"Really?"

"Would I lie to you?" There was that smile again. She caved.

"What do you do, Todd, I mean besides run on the beach for my entertainment?" Her hand flew to her mouth. "Did I say that? I meant to think it."

"I'm a golf instructor, which could also be for your entertainment, but it would be my pleasure."

Mallory blushed.

"Speechless? Finally? Lessons are in an hour." He winked.

"Sorry, my game is tennis."

"Will you at least wave when you walk by the driving range?"

"You don't waste time."

"Can't. The week flies by here, but they say one week in Club Med is like six months in the real world."

"A week of this weather might feel like six months," Mallory said.

"I'm supposed to say it's always nice here, even when the skies are gray and crying."

Mallory smiled. "Oh, don't tell me—"

He nodded and winked. "More time for indoor activities ..."

"Then I should get some tennis in while it's still dry." Mallory reached for her book, and Todd stood, extending his hand to help her up.

"Dinner?" He asked, reaching for her towel.

"Sure."

Todd nodded. "Okay. See you then." He handed Mallory her towel.

"See you," Mallory said, and she turned and headed back to her room. She could feel his eyes on her and she put a little extra saunter in her walk just for him, glad he couldn't see the girlish smile on her lips. Mallory unlocked her door, almost wishing she had a roommate with whom to share her beach encounter. This was shaping up to be a good vacation. As she prepared for dinner, Mallory found herself humming, and she couldn't stop smiling.

– € –

The next morning, Mallory woke remembering a dream she'd had on the plane to Nassau. The dream had been about Tom, her one and only lover. He had been her freshman French teaching assistant. Mallory had thought he was cute, but that was all the thought she had given him until the following year, when she was having lunch alone at Varsity Pizza and Tom slid into the seat across from her with a pitcher of beer and three slices on a plastic tray. He had been charming, and cute, and he even though he was not French, he'd spoken with the accent. It was cheesy, but so was the pizza and Mallory had fallen for it, hook, line and sinker. In the beginning, Tom had been kind and gentle, and Mallory had been drunk on the attention from an "older man." And the sex was fantastic. Tom was in the right profession, because he liked to teach and she was an avid student; there had even been some exploits with blindfolds and closets (which is where Mallory had discovered her aversion to closed spaces). Exactly a year later, Tom had dropped Mallory as swiftly and as smoothly as he had picked her up. He found a new student and stopped calling with no explanation. Mallory had spent a long fall week in her room, nursing the wound, but then she had rallied, and made herself get back to her life and her love of printing. Mallory had returned to the world, but with a new wariness, a trepidation that hadn't been there before.

Mallory pushed the memory from her mind and threw back the covers. She was on a beautiful island and the sun was actually out this morning, Todd was cute and had been very attentive at dinner, and Mallory had just decided that she was going to let go this week and have some fun.

As she walked down to the tennis courts, Mallory looked for the driving range and a glimpse of Todd. It didn't take long for her to find both; the driving range was on the same path as the courts. Todd had three students, but he still managed to spot Mallory, and when he did, he smiled and waved. Mallory blushed and waved back, but continued on without stopping, hoping Todd was watching.

Her tennis was a little rusty, but by the end of her hour lesson, the consistency had returned to Mallory's strokes. Her instructor was giving her some "hands on" advice on how to improve her backhand and flirting more than a little when Todd walked up with a racket in his hand.

"Time's up! Lesson's over. Want to hit some?" he asked Mallory. He cocked his head and smiled at the tennis instructor, who reluctantly let go of Mallory and disappeared without another word.

"I thought your game was golf," Mallory said.

"It is. Among others."

She laughed. "What was that?" She imitated the gesture he made to the tennis instructor. "Guy code?"

"Yep. Letting him know I saw you first."

He directed Mallory to the court furthest from the pro shop.

Intellectually, Mallory wasn't sure how she felt about having just been "claimed," but her insides were turning to mush. How was she going to play tennis? "You've played before?" She asked.

"Not since I was little."

"That was a long time ago?"

"I've been this tall since I was seventeen."

Mallory blushed again, imagining him in high school and feeling that now familiar rush when she was near him. She turned and went to her side of the court. She started easy, but Todd seemed to be holding his own, and soon they were hitting long rallies and moving each other all over the court. After an hour, Mallory was exhausted and invigorated at the same time. They filled cups with water and flopped onto the bench next to the court. "I don't believe you haven't played since you were a kid. You're too good."

"I swear," Todd said, and he wiped his brow with his forearm, "I'm just so athletic, most sports I can fake."

Mallory smiled. "And modest, too."

Todd laughed and draped his arm around her.

"What time is lunch?" she said.

"We have some time."

Mallory stood and cocked her head in the direction of her room. She turned and walked off the court. He picked up her tennis bag and followed.

He walked right in, dropped her tennis bag on the floor and hopped into the bed. She smiled at him. He patted the bed next to him.

"I'm all sweaty," Mallory said.

"I know!"

She laughed and turned away. He stood, picked her up, and kissed her deeply on the lips. She nuzzled his neck. He traced her face with his lips, his nose, his cheek, like he was memorizing her.

She whispered in his ear, "Put me down."

He laid her gently on the bed. She kicked off her shoes and wiggled her toes at him. He took the hint and slowly removed her socks, stopping to sniff each one before he dramatically threw it across the room. She scrunched up her face as he smelled her socks.

"No, no my dear, it's perfume. Sweet, sweet perfume," he assured her.

Again she laughed. This guy was funny.

"Take it off, buddy," she said, "Oh, and make it slow."

A wicked smile took over Todd's face as he slowly revealed his chiseled abs and muscled chest inch by inch, until his shirt was over his head. He twirled it over his head three times and slammed it to the floor.

Mallory giggled. "We need music."

Todd grabbed the remote and found a TV channel with easy listening music.

Mallory laughed. "Not exactly rock my world."

Todd laughed, too, and tossed her the remote. "Okay, Ace. You choose."

Mallory surfed until she found a channel with rock and roll, and turned up the volume, very glad now that she didn't have a roommate this week. She tossed the remote onto the floor, whipped off her top, and, suddenly embarrassed about her industrial strength sports bra, she crossed her arms over the garment. Todd flopped down next to her on the bed and pulled her arms gently apart. He kissed her just above where the bra covered her breasts. Mallory sighed and raised her back. He expertly unlatched the bra and his mouth dropped over her left nipple. The tempo increased and events seemed to fly by. They were naked. They were exploring. They were laughing. They were one, moving together and then the explosion, the climax ... or so she thought. Afterward, lying with Todd was just as amazing as the sex. He made no move to leave; unlike Tom, it seemed Todd actually enjoyed cuddling. It was crazy, but Mallory found herself thinking of a life with him. God, he made her laugh.

"I don't usually do this," said Mallory.

"Have great sex?" Todd said.

"Sleep with a man I've just met." She stood and wrapped the sheet around her.

Todd took her hand and tried to pull her back into bed. "Aw, you care what I think?"

She resisted. "Thinking you'll be avoiding me for the rest of my stay."

"Not a chance, baby. You're mine all week."

She landed back on the bed next to him. "The whole week?"

"That a problem?" He kissed her.

Just a week? Already berating herself for dreaming about a future, Mallory thought: *stupid, stupid, stupid.*

"Mallory? Hello? Anybody home?"

She nodded. "I'm back. Want a shower?"

He made a beeline for the bathroom. They never made it to lunch.

— € —

As the week went on, Mallory continued to be happy she had a single room, because she never spent a night alone. During the day, she learned some golf, and she and Todd played tennis, hung out on the beach during his breaks, and returned to her room when it rained, which was quite often. Mallory found herself learning to love both gray skies and Todd. She began to understand what Todd had meant about a week at Club Med; by the third day Mallory felt like she'd known him all her life and yet she didn't know much about him at all. But like the percussive sound of the rain on the roof, Todd entranced her. Everything about him was entrancing: The small of his back, his wacky sense of humor, his hands, his arms, his lips—he captivated her. She was drawn to him in a way that wasn't rational, but instinctive, animal. Mallory didn't know how she was going to leave him.

"Todd," she asked one rainy afternoon. "Why are you here?" She stroked his bare chest.

"I really like sharing a bed with you?"

"Not what I mean."

He smiled. "Ah, working at Club Med instead of a real job." He sat up and turned to her, startling her with his steady, intense gaze. "That's not an easy question to answer."

"Did I just break a Club Med Magic Week rule?"

"Yeah, we don't talk about deep stuff here."

"I didn't realize it was a deep question."

He shrugged. "I could give you the standard Club Med answer: I wanted some time to find myself."

She smiled. "And the real answer?"

He looked at her again for a few moments. "I'm a fuck-up."

Mallory shook her head.

Todd sighed. "I was supposed to play football professionally. My granddad was a pro, my father was one, and I was supposed to be one, too."

"And?"

"I was a little hung over for a game early in my senior year of high school. I got hurt, my knee."

"The limp?"

He nodded. "Once the initial injury healed, I didn't FEEL hurt anymore, but the docs said I couldn't play, that it would just get worse and worse with time, and if I got hit a certain way, I might never walk again. So, I couldn't play football. And I couldn't do anything else." He got up and walked to the open window and stared out at the sea.

"That's ridiculous."

"No, no it's not. I'm great at drinking and getting high. I guess I'm pretty good at sex."

"Oh, honey, you're very good at sex."

Todd turned and smiled. "But not exactly a career."

Mallory nodded.

Todd nodded, too, and started to pace the room. "If I couldn't play, my father wanted me to become a coach; he was always bugging me about it. But I couldn't stand to even watch a game anymore. I knew then—and I know now—that if I can't play, I can't coach. I can't watch healthy kids stealing my dream day after day after day."

"But is it really your dream?"

"What do you mean?"

"It sounds to me like you never had a choice. You did what your family expected you to do. Your dad's dream became your dream."

Todd thought about this for a moment and then nodded. "I guess I never looked at it that way." He crossed the room, sat down on the bed, and stroked the side of her face. "Mallory, how did you get so smart?"

"I'm not so smart; sometimes it's just hard to see what's going on when you're in the middle of it." She sat up and kissed him on the forehead. "What about college?"

"University."

"Fine. University?" She rolled her eyes.

"University of BC. British Columbia, in Vancouver."

"But you grew up in Quebec. Why so far from home?"

"Did I mention the relationship with my dad?"

"Oh, running from Daddy."

He smirked. "At first, but I wound up loving it there. You should see the coast north of Vancouver. The most beautiful country you can imagine. It's quiet, not many people. Some people think this is paradise, the palm trees, the turquoise ocean, the heat. Not me, give me the Sunshine Coast any day."

"The Sunshine Coast? My father fishes there! In Roberts Creek."

Todd brightened. "Have you been there?"

"No, I don't even know exactly where it is, somewhere in western Canada."

"It's the coast of British Columbia. You have to take a ferry to get there. Most people are just passing through. The coast is craggy; the whales are incredible. The water is amazing. It changes color all the time: blue, green, purple, orange. It has the full spectrum."

"You sound like an artist."

"Nah," Todd said. "Well, I do love photography. I'm a decent amateur."

"Take my picture?"

He smiled. "Love to." He shrugged. "No camera."

Mallory got up and opened the room safe. She took out her Tamrac camera bag and handed it to Todd. He unlatched the bag, saw the Minolta Maxxum 5 and two lenses and whistled. "Wow, this is great stuff!"

"It's yours for the next few days. I've got tons of film and haven't taken a single picture."

Todd was already focusing the lens on Mallory.

Within ten minutes he had shot almost an entire roll.

"Hold on. I need at least one shot of you." Mallory grabbed the camera and took the last three shots of him. Through the lens she saw something in his eyes she hadn't seen before. It made her shiver. She wasn't certain, but she thought it was love. Perhaps it was just wishful thinking, but it seemed to Mallory that they were changed. That their conversation had changed them. That on this gray rainy day, they had become a couple.

For the rest of the week, the only time Todd wasn't wearing the camera was when he was working or when they were in bed. By the last day, Mallory was wondering if she should stay. Quit school. Give up the ink quest. Get a job at Club Med and be with Todd. She knew he cared about her, but she also knew that this was Club Med, the birthplace of the vacation fling. That morning, as he was dressing to go to work and she was still lying in bed, Mallory took a deep breath and then took the plunge. "Are we going to keep in touch?" she said.

"Sure," Todd said.

"That would be a no."

He grabbed a pen and paper from the bedside table. "Give me your email, and I'll give you mine."

"Email?"

Todd sighed. "Mallory, what do you want from me? You'll go home to your life. I'll be here. What we have is here. You can come back and visit, but I'll be somewhere else by April. Just another golf pro at another Club Med. It's what I do." Mallory pouted and turned over. Todd sat on the bed and rubbed her back. "I just want to be straight with you."

"That's why I asked," she whispered.

"Mallory?"

She rolled over to face him. "I guess I was just hoping it would be different. You were right, this week with you has seemed like six months. That makes it hard."

Todd frowned. "It's synthetic, trust me. I've seen it a hundred times. Lots of couples are fabulous here and fall apart as soon as they hit the tarmac back home."

Mallory shrugged.

"I know it sounds cold but it is what it is." He smiled at her. "We're great together here. And I'm definitely going to look for you when and if I'm ready to return to the real world. Who knows, if we're both in the right place at the right time, maybe we could make it work. But not right now, sweetheart. You've got school to finish, my smart one. And that ink, you've got loads of places left to go."

"Will we become a cliché?"

Todd smiled and kissed her gently. "Never."

— € —

After lunch, Mallory purchased ten new rolls of film in the boutique and tucked them into her camera bag. Her luggage and Todd were already gone, downstairs, waiting for her in an airport cab. Mallory glanced around the room one last time. It had been a wonderful week. But it was over.

She'd had to keep reminding herself of that all morning.

She had to remind herself again now.

– € –

At the airport Todd unloaded Mallory's luggage from the cab's trunk and shut the lid. He turned to Mallory. "I can't stay. I've got afternoon lessons to get back to, but I wanted to see you off properly."

Mallory nodded. Lessons AND bed sessions. IT'S OVER.

"I guess this is it," Todd said.

Mallory nodded, blinking back tears. "Here." She held out the camera bag.

"Mallory, I can't take that."

"Yes, you can. You need it. I want you to have it. I'll send you copies of the photos you took this week."

He paused, but she put the bag on his shoulder. He wrapped her in his arms and held her until the cabbie honked his horn.

"Just a minute!" he snapped.

"You should go." She placed her hand on his chest and kissed him softly on the lips. *I love you,* she thought.

Todd kissed her forehead. "I won't forget you," he said.

She smiled. "Nor me you." She turned and walked a few steps.

"Mallory."

She turned around.

"Don't forget to send the photos. And thank you."

Mallory nodded. "Good-bye, Todd." She walked through the airport doors without stopping, letting the tears fall. She would send the pictures, and she would email him, but she doubted already that he would respond.

It had been lovely, but it was over.

CHAPTER 5

FEBRUARY 1999

Forget hearts and flowers, February was Syracuse's cruelest month. There was snow and more snow and cold and more cold and sleet and hail and ice and cold and cold and cold and cold. If the sun came out for more than an hour the entire month, it was considered a balmy February. Yes, forget hearts and flowers, for, not surprisingly, they hadn't been forthcoming. What got Mallory through February were the memories of Todd and the Club Med photos, which covered her dorm room walls. Todd was only in three: those Mallory had taken the day she'd first brought out the camera. There were no pictures of Mallory and Todd together, but Mallory saw everything she needed to see in the photos he had taken of her. She looked so happy, completely content, when the camera and Todd were focused on her.

Mallory had sent copies of the photos to Todd the week after she'd returned to school. She had sent emails to him every three or four days for a while; she had wanted to email every day, but she had been religious about restraining herself. He had replied twice, briefly. He had responded to her first email, and he'd thanked her for the photos when they arrived, and that had been it.

It was over.

Mallory picked up the I Ching book her mother had given her when she left for college. When Mallory was at a crossroads, or had a problem she could not solve, she would pick up the Chinese fortune-telling book and let it drop open randomly on her desk. What the passage on the page revealed was supposed to be the perfect solution to Mallory's problem, and believe it or not, the ancient Chinese art usually provided exactly the perspective Mallory needed.

Mallory dropped the book now and the pages fell open.

"Grace" was the heading revealed.

You have been given the grace of knowing feelings like this are possible. Treat them as a passing blessing that lets you know of the possibility. DO NOT rely on them as a constant in your life.

"Perfect." Mallory sighed aloud. "Sad, but perfect. So back to work for you, girl."

She set the I Ching book aside, looked up at the pictures of Todd and her happier self one more time, and then she shook her head, and went back to work on the hacking project that she had promised Warnock she would assist with at the end of last semester.

Mallory's assignment was to push the tracer program back to give the hacker more time to shut down the hack before being caught, as she had been by the Bank of France. Mallory needed to be able to identify and send an alert that a trace had been started before said trace hit her computer. In order to do that, she had to find a way to route her routines through a network node that couldn't be traced back to her.

Mallory sighed again, and stretched her arms up over her head.

She had been at this for hours with no luck.

She had no doubt she would find the solution eventually. That was a given. The problem was Mallory had no enthusiasm for this project, partly because she had lost her enthusiasm for the sport of hacking in general, and partly because she was basically being blackmailed by John Warnock: Do the work or fail his class, and Mallory wasn't fond of blackmail. Let's face it: hacking was supposed to be fun and it wasn't fun when the hacker was under duress. And Mallory was under duress, on more than this front. She wasn't feeling creative and that made her unproductive. She needed a break. She dressed herself in layers and fought the frigid February air to the chapel café for coffee, an everything bagel, and the newspaper.

The Tuesday *New York Times* carried not only an easy crossword, but The Science Times, which today featured a half-page photo of a rainbow over Guadeloupe. The rainbow, according to the accompanying article, had been visible for nearly an hour, which was quite remarkable, since a typical rainbow is only visible for about ten minutes. Reading the article brought Mallory back to her week in the Bahamas and thoughts of Todd. There had been rain. And there had been rainbows. Almost every day. Mallory shook her head and reminded herself yet again: It's over.... She turned to the crossword puzzle which, unlike her hacking project, was way too easy to decode, and she finished it in record time. Following that success, Mallory returned to her dorm room and the hacking project, but discovered upon arrival that she was even less motivated than she had been before. Without removing her outer layers, she grabbed her tennis bag from her closet and braced for the cold once again, headed for the indoor courts a few blocks away.

— € —

The sound of the tennis ball hitting the strings and the feel of power she got from striking the ball correctly had always helped Mallory to focus. She had often wished she could find another sound or motion that she could use as a substitute, but she had yet to make that connection. What Mallory also needed was the physical exertion, a good hot sweat, something to get her mind off Todd.

She dropped her bag on the bench of an empty court and pulled out her racquet. She stretched for a few minutes, then pulled a cart of balls to the far end of the court and started to hit serves. Taking it slow and easy at first, she gradually made contact with more and more power. Her rhythm was steady. Thwack. Thwack. Thwack. She delivered into the service box, the center line, the far back corner, and then straight into her imaginary opponent's stomach. Feeling confident, Mallory tried a spin serve. She had been trying to master this skill for years, and it still wasn't ready for prime time. Her toss was consistent, always in the same place, but she hadn't conquered the long, swooping brush stroke on the ball. When she did get it right, the result was pure magic: a loose, looping spiral that hit the ground and corkscrewed off in an unexpected direction. When she missed, the serve generated a soft lob that would allow any decent opponent to smash a devastating and unreachable cross-court return.

Mallory hit a series of serves, none quite right, and paused to wipe the sweat from her brow. The indoor court lights caught a droplet of sweat on her hand, and a light bulb went off inside Mallory's head. She stared at the back of her hand. It was the liquid, she thought, *that's what makes rainbows work.*

And if it makes rainbows work.

It could make the ink work.

Mallory laughed out loud and kissed the droplet on her hand. She started picking up tennis balls, trying to figure out where she could get a substance that would remain in semi-liquid form when applied to paper. She thought all the way home and went directly to her laptop, forgetting about Warnock and his project and Todd, and started researching ink. And then she realized that she had access to a source that was better than the Internet.

Her mother.

Emma Richards was one of the foremost currency experts in the world. She had been working in the field for over twenty years, developing ink and providing quality control specifications and counterfeiting protection for the United States. Ten years ago, when the Internet had begun to make remote work easier, Emma had broadened her client base to include Canada and Europe. She had always loved her work, but she'd loved it even more after the Internet allowed her to work from home and care for her daughter. She had set up her own printing press in their home and that's where Mallory had nurtured her future love for the field. Her mom, Mallory knew, would have access to ink sources that weren't public knowledge or mass produced yet.

The next morning, Mallory was up bright and early, too excited to sleep, and dialing home. "Mom, I need your help."

"Mallory? Are you okay? Is something wrong?"

"Yes. And no. I'm fine, fine. It's about the ink."

"Tell me," her mother said.

"I need something ... something I can apply to paper that will stay in liquid form."

Her mother thought for a few minutes, which felt like hours to Mallory. "Hmm. Well, I do have a contact at Monsanto who might have something like that. I'll get in touch with him and send you an email," Emma said.

"Okay. Thanks, Mom. Um, could you call him now?"

"My pleasure, honey. But no." She laughed. "It's 6 a.m. Eastern time, sweetheart. You're going to have to wait a few hours. Go get some coffee and the *NYT*. It's Wednesday; the crossword should give you a little mental workout at least."

— € —

Dr. Cartman had kept her word and had cancelled Mallory's favorite printing class due to low enrollment, but, due to Mallory's dedication and determination, her instructor had softened on the subject and had agreed to allow Mallory to use the lab on Monday when it was unoccupied.

Mallory set the FedEx box she had received that morning on the lab table, and silently thanked her mother ... again. She took a deep breath and opened the box from Monsanto. Inside was another small box, and Mallory opened this, too, to find a small vial of liquid crystal nestled in a bed of Styrofoam. She reached for a piece of test paper, set it in front of her, and then she opened the vial, pulled out the dropper, said a brief prayer—please God, let this work—and carefully applied the liquid crystal to the paper. Her Walkman was playing The Beach Boys' "Help me Rhonda", and Mallory hummed along while she waited for the liquid crystal to start to dry. When the time was right, she spread some green ink on her print plate, placed the liquid crystal–coated paper on top of the plate, picked up her roller, and firmly pressed back and forth, back and forth. She flipped the plate and paper over and repeated the rolling process, and then she removed the plate and set the paper aside, waiting for the green ink on the liquid crystal–coated paper to dry completely.

Dr. Carlson stopped in while Mallory was cleaning the printing plate with turpentine. Even though Mallory hated the smell of the cleaning fluid, she was still humming and smiling, beaming really, because she was certain she was on the precipice of something big.

"You look excited," her former instructor said.

Mallory nodded and set down the plate. She crossed her fingers. "I think I've got it."

"That's great, Mallory! Let's see."

Mallory winced. "I haven't checked it yet myself."

Dr. Carlson laughed. "No time like the present."

Mallory nodded and reached for the print. She held it up to the light and rolled it from side to side, and where she did, the ink color changed from light to dark green. "It works!"

"Congratulations, Malloy. This is wonderful work," said Dr. Carlson.

"I guess we should let it sit for a few days before we declare complete victory."

Dr. Carlson nodded. "Yes. And you should also make a few more prints. Take all the lab time you need. And when you're ready, come see me." She turned to leave and then turned back. "I'm thinking I'd better put that class back on the roster for next semester." Mallory smiled, "I'd like that," she said, and then she set to work, making five new identical prints. She hung them on the print line, cleaned up her work station, and then used the lab camera to take pictures of each print, trying to catch the color movement in the photograph. At that moment she missed her Minolta more than she missed Todd; still she wouldn't have taken the camera back for the world. He needed it. Of that she was certain. Mallory vowed to return to the lab every day for the next five days to check the prints and make sure the color variegation remained in The Ink.

When she returned to her dorm, Mallory sent an email to Todd to tell him about her Ink breakthrough. She hadn't heard back from him in several weeks and she didn't expect a response today. Lately, writing to Todd had become more like journal writing for Mallory; her daily successes and failures immortalized in computer bits and bytes because she couldn't have a conversation with someone who obviously wasn't there. It was over. Still, Mallory wrote to Todd and responded to herself in the way he had responded to her once upon a time. It was soothing. Comfortable. And there was no one else she wanted to share her news with. When Mallory finished writing to Todd, she saw that she had an email from Dr. Warnock.

It was succinct. *Deadline looming. Two weeks. Where the hell have you been?* John.

Mallory closed the email quickly and marked it as unread.

CHAPTER 6

MARCH 1999

Mallory realized that she could not procrastinate any longer; she needed to get to work on the tracer. She had to stop looking for inspiration and just power through this, and she decided to ask for help. She sent an email to MafiaBoy, a fellow hacker in Canada with whom her alter email persona, MagicGirl, had shared code in the past.

Mallory was pretty sure MafiaBoy would answer. Hackers firmly believed that there were so many problems in the world that none should ever have to be solved twice. It was a waste of think time, and in this case Mallory had wasted a lot. Hackers weren't proprietary; in fact, they loved it when people used their code to do evil deeds or just engage in some hacking mischief. Mallory was partial to MafiaBoy, for it was his code that had first allowed her to hack into and follow her Stories.

While she waited to hear back from MafiaBoy, Mallory carefully crafted a response to Warnock's "Deadline Two Weeks" email.

Good Morning John,

I'm making progress on the tracer. Give me a few more days and I'll have something to show you. Thanks for the laptop and The Bank pass key. That should help. I'll be in touch.

Mallory.

She sent the email and got up to make coffee. She pulled her favorite beans from her tiny dorm refrigerator, breathed in the aroma and smiled broadly. The resonant *ping!* that rang out as each bean dropped into the coffee grinder was one of Mallory's favorite sounds. The grinder whirred, and a rich fragrance filled her dorm room. Mallory poured filtered water into the coffeemaker on top of the refrigerator, set up the filter and spooned in the grinder's fragrant contents. She pulled her favorite mug from the shelf and added her allocation of half and half. When the coffee started to drip, she pulled the pot away and replaced it with her mug.

Coffee in hand, Mallory returned to her desk and logged back into MagicGirl's email account. MafiaBoy had responded and, reading, Mallory smiled. The information was exactly what she needed. Now she could get to work.

For Mallory, writing code was like creating a painting. You had to nail the composition before you started applying the color or it would be a hot mess. MafiaBoy had provided the key to the composition; the rest would almost write itself. She connected through five network servers and planted the trace on the fifth server. She connected to five more nodes and then to The Bank. She used The Bank pass key that Warnock had given her to find the security trace and open the microscopic back door that would allow her to access the site anytime, going around the trace, and then she closed the door, so The Bank trace was tracking her again. Mallory set the timer and sat back with her coffee. It was lovely that she didn't have to sit in the claustrophobic computer lab any more. The laptop alone had been worth the trouble to do this. She finished her coffee and got up for another cup.

At 45 minutes, the trace alert started to sound. Mallory reset the timer, and seven minutes later the alert sounded again. Thirty seconds later the trace had made its way to her PC and had her IP address. At that point, Mallory would have been busted, but she quickly sent a message packet to The Bank with the pass key. Two minutes later she got an acknowledgement. That was it. She had struggled for weeks to find the tracer, and one short email to

MafiaBoy had given her what she needed. Mallory shook her head and vowed not to be so proud about asking for help in the future. She tested the composition multiple times—minus the foray to open the back door. It worked perfectly each time. Seven minutes was more than enough time to get out of the site before getting caught, even if one were lingering. Mallory emailed Warnock asking to meet the next morning. She thought about emailing Todd with news of her victory, but it was too soon. Once a week was her new rule.

— € —

The next morning Mallory arrived at Warnock's office early and, finding it unlocked, she decided to be ready when he arrived. She set up her laptop and plugged into his network cable. She launched her composition and watched as it connected to the first five servers, installed the trace, and continued on to the next five nodes. Warnock arrived just as she was accessing The Bank of France's Web site.

"Am I late?" He asked.

"No, no, I just wanted to be done with it."

"Has it been that painful?"

Mallory shook her head. "Just stressful. Look here—I'm into The Bank."

Warnock leaned over her and Mallory squirmed to the side to avoid contact.

"Tell me what you did," he said.

Mallory pointed to the screen. "You can see it in this window. I connected through all of these servers," she said. And then these."

"But don't you normally connect through multiple nodes?"

"I do, but this time I installed a trace on this server—halfway through."

"Ha ha! That is genius, how did you figure that out?"

Mallory smiled. "My little secret. I'll give you the program for The Bank, but how I came up with it wasn't part of the deal."

"Fair enough. Let's see what it does."

They watched until the first alert went off and then Mallory hit the timer. Seven minutes later the second alert sounded, and thirty seconds after that, the final alert sounded.

"Seven minutes' warning—that's incredible," Warnock said.

"I know, right!" Mallory said. "It's all buttoned up on this thumb drive."

Warnock took the thumb drive and reached to hug her. Mallory moved back and stuck out her hand. Warnock shook it.

"Mallory, I'd like you to continue to work for me," Warnock said.

"Dr. Warnock ..."

"John."

"John, thank you, but I'm not interested. I have had enough of hacking. Too much stress when you do it because you have to, not because you want to."

"But you'll be wasting your talent."

Mallory shook her head. "I'm done." She closed her laptop, unplugged from the network and left Warnock's office. As she walked down the hall she felt lighter, like a weight had been lifted from her shoulders. As she crossed the Quad, she was singing to herself.

— € —

Focusing on her Ink and her studies got Mallory through the winterlike spring semester. She was still emailing Todd every week, wondering if he was even reading them anymore. She talked about her feelings more openly in her messages to Todd than she did with anyone else; it didn't matter if he was reading them or not, she would never see him again. She just felt freer when she was writing to him. She wrote about her work for Warnock, how she had felt when she ran into her former French TA lover at the Varsity with his new student, her breakthrough with The Ink, and her dream to work on the euro printing project that was slated to begin any day now.

— € —

Mallory finished the semester with flying colors, and spent the summer at home in New Jersey, working with her mother to improve her Ink. Once they had perfected the process, her mother thought there was a good chance the Canadians would want to employ Mallory's new technology. In her downtime, Mallory, back to hacking, but only for fun, found a new email thread to follow. The email account was held by a man who worked for Club Med. Reading his emails made Mallory feel better, as though she were reading about Todd. She didn't know this man, and yet she felt she did.

TO: Turkoise Scuba Blu [BluScuba@hotmail.com]
FROM: Andrea [AAZ@excite.com]
DATE: March 10, 1999
RE: Missing you already

Back in the real world. Totally missing the sand, the sea and my beautiful man. I'm already thinking about coming back. Work is a hassle, the train was late today and I have this weird smile on my face. What's new with you?

TO: Turkoise Scuba Blu [BluScuba@hotmail.com]
FROM: Lori [LoriJohnson@yahoo.com]
DATE: March 10, 1999
RE: Heading back

Hi Blu.

I have another vacation coming up and I'll be down the week of March 27th. Is there anything I can bring you? Can't wait to see you.

Little Lori

TO: Lori [LoriJohnson@yahoo.com]
FROM: Turkoise Scuba Blu [BluScuba@hotmail.com]
DATE: March 10, 1999
RE: Heading back

Hey Luv–

Great that you're coming back. I'm excited! Thanks for asking about what you can bring. It's hard to get stuff here. I could really use a couple pair of board shorts–size 34. My favorite colors are orange and olive green.

I'm already thinking about what I'm going to do for you every night.

SWAK–Blu

Mallory had had enough. At some point reading Scuba Blu's emails had become depressing, but she kept his account in her rotation. It wasn't just the misery loves company thing; it was interesting to see when and if and how Scuba Blu responded to these women. She wondered if it was actually a good thing that, after the first two, Todd had chosen not to respond to Mallory's emails. At least he wasn't stringing her along or keeping her as part of his Club Med harem like Scuba Blu.

— € —

For her senior year at school, Mallory said good-bye to roommates and dorm life and rented a studio apartment by herself. She had her laptop, a desk, a tiny kitchen, and a great coffee maker, and that was all she needed. The fall semester flew by and it was time to head home for Christmas. Mallory was packing and planning her final semester's class schedule while she ran the program that she had run faithfully every week since February. Mallory watched as the program connected to node after node and finally to The Bank of France and through the microscopic opening she had left just for herself. It was still open, and today Mallory decided to linger for a few safe minutes to check on the progress of the euro printing. Her search revealed that €500 notes were almost completed. Mallory smiled wistfully. She would graduate in May. She wondered if she could find a way to get on the team. An internship, anything. She decided she would talk to her Mom when she got home and see if she might have any connections to the project that Mallory might tap into.

– € –

The bus trip home for Christmas was long and snowy; the trip that normally took four hours took six. Mallory was happy to see her father bundled in his down coat, waving to her by his car, parked illegally at the taxi stand by the George Washington Bridge. He hugged her, but they both had on so many layers they couldn't really feel each other. As they approached the house, Mallory's face lit up at the sight of the simple Christmas lights. Her father pulled her heavy suitcase up the walk and opened the front door.

Her mother was there to greet her with a cup of coffee. Dad took off his coat, scarf, and gloves before giving Mallory his signature bear hug. Mallory took off her coat, grabbed the coffee and they all headed into the living room where the nine-foot tree was waiting to be decorated. The lights and the ornament boxes were lined up across the room.

"We thought we'd wait for you this year," Emma said.

"You seemed disappointed that we'd already done it last year," Andrew said.

"I do love to decorate," Mallory said.

They decorated the tree, had dinner, and at 10:30 they made their annual pilgrimage to church to sing carols and listen to the Christmas story. Mallory thought maybe she should visit church more often. She loved this time with her family.

She woke early on Christmas morning to the smell of cinnamon. She padded downstairs to the kitchen in her bare feet.

"Smells heavenly," Mallory said. "Mistake cake?"

Her mother nodded. "It's my Christmas present to YOU this year."

Mallory paused. "Mom, what happened to the oriental rug and the antique dresser in my room?"

"I'm redecorating," Emma said.

"With IKEA? What's going on?"

Emma Richards sighed and turned to her daughter. "Your Dad had a little business setback this year. Nothing serious."

"Mom?"

"We live just fine on my salary. He's ramping up for another project and he needed some seed capital." Emma smiled. "Honey, it's temporary, don't worry."

"Morning, how are my girls?" Andrew Richards bounded into the room. He kissed Mallory on the head and dipped his wife.

"You're in a good mood," Mallory said.

"Yes, I am! It's Christmas, that's the default!"

They sat in the kitchen chatting, drinking coffee and eating mistake cake. Mallory thought it was the perfect Christmas morning. She didn't need gifts, particularly since her parents were selling furniture to raise money. The day was spent assembling a 1,500-piece Christmas ornament jigsaw puzzle that Emma had brought down from the attic. The last piece was in place at 10:28pm.

The rest of the week was spent sitting by the fire, reading, doing more jigsaws, and baking. On New Year's Eve Andrew announced he was taking his wife out for dinner and dancing, no ifs, ands, or buts. Emma was delighted with the surprise; they hadn't been dancing in years. Mallory smiled as she watched Emma light up with pleasure, and winked at her father. The romantic evening was a gift from Mallory to her parents. She had gone to her dad and presented her plan and its payment, and she had refused to take no for an answer. Her parents had been struggling in secret for months, and they deserved a fun night out on the town and a fresh start to the new year. When she found out about the gift, Mallory's mother wiped the tears from her eyes, enveloped her daughter in a long hug, and then she grabbed Mallory's hand and pulled her upstairs to help her pick out a dress.

CHAPTER 7

JANUARY 2000

An insistent doorbell interrupted Mallory's sleep. She grabbed her robe and wrapped it around her as she descended the stairs. The Christmas tree lights in the living room blinked her path to front door.

"Yes, what is it?" she said as she looked through the peephole.

"Captain Carpenter of the Fort Lee Police Department," an authoritative voice said.

Shoulders hunched, the captain had his collar turned up to shield him from the icy rain. Mallory squinted to focus as he displayed his badge. She opened the door and stood behind it.

"Ms. Richards?"

Mallory nodded.

"Daughter of Andrew and Emma Richards?"

Mallory nodded again.

The officer sighed. "I'm sorry to deliver this news. Your parents have been involved in a car accident."

Mallory blanched. "Oh my God! Where are they? Are they ok?"

"I'm sorry, Ms. Richards—" he hesitated.

"What? What is it?"

"Your Father ..."

"What, please!"

"He didn't make it."

"Didn't make it?" Mallory repeated. She struggled to wrap her mind around what the police officer had said. He didn't make it. He was dead. That wasn't possible—Mallory was certain she would have felt that.

The captain shook his head.

"My mother?" Mallory said.

"In the hospital."

"This is my fault," Mallory said.

"No. It was a truck. A semi. It jackknifed right in front of them. I'm sorry, Ms. Richards. I need you to come to the station with me, and then we'll get you to the hospital."

"Why can't I go right to my mother?"

"We need you to identify ..."

Mallory stepped back. "No ..."

The captain shook his head again. "No, not ... just personal effects."

"I'll drive you?"

— € —

The police department was housed in a double wide trailer in the middle of a large parking lot. The captain put Mallory in a small interview room and introduced her to the officer who had been the first to arrive on the scene. The officer gave Mallory his condolences and then he opened a manila envelope and poured its contents onto the table. There was a wallet, some change, and a wedding band, but they could have belonged to anyone. Mallory's hopes rose. Maybe this was all a mistake. The officer reached into the envelope to make sure it was empty, and the sight of what came out in his hand made Mallory's insides twist. The I Ching coin was her father's favorite memento from a trip to China twenty years earlier. It was 24-carat pink gold, and Mallory had never seen another like it. Her father always wore it on a simple box chain around his neck. He would not part with that piece as long as he had breath in his body. Mallory thought about the last time she had read the I Ching. *You have been given the grace of knowing feelings like this are possible. Treat them as a passing blessing that lets you know of the possibility. DO NOT rely on them as a constant in your life.* This did not feel like grace.

"The road was icy, we're not sure if alcohol was involved. New Years' Eve and all. His side of the car took the brunt of the impact, but his passenger."

"My mother," Mallory said.

"Sorry Ma'am, your mother was thrown from the car. It probably saved her life. The car was fully engaged when we arrived."

"Engaged?"

The officer looked down. "On fire."

"I need to see my mother."

— € —

Mallory stood at the door to her mother's hospital room, listening to the respirator fill with a swoosh and deflate with a slow hiss. She became conscious of her own breathing, which matched the deliberate rhythm. Her mother's head was swollen and bruised; the face was not her mother's face. Mallory had to look away. She felt like crying but she couldn't let herself. She pulled the chair to the bedside and took her mother's hand. It was cold. Mallory tried to warm it by holding it in both of hers. Emma's hands didn't look like they had been in a car accident. They looked like her mother's hands. Emma made her living, her reputation with her hands. Mallory examined Emma's smooth hands and compared them to her own. They were very similar; along with the faint traces of ink under their nails, they shared the same long tapered fingers and broad palms. Mallory squeezed her mother's hand tightly, disappointed when there was no response. She lay her head down on the bed and wept.

CHAPTER 8

JANUARY 2000

The doctor shook her lightly. Mallory woke and took a few deep breaths as she tried to remember where she was and what had happened.

"Hello, Ms. Richards. I am Dr. Sparks. How are you doing this morning?"

Mallory blinked her eyes to make them stay opened. "I'm okay ... I guess."

Dr. Sparks sat down next to Mallory. "I know this has been a great shock," she started. "I'm so sorry."

Mallory looked into Dr. Sparks' eyes and saw compassion. At first, she was grateful, and then she was suddenly terrified. Dr. Sparks turned away. Mallory's pulse quickened. "What is it?"

"There's no easy way to say this ..." Dr. Sparks paused and took a deep breath. "Your mother's condition is stable."

"That's good news, right?" Mallory said.

"The EEG revealed that your mother has very limited brain activity. It is unlikely she will regain consciousness."

"Ever?" Mallory said.

Dr. Sparks shook her head.

"Are you certain?"

"As certain as one can be in these circumstances."

"Meaning she could wake up, but there is no way of knowing when or if?" Mallory said.

"Yes, but it is highly unlikely," said Dr. Sparks.

Mallory thought she should cry or scream or something, but she felt nothing … but guilt. The world as she knew it was slipping away and it was her fault. Her fault. Her fault.

"Ms. Richards?"

"Mallory."

"Mallory, are you ok?"

"What happens now?"

"Does your mother have a living will?"

Mallory shook her head. "I don't know."

"I would advise you talk to your family lawyer. He will probably know. There is nothing you can do here, why don't you go home and see if you can figure things out. We will keep your mother here for a few more days, until her condition has fully stabilized, but by next week she should be transferred to a long-term facility that can best see to her needs."

"Facility …" Mallory repeated.

"Let's talk again in a few days," said Dr. Sparks. She shook Mallory's hand and left the room.

Mallory sighed and closed her eyes.

— € —

Her parents' lawyer, Dennis Kenny, having seen the news in the paper, contacted Mallory the next day, and was helpful and kind. Although there was no living will that he knew of, he helped Mallory find an excellent facility for her mother. Without an explicit legal document expressing her wishes, he recommended that Mallory wait at least three months before making any decisions about her mother's long-term care. He assured Mallory that with her father's life insurance there was enough money for Emma's care for now.

There were only three people at her father's grave site: Mallory, Dennis Kenny, and a minister. It was raining, pouring actually, as it had been since the night of the accident, but Mallory doubted the weather had any influence on attendance. Her parents had always been loners; they didn't have a lot of friends. At the end of the short service, Mallory dropped a long-stemmed rose into the grave and then a handful of dirt, a Jewish tradition. They weren't Jewish, but it seemed like the right thing to do to let go of those who were gone. Mallory let go of her father as the soil dribbled out of her palm. She still had her mother, but she felt alone, completely alone.

Mallory realized that her parents' insular life had created one for her, too. Her mother had worked from home and despite the fact she had been at the top of her field, she rarely had met with her clients. Her father had done most of his work overseas. When he was at home, he was focused on Emma and Mallory. That had always made Mallory feel like a princess, like she was the most important thing in his world. But now she was his only legacy, the only person who would remember he had been on this earth. When she thought about her life, she could now see that she was following a similar pattern, and that her parents had been worried about that, which is why they had sent her to Club Med last Christmas.

After the funeral, Dennis Kenny drove Mallory back to her parents' house. It embodied them. It was comfortably decorated with treasures from her father's travels. Well, those her mother hadn't yet sold.

"Would you like tea?" Mallory asked the kind attorney, as she directed him to a seat in the living room.

"Tea would be nice," he nodded.

As Mallory lifted the tea kettle from its designated place on the stove, thoughts of her mother flooded in. Tea was her mother's solution to any problem. Acne and lack of a prom date had been soothed over a strong cup of tea with her mother. Mallory had since moved on to coffee, but today tea seemed most appropriate. She reached into the cupboard and pulled down the can of Emily Rose Orange Fountain. Emily Rose was a recent discovery. Mom had a client in the Bahamas who had sent her a case of assorted teas as a thank you for a job well done. Green Lime was her mother's favorite; it was caffeinated but light and a little fruity. Orange Fountain tasted like hot orange Kool-Aid. For Mallory it had the same odd appeal as a Creamsicle; it tasted like her childhood.

Since they rarely had guests, Mallory was unaccustomed to entertaining. It occurred to her as she carried the tea tray into the living room that she should have asked what kind of tea Dennis—as he insisted she call him—wanted. Dennis surprised her by taking several quick sips from the cup. "I'm not much of tea person, but this is outstanding. Where did you get it? My wife would love it."

"Actually, it's from the Bahamas, but I'm pretty sure they have a Web site," Mallory said automatically. The small talk was making her more apprehensive.

Finally, Dennis said, "Mallory, I need to discuss something with you."

Mallory winced. "I don't care about the will."

"It's not the will. Because your mother survived him, the will won't be in effect until she passes. There is, however, a $200,000 trust fund for you," he said. "I hope you will be able to make that last for a while, but I have to confess I'm a little concerned with the cost of your mother's long-term care."

"Isn't there insurance?"

"Some health insurance, but when she is transferred into the long-term care facility, that will not be covered."

"How long will we be able to pay for it?"

"I think we can manage a year and a half or two with your father's life insurance, keeping your trust fund intact. But that's not what I need to discuss with you today."

Mallory winced again. She didn't want to think about her mother lying in a coma for more than a year. She changed the subject. "If it's not my father's will or my mother's medical expenses, then what is it you need to discuss with me?"

"I have a letter for you. From your father."

Mallory stared at him for a moment. "A letter?"

"Yes. And your father was very specific about its delivery. In the event something happened to him, he wanted you to have it immediately."

"Immediately?" Mallory echoed. And then she wondered: had her father expected to die?

The attorney nodded. "And he requested, rather, instructed, that you read it in his study."

Dennis handed Mallory a sealed envelope and stood. "I'm going to leave you with it for now. You've had a lot to process. Please don't hesitate to call with any questions or if there's anything else you need from me." He smiled. "Thank you for the tea."

Mallory stood and shook his hand. "Thank you for everything."

— € —

Mallory closed the door behind the attorney and, in a daze, carried her mug of tea and the letter downstairs to her father's basement study. The study was large, but had very little natural light, and Mallory had never much liked going down there, even when her father was there.

But this is where he had wanted her to be.

She sat down in his worn leather desk chair and set the document on the desk in front of her. Thinking of it as a document rather than a letter somehow comforted Mallory. It distanced the content, made it less personal. Mallory breathed deeply. She could smell the lingering scent of her father's after-shave in his office, and that comforted her, too. She had a clear view of the family pictures on the bookcase, and she focused on them for a moment. She ran her fingers across the top of the desk, feeling the little bumps and grooves of age in the wood. Enjoying the feeling, she reached under the drawer and brushed her hands along the bottom of the desk as well, stopping abruptly when her fingers tripped over a smooth, round something. Mallory bent down and examined the spot. It was a button. It was small, black, and connected to a wire that ran down the desk leg and under the carpet. Her natural curiosity getting the better of her, Mallory pressed the button, and jumped at the sudden mechanical sound above her, bumping her head. She sat up, rubbing her head, and watched in wonder as a large panel across from the desk slowly opened up to reveal a painting. Not just any painting, but Mallory's all-time French favorite: Monet's *La Barque* or *The Boat*. Even from across the room, Mallory could see it was an extraordinary reproduction. It was so beautifully lit it almost sparkled. Mallory stood and walked over to the painting, running her fingers along the deep ridges of the oil paint on the canvas. It was amazing. She had a print of "La Barque" upstairs in her bedroom; her mother had bought it for Mallory at a Monet exhibition at MOMA they had attended on Mallory's fifteenth birthday. Her mother, who's breath had caught at the sight of the painting, had tried to steer Mallory in the direction of the more famous *Water Lilies* when they went into the museums' gift shop, but Mallory would not go. *The Boat* had moved something deep inside of her.

And her father, too, it seemed.

Mallory went back to the desk, logged on to her father's computer and Googled "La Barque." The original, she learned, was hanging at the Musée Marmottan, Paris. It measured 146 x 133 cm, and was painted in 1887 when Claude Monet was 47, fifteen years after he'd started the Impressionist movement. Mallory looked up and pondered the stunning reproduction. Whomever had created it was good. Very good. Mallory could not stop staring at it. She felt elated, even invigorated, as though she had just received a gift from her father. This thought reminded Mallory of the letter, or the document. She turned away from the painting and reached for her father's letter opener. She paused, took a deep breath and then slit the envelope open in one clean motion. The envelope contained one handwritten page.

Dear Mallory,

If you are reading this letter, then I am gone. And if I am gone, there are two things I want you to know and carry with you: First, I love you. You are the bright light in my life and your mother's. You changed our lives when you came into this world and now that it seems I've left it, there's one more thing you need to know.

There is no easy way to couch this, so here goes. Honey, my profession was appropriating things. I guess you would call me a thief. You might call it the family business, your grandfather and great-grandfather did the same thing. I learned at the feet of your grandfather and I was planning to ask you to join me in a job after you graduated from college. No obligation, just so you could understand what your family has always done, to see if you wanted to follow in my footsteps.

When my father first told me what he did for a living, I didn't want anything to do with it, but he convinced me to come along with him when I was about your age, and from the first moment, I was hooked. I urge you to give it a try and make your own decision from a place of true understanding. Don't dismiss it without serious consideration.

I fear your mother and I may have done you a disservice by being so protective. You have lived a sheltered life and I fear you are missing out. You need to go out and really live. Take chances, follow your passion and love deeply. Whatever you decide to do, you will be brilliant.

I know you must have a million questions, and I'm not sure you will get all the answers you want. If you use your nickname, you'll find some answers behind "Le Barque". You are my sweet girl. I love you!

Dad

As Mallory read the letter, it seemed her father was in the room with her. She thought she felt his hand on her shoulder and she was now certain she detected the scent of Old Spice. She set the letter on the desk and walked the study in a semicircle, contemplating the Monet mounted on the panel. Finally, she reached out, lifted the canvas, and found a safe behind it. Mallory had to laugh: how cliché it was to have a safe hidden behind a painting.

The safe did not have a combination dial, but an electronic keypad, similar to a touchtone phone. Mallory remembered her father's instructions, and punched her childhood nickname onto the keypad: LORY.

The safe popped open.

Inside, Mallory found five bound journals and a thick green folder labeled "No Doubt."

CHAPTER 9

JANUARY 2000

Both excited and afraid at the same time, Mallory slowly opened the green folder, and to her astonishment, discovered that the papers contained therein outlined a detailed plan to abscond with thirty million euros. Euros that had yet to be printed. From the very same French facilities Mallory had found while hacking into The Bank of France Web site. The plan was to take the euros before they were actually in circulation. The euros were now electronic currency, in the process of being printed. It was ingenious, albeit A CRIME, to steal something before it was worth anything. Mallory was shocked at her father's audacity and the sheer coincidence of their shared fascination with the euro, but she had to admit it was a brilliant plan. Shame to waste it. She turned the last page and her eyes fell on a Post-it note tucked in the back of the folder. Mallory winced at the sight of her father's handwriting. It looked so alive.

"You can do it Lory, you don't need me."

What?

Mallory read the note again.

Her father wanted her to carry out his plan?

What?

Her father thought she was capable of carrying out his plan?

What?

Her father wanted her to become a thief.

Mallory closed the folder. What puzzled her more than wondering if she could do it was why her father would WANT her to do it. Why he would encourage her to become a thief. Why he had become one. When, where, and for how long? Was Mallory's whole life based on a lie? Did her mother know?

Looking for answers, Mallory picked up the first journal.

October 20, 1969, New York, NY—
Unusually Warm, Magritte Sky
There was a Caravaggio painting stolen yesterday in Italy. It was called "Nativity with St. Francis & St. Lawrence". Made me think of Dad. I wonder if our old buddy Gus took the painting. If he is still in France. I wonder how he will get rid of it. I wonder how to get in touch with him. If I'm finally ready to follow in Dad's footsteps without him here beside me, to guide me.

October 31, 1969, New York, NY—
Brisk and on the edge of rain
I think I've found the perfect first job as a second-generation art thief. My girl is taking an art class copying masterworks. She's good. Very good, and I'm wondering if I could replace the piece I took with a really good copy?

I've borrowed her art history books, and am looking for an oil painting on canvas, one that will hold up well in transit. The painting can't be too large or it will be a transport issue, and Emma tells me she is a better copyist when imitating an artist she loves—so I'm thinking Degas, Sargent, or Monet. My thought is this: We produce a reasonably good copy and replace the original so the heist will be less likely to be discovered right away. We will need some good distance between us and the job before it's discovered. Most people are caught because they commit crimes in their neighborhood or they succumb to the cliché by returning to the scene of the crime. It's a good plan. Now I just have to convince Emma to join me.

December 1, 1969, New York, NY—
First snow fall, just a dusting but magical
Emma still thinks I am joking, I tell her I need her; that her work will be hanging in a museum (unaccredited) and she can pick the painting. Still no dice, but I will not give up.

Who's going to get hurt here? We're replacing the painting. It's a victimless crime. I am not going to let it go. Today, I brought out the big guns. I told Emma it's the family business. That my father had made a very good living lifting art. That he had been teaching me the business before he disappeared. I told her I had gone along on only one job. My father didn't let me do anything, just watch. It was fascinating, all the planning. I was sixteen. I hardly ever saw him when I was growing up, and now I knew why. And now he was bringing me into the business. It was his way of bonding with me. It was wonderful. He taught me a lot. He was so wily, nothing ever fazed him. We were just starting to form a real relationship, then he was gone.

January 15, 1970, New York, NY—Frigid and overcast
EMMA has AGREED! Don't know how I finally got through, but I did. I'm exhausted.

February 14, 1970, New York, NY—
Lots of snow, settled in for the day
Two variables remain: the painting and the location. Emma narrowed the list to Monet and Sargent. Sargent was eliminated quickly because he painted fewer oils than Monet. So we are focusing on small museums and private collections.

March 27, 1970, New York, NY—Spring thaw
The Musée Marmottan, a small museum in Paris, is housed in an old private mansion in a quiet residential section. Over sixty Monets are on display there, even

one of his most acclaimed, "Impression Sunrise." Our final choice is "La Barque," a relatively obscure painting, considered second-tier by the art world. The image is a brightly lit rowboat in the top right corner. It has one other feature that makes it desirable for our purposes. Monet didn't sign it.

"La Barque" will be the center of our world for a while.

Mallory read through the rest of the first journal, taking in her father's musings about going to France and creating the plan. The second journal started.

June 26, 1971, Paris, France—Magnificent weather
We are in France. Our small hotel is near the musée. It overlooks a sun-dappled park replete with maple trees. Out the window we can see the musée just across the park.

We met the painting for the first time today. We walked through the park to the musée. Once inside, I scoped out the security system; Emma went directly to the basement gallery where "La Barque" hangs. I finished quickly and went downstairs to join her, but found her still standing at the entrance to the gallery, taking in the painting from a distance. Her eyes tracked over the canvas, taking in each inch, cataloguing it in her mind's eye. It isn't a widely documented painting; we only found two reproductions in our research, and neither does the work justice. Finally, Emma approached the painting. She surprised me and touched it, she tilted her head as she ran her fingers up and down the ridges of paint. When I approached, she told me, "I need a photograph. Several actually. Can you get a small camera that doesn't need a flash?" She opened her sketchpad and started drawing. She didn't stop for three hours. At that moment, I knew she was really in.

Mallory started skimming the journal entries—she wanted to get to the good part, she wanted to know what happened.

July 4, 1971, Paris, France—Beautiful summer's day
Met Gus in the park today, took Emma along and she loved him. We reviewed the basic plan and cased the musée together. Gus gave me a few suggestions, but agreed it was a solid plan. He offered to help, but I declined. I feel I need to do this first job solo. Plus we aren't going to make any money, so I don't want to put Gus at risk for no reward.

May 26, 1972, Fort Lee, New Jersey—Mild and sunny
Getting married at City Hall. We've bought a home in Fort Lee, New Jersey.

June 5, 1972, Fort Lee, NJ—Light mist and very muggy
Emma configured a small printing press and is set up to do intaglio printing. In that well-lit basement room, Emma and Andrew Scott were born—new identities for our new lives. Emma forged passports, driver's licenses, and a credit card for us.

To create an effective forgery of the Monet painting, Emma needed to acquire a special ingredient before we left the States. Monet used flake white paint powder, which contains lead and is illegal in France. She found a small apothecary shop in Greenwich Village through one of her old art professors at NYU. She had to tell the owner that Professor Jones had sent her before the old man would even admit he had it for sale. We paid cash and left via the back alley. It seemed an appropriate start for what we are about to embark upon. Everything else Emma needs we will acquire in France.

June 15, 1972, Paris, France—Sunny day
We are settled in a small pied-à-terre attached to an artist's studio a few blocks from the musée. When we arrived, our forged passports weren't even given a second glance. My wife is fitting well into the family business. She has a flair for the work. We popped the cork on a bottle of champagne in our temporary flat and toasted the plan.

The museum is the perfect place to test our skills, in a residential part of Paris and not particularly well known. In addition to "Impression Sunrise," the seminal painting of the Impressionist movement, the museum's Monet collection includes a number of relatively unknown paintings that were donated to the museum upon the death of Monet's son. It's a small collection and housed in a building that was previously a private home, so security is not as tight as at the larger, more famous museums.

August 23, 1972, Paris France—Hazy, hot and humid
I've spent two months getting to know the museum, watching the security guards closely. The guards leave when the museum closes at five, and do not return until 8:45 the next morning, shortly before the museum opens. They sit and have coffee on the porch until nine. The alarm system is basic and easily subverted. There are no motion detectors or sensors on the paintings. An audible alarm sounds for a few moments every morning when the guards enter the building. The windows and entrances are wired, but a small piece of aluminum foil strategically placed would keep the circuit in the window of the men's room complete while we use it to enter the building. I have unscrewed the latch on the window and reattached it backwards to appear as if the latch is locked in place when in fact it is open. Just to be certain, I tested it tonight—carefully inched the window open from the outside: no alarm sounded. Ah, success!

August 30, 1972, Paris, France—Relief!
It has been really hot and finally today the wave broke. I spend my days lingering in the museum, pretending to be a typical lazy American in love, while Emma works on her Le Barque. The painting is hanging unframed in the museum on stretcher bars. Oils are not Emma's forte, and she still is unsure she can produce a suitable reproduction. It doesn't need to remain undiscovered forever, just long enough for us to get our treasure out of the country. We are thankful a photo of Le Barque does not appear in the brochure that patrons carry into the museum.

August 31, 1972, Paris, France—Hot again!
We should have rented a place with air conditioning.

The canvas is hung and finally dry and almost ready to work on.

La Barque was not a large canvas for Monet, but it's the largest Emma has ever painted, measuring 57 inches by 52 inches.

September 1, 1972, Paris, France—Hotter
Emma works quickly and confidently because tentative strokes would scream forgery. Monet's paintings typically shine with light. La Barque is dark; only the top of the boat reflects sunlight.

September 10, 1972, Paris, France—Feels like Fall
Emma has completed the painting in only nine days. Now she has the door to the studio closed and she has turned the heat up to 85 degrees to encourage the paint to dry. She used purified linseed oil to mix the paint. It was the fastest-drying oil paint on the market in Monet's day. And again we wait. I'm ready to go. I am not good at watching paint dry. But patience, as Dad taught me, is priority one in the family business.

September 17, 1972, Paris, France—Rainy
Paint dries more slowly when it is raining, but finally Emma can apply a layer of varnish. She says the forgery has to be completely dry before she starts to age it. I can't believe it will be another two weeks.

September 23, 1972, Paris, France—
Leaves are starting to turn, cool
Emma and I combed the city for the perfect tool to age the painting. We looked in art stores and antique stores and finally found it in a woodworking shop. We also had the shop owner lathe a wooden rod that is 162 centimeters long, and five centimeters in diameter.

October 1, 1972, Paris, France—Bit of a chill in the air
Today we began to age the painting. Emma laid a clean bed sheet on the floor of the studio and placed the painting face down upon it. We worked together to roll the canvas tautly on the woodworking shop rod. The painting cracked perfectly, every quarter inch or so parallel to the rod. We repeated the process on the perpendicular side, and then Emma reattached the canvas to its stretcher bars. The new painting looks as good as the old. It is incredible! The color, patina, and tiny cracks of a painting nearly a century old. And now it is time.

October 5, 1972, Paris, France—Still and cool
It was moonless, on the stroke of midnight. I raised the museum window and boosted Emma into the men's washroom. I handed her the rolled-up painting and vaulted in behind her, scarcely giving Emma a chance to get out of the way. Clad in black from head to toe, it was difficult to see each other. I held a small flashlight, but we moved into the windowed main floor in darkness. We both knew the museum layout by heart. We went down

into the basement gallery where La Barque is housed. Emma pulled a bag off her back, withdrew the bed sheet, and spread it on the floor, while I removed Monet's La Barque from the wall, laying it face down on the sheet.

I held the flashlight while Emma removed a hammer from her bag and started removing the nails that attached Monet's canvas to the stretcher bars. She carefully placed each nail in a small ramekin. When all the nails were removed, I lifted the support and leaned it against the wall. We each grabbed an edge and turned the painting over. We rolled it up and tied it with the same wide cloth strips that had bound the forgery.

We unrolled the copy face down and put the support on top of it. Emma had marked the exact spot for the frame on the back of the canvas. I held the light while she made the small adjustments. Emma secured the canvas in four places using the old nails. I lifted the painting for Emma to inspect the placement. She nodded and I replaced it on the sheet. Emma methodically placed and hammered in the remaining nails. She took the flashlight as I hung the forgery on the wall. Emma quickly balled up the sheet and stuffed it, the hammer and ramekin back in her bag. I held the light for her and she adjusted the hanging copy by a hair and then we headed back to the men's room in the dark. I went out the window first and Emma hoisted the original canvas out to me. She shimmied out after it, I carefully closed the window, and then we skulked through alleys to our studio apartment two blocks away. Mission accomplished!

October 6, 1972, Paris, France—
Looks like London out there
The original La Barque is now wrapped inside a Persian rug bought at the Moroccan market a few days ago, and is on its way to Fort Lee, New Jersey, via airmail. Emma and

I will follow shortly. For now we will spend our days at the museum, Emma sketching Monets, and me still pretending to be a lazy American boyfriend. We are amused at the patrons examining Emma's La Barque. I feel curiously proud. Thus far, no one is the wiser.

October 10, 1972, Fort Lee, NJ—
Gorgeous Fall day—full of color!
Our trip home was blissfully uneventful. Soon we'll have our prize. I'm waiting for the phone call from the shipper.

October 15, 1972, Fort Lee, NJ—
Crisp, cool and windy, leaves all over the place!
The rug and its precious contents arrived today. I know we can't sell the painting. I don't want to sell it. I want to keep it. The theft has not been discovered and probably will not be unless Emma's forgery, tucked away in the windowless basement museum gallery back in France, were to be professionally appraised, which is not likely to happen any time soon. I have hidden the real Monet in a basement of its own, right here in my office.

Now it's time to plan the next job.

Mallory read and read and read.

Her father's journals outlined each job he had executed, and after a while her mind started to click into autopilot. She found herself accurately predicting what would come next. Not like when she could guess the ending of a movie halfway through; it was as if someone had gotten into Mallory's head and had overtaken her thought patterns. It was a little eerie. It was like HACKING. That was it. She felt like she had been hacked. And she didn't hate it. In fact, Mallory was totally intrigued with her father's life as an art thief. Now she knew where he'd really been when he was away "on business" and she got lost in the pages. As she read, it was as though her father were in the room with her, whispering in her ear. It emancipated Mallory from the grief that had immobilized her since the accident.

Christophe Rabat and Gustavo Lattanzio had been essential participants in her father's recent jobs. Gustavo or Gus, his longtime partner, was an Argentinean with Italian blood. The Frenchman Christophe was only eight years older than Mallory. They had both worked loyally for Andrew Richards, but he hadn't been in contact with them in more than a year. He'd gotten them to agree to do another job and had said he would be in touch. This must have been the euro job her father wanted her to take over. Both men had cell phone numbers that Andrew had used to contact them, but Mallory was far from certain that she wanted to do the job, let alone try to convince his partners to join her. They had trusted her father. But they probably didn't even know Mallory existed.

The euro job made Mallory sad and excited at the same time. The thought of doing the job without her father terrified Mallory, but she felt flattered that he'd thought she was smart enough to carry it out on her own. WAS she smart enough to be in charge of a job of this magnitude, with no experience other than her father's journal/textbooks?

With the morning came doubts.

In order to do the job, Mallory would have to leave school, and she wasn't sure she was prepared to do that. She was a second semester senior. Actually, that was to her advantage. She could always finish that last semester later, and it wouldn't take much doing. This was the school of life and her father had wanted Mallory to learn from it, too.

How could she leave her mother?

But what could she do for her right now?

What her mother needed was long-term care, and in order to provide and maintain that care for possibly years and years to come, Mallory needed money. And lots of it. And she would most likely need it within the next year. Where would she get it?

The euros.

How could she not accept her father's challenge? It was a chance to be close to him, to redeem herself for having sent him out in that storm, to care for her mother who was lying in a coma because of Mallory. More so, she wanted to see and feel and try to understand what their life had been like that year in Paris; what it felt like to plan and execute what her father referred to as "a caper." Mallory longed to feel the rush, to have a partnership with Gus and Christophe, like her father had had. To live an exciting, secret life, like he had. She got a vision of herself dressed in black, "casing a joint," with a pen flashlight.

The thought made her laugh.

And that was the best reason of all to accept the challenge.

Mallory was tired of crying.

— € —

The next morning's mail put the seal on the deal. In the middle of the stack was a letter addressed to Emma Scott from the European Common Bank. Mallory felt a shiver of knowledge run up her spine.

She opened the letter and read:

> Dear Ms. Scott,
> We are very pleased that you have agreed to join our Quality Management team at the Bank of France in Chamalières. Our printing standards for the euro, of course, are strict, and retaining the appropriate personnel to oversee the project in that region of France has proven impossible. The enclosed contract outlines the details. We look forward to your start on June 15.
> Regards,
> Wm Reinhert, Chairman, European Common Bank

Mallory could not believe it. Again the sheer coincidence. It was the job she'd dreamed of just a few months ago. And it had just fallen into her lap. Her mother must have been looking for work because of the money issues her father had been having. Mallory still didn't know what they had been. Only that her father had not pulled a job in more than a year. Maybe Gus and Christophe would know what had happened. And then Mallory realized: No. This was no coincidence. Her mother had obviously gone back into the family business to help her father. This job was the part of The Job. Still, it was her dream job. And Mallory was going to take it.

She was going to take both jobs.

Big and little.

But first she had to become Emma Scott.

CHAPTER 10

FEBRUARY 2000

Mallory walked up to her bedroom and took the I Ching necklace her father had worn out of her jewelry box. She fastened it around her own neck and nodded at her reflection, her new resolve, and then she headed for the hospital.

She stood at the door of her mother's room and tried to decide if she looked any better. Her mother seemed peaceful, if you could ignore the respirator. Mallory took a deep breath, stepped into the room, and closed the door behind her. She didn't know if her mother could hear her or not, but she needed to talk. "Mom ..." she said softly. "There's something I need to tell you." Mallory walked over to her mother's bed. "Dad left me a letter and file about The Job. He wants me to do it. I can't imagine it, I can't believe everything I've seen and read in the past 24 hours, but I think I'm going to do it. To try." Mallory paused, waiting for an answer, then remembered none would be coming. "I never knew you were a fine artist—I can't believe that you painted *Le Barque* and that it's been hanging in a museum in France all these years and everyone still thinks it's a Monet. I can't believe the original is hanging behind a secret panel in the basement." Mallory sat on the side of the bed and took Emma's hand. It didn't feel as cold today. Mallory stroked it softly. "There is so much I don't know about life, Mom. Yours. Dad's. Mine. Please don't leave me while I'm out there trying to learn."

— € —

Mallory was going through the contents of the No Doubt folder again. She was trying to think of how best to proceed when she noticed a handwritten note on the inside of the folder.

It read, ejob@yahoo.com, Scott.

Mallory turned on her computer and tried to log in to the Yahoo account with the password Scott. She got access and started exploring. There was nothing in the inbox or the sent folder, or the contacts. Her elation about finding the email was fading. She looked in the trash folder, nothing.

She clicked on the drafts folder and found one email draft with no subject title. Mallory opened the file.

> Scotty–
> It's a perfect time to do The Job: before the new euros are issued. It's a near perfect plan. But you'll need someone on the inside who knows both computers and currency. You might want to think about a shell game–take twice as much as you need from each warehouse and put half back each time you visit the next warehouse. That way if you're somehow discovered, it will take the bank officials longer to figure out how much was taken or even if any was taken, because the serial numbers on the euros you put back will actually belong in a different warehouse. After the job, you'll need to put as much space and time between you and it as possible.
> Coach

Mallory frowned. She assumed Scotty was her Dad, but who was Coach? What was his older partner's name? Gus—that was it. Could Coach be Gus? Well, she thought, there was only one way to find out. Mallory turned back to the green folder. "No Doubt." That was a pretty optimistic moniker. Did it mean her father and Gus had no doubt that it would work? It was possible. Mallory brought up the project management software on her laptop. She methodically logged each step of Andrew's plan into the software. This was a framework that she knew well and in this format the plan made more sense. It was impressive as far as it went; the question was could Mallory execute it without her father. Mallory shook her head in amazement. And she'd thought all these years that her father imported Persian rugs.

Mallory couldn't sit still; she suddenly felt like the walls were closing in on her. She went upstairs to her mother's office, sat at her desk, and took in the room. This office was much more comfortable than the basement. It was big, it had to be; it contained a small printing press and even a small press required a fair bit of space. The office furnishings—a large upholstered chair and ottoman and a sizable desk—were more comfortable up here, too. Most enticing to Mallory were the four large windows; there was nothing claustrophobic about this room. Although she would miss looking at *Le Barque,* Mallory decided to move Her Operation—as she was starting to think of it—to Emma's office.

Suddenly Mallory wondered ... her father's office had a secret hiding place. Maybe her mother's did, too. She ran her hands along the bottom of the desk. She opened the desk drawers and examined the bottoms of them. That would have been too obvious, she thought. She flopped down into the upholstered chair and put her feet up on the ottoman as she looked around the room. The light blue/gray walls reflected the afternoon light. Ivory painted wainscoting rimmed the room, but there were two little breaks in it. Mallory walked over and examined the breaks. She pushed lightly on the top break and it swung open. Inside was a refrigerated safe. Mallory thought she knew what was in the safe, and if she was going to do the job she was going to need it. She tried the first password that came to mind: LORY.

It worked.

Mallory couldn't believe that her parents had been so naïve; their passwords were terrible, way too easy to guess. She should have taught them better, but she'd had no idea they'd needed the security. Or maybe they had made it easy for her. Maybe they had thought she might need easy access one day. Mallory sighed. There was so much about them she didn't know and probably never would know. But she was right about what was in the safe. It was paper. Not just any paper, but passport paper for the United States, France and Italy. There was a manila envelope at the bottom of the safe. Mallory opened it and found detailed instructions on creating forged passports. She put everything back inside, closed and locked the safe, and spent the afternoon moving into her mother's office. She carried her laptop, Andrew's journals, and the green folder upstairs, and hooked up a network connection, already feeling more comfortable and productive in the brighter space.

She opened the ejob@yahoo account again, took a deep breath and started typing.

> **Dear Coach,**
>
> **I'm sorry to tell you that Scotty—my father—died in a car accident a week ago. My mother was with him. She survived but is in a coma, her doctors believe it will be a persistent vegetative state, and that she will not recover. After my father's funeral, our family attorney gave me a letter from him encouraging me to pursue No Doubt. It is clear from the previous message that you have been helping him plan this operation, and I am asking if you will continue to help me carry out his final wishes. I am all alone.**
>
> **Sincerely,**
>
> **Mallory [aka MagicGirl]**

Mallory read and re-read the email. It was direct, blunt even, but she couldn't think of another way to say it. So she hit the SAVE button and then she sat back and waited.

CHAPTER 11

FEBRUARY 2000

After two hours with nothing from Coach, Mallory ate an early dinner and carried her laptop up to her room. She checked her email. Nothing. She tried, but could not sleep. She turned on the television and, in what was turning out to be a series of now somewhat creepy coincidences, happened upon the original *Ocean's Eleven,* starring Frank Sinatra. She watched the movie—they got away with the heist—and checked her email. Nothing. She brushed her teeth. And checked her email. Nothing. She took a shower. And checked her email. Still nothing.

Mallory sat on her bed, pondering her parents' secret life.

She didn't understand. Did she want to understand? She did. Her father was right; her life thus far had been fairly safe, books and brains and not much beyond. Now she wanted to be in the scenes in the journals, not just reading them. She wanted to take risks, she didn't want the most exciting week of her life to have been the one at Club Med. She wanted to feel alive. She wanted real excitement. Mallory wanted to do it. She felt she OWED it to her father and mother to live a larger life now: one for all three of them.

Mallory closed her eyes and opened them again. She checked the email draft folder. Nothing. She stared at the dark ceiling. Occasionally a car headlight outside bounced off the wall and drew her eye. She followed the lights as they traveled across the wall and onto the ceiling. Mallory closed her eyes again, longing for sleep to quiet her mind, and finally, just after midnight, it did.

She woke in the morning and checked the email draft folder: still only the two drafts, one from Coach to her father and one from her to Coach. Mallory opened each of them just in case. "Damn it," she muttered, "I want to do this, but I need your help, Coach." She closed her laptop and carried it downstairs to make breakfast. As the aroma of fresh brewed coffee filled the kitchen, Mallory opened her laptop and checked once again for good measure: NOTHING. She sighed. Her mother always said a watched pot never boils, but really that wasn't true; it boils, it just seems to take forever. Mallory waited for the entire coffee pot to fill before she poured her first morning pick-me-up. She hated that she had to keep checking her laptop, but there was no easy way to set an alert when a new draft showed up in the email folder.

She made toast, and while she ate it, she drafted a letter to The Bank of France confirming "her mother's" acceptance of the Quality Management job at the euro facility in Chamalières. Once that was done, Mallory worked on creating a new passport in Emma's name with her own photo, although she didn't know, if she didn't hear back from Coach, that she would ever use it. She created a new background for Emma Scott, just in case anyone checked. Most of her mother's reputation had been built upon work that had taken place in the past five years, and to add credibility, Mallory aged herself from 21 to 29. Changing the records was a snap in the TRW Credit Services and Social Security databases. She opened the safe in her mother's office, took out her forgery instructions, and started reading. She used her mother's passport as the base for her new one. With the equipment in Emma's office, Mallory forged the date of birth, changed the photo, and replaced the seal. Her last act as Mallory Richards was to memorize her new Social Security number and place her old documents into the climate-controlled safe.

She was now Emma Scott.

Next, Mallory started on a French passport for her father's partner, Olivier Christophin, and an Italian passport for Gabriel

Ustinov. Or Gus. She took the paper from the official passport paper stores for six different European countries in her mother's safe. It was a very sophisticated temperature control system. It was critical the paper be kept at 70 degrees and moisture free. Only paper stored in this way would yield the appropriate results when ink was applied.

Mallory checked the email; STILL ONLY TWO.

She opened the packet from The Bank of France. It contained the specifications for each euro denomination. Quality control involved all aspects of production for the currency: the paper, the ink, the printing, everything. There was also an approximate schedule for denomination printing. Mallory knew the project was on schedule from the last time she'd hacked into the Bank's Web site. She was so enthralled with this project, one would have thought she was reading the latest popular thriller. Like her mother, Mallory was a printing geek. She actually forgot about the email.

She sat at the computer and started to crunch numbers. There would be too much paper volume with tens. They'd be harder to use, too. You can't really pay for a new car with ten-dollar bills, although it would be just as awkward with twenties. The crux of the plan was to take the euros without being detected, which meant that Mallory would need to replace them with fake paper packets that looked just like the printed euros. She tried to calculate how much paper she would need. Mallory's paper contacts, well, her mother's contacts, were on this side of the Atlantic, where the specific measurements would be less recognizable. She could call Canada to get the paper. The euro, she had learned, was going to be printed on 15lb paper with a unique mix of pulp and fiber. Because she wasn't going to be counterfeiting the money, it didn't matter what the paper was made of; only its weight mattered. Ink and the intaglio process would add another pound, so Mallory ordered 16lb paper. The twenty euro notes were spaced at ten notes up and five notes wide. The individual twenties were 133 mm wide and 72 mm high and were set up in stacks of 1,000. A packet of twenties measured 665 mm x 750 mm and contained 1,000,000 worth of euros. Mallory did the math. She would need thirty packets of fake euro paper.

She was finishing her fourth cup of coffee and trying to figure out what to do next when she looked down at the computer and noticed that now there was LESS THAN NOTHING.

One of the emails had disappeared.

CHAPTER 12
FEBRUARY 2000

Mallory stared at the computer screen, wondering why and how one of the two emails would have been deleted. She thought she'd better open the other one before it was deleted, too.

She clicked on the email, cursing herself for not having printed them.

The email opened:

> **MagicGirl,**
>
> **If we are going to continue this conversation, you need to delete each draft when you finish reading it. There should only ever be one draft in this email account. It is unlikely that someone would see a draft, but deleting the drafts makes it less likely they could be traced.**

Mallory laughed out loud. She could have easily hacked this account, the password was so simple and they used it in how they addressed each other. Now the fact that there was hardly ever anything in the account made it less of a target, but so naïve. Still she printed the draft and deleted it.

And then she read:

> **It naturally follows that we won't use our real names to communicate, and don't write anything that might help someone**

identify you. Thank you for letting me know about your parents. I will miss your father very much. I hope that your mother is improving, and that you are holding up after such a shock. It sounds as though you are.

Let me know if there is anything else you want or need to know.

Coach

Mallory replied:

Dear Coach,

Thank you for your kind words. I will follow your instructions precisely. As I mentioned previously, my dad left me a letter and folder on the job you and he were discussing prior to his accident. Do you think I can do it?

MagicGirl

Mallory hit save and again she waited. Darn it, she thought, I forgot to print. She watched as the number of drafts went to zero and shortly back to one. Mallory opened the draft, it was succinct, just two words and a punctuation mark.

No Doubt!

Mallory smiled, printed the email, and then deleted it.

She addressed an envelope to The Bank of France and slipped the letter she had crafted earlier inside it. She rummaged through her mother's desk to find an airmail stamp, licked it, applied it to the envelope, and then she walked to the public mailbox on the corner and dropped the letter in the slot. "No turning back now," she told herself. "I'm officially Emma Scott."

Mallory had butterflies in her stomach but she felt better than she had in a week.

Dear Coach,

I need to order supplies for the operation. I think I need enough paper to replace 30 euro packets, but I was wondering how you saw the shell game working. Do I need more and if yes, I think I need a plan to get rid of any leftovers at the end. Your thoughts?

MagicGirl

Mallory hit save and waited. She knew it was unreasonable to just sit here and wait for Coach's response, but she couldn't help it. She was anxious to move forward. After ten excruciating minutes, however, Mallory ran upstairs and changed into her running clothes. When she came down, she squelched the urge to check the drafts folder, and went right out the door. She needed to run, to push herself, hard. She needed to be in good shape, tough and ready. It was a beautiful day, cool but sunny, and Mallory managed five miles in a little over an hour. She returned to the house, grabbed a water from the kitchen, and headed to her office. There was one draft in the folder. Mallory smiled and sat down at her desk.

Dear MagicGirl,

The concept is to take twice as much as you will keep from each target and put half back in a different target. That means you will need to be able to replace 40 palates. It will go like this:

Target 1–Take 20 replace with equivalent paper

Target 2–Take 20 replace 10 with paper, 10 with original from Target 1

Target 3–Take 20 replace 10 with paper, 10 with original from Target 2

Back to Target 1–Replace 10 of paper with 10 original from Target 3

This way each Target will have both a missing palate and a

palate with incorrect serial numbers. This will add to the confusion in the event you are discovered.

Coach

For the next few days Mallory continued her consultations with Coach as she fleshed out the operation. She entered each new item into her project plan, then started ordering from four different paper suppliers across Canada: Vancouver, Toronto, Halifax, and St. John. The paper was delivered to a holding warehouse Mallory had reserved in Milan, Italy, under the name Gabriel Ustinov.

Mallory, as Emma, also arranged for an Italian-scale shrink-wrap machine with supplies to be delivered to the warehouse in Milan. If all went well, her father's partner would be driving the truck and supplies to France.

Dear Coach,

I think it is time to contact the help I will have in France. Gus first, then Christophe. Do you know them? Any advice?

Thanks,

MagicGirl

Mallory thought if Coach WAS Gus, perhaps he would fess up now. She was nervous about calling Gus; if he said no, the operation was probably over. She wanted to put off the call as long as possible because, until she actually spoke to him, anything was possible.

Coach didn't waste any time responding. As Mallory watched, the drafts count went from one to zero and back to one.

Dear MagicGirl,

Go ahead and make contact. Just be yourself, you will be fine. They are good men, and you have your father's good plan as guidance. Let me know how it goes.

Coach

Mallory smiled. With Coach's blessing, she was ready for her first challenge of the job. Her palms were sweating, her heart was beating almost out of her chest. She actually started to feel a little woozy. She got up from the desk and went over to the upholstered chair. She sat down, put her feet up on the ottoman, and told herself to breathe. *No need to worry, she thought. If Gus says no, I can still go to France and do the Quality Management job as Emma; and I will still get to be a part of the euro printing. Maybe that would be BETTER for me.* And that's when Mallory realized how much she was invested in this operation. It was as though her father was still here guiding her. She wanted it.

Mallory got up from the chair.

It was time to call Gus.

Gustavo Lattanzio was born in Argentina and moved with his family to Italy at a young age. He spoke fluent Spanish, Italian, and English. His French and Greek were good, but not fluent. Gus didn't exactly remember when he'd started his secret life; his wife knew what he did, his children did not. By the time he'd started working with Mallory's father in 1977, he already had years of experience with Mallory's grandfather under his belt.

Gus knew about Mallory and her mother, but not their whereabouts. This knowledge indicated the strong bond between Gus and Andrew Scott. They trusted each other completely. Well, as completely as thieves could. Gus and Andrew had done their work without the benefit of technology for years. Andrew had updated his skills somewhat to deal with modern security systems, but both he and Gus had been relieved when Christophe had proven to have a natural aptitude and interest in computers.

Gustavo had been the muscle of most their operations and Andrew Scott's most trusted friend. Gus drove trucks, lifted weights normal men would collapse beneath, and he was SMART. This combination was quite unusual, and very valuable to Andrew Scott. Gus had been willing to use physical force if necessary, but fortunately, with the help of his brain, those occasions had been rare.

When the phone rang, Gus almost didn't hear it because the cell phone was in the bottom drawer of his desk and had been for more than a year. If he hadn't been in his office, the call would have gone unanswered. When he realized what it was, his heart started pumping. It had been a while since that phone had rung. He threw the drawer open and answered the call.

"Hello, Gus."

A woman? Why was a woman calling? No one but Andrew and Christophe had this number. "Who the hell is this?" he said.

"My name is Emma Scott. I'm Andrew's daughter."

Andrew's daughter? My God. She had to be, what twenty-one now? And if it was her, there could be only one reason for the call.

"I do know an Emma Scott," Gus said. "But you are not her."

"Technically, no. You knew me as Mallory. Emma's my mother. But let's just say I'm Emma now."

"The only reason I believe you is that you reached me. Andrew must have given you the number. Tell me what has happened."

"I'm afraid I have bad news. My father was killed in a car accident a week ago. On New Year's Eve."

Gus had known what was coming; still, the news shook him. His heart palpitated and he struggled to compose himself. "I'm sorry," he said. "Your father was a great man and a dear friend."

"Thank you. He said much the same about you."

Gus's heart returned to its normal rhythm. He assumed that this was just an informational call and that the phone would never be used again.

"Gus, I know that you and my dad were very close. Are you okay?"

"Been better, *Cara*, been better. I will miss him."

"Me too," Mallory said, her eyes stinging.

"And how are you?"

"Busy. He left me a job to work on."

"Did he?" Gus said.

"Yes, I believe he'd already had a preliminary discussion with you. You are one of the key players."

Gus smiled. "Of course I am."

"Are you still interested?"

"Are you going to run it?"

"With Dad's blueprint for guidance, yes, that's the plan."

"Think you can handle it?"

"He left me the plan and several motivational messages, like he knew he wasn't going to be here. I am realizing that I am my father's daughter."

"No doubt."

"That's funny."

"What?"

"No Doubt was the name on the file. I assumed it meant the outcome of the job was not in doubt, making it the perfect crime."

Gus laughed. "Your Dad had quite the sense of humor."

"I don't get the joke."

"That was our battle cry when we went out to do a job. Andrew would ask me if I thought it would work and I would reply, No doubt. Christophe picked it up, too. Has he signed on?"

"I haven't talked to him yet," she said.

"Emma," Gus said.

"What?"

"It's all very exciting now, but things will come up. Difficult and possibly dangerous things. You have no experience."

"I know," she said. "But what I do have is a job on the inside waiting for me."

"Do you? That's very good news. Still, I'm just going to ask you to be open to suggestions and willing to listen when I think there might be a problem."

"I would welcome your guidance, Gus, but I need to have your word that you will trust my judgment. Someone has to be in charge. When we meet I will give you the whole picture. If you are still not convinced it will work you can walk, no hard feelings, no consequences."

"You'll call it off?"

"Yes."

"Good answer. Promise me something," Gus said.

"What?"

"If I walk away, you will walk away."

"I guess," Emma said.

"If I walk away, you will know it's too risky, and you shouldn't try to do it without me. Your father used to make that call. He aborted the last job and that was wise. But it was his wisdom, his experience that prompted him to make that call. I'm asking you to let me make it. I know I'm not your father, but I'm the most experienced person on the team."

"You're right, Gus. You should make that call."

"What's your next step?" Gus said.

"I have a few more things to do here and then hopefully I'll be off to France to meet with Christophe and get started," Emma said.

"Be careful with him, *Cara*," Gus said. "He is first a man."

Emma hesitated but replied, "I will." She was wondering what Gus meant, but something stopped her from asking.

"Can't wait to get started," Gus said. "Ciao for now."

"I look forward to it, too. Ciao."

— € —

Her mother's new private room in the long-term care facility overlooked a lovely courtyard, for all the good it would do Emma. Still, it made Mallory feel better that her mother was out of the hospital. Pangs of guilt hit her as she realized once again what she had done, and that she was leaving her mother alone.

Mallory reached for her mother's hand and her eyes landed on the gold Cartier watch that had been a wedding present from her father to her mother. When it had stopped keeping time, her father had tried to convince her mother to let him take it to a jeweler. But she had refused to take it off. A few months later the watch started again, on its own. Emma had never taken it off, but Mallory was concerned about leaving the expensive watch on an unconscious patient. She removed the watch from her mother's wrist and put it on her own. Now she had her father's necklace and her mother's watch.

Transformation complete, she thought.

The next day, Emma Scott emailed Coach that she was going to France. Her lawyer would set up a Swiss bank account for her and deposit the proceeds from the trust. It was time to go. Her father had given Mallory the gift of a new and exciting life, and she was ready to take advantage of it.

CHAPTER 13

JUNE 2000

The wheels touched down on the tarmac at Charles de Gaulle Airport, and Emma let out a deep sigh. As the plane slowed to a crawl, she smiled. Rainy and gray, the weather seemed more like London, but she was in Paris and starting a new life, however temporary.

Once through customs, Emma hailed a cab and directed the driver to 2 rue Louis Boilly. She stepped out onto the damp pavement and took in the stone façade of the Musée Marmottan. If it weren't for the banner out front, Emma would have mistaken the art museum for a private home, albeit a very nice home. She entered, paid the admission fee, and took a brochure, which included a map of the public areas.

"Ou et La Barque?" Emma asked a nearby security guard.

The guard replied in French, which made her smile. Although her French was fluent, Emma had never been to France, and she knew that was the true test. The guard would not have answered Emma in French if there had been even a hint she was not a fellow countryman.

She had cleared her first hurdle.

She thanked the guard and headed in the direction of Monet's *The Boat,* which was not really a Monet. She descended the carpeted stairs and as she entered the basement gallery Emma gasped. Just as her Dad's journal had described, four large paintings hung in the basement, three original Monets and one Emma Richards forgery. Emma went directly to her mother's painting. She examined the brush strokes and the colors. She withdrew a piece of paper from her coat pocket and unfolded it. It was a museum-quality print of La Barque. Emma had seen the original up close and personal; this was just a reminder. As she gazed back and forth from the picture in her hand to the painting on the wall, Emma came to the conclusion that her mother had been a superb forger. Her painting had hung in this tiny museum for twenty years and no one had noticed it was not an original. Emma was in new awe of her mother.

— € —

Christophe Rabat was a security systems expert. Andrew had not encountered a system that Christophe could not circumvent. In the time they had been together, Andrew had taught Christophe everything he knew about bypassing most barriers to entry, and the boy had been extraordinary at figuring out what remained. Andrew had written in the No Doubt file that without Christophe many successful jobs would have been impossible. Christophe wouldn't always choose the electronic solution; sometimes it had been better, easier, to get around the security system manually. Christophe's aptitude and talent with security systems was beyond reproach, and he was quite capable with computers, as well. Andrew, Emma had learned, structured a job team very carefully. Each member of the team was critical and without even one of the members the job was unthinkable.

Emma sighed.

And here she was, considering this heist without its real mastermind. Crazy.

Christophe Rabat was his given name, but Christophe never used it. He had no real friends and all of his acquaintances knew him as Christophe or by one of his many aliases. Raised in a small village in the French Alps, the ski lift right outside his front door, Christophe had been skiing since he was two; it was as natural to him as walking.

His father had left the family when Christophe was eight, and had died when Christophe was seventeen, under what his mother had said were quite suspicious circumstances. The official cause of death had been a heart attack. According to witnesses, his father had skied off a cliff; recovering the body had been impossible. Christophe hasn't skied since. Though there was no tangible evidence to the contrary, Christophe believed his father had been assassinated. His father would have never skied off a cliff. He had tried to investigate for a while and had found some debts his father had owed, but when he'd questioned his uncle—the family's financial counselor—about the debts, he had been told to mind his own business, if he knew what was good for him.

An assassin is what Christophe had intended to become when he left his mother's house six months before his eighteenth birthday. He was filled with fury and he'd hoped that killing people the way his believed his father had been killed would stem the rage that possessed him. He hadn't been sure how to pursue that particular career path, but he'd definitely had a passion for it. When he met Andrew Scott, the older man recognized right away that Christophe was smart and motivated. Andrew recruited Christophe to be one of his operatives, and he had turned out to be one of the best. Christophe liked being the best at something and the urge to kill had waned. For ten years Christophe had worked on every job Andrew had executed.

— € —

Emma closed her father's journal and looked at her hotel room clock. It was four o'clock in the morning in Paris. That was the time Andrew had always called Christophe. Emma didn't know why. She did know that when Christophe saw this number come up on his cell phone, he would expect to hear her father's voice at the other end of the line, so when he answered, in order to keep him from disconnecting, Emma launched right in. "Christophe, my name is Emma Scott. My father was Andrew Scott. He passed away in a car accident."

Christophe was silent for a moment then said, "I didn't know Andrew had a daughter." He had just a trace of a French accent when he spoke.

"Until recently I didn't know about you, either. I guess that puts us on a par," she said.

"Yeah, I guess it does."

"I'd like to meet," she said "to talk about my dad."

"I don't know ..."

"I thought you might be skeptical, but Christophe, you knew a side of him I never had a chance to see. He left me a project and I'd like to talk about that, too. The more I know about my father and his past projects, the greater my chances are of success with this new one."

"How did you get my number?"

"It was in the project file."

"When is the last time your father and I spoke?"

"About a year ago."

"And this new project: What, when, and where?"

"I'd prefer to discuss that in person, if you don't mind. Will you come?"

"Where?" Christophe said.

"Do you know Le Bistrot du Dôme in the 7th arrondissement?"

"Yes. So you are in Paris.

"Yes."

"How will I know you," he said.

"I'll meet you out front at 5:30 tonight. I'll be dressed in black," Emma said.

"That won't set you apart in the 7th arrondissement."

She laughed. "Don't worry, I know what you look like."

— € —

The rue Delamabre in the 7th arrondissement was bustling when Emma arrived and a took a seat at Le Dôme at 5:15. The bar was across the street from Le Bistrot and provided Emma a good view of the entrance through the reflection in a shop window. She wanted to get a look at Christophe before she had to speak with him. Although she had seen a photo, Emma's first look was a direct hit. Physically, Christophe was not an imposing figure; in fact he was almost short, but he had a handsome, chiseled face. Emma watched from across the street as he walked toward the bistro. He made eye contact with each woman he passed. Emma wondered if he always did that or if he was looking for her. She crossed the street behind Christophe and as she approached, her nose was assaulted by a sharp scent. It was vaguely sweet and a little musky, but an unmistakably masculine smell. She was trying to identify the scent when he turned and smiled.

"Hi Christophe, I'm Emma," she said, then took his hand and kissed each cheek. "Sorry I'm late."

Christophe responded in kind, then stared at Emma.

"What's wrong?" She said. "Is there something on my face?" Her hand instinctively touched her cheek.

"No, *pardon*," he said. "You look so much like your father."

"What did you expect?" She said with a shy smile.

"I don't know what I expected. I was surprised by your call. I've been wondering when Andrew would call." He pointed at Emma's neck. "You're wearing his charm," he said, and looked down quickly. He seemed to regret the comment. "Let's get a table," he said.

They asked for and got a small table on the patio. It was early enough in the evening that they had some privacy. Christophe pulled out Emma's chair and brushed her shoulder with his hand as he pushed it back in. He took the seat opposite her, and looked deeply into her eyes, silent. Emma felt herself warming to him. She couldn't help but smile. She was playing with the I Ching charm around her neck—a recent habit that was more calming than nervous—sliding the coin back and forth. Christophe watched her intently. "I wear this to remind me of him."

Christophe nodded. "He was the great man. He found me when I was only seventeen. Tried his best to discourage me from this life, but I so wanted to be like him. Andrew was a father to me." Christophe looked guarded.

"So I guess that makes you my brother." Emma encouraged him to share more. "But you got to know the REAL him."

"I don't want you to think about me as a brother."

Emma grinned. "Yeah, well, you don't have to worry about that."

Christophe took Emma's hand in both of his and caressed it. The hair on the back of her neck stood up. "He was a remarkable man," Christophe said. "It would give me pleasure to tell you what I know about him." He smiled ruefully. "However, let's walk and talk. I don't like talking in small spaces, you never know—," He tossed a handful of bills on the table.

"—who might be listening—Dad." Emma grinned again.

Christophe laughed, and as they exited the restaurant, when he put his hand on the small of her back to lead her out, Emma thought she could hear him breathe in her perfume. As they walked, Christophe trailed Emma just the slightest so that he could assess her body. She had already assessed his. Christophe lit a cigarette and Emma smelled that slightly sweet scent again. She turned to find him boldly appraising her.

Emma's body was lithe, borderline too skinny. She knew Christophe could see her toned muscles wrapped in tight Lycra slacks. Emma was strong and walked with the confidence of a seasoned athlete.

"Oh, I see we're in the assessment phase." Emma opened her jacket, stretched her arms out and turned slowly. "Do I pass?"

Christophe rushed over and wrapped Emma's jacket around her. "No scenes, please," he said. You look fine, fabulous in fact." Christophe directed her to a nearby bench. "Sit with me. Now, tell me about the job."

"What kind of cigarette is that?"

"I roll my own. Why?" Christophe said.

"Smells sweet."

He smiled. "Don't worry, *chérie*. It is tobacco. The job?"

Emma sighed. "Okay. But just so you know, this was basically Dad's plan. He just wasn't around long enough to execute it."

"Good, Andrew was a great planner."

"Frankly, I haven't decided yet whether or not to do it. I need your help."

Christophe nodded. "Talk to me."

"Are you familiar with the euro?" Emma said.

"The new European currency?"

She nodded.

"It's only electronic right now, there won't be paper until 2002," Christophe said.

"That's true, but do you know why?"

"Because they want people to get used to the idea."

Emma shook her head. "Actually it's because it will take that long to print enough notes and mint enough coins to replace the currency that is currently in circulation."

"Really. Two years. Where are they storing it?"

Emma smiled. "You think like Dad. Warehouses, in the south."

"How do you know?" Christophe said.

"Now we're treading on some confidentiality issues. How do I know I can trust you?"

"Your father trusted me. What's the downside? You said yourself that you weren't sure if you wanted to do the job and you need my help. Trust works both ways, Emma."

"I have a contact at The Bank of France."

"A trustworthy one?"

Emma gazed at him through confident eyes.

"So you have procured a job with The Bank?" He said.

Emma blinked. "How did you know that?"

Christophe smiled and shrugged. "Your father may have been the brains of the team, but he taught me a lot. Part of being good at the job is having good intuition. I didn't know. I made an educated guess."

"Large portions of the bank notes are being printed near the Loire Valley and stored in several facilities in the area."

"So the plan is to take the bank notes," he said.

"In a nutshell, yes," Emma said.

"Before they are in circulation?"

"Yes. Enough so we'll all be happy, but not enough to delay the circulation date. Even if they discover the theft."

"And you've determined how much enough is?"

"Thirty million."

Christophe whistled. He looked at her silently for a moment. "What makes you think you can pull this off? You're a novice," he said.

"Exactly. Which is why I need you. Dad said you would help me."

Christophe smiled and shook his head. "I don't know."

Suddenly Emma felt even more passionate about the job.

"He asked me to do this. It was his last wish. Please, I need your help," Emma said.

Christophe stood. "Emma, no offence, but this is dicey work. You have no idea." He dropped his cigarette and snuffed it out with his boot.

"You were a novice when my Dad took you on. I'll have you and Gus," Emma said.

He was studying her. "You have Gus?"

"Are you in?" She asked.

"Do you have Gus?" Christophe repeated.

"Yes."

"And Andrew's original plan? In writing?"

"Yes," Emma said.

He nodded and reached for her hand to help her up. "Okay. Oui, I am in, too. Come to my place and we will look at your plan and see how Christophe can make it better."

"Your place?"

"We need privacy. You have a better idea?"

Emma shook her head.

Christophe hailed a cab and opened the door for Emma. He slid in next to her and his thigh pressed against hers. She closed her eyes and took in his aroma. When she opened them, he was smiling at her. Emma looked out the window, but Christophe's smile was imprinted on her brain. She was getting distracted, very distracted.

— € —

Christophe was focused as he slowly read the No Doubt file. Emma paced the small studio. Christophe was sitting on the bed; it was the only place to sit, and it was a BED and Emma was trying to focus, too. She stopped, looked out the small window, and then turned to pace again.

"Emma, you're distracting me. Please sit down."

You have no idea, Emma thought. She plopped down on the floor.

"Where are you?" Emma said.

"Almost done. Hush."

A few minutes later he carefully closed the file.

"Well, what do you think?" Emma asked.

"I think if we are going to do this, you need more patience," Christophe said.

"It's not the first time I've heard that."

"Patience is critical in a job like this. You can't rush anything. You have to wait until the moment is right. Can you do that?"

She looked at him wide eyed and nodded her head.

"Good. This is a really interesting idea, but there are still a lot of unknowns. We have work to do," he said.

"I know, the job at the warehouse is really undercover work," she said.

"Are you up to it?" Christophe asked.

"The computer stuff, yes. It is the security stuff I'm not sure about."

"I can coach you through that, but I'll have to go down there with you. What concerns me is that you need a poker face, you need the intuition I was talking about earlier. That can't be taught," Christophe said.

"Do you really think we can do this?"

"Too soon to tell. When are you supposed to start work?" Christophe said.

"Monday in Saint-Étienne."

"We can work together until you leave. I will join you a week or so later and make sure the details are falling into place," Christophe said.

"Fine," Emma said. "But we will be working at MY place. I need a place to sit."

— € —

Emma and Christophe spent the next three days in Emma's hotel room planning and running different scenarios. She filled a notebook with questions that needed answers before the job could be completed successfully and as she ran through them with Christophe, she felt more intellectually stimulated than she had since she'd left college six months ago.

On the afternoon of the first day, Emma pushed a protesting Christophe out the hotel room door not long after lunch, with the promise that she would be available twenty-four hours for the next two days. After he left, she put on her business suit and left for her appointment with William Reinhert, Chairman of the European Common Bank in Paris.

"Madame Scott, so pleased to meet you," Reinhert said as he rose to shake her hand.

Emma extended her hand and shook firmly. "A pleasure, Monsieur," she said as she sat down in the chair across from the desk. "I'm looking forward to working on this project."

Reinhert nodded. "We are so pleased to have a woman with your credentials, although I must admit you look younger than your reputation would indicate," he said.

Emma smiled. "I get that all the time. I'm fortunate to look younger than I am. Of course, I hated that when I WAS younger, but now I love it," she said.

Reinhert laughed than sobered. "Our quality control processes have not been up to our usual exacting standards. There is just so much volume. Anything you can do to raise the bar would be greatly appreciated."

"I'm sure I can make a difference, but I can't be specific until I actually get on site. That won't happen until next week. Speaking of which, would you like me to check in regularly with you while I am on site?"

"That won't be necessary," Reinhert said as he rose, indicating the brief meeting was over, "I have my sources."

"Thank you again for the opportunity to work on this project. It's a dream job for me," she said.

"Madame Scott, the thanks are all mine. You are my secret weapon. We need better quality euro than those damn Germans," he said.

"I'll do my best," Emma said.

— € —

On their second work day together, Emma started flirting a bit with Christophe; she couldn't help it, but he remained focused—singularly, frustratingly focused—on the job. Until the last night, when their paperwork was finally done, after they had ordered dinner and wine from room service.

Christophe smiled as he took Emma into his arms. "See," he said, "Patience."

He picked her up and laid her gently on the bed.

"What about dinner?" Emma asked.

"This is France. They will leave it outside the door."

Emma smiled and pulled him down to her. Christophe was patient and thorough. Emma was appreciative and fulfilled, but something was missing. Afterwards, after dinner, Christophe was smoking a cigarette and Emma was sipping a glass of red wine and pondering what had not gone quite right between them, when she had an idea. She looked up at him and said "Christophe?"

He smiled at her. "Yes?"

"My mother's name is Emma," she said, thinking that sharing something, some truth of her old life might make being with this new man feel more right.

He put out his cigarette. "Same name?"

Emma nodded.

"She was in the car, too. She was thrown clear. She lived but she's in a coma." Emma started crying.

Christophe pulled her into his arms and stroked her back.

"I don't think she will ever wake up."

"Where is she?" He asked.

"New Jersey, in a long-term care facility."

"I'm sorry," Christophe said.

Confession may be good for the soul, but it obviously wasn't good for post-sex connecting. Not for Emma and Christophe anyway. She didn't feel at all connected to him. Not the way she had with Todd. Emma shook her head. She was Emma now. Not Mallory. She set down the wine glass, got up from the bed, and went into the bathroom to run a hot tub. When she came back, Christophe was sleeping with his back to her. Emma lay down next to him, not touching, and before she fell asleep, she realized the problem had not been her, but Christophe. She felt he had simply serviced her. He had done all the right things, but the whole experience had been hollow, mechanical. There had been no romance. No laughter.

And then, too late, Emma remembered Gus's warning.

CHAPTER 14
JUNE 2000

Emma didn't sleep well, and was up and dressed by 4 a.m. She was trying not to wake Christophe—and trying to forget what she had given into the previous evening—when he stirred and rose up on one arm. "Where are you going?"

"Want to get an early start on the trip," Emma said. She went over to him, gave him a quick peck on the cheek, told him she'd call and then she grabbed her bag and sprinted out of the room.

She picked up her leased BMW and drove through a drizzly Paris morning with a cup of strong French coffee in her cup holder. The part of France she was driving through wasn't the most picturesque, but it gave her time to think, and by the time she passed through Lyon the sun was shining and fluffy Magritte-esque clouds dotted the cerulean blue sky over Saint-Étienne, her new home for the next three months.

She had chosen to live in Saint-Étienne because the bucolic town was centrally located between the three warehouse facilities she was going to be responsible for: Le Clapier, Terrenoire and Grange Neuve.

Emma pulled the BMW up to the house The Bank of France had rented for her and gasped in delight as she gazed out at the charming, compact stone cottage. Upon entering the cottage, Emma found her luggage waiting in the foyer. A comfortable, well-appointed living room was to her left and beyond that a roomy kitchen, painted a cheery bright yellow. Two bedrooms and a bath were to the right.

Emma chose the back bedroom. The front bedroom had east-facing windows, and she couldn't sleep with sunlight streaming in early in the morning.

Emma sat on her bed and smiled.

"Here we go, Dad."

Emma arrived at The Bank of France printing facility in Chamalières, the largest of the five French euro printing facilities, on June 15th. The day was filled with meetings and introductions to the existing Quality Management personnel. Emma's staff consisted of only two people, both very inexperienced. That was not surprising to Emma; printing currency was, as Dr. Warnock had said another lifetime ago, a rather esoteric trade.

Emma was given an office, computer access, and a Bank of France email account. She would be designing and implementing a quality control and testing program that would ensure the euro banc notes printed at this facility were held to a higher standard than the rest of Europe. Due to these stricter standards, it was possible, if not plausible, that this facility could be shredding a lot of sub-standard currency. It was Emma's job to catch any quality issues early in the printing process and correct them. It was a big job and she was only now realizing how big.

Emma stayed at the printing facility late into the evening, mapping out her visits to the three storage facilities. This main office was not where Emma would be spending most of her time, but the computer access here was critical to the success of The Job. Before she left the office, Emma checked to ensure she could still access the microscopic opening she had left in The Bank's Web site back at school. It took a little longer than it had at home, and at one point Emma thought she was going to have to hack into the site again, but it finally opened. The slowdown, Emma realized, was The Bank's own network, which made sense, and she made a mental note to access the site from her home and personal laptop next time.

Later that evening, Emma poured herself a cup of decaf and called Christophe.

"How's it going?" he asked.

"Fine, just getting settled. I won't know for a couple of days if I'll need you to come down."

"I'm coming."

"You know we can't be seen together," Emma said.

"I'll stay in Lyon; we need to find a place there for me and Gus. You can come to me."

"Not sure that is a good idea."

"Emma, I miss you," Christophe said. Again, the words were right, but the tone, something was just slightly off.

"I've got to be at my best here at the start. Give me a few days."

– € –

The next morning Emma returned to the Chamalières facility, where she was issued a uniform from an unlocked storage closet on her floor and a security pass for the warehouses. While waiting for her photo ID to be processed, she noticed a box of blank badges next to the door. The guard handed Emma her security pass and turned to deal with a question from a coworker. Emma slipped a few blank badges into her coat pocket.

This might be easier than she had imagined.

Within a few days on the job, Emma discovered that the people who hired the truck drivers to transport the euros from the printing facility to the storage warehouses never came into personal contact with the truck dispatch personnel. All communication was handled by computer. Emma also noted that there was a lot of driver turnover. Perhaps it was the nighttime hours, Emma thought, and a salary that was not particularly attractive for night work. She set up a computer worm to notify her whenever they lost a driver, and when one quit the following day, Emma intercepted the communication from Dispatch to Employment. A few days later, she sent Dispatch an email reporting the two open positions had been filled. Christophe and Gus, under their aliases, would work for a few months prior to The Job.

Long enough for them to become known and trusted both at the printing facility and the warehouses. The uniform seemed odd to Emma; she didn't understand why she needed to wear coveralls in that horrid bright blue color. They were required on the warehouse floor. The color was undeniably noticeable. It would make it difficult to skulk about and not be spotted.

Emma donned the uniform and headed out to tour the warehouses. Her easy feeling from the badge pilfering was allayed when she reached the first warehouse in Saint-Étienne. It was located in the western part of town dubbed Le Clapier, the carpentry district. Le Clapier translates as "the hutch," the dining room furniture centerpiece that the tiny hamlet was famous for. The security was intense; Emma was quite sure the management here was unaware of the badges that lay out for the taking back at the home office. After passing through a metal detector, Emma was physically patted down. She hoped the pat down was a new employee security measure; it was not an experience that she wanted to endure every day.

Another security guard—they were everywhere—led Emma to her office, a large but spartan room, with military gray metal furniture and no personal items to be seen.

A small, serious-looking man entered the room. He was not wearing a uniform.

"Madame Scott. We've been expecting you," he said in perfect English. "Sorry about the security checks, but we can't be too careful here at Le Clapier. Lot at stake and all that."

Emma was surprised the man was a Brit, and the expression on her face must have betrayed that.

He nodded curtly. "Weren't expecting an Englishman? Not much call for security in France unless it's the military. The Bank wanted private citizens for this project, so here I am, as are you. Roger Coltman, at your service."

Coltman was short and carried himself in a polished manner. His suit was well tailored, and his tie was worn a little longer than most, giving the illusion that he was taller than he actually was. His booming bass voice announced his presence with authority. Emma could tell he'd had his share of female attention when he was young.

His confident air extended his height by a foot. His rugged features and intense brown eyes completed the package.

Emma smiled. "It's mademoiselle, actually. And please, call me Emma. I'm hoping you will have a small office that we Quality Management folks can use while we're here?"

"Hmm," Coltman said, thinking. "There's nothing in this part of the building, but if you don't require anything this fancy, I might have something on the warehouse floor."

Emma winced. If this office was fancy, she couldn't imagine what the warehouse might have to offer. But she wasn't in a position to be picky.

"That would be perfect," she said. "Just a place to write reports and do some quiet analysis work. How is the lighting?"

"Very bright," he said.

"Fine, that will do nicely. I'd like to see the floor," Emma said.

Coltman bowed slightly. "Shall we talk while we walk?"

Emma smiled. "Lead the way."

They exited his office through a back door which led to a catwalk above the warehouse floor. The warehouse was tremendous. Emma had never been in a building that large. It was at least five city blocks long and equally as wide. There were openings between the euro stacks big enough to drive a truck through. In fact, that is precisely what they did.

"How many notes are stored here now?" Emma asked.

"About 120 million. Almost all of the big notes have been printed," Coltman said.

"Won't you ultimately have almost a billion?" Emma said.

"About 850 million."

"It looks full now," Emma said.

"It is full now, all the printing paper is stored here as well. Once or twice a week we get a shipment of printed notes and send back a shipment of blank paper. It's pretty efficient and the paper is almost as valuable as the currency. Having the paper would make it easier to counterfeit. Ergo, the stringent security."

Emma made a face. "And the overalls."

Coltman laughed.

"But it does make sense," Emma said, and despite the overalls her mind raced with excitement. It was going to work, Andrew's "perfect plan." She felt like dancing along the catwalk, but restrained herself.

"Would you like to see the available office?" Coltman asked.

Emma nodded and followed him down the stairs and all the way to the end of the warehouse. It was a long walk, but that was ideal for Emma's purposes. She could be in the warehouse, but in a less occupied part of it. In addition, the printed currency was in the back of the warehouse and easily accessible.

"Sorry, no computer," Coltman said. "I hope this works for you. The Powers That Be want you to be happy here. There are carts you can use to get back and forth."

"It's perfect. I'm a BYOC kind of girl. I expect to be here all of next week and then a day or two a week after that," Emma said.

"BYOC?"

Emma laughed. "Bring Your Own Computer. And coffee. I live on it."

Coltman nodded. "American. Well, whatever you like. Just let security know what you expect your schedule to be. They only pat down first-time and unexpected visitors."

"Will do," Emma said. Anything, she thought, to avoid another pat down. "So tell me. Why you aren't wearing a uniform? I was told they were required."

"Don't fancy it?"

"Oh no, it's *très chic.*"

"I had my time in it. But everyone knows me here now and I don't spend a lot of time in the warehouse itself. It IS technically a violation, and I do have a uniform hanging in my office, but I only put it on when we're being audited."

"Audited?" Emma asked.

"About once a quarter every warehouse gets audited for security and to review the currency and paper storage. We never know exactly when it's going to happen. Could be twice in one week, or none for many months. The Bank makes it quite random to keep us on our toes," Coltman said.

"Sounds like The Bank has thought of everything," she said.

Coltman grinned, and Emma thought again how he must have once been quite the lady killer. "One can never think of everything." He bowed slightly again. "Make yourself at home and let me know if you need anything. Good to have you here."

"Good to be here," Emma said. "And thanks."

— € —

When Coltman had gone, Emma ran her hand along the gray metal desk and picked up a finger full of dust. It needs work, she thought. She gave the office another cursory glance, then she closed and locked the door and set out to explore the warehouse floor. As she walked among the stacks of colored notes, Emma couldn't help but think about "the other job." She couldn't wait to get started. She turned a corner and almost bumped into a man in a security guard uniform. He looked at Emma suspiciously. "Parlez-vous Anglais?" she asked in a friendly tone.

"Yes, the boss insists on it. He doesn't speak French. Can you imagine living in France and not speaking French?" the man said as his faced flushed with color.

"Don't worry, I speak French, too. I just prefer English, if you don't mind. I'm Emma Scott."

"Oh, the new quality guru," he said.

"Yeah, I guess, although I've never been called 'guru' before. I kinda like it." She smiled.

"Giles." He extended his hand. "Giles Fougerouse. I'm just one of the security guys. Nice to have a woman around." He smiled broadly and then broke into a laugh.

Emma stopped for a moment to appraise him. He was quite plain, but had genuine warmth about him. She had never seen a nose quite like his, so prominent, yet it fit his face. He almost reminded her of a cartoon character because he was so small in stature that his oversized head seemed precariously balanced on his shoulders. Bushy eyebrows slightly obscured his eyes. And he had a most remarkable laugh. It was infectious and Emma could not help but smile.

"Lovely to meet you, Giles. Been here long?"

"Since it opened. Back in '98. We just had paper then, walking the stacks was pretty boring. Now at least there's some color."

Emma must have looked confused. When seen from the side, the bank notes looked exactly like the unprinted paper, except the notes were cut. Sensing she didn't get it, the guard pointed to the colored palettes that were under the printed money.

Giles asked her if she wanted an expert's tour of the warehouse and Emma quickly accepted. They walked the aisles for what seemed like hours. The place was truly massive, but Giles knew every nook and cranny: where the paper was stored, where the money was stored. He knew every driver who brought the euros in and took them out of the warehouse. He knew where the trucks came in, how they were checked for security.

He knew everything.

And he liked to talk.

The security guard had already proved to be a very valuable resource, and on top of that, Emma liked him. She wondered, for not the first time, if she was cut out to be a thief. She felt bad that Giles would probably bear some of the blame for The Job when it was discovered. IF it was discovered.

Emma shook off her doubts, and returned to her large warehouse office, where she typed for an hour, recording all the information Giles had given her in a secure section of her computer.

She smiled when she had finished.

This could really work, Emma thought.

It *will* work.

— € —

The next day Emma set off for the Terrenoire warehouse on the southeast side of Saint-Étienne. Terrenoire was named for its loamy, fertile soil. It was home to many farms that thrived on its "black earth."

Although the warehouse's physical set-up was identical to the Le Clapier site, the Terrenoire personnel couldn't have been more different. The head of the facility, Albelard Beaumont, was French. He was late for their meeting and Emma thought he smelled a bit of alcohol, but figured she'd give him the benefit of the doubt. He, too, gave her an office, but this time Emma found her own way around, specifically choosing not to befriend a security guard here unless it became absolutely necessary. She didn't need any more emotional attachments. The security was lax and there seemed to be no sense of discipline. At least Terrenoire looked like it would be easier than Le Clapier.

Emma left the warehouse humming.

— € —

Emma was scheduled to visit the third and final warehouse in Grange Neuve on Thursday, but she decided to go to the main printing facility in Chamalières and test the security badges she had lifted a few days earlier to see if they were still in working order. She looked around to ensure she was alone before she inserted one of the badges into the door's security scanner. The telltale click sounded and the scanner flashed "Security level 6." Emma opened the door and let it shut again, then returned to the scanner and scanned her own badge. It was also Security level 6, so she assumed the other badge would work in the warehouse as well. There were holes in the security; Emma knew that now. She didn't know how or when she might exploit this particular hole, but knowing that it existed encouraged her. She spent most of the day meeting with the Printing Quality Management team to get up to speed on their current efforts, which she quickly determined were sadly inadequate. Emma decided to spend the next week at the main facility, working on a detailed quality plan to implement in the next month. She figured, if The Bank of France was paying her to ensure the superior quality of the French euros, she would give them their money's worth. Any lingering insecurity about her ability to perform this job was gone.

— € —

Emma's new quality control procedure was implemented within a week. From every 3,000 sheets printed, one was pulled and manually measured for exact ninety-degree angles. Color charts were created to match ink saturation levels. Initially, many defective batches were found and the press had to be re-calibrated. The defective currency was shredded and documented. The serial numbers were not repeated. Emma received high praise for her efforts. She had already proven herself worth her salary, and she was happy to have been able to put her mother's knowledge of printing and her own years of study to good use. It took a little of the sting out of knowing what she was about to do.

At the end of the week, Emma finally visited Grange Neuve, home of the third and final warehouse facility. Grange Neuve—the "New Barn" that the small hamlet had been named for back in the 1500s was now a dilapidated stone and wood structure that sat next to the entrance of the warehouse. The warehouses had all been built specifically for storing the pre-issue euros, so it was not surprising that they all had exactly the same floor plan and physical set up. That was where the similarities ended, however. Grange Neuve had a very earnest, not-so-bright Frenchman in charge. He was much younger than the other two managers. Emma found out later that Fabrice Martin had been awarded the job because his father was important locally, and the appointment had been a kickback of sorts. Martin seemed to want to do a good job and was very cooperative, but clueless. Emma suspected that the functions in the warehouse would reflect that as well. The best organizations worked from the top down. Emma was certain this would not be an exception. As she was contemplating the plan for the last warehouse, her cell phone rang.

"I've found a place in Lyon. I need to see you," said Christophe.

"Glad you called, it's time for us to talk about a job for you."

"Of course. That is why I called."

"Not The Job, a job," Emma said. "Can't talk now, I'm at work." I'll meet you in Lyon tonight. Le Musée on rue des Forces at 7?"

"You will be wearing black?"

Emma laughed as she hung up, wondering how she was going to manage to sleep alone that night. The office phone rang.

"Hi Emma, it's Giles from Le Clapier."

"Hello Giles, what's up?" Emma said.

"I was wondering if you'd like to get a coffee sometime."

Emma thought for a moment. She wasn't at all interested in this man but his allegiance might come in handy at some point.

"I'll be in Le Clapier next Tuesday. How about I stop by and see you when I get there and we can set a time," Emma said.

She felt his joy through the phone. She hoped that wouldn't be another mistake.

When she arrived at Le Musée at 7, Christophe was already seated and talking to the chef. He jumped to his feet when Emma approached the table, wrapped his arms around her in a full-on kiss. Emma pulled away and sat quickly.

"*Chérie,* this is Luc," Christophe said.

"Bonsoir, Mademoiselle," said Luc. He took her hand and kissed it. His lips lingered longer than they should have. She wondered what was with the men in this country.

"I have prepared a special meal for you at Christophe's request. Excuse me."

"Enchanté," she said.

Christophe eyed her suspiciously.

"What?"

"My question exactly."

"I don't think a romance is a good idea," she said.

"If you think it is romance you have not had a romance."

"Fine, I don't think us having sex is a good idea."

"Ever?" Christophe said.

"Not during The Job. I … we have to be focused, any complication would be distracting," Emma said.

"Okay, I can't disagree with that," Christophe said.

Every muscle in Emma's body relaxed, relief flooding through her.

"However, I need you to know something."

Emma felt the tension creeping back in. She sat straight up in her chair.

"After we finish The Job, I intend to romance you, court you, woo you, win you, marry you, and love you forever. I know we haven't known each other long, but I feel it and I know that you do, too. We are meant to be together."

He was looking a little wild eyed to Emma, he was scaring her a bit, but she didn't want to let on. Emma needed to exercise her new found patience and get through The Job. And she needed Christophe. She had lots of time afterwards to plan her escape, and he had time to change his mind.

"I know you are thinking this is crazy, we hardly know each other. I assure you this is the sanest I have ever been. It is going to happen. We will be together."

Emma calmed herself, quieting the butterflies in her stomach. She tried to smile at Christophe, but the best she could manage was a small shrug. "You start work next week as a driver."

"Driving what?"

"A truck. You will be picking up the newly printed euros from the main printing facility, delivering them to the warehouses, and returning with blank paper for more printing. I need to know if there are any security measures in place at the printer. As a driver you'll have the best access," Emma said.

"Sounds perfect, you can arrange this job?"

"It's done. I will have one for Gus, too, when the time is right. It's better that you don't start at the same time. The Bank of France provides housing for its employees, so you can stay close to the job," Emma said.

Christophe nodded, all business now. "Anything else I can do?"
"Maybe find a staging area where we can do our paper/currency swap. I'm thinking the best location is a town called La Dame. It's equidistant between the three warehouses and the printing facility."

— € —

Emma fell into a regular routine of having coffee with Giles when she went to Le Clapier. They became quite congenial, and occasionally Roger Coltman would shed his gruff demeanor and join them. Emma's office, deep within the bowels of the warehouse, became their coffeehouse. She shopped for special coffees and kept little treats stored in her bottom desk drawer. The aroma made the office seem less dismal.

Today was a Le Clapier day, and Emma wasn't in her office long before there was knock at her door. "It's open," she called.

"Hey, Emma!" greeted Giles.

"Come on in—the coffee is on," she said. "Is Roger coming?"

"He might stop by later. Right now he's on a call with Paris."

Emma opened her desk drawer and pulled out a cookie tin.

"Ooh, my favorite. Emma, you are wonderful."

"And I have a new coffee. Chocolate covered cherry," Emma said.

"Ah, *bien, bien.* You know, everyone is talking about your new quality management process. I think that is what Roger is talking to Paris about. You are causing quite a stir."

"It's what I do best. Shake things up."

"Oui. C'est vrai," Giles said.

Roger wasn't as friendly as Giles, nor nearly as revealing, but to her surprise, that very afternoon, he called to invite Emma to his home for dinner with him and his wife.

— € —

Emma rang the doorbell of the large redbrick home—completely out of place in a neighborhood of small cottages. It stood out in its grandeur, and Emma suspected that was what had appealed most to Coltman when he'd chosen it.

"You must be Emma," a lovely woman held out her hand. "I'm so glad you came. I'm Julia Coltman. It's lovely to meet you."

"Thank you for inviting me," Emma said, holding out a bottle of wine. "French food is wonderful, of course, but it will be nice to have a home-cooked meal for a change." Emma was surprised by the aura that emanated from Julia; she had never pictured Roger with such a warm woman—he was kind of a cold fish.

"Emma, you're here." Roger seemed warmer at home, although he drew the line at hugging. He shook her hand.

"I love to entertain and so rarely get the privilege since we arrived here," said Julia, leading them into them into the dining room.

"Oh my, the table is magnificent. All this for me," Emma said.

"Well, THIS time it's only you," she said. "Maybe next time you'll let me fix you up."

"That's sweet of you Julia, but I'm not here looking for love. Just doing my job."

"And a fine job you are doing," said Roger, "I have to apologize for my wife, she thinks she can make everyone happy. Actually I think she's just bored. We can't get work papers for her here, so she's a housewife."

"Well this is lovely, it looks delicious," Emma said.

It was a long evening with lots of wine. As Emma drove home she had to really focus to stay on the road. She hoped the driving while intoxicated regulations in France were looser than they were in the States. She focused on the road, sang loudly along with the radio, and pulled into her garage so tired she contemplated just closing her eyes and sleeping in the car.

CHAPTER 15

JULY 2000

Christophe called Emma and asked her to meet him in La Dame. He had discovered a vacant barn that could be suitable for the staging area. Equidistant from each warehouse, it was an ideal location. Emma loved the name, translated as "The Lady," and the barn was perfect: large enough for a slightly larger truck than the ones used in the regular deliveries of the printed euros, and with room to house the packets of paper Emma had shipped from Canada. There would be room to work, but not a lot to spare. The barn was fairly rustic, and Emma considered herself lucky it had working electricity. Best of all it was isolated, so their middle-of-the-night activities would be much less likely to be interrupted or intercepted.

"Nice," said Emma.

"I can get a six-month lease. That will be long enough?"

"Should be more than enough."

Christophe shrugged. "Done."

Emma nodded. "Have you discovered any new glitches or gimmes while you've been driving?"

"Andrew had it right for the most part. I would like to check out the colored palettes. I suspect they have chips in them. Microchips. Might not be a problem since we're not 'keeping' those, but we should know how they work."

"Agreed, how do we do that?"

"I'm working on a scanner that I hope will be able to read a chip remotely, but the best thing would be for me to get one of the palates alone to examine it. Can't do that with my current driving partner."

"Then it's time to call Gus," Emma said.

— € —

Gus hung up the phone.

His wife, Sherry, was standing at the door.

"What's wrong?"

"That was Andrew's daughter."

She went to him and sat on his lap. She knew what this meant.

"Sherry."

"When do you leave?"

"Tomorrow."

"Tomorrow? So soon?"

He nodded. "I have to do this for Andrew."

"I know. It's fine. I was getting tired of having you around the house anyway," she said. "How long?"

"I don't know. Two months, maybe three."

"I'll get your bag," Sherry said. "Is it still packed?"

He nodded and held his wife in a tight embrace. "*Cara mia.*"

"Me too." She kissed his nose and turned to go. Gus swatted her still-toned behind. She giggled as he chased her down the hall.

— € —

Gus picked up his plane ticket and instructions from the usual drop point and headed to the gate with only a small carry-on bag. He never took much luggage on a job. He preferred to purchase what he would need at the site. As he slid into his assigned seat and fastened the seatbelt, Gus realized how much he had missed this feeling. He had been idle only for a year, but it had been long enough. And now here he was again, flying off into the unknown—for who knew how long—to partake in something very dangerous and potentially very lucrative. Was there any better feeling? He didn't think so.

He arrived in Milan and took a taxi to Parco Sempione as instructed. He paced a bit outside the gate. He was excited and did not feel like sitting still. When he saw Emma walking toward him, Gus smiled. No mistaking that resemblance.

"Meeting someone?" Emma asked.

"Emma?" Gus said.

"Yes."

She held out her hand, but Gus stepped in and enveloped her in a bear hug which—because it reminded Emma of her father's hugs—she returned enthusiastically. After a minute, Gus let go and held Emma out in front of him. "Turn around, let me look at you."

Emma obliged, noting how deftly her father's best friend had gotten her to the assessment phase. Gus was average height but he was strong, she'd felt it in his hug.

He pointed to a park bench inside the gate. "Come. Sit here with me. Tell me, how is your mother?"

"Mom is ... the same." Emma looked down.

"I'm so sorry," Gus said.

Emma swiped a tear and blinked back the rest. "It was my fault. I sent them out that night on a date."

Gus shook his head. "No. It was an accident." He looked at Emma sharply. "Is this why you're doing The Job?" He said. "Out of guilt?" He shook his head again. "Is all the wrong reason."

Emma took a deep breath. "Yes and no. I'm doing it mostly because my father wanted me to. He thought my world and my life were too insular, too insulated. He wanted me to take a chance."

"But he's gone now," Gus said. "His wishes for you are done. Your wishes for yourself are what count now."

"I want to do it," Emma said.

"The money?"

"I won't deny that's a part of it. But I want to know my dad. Why he did this. Why he loved it. I don't know what happened the last time out, but I know he was hurting for money and that he believed this job would be the perfect last one for himself. And for me." Emma turned to Gus. "But make no mistake about it, this is a one-time deal for me."

Gus nodded. "Fair enough. So what's The Job?"

"Thirty million euros," Emma said.

"Euros?" Gus was puzzled. "They're not out yet."

"Yes, but they're already printing the bank notes, even though they won't be distributed until 2002."

"The perfect time to take a few," Gus said.

"Exactly."

"Where?" he said.

"France," she said.

"Won't they miss 30 million?"

"Ultimately, but it's the perfect amount," Emma said.

"Because?" Gus said.

"It's not enough to make them want to reprint. It's little enough that they won't want to admit publicly that someone's taken it, and little enough so it's transportable and can be hidden easily."

"What's the schedule?"

"I need you to pick up a truck here in Milan this week. Both you and Christophe will need to be in Lyon for the duration, which I expect to be three to four months," Emma said.

"I'm still concerned that you don't have the experience."

Emma nodded. "I know. And I still remember my promise to walk away if you call it off. But I've got an inside job with The Bank of France and I've got the printing knowledge and computer skills. I just need you and Christophe to help me with the rest. I'll tell you what, bring the truck to France. We'll discuss the entire plan—you, me, and Christophe—and then you can make your decision."

Gus nodded. "I can do that," he said.

"Great." Emma stood and extended her hand. "A pleasure!"

Gus grinned. "Same here." And he pulled her into another big hug.

— € —

To pass the time on the flight back to France, Emma scanned through her Stories, looking for something to disappear into for a bit, but came up empty. The Club Med guy was too familiar, and too depressing, and Pandora had obviously finally been caught by her husband for she was nowhere to be found. Emma decided to look for a local story thread to follow. She had scanned accounts for a little more than an hour when she happened upon JCMI5. The email account belonged to a British housewife who was living in France with her husband, whom, apparently, was more interested in his job than their sex life. Being an independent woman, JC had decided, it seemed, to mitigate that need elsewhere. René was her current beau, although there was a history that included at least six other men. Emma blushed as she read about their exploits. She wondered for a moment if the woman could possibly be the warm and perfect hostess at whose home she had recently had dinner. Emma shook her head. Julia Coltman? Still she would hang on to this one.

CHAPTER 16

AUGUST 2000

A week later, Emma arrived at La Dame, pushed the opener for the bay door, and pulled the BMW behind the barn. Gus was walking the barn, checking out all the corners. "I didn't start unloading. Not sure where you want stuff," Gus said. He gave Emma a hug.

"No worries, Christophe should be here soon. He can help."

On cue, Christophe pulled up in his green Renault. He got out of the car, closed the bay door behind him, and gave the older man a kiss on each cheek and a tight embrace.

"I've missed you, my friend," said Gus.

"It's good to be working with you again," Christophe said.

"Behaving yourself, I trust?"

Christophe grinned. "Always."

Gus laughed. "Nice try."

"Okay, okay," Emma said. "You'll have plenty of time to catch up later. We've got work to do."

Gus opened the back of the truck and pulled down the ramp.

"What is all this?" said Christophe, peering into the truck.

"Paper to replace the euros. And a shrink-wrap machine. The scale will be the final check. I've calculated the weight very carefully. We will replace the top sheet on each euro palette with an official cover sheet and re-shrink the package. This should be all we need, other than time."

"Where will you get these cover sheets?" asked Gus.

"It's taken care of," Emma said.

Gus sat on the truck ramp and took off his left boot. He pulled a small piece of paper out of the boot and handed it to Emma.

"What's this?" she asked.

"The receipt for the truck rental," Gus said, replacing his boot. He saw her staring at his feet, and grinned. "Bexleys are great for safekeeping. No one ever searches the shoes."

"Bexleys are the best," agreed Christophe, pointing to his own.

Emma grinned. "Good to know. There's a Renault waiting for you in Lyon," she said to Gus. "You'll be starting as a driver a week from Monday. It's important for your cover. The best chance we have at successfully pulling this off is if they don't discover the money is missing until quite some time after it is gone. To accomplish that we need to fit in and be seen as regulars at the warehouses."

"Right. Details?" Gus asked.

"Five nights a week you will transport new euros from the printing facility to the warehouses and return with blank paper for the next day's printing. You start at 7 p.m. and work until 3 a.m."

"It's not bad Gus, I've been doing it for a couple of weeks," Christophe said.

"Is that how we're getting the money out?" Gus asked.

Emma nodded.

Gus stood up and headed up the truck ramp. As he and Christophe unloaded the supplies, Emma pointed out their destinations. She had drawn out a plan for each piece of equipment, placing it where the appropriate outlet was located, and making sure they would have room to work. At the end, she decided they needed another long table and Gus volunteered to source it.

They sat at the small table and chairs that Emma had brought to the barn the previous week, and Christophe took Gus step by step through the plan. He listened carefully, asked questions here and there, and smiled when Christophe had finished.

"It's very thorough," Gus said.

"So, are we good?" Emma said. "Are you in?"

"I'm going to reserve final judgment until after I'm able to case the warehouses," Gus said.

"I can arrange that. I'll make sure you're on the schedule for each warehouse we are going to hit by Friday," she said.

"How will you do that?" Christophe asked.

"I've infiltrated the computerized driver scheduling system—that's how I got you your jobs—and I can manipulate the schedule to send you to specific warehouses. I can also ensure that the two of you will be working together the week of The Operation."

"Perfect," said Gus. "Let's plan to meet here on Saturday morning after I've seen the warehouses and we'll have a final Go or No discussion. In the meantime, is there somewhere we can eat? I'm starved."

Emma shook her head. "Not around here, don't want anyone to see us together. I'll meet you two in Lyon in a few hours."

— € —

They had dinner at a small bistro next door to the inn where Gus and Christophe had rooms. With a lovely bottle of Bordeaux, they toasted to future success.

"To Emma," said Christophe. "Your father would be proud."

"No doubt," said Gus, smiling.

Emma raised her glass. "To my dad and his good friends."

"Salute," said Gus.

"Salute," said Christophe.

The wine was good, and Emma finished half her glass with the one toast. She felt safe in the company of these men; it was nice to let go for a bit, but she kept it to one glass. Another one and she might start to lose control, and this was not a time for that. As if to prove her right, Christophe's hand brushed softly against her thigh. Emma pulled away sharply.

Christophe got the message and removed his hand.

The waiter arrived with their food, and they ate a leisurely dinner, enjoying the company.

"Did you hear the story about how your Dad and I met?" Gus said.

"No." Emma said. "It wasn't in his journals. Please, tell me."

"I started this life work with your grandfather," Gus said. "I met your father on our last job together. He was a quiet kid, hardly said a word during the whole job. His father and I didn't think he was cut out for the work; it didn't seem to suit him at the time, but as it turned out he had just been too busy soaking it all up to bother with small talk." Gus smiled. "He contacted me when he and your mother were headed to France to obtain *Le Barque*. I came to Paris to meet them. We met at a little café near the musée. Your mom was very fond of the café au lait there. Andrew laid out his plan and asked for my advice. It was a good plan, but it had a few bugs and I helped him work them out."

Emma frowned. "You worked that job? He didn't mention you in his journal until a few years after *Le Barque*."

Gus smiled. "No, I didn't work *Le Barque*. I offered, but your father refused. I suspect he felt he had something to prove to HIS father by going solo." Gus shrugged. "It was okay with me. It was obvious that he wasn't going to profit from the job and I don't make a habit of taking risks without reward. He didn't call me again until your mother got pregnant with you. That is when we became partners."

"I didn't know this story," Christophe said.

Gus grinned. "Got to maintain my air of mystery, brother."

"And you, Christophe, do you have a story?" Emma asked.

"OH, YES ..." Christophe said. "I HAVE A STORY."

"Ha—I bet I know the one," Gus said.

"Tell me," Emma said, leaning in with anticipation.

"I think it was the third job we did together," Christophe said.

"That's about right," Gus said.

"We were taking something from a very sophisticated safe in a small house in the French countryside. My job was to crack the safe. Typically, Andrew was the safe cracker, but this was not a manual safe, it was electronic, and electronics were my forte. I had never cracked a "live" safe before, although I'd had lots of practice and I had very good equipment."

"The best," said Gus. "Andrew never skimped."

Christophe nodded. "It didn't take long to open the safe, and I reached in eagerly for the contents, very pleased with myself when something or someone inside the safe grabbed hold of me and the alarm started screaming. I was screaming, too, and cursing and trying to pull my hand out of the safe, but I couldn't get loose when Gus came into the room and said 'Man, we're blown. We gotta get outta here. NOW.'"

Gus chuckled.

"'I'm stuck!' I said, and Gus started to laugh like he's laughing now. I didn't see the humor. 'I'm stuck man,' I yelled. 'Something's got me. Stop laughing and HELP ME.'"

Gus lost it and dissolved into laughter.

"WHAT," Emma breathed. "What had you?"

"Your father," Gus said, wiping tears from his eyes.

"Yes, Andrew," Christophe said, laughing now, too. "He released my hand and came out from the next room. I wanted to kill him. I'd never been so scared in my life, and I haven't been since."

"But why?" Emma said. "I don't get it."

"He was teaching me patience—to look inside the safe rather than simply grabbing for the loot. Many safes have booby traps inside them. Trust me, I learned that lesson."

Emma's eyes filled with tears, but hers were not of laughter.

"*Cara,*" said Gus. "Is this too difficult for you? These stories? Too soon?"

Emma shook her head. "No, it just brought back a memory."

"Tell us," Christophe said.

"Yes, *Cara,*" said Gus. "Tell us."

Emma wiped her eyes with her napkin and set it down on the table. She took a breath. "When I was a little girl Dad would make me go on a treasure hunt for my birthday gift. He would stay up the night before, making up and hiding the clues. He would never give me even a hint. I had to find them all for myself. Every year the hunt got longer and harder, but I learned to love them. Almost more than the gifts themselves." Emma blinked back fresh tears, and then she took another breath and continued. "When I turned 14, it took THREE DAYS to figure out all the clues. By the third day I wasn't loving it so much, and I begged Dad to give me a hint, just one hint, but he refused. He said I needed to develop patience; that patience was the best gift he could ever give me, and it would only come with practice."

"And did you find the gift?" Christophe asked. "The actual gift, I mean?"

Emma nodded. "Finally, I did. It was a computer. I learned to hack on it."

Gus clapped his hands. "Perfect! You learned patience and became a little thief! It sounds just like Andrew."

Emma smiled. "Thank you both. Listening to your stories made it seem as if Dad was here with us."

"He is here," said Gus. "Whenever the three of us are together, he will also be here."

Christophe waved down the waiter and motioned for another bottle of wine. "We will drink to Andrew," he said.

Emma shook her head. "This has been lovely, but I've got a long drive home and a lot of work to do in the morning." She reached into her purse and pulled out three hundred fifty francs and laid them on the table. "You two stay, have the wine, and get caught up. I will see you on Saturday at La Dame." She rose from the table. "Gus, there are working papers, a passport, and credit cards in your new name waiting for you in your room."

"What is my name?" asked Gus. He loved this part of a job. He was born again every time.

"I'm Olivier Christophin. That way you can still call me Chris," said Christophe.

Emma nodded. "And Gus, you are Gabriel Ustinov. That way we can still call you Gus."

Gus grinned. "For a beginner you're pretty good at this."

"Actually, Dad made up the names. They were in the file." Emma said. "Okay, I'm off. See you Saturday, boys." She waved and walked out of the bistro.

Christophe looked after her a little too long.

"What's up?" Gus said.

"Nothing."

"Please. Who are you talking to?"

"What?" Christophe said.

"The girl. It's a problem," said Gus.

"What about the girl?"

"Chris."

"Not a problem."

The older man sighed and shook his head, feeling certain he was too late. "I don't know what I missed, but know I missed something. I also know the girl is trying to stop it. And she's right and you know it."

"Did she talk to you?" Christophe asked.

"No, but I can see it. Anyone can. Leave it until after The Job."

"But I ..." Christophe said. "This is not the same."

"Leave it," Gus commanded.

Christophe knew this tone. If he didn't agree, Gus would abandon The Job.

"Okay," Christophe said. "I will wait. But I will have her, Gus. She's mine."

Gus shrugged. "We'll see, my friend. We'll see. I don't think Emma's the type to belong to anyone. Not if she's her father's daughter, and from what I've seen thus far, I believe that she is." The old man smiled. "No doubt," he said softly.

CHAPTER 17
AUGUST 2000

Christophe was working with Gus, quizzing him on the complex details of the upcoming operation, when Emma arrived at La Dame.

"So it is Go or No?" Emma asked.

Gus smiled. "Go."

Emma smiled back. "Great. Okay, you will be in training with one of the euro transporters for a few weeks and then you'll be given a permanent assignment with Christophe. You both need to be as diligent as possible and do everything by the book. Stay under the radar. Report back with any issues that might compromise The Job."

"Right," said Gus.

"Got it," said Christophe. It was clear he was getting antsy.

"Don't do anything to draw attention," Emma continued. "You don't know each other yet, so if you bump into one another remember that. During the work week you will be living in small accommodations next to the warehouse facility in Saint-Étienne. The living quarters are pretty small, so you're bound to run into each other."

"We've done that before," said Gus.

"Once you're on The Job, you need to work as slowly as is acceptable."

"Why?" both Christophe and Gus said at the same time.

"Because when we pull The Job, you will need wiggle room for the time it takes to replace the cover sheets on the pallets. I may be there to help, but I may also need to provide a distraction, so we cannot count on that. Trust me, right now, the slower you work the better, but within the acceptable limits of the job."

"What kind of distraction are you talking about creating?" Christophe asked, grinning.

Gus looked sharply at Christophe, and he dropped it.

"We're good to go?" Emma asked.

"Yes," said Gus.

Christophe nodded.

— € —

For the first time in their lives, Christophe and Gus had regular jobs.

Christophe actually liked the routine and thought he might be able to do something like this for the rest of his life—as long as he knew he didn't HAVE to do it for the rest of his life. The job called for the partners to carry side arms, which made Gus happy. He had never carried a legal gun before. He mentioned to Christophe that Emma must have done a masterful job with their credentials to get them licenses to carry firearms.

"She knows what she is doing, though she is very young," said Christophe.

"And very beautiful," said Gus.

Christophe nodded, but he didn't take the old man's bait. He had said he would wait, and he was a man of his word. Andrew had demanded that.

Gus had finished his training, and he and Christophe were driving their first night shift together. The euro trucks were weighed both on arrival and departure from the printing facility and the warehouses, to ensure that the same amount of money and paper were exchanged, so after their first euro pick up—and prior to delivery—they took a quick detour to La Dame to check things out.

Gus pulled the company truck into the barn, and Christophe jumped out of the passenger's side, pulled down the back gate and started to work. He used a flashlight to examine every nook and cranny of the money palette. He found a sensor in the far-right corner, and used the scanner he'd crafted to analyze it.

Gus appeared in the truck door. "How's it going?"

"I found something, give me a second," said Christophe. "Here we go," he said, pointing the flashlight beam toward the back of the pallet. "It looks like it's just an identifier and a weight indicator. No alarm."

"So we'll have to match the weight exactly. Good thing we have the scale," Gus said.

Christophe jumped to the ground and closed the truck door. "Let's roll."

— € —

Two months later, Emma visited the boys on a Saturday morning in Lyon. They sat outside at a small café, sipping coffee and eating croissants and speaking English—though they all spoke French—so their conversation, if overheard by the café owner or the few other guests, would not be understood.

"So, are we ready?" Emma asked.

"But of course!" said Christophe.

"Absolutely!" said Gus.

"Okay, we will start Tuesday night, but we'll meet tonight at La Dame for one last run through."

— € —

"Let's review," said Emma the following night as she stood in the empty barn. "Ultimately we are taking ten million euros from each of the three warehouses, but we are also moving some of the printed money around."

Gus and Christophe nodded.

"You've been delivering to our chosen three warehouses for the last few months," she continued.

"Right, Le Clapier, Terrenoire and Grange Neuve," said Christophe.

"The operation will take four days and we will be taking forty million in euros."

Christophe said. "Forty, I thought—."

"Yes," Emma said. "We are only keeping thirty million. But we are taking forty and putting ten back at the end. At the first location we are taking twenty million, but only keeping ten. Each subsequent night we will move ten million from one warehouse to another. That way, if the theft is discovered the incorrect serial numbers will add to the confusion and make it more difficult to identify which serial numbers are actually missing."

"Makes sense," Gus said nodding.

"Tuesday, as usual, you'll pick up forty packets of euros from the printing facility. You'll stop here, drop off twenty packets of euros. You'll replace them with twenty packets of blank paper. I've obtained cover sheets for the packets so we can prepare ten packets before we start, so let's go. Timing is essential, as well as weight, so let's see how it goes."

Emma looked at her watch—her mother's watch—and they began.

Christophe loaded a packet of blank paper into the shrink-wrap machine, pressed a button, and the wrap was cut from the paper and stripped from the packet. Emma placed the cover sheet on the top of the paper packet, pressed another button and the machine wrapped the packet up tight. They repeated the process for nine more packets.

"Great!" Emma said. "That took less than fifteen minutes. I imagine it will get faster as we go. You'll arrive here on Tuesday from the printing facility and unload twenty packets of euros. We will need to unwrap and remove the cover sheet and rewrap ten of those packets." She turned to Christophe. "Remember, you need to check the sensor to get the expected weight and weigh the palette to be sure we're compliant. We will repeat the process we just went through and you will have twenty packets to load back in the truck and drop off at Grange Neuve. You'll continue on your route back to the printing facility to drop off the paper from Grange Neuve. Then we'll meet back at La Dame."

Gus and Christophe nodded again.

"Wednesday, again, you'll pick up forty packets of euros from the printing facility. You'll stop here, drop off twenty packets of euros, take the ten euros that came from Grange Neuve that still have to have cover sheets on them. Replace the cover sheets, load up them up along with the new ten packets of paper, and you're on your way to Terrenoire."

"And Thursday ..." Gus said.

Emma nodded. "Thursday, it's a repeat at Le Clapier. They'll get ten packets of paper and ten of euros from Terrenoire. Friday is the tricky one. We need to switch the truck, so they don't realize there are fifty packets in the truck. Once in Grange Neuve, you will need to load ten of the plain paper packets you left there on Tuesday and leave ten packets of euros from Le Clapier."

"Frankly, Thursday is the tricky one," said Christophe. "Le Clapier has the tightest security."

Gus nodded in agreement.

"Well, just be careful. Okay, I think we've got it covered," said Emma. "Agreed?"

Gus and Christophe nodded a third time.

— € —

Emma went into the Chamalières office on Sunday morning, reviewed her email, and logged in to the scheduling systems for the warehouses. She revised the driving schedule so that Christophe and Gus were visiting Le Clapier on Monday, Grange Neuve on Tuesday, Terrenoire on Wednesday, Le Clapier on Thursday, and Grange Neuve again on Friday.

— € —

On Monday, Gus and Christophe ran their regular job run of forty million from the printing facility in Chamalières to the Le Clapier warehouse, deviating from the schedule only for a 20-minute stop at La Dame.

"A little late tonight guys," said Giles as he weighed them in.

"Really?" shrugged Gus. "Maybe more traffic. I dunno."

"Maybe because he just drives like AN OLD WOMAN," Christophe yelled across the driver's seat.

Giles laughed and waved them in.

Watching the delivery from the door of her Le Clapier office, Emma smiled, too. They were good. She could see why her father had refused to pull a heist without them. When they lifted up the last palette and slid it into the truck for the return trip to Chamalières, Emma smiled with relief.

This is going to work, she thought.

— € —

Tuesday was The Launch.

Emma was waiting for Gus and Christophe at La Dame.

The plan, her plan—Yes, now it was Emma's plan—was about to be put into action.

This was it, no turning back.

The boys slipped the truck into the barn at 8:49 p.m., a little ahead of schedule, and the three of them were starting to work before the barn door was even completely closed. Gus unloaded the packets and Christophe slid them into the shrink-wrap machine. Emma pushed the button to remove the wrap, slipped out the blank sheet, replaced it with the cover sheet, and pushed the button to re-wrap the packets. The process was repeated nine times. The new packets were scanned and weighed and reloaded, and Gus and Christophe were ready to pull out of the barn in less than fifteen minutes.

Emma instructed them to wait ten minutes more before proceeding to Grange Neuve, and then she jumped in the BMW and drove to her Grange Neuve office. The truck pulled in at precisely 10:30 p.m. Emma smiled. The boys had been so good at being slow before, now they had time to drink a cup of coffee before leaving the warehouse. But their task was only partially completed. After dropping off the euros, and reloading with paper for the next day's printing, they drove back to Chamalières, dropped off the truck, and then drove their separate cars to La Dame.

Emma was waiting for them once more.

She was staring at the money.

Christophe arrived first.

"Where's Gus?" Emma said.

"He'll be along in a minute. He drives like an old woman."

Emma laughed. "I heard you say that. It was funny. It was good."

Christophe grinned. "I was telling the truth!"

Emma sighed, looking at the euros on the table. "Wow. Pretty amazing, all that money."

Christophe nodded and took his own mental inventory of the notes.

"It's all there," Emma joked. Gus arrived just then and took his own inventory as well.

Emma supposed this was to be expected. There may be honor among thieves, but they were thieves nonetheless.

Gus yawned. "So far so good. I'm off to get some sleep. Christophe, you coming?"

"I'll be along," Christophe said.

There was a long silence when Gus left. Emma was staring hard at the floor then the walls, then the ceiling. Christophe was looking at her. "So that went well," she finally said.

He nodded. "Nice job."

"This was the easy one," Emma said. "We've got a long road ahead."

"No, I'm serious. I was skeptical, but you've got it planned well," Christophe said. He stared at her.

"What?" Emma said.

"I want to tell you something," said Christophe.

"What's that?" Emma said.

"My name," Christophe said.

"Why would I—"

"I want you to know my real name. Christophe Rabat."

"I know your real name," Emma said.

"OK, how about my mother's name?" Christophe said.

"This is ridiculous."

"No, I want you to know I trust you."

"Fine," Emma said.

"Laurence Front," Christophe said.

Emma nodded. "Okay. I've got it. Now, I've got to get some sleep, too. I have to work in the morning."

"Wait, it's important. You must promise me you will remember this," Christophe said.

"Why?" Emma said.

"Just promise me. Laurence Front."

"OK, OK. Laurence Front is your mother. How about your father?" Emma said.

"No just my mother," Christophe said. "My father is dead."

"Laurence Front is your mother. Goodnight Christophe."

– € –

The next night things went just as well at Terrenoire.

Afterwards, Gus broached a difficult subject. "Emma, I'm a little worried about tomorrow. Le Clapier is run by that anal Brit Roger Coltman, and his henchman Giles is much more on the ball than those other security guys."

"I know, but I'm not concerned. I will distract Giles," Emma said.

"We already have 30 million in our hands. Why not just cut and run?" Gus said.

"No. The missing euros can't be discovered before we are gone. Part of what makes this plan work is that they won't discover anything is missing, let alone exactly what is missing, for months. If they are able to identify the serial numbers that are missing before distribution, what we've taken will not only be worthless, but there is a good chance we will get caught if we try to use them," Emma said.

"How do you plan to distract Giles?" Gus said.

"We often visit when I'm at Le Clapier. I'll ask him into my office for coffee and cake. You shouldn't have any trouble. Just call the cellular when you are ten minutes away and my office phone just before you start loading the paper."

"Ok, see you tomorrow." Gus waved goodnight and left the barn.

Christophe and Emma stood there for a minute, neither of them knowing exactly what to say. She finally broke the silence. "Goodnight then."

Christophe looked in her eyes. "Don't you see I'm in love with you?"

"Christophe, we've talked about this ... you and me ... it is not going to happen." She got into her car and drove home.

CHAPTER 18
AUGUST 2000

Le Clapier scared Emma too, but she would never let on to Christophe and Gus. Giles needed to be distracted; he WAS very sharp and had to be out of the picture. Any flaws in Emma's plan, no matter how tiny, were at risk of being discovered at Le Clapier.

Emma received the cell call from the boys, waited five minutes, and phoned Giles.

"Giles, it's Emma."

"Well, hello Emma, you still here?"

"Yes, and I was hoping you would come see me."

"I'm just weighing in tonight's delivery, can it wait?"

"I can wait a little while, but not long," she said.

"I'll get there as soon as I can."

Emma closed her office door and started the coffee pot brewing. She put a cloth over her desk and placed the cheesecake that she had baked a few nights before—so it would age properly—on the desk. She put out plates and a cake knife. She could already smell the cinnamon of the coffee. She turned off the harsh overhead light and turned on the small lamp on the credenza behind the desk. She smiled. It was perfect. Her offices at the other two warehouses were still as stark as the day she'd moved into them, as was her office at Chamalières. Emma had taken care to "warm up" Le Clapier—and to invite Giles in for cake and coffee one evening a week—just for this moment.

Giles knocked lightly.

"Come on in," she said.

"Wow," he said, eyeing the cheesecake. "That looks fabulous. And what is that lovely aroma?" Giles said.

"It's the coffee I told you about. I figured about this time of night you could use a cup," Emma said.

"It has been a long shift."

"It's almost ready. Let me cut you a piece of cheesecake."

"Oh," Giles said, "I LOVE cheesecake."

"I'll let you guess the flavor," Emma said as she sliced cleanly through the cake and served it onto his plate. Then she cut a piece for herself.

Giles lifted his fork and inhaled deeply. "Smells like, lemon ... and maybe white chocolate."

"You're amazing!" Emma said.

"I'm right?"

"Yes, you are."

He took a bite and savored it. "Mmm ... it is possible, Emma Scott, that you make the best cheesecake in the world."

"That's quite a compliment coming from you," Emma said.

"I am a connoisseur. How about some of that coffee?"

Emma poured him a cup, knowing he took it black. She poured herself a cup and cut it with half and half.

"This is great, I would have never thought to add cinnamon," Giles said.

Emma's office phone rang.

"You still on the clock?" Giles asked, surprised.

"No, but I'm expecting a call from a friend who's arriving from the States tonight, that's why I couldn't wait too long," Emma said, reaching casually for the phone. "Hello."

"Almost done," Christophe said.

"You're here! I can't wait to see you! The key is under the mat. Let yourself in and I'll be there in ..." Emma looked at her watch. "Ten minutes."

Christophe hung up.

"Okay. See you soon!" Emma said. She turned to Giles. "I have to run. Please, enjoy your cake and coffee and feel free to have another piece. Take some home with you tonight. Just put what's left the mini-fridge when you're done and lock the door behind you?"

Giles nodded. "Oui, yes. Will do."

He was halfway through his second piece of cheesecake and just pouring a second cup of the delicious coffee when his beeper sounded. He set down his coffee and reached for the beeper.

Where are you? R. Coltman.

Giles swore softly. Of course, Coltman would choose to make one of his surprise checks tonight, when there was cake and lovely coffee. He quickly cleaned up, turned off the light, and locked the office door behind him.

— € —

"I still don't think it's a good idea," said Gus.

"What?" Christophe said.

"You and Emma."

Christophe paused before responding, "Why, do you think we'll cheat you?"

"Nah, you know better than that. I trust you. I just think it's a bad idea."

"You asked me to wait until the job was done. It's as good as done now. You can't stop me." Christophe said firmly.

Gus nodded. "No, I cannot." He pulled the truck up to the Le Clapier weigh out station and a disturbing sight greeted them. Giles was at the scales, as usual, but Roger Coltman was standing there as well. Giles was looking quite sheepish and Coltman's eyes narrowed.

"You were late arriving tonight. Why?" Coltman accused.

"Construction on La Lille," said Gus calmly. "They have been working nights all this week and we've had to detour. We've been late every night this week, haven't we Giles?"

The security guard nodded, happy to have Coltman's attention on something other than the fact that he had not been at his station when he should have been.

Coltman seemed to relax, as much as a guy like that could relax. "Yes," he said, clearing his throat, "I guess I read something about that. Carry on."

The truck eased on to the scale and was given clearance by the computer. Gus drove slowly out of the warehouse. "Keep an eye on the rear view," he said to Christophe. "I don't trust that guy."

Christophe laughed out loud. "You don't trust that guy. We're the ones stealing from him. That's rich."

"Not funny. He could blow this wide open," Gus said.

Christophe scanned the road behind them. He saw no one. They dropped the new load of paper at the printing facility, and arrived at La Dame without incident. Emma was waiting for them in the barn.

Although they had one more night to the job, each of them felt relief that the Le Clapier leg of the journey was over. It showed on their faces, especially Emma's.

"Is everything okay?" Gus said, alarmed.

"Everything's fine. I'm just tired and glad that's over," Emma said.

"We won't need you at Grange Neuve tomorrow," Gus said. "Maybe you should get some sleep."

Emma shook her head. "I'm in it for the long haul." She grinned. "No pun intended."

Christophe stepped toward Emma. "Let me drive you home."

Emma shook her head. "Nothing can change. The routine is set. It's working so far. I'm fine on my own. It's not over yet."

"No," said Gus, eyeing Christophe. "It's not over yet."

"See you tomorrow," said Emma.

"Yes, you will," said Christophe.

— € —

The next night Emma, under the facility dispatcher's ID, sent an email to Grange Neuve security telling them to expect a different truck that night, and asked for an immediate reply to acknowledge. When the email response did not immediately come, Emma set up her computer to monitor and intercept phone calls from the floor of the warehouse. She had just switched to the telephone monitor when she caught a call from the warehouse to the dispatcher. She went into action. "Monsieur Laurent's office," she said in a husky voice.

"May I speak with him please, security from Grande Neuve here."

"I'm sorry, he just left for dinner. May I help you?" Emma said.

"Yes, I just received an email about a different truck making the delivery tonight. I wanted to confirm," the guard said.

"One moment Monsieur, please, I'll check," Emma said.

She returned. "Yes, there was a mechanical issue with the regular truck. Is there a problem?"

"No," the guard said, "just checking. Thanks."

Emma continued monitoring both the phone and the email. An affirmative email response came back a few minutes later, and Emma sighed in relief. She replied and then deleted the email, but she continued to monitor the situation until the boys phoned to say they had left the warehouse. She smiled, shut down her computer, and headed for La Dame.

— € —

Emma popped a bottle of Perrier-Jouet and poured them each a glass.

"To Andrew," Emma said, raising her glass.

"To us," toasted Christophe.

"To my last job," said Gus.

"Mine too," Emma said.

"But we've only just begun," Christophe said. "We make a good team."

"Nope, I'm done. I just wanted to see what it was like," Emma said.

"Does that mean I can have your share?" Christophe said.

"Funny," Emma said, yawning. "I don't think so."

"You should go home and go to bed," Gus said.

Emma nodded. "On my way. See you guys tomorrow."

"But we have to celebrate," said Christophe. "The night is young."

"And I am old," said Gus. "Let's go Christophe. We have business to wrap up tomorrow."

— € —

Gus rented a truck for the trip back to Milan, and they loaded the supplies. They shredded the leftover paper and loaded it into garbage bags, and loaded the garbage bags into the truck. Gus would dispose of the bags at different points along the journey to Milan. They left the truck in the La Dame barn and went back to their jobs as normal.

For the next week, Emma monitored all company email closely to see if there was any hint of suspicion. There was not. A week later she finally felt it was safe for Gus to quit. He had the farthest to go, and he had to deal with the truck, so it seemed fitting that he be the first one out.

They loaded Gus's share of the take into a compartment Gus had built into the truck, Emma's and Christophe's into smaller vans they each had rented, and then it was time to say farewell.

Gus shook the younger man's hand. "Be careful," he said. "Be wise. And be well."

Christophe nodded. "You take care, old man. And don't drive to Milan like an old woman."

Gus laughed. "At least there are no longer border checkpoints between France and Italy." He turned to Emma, hugged her tightly and kissed her forehead. "Thank you, *Cara*. It was fun, but it is time to retire. I am tired."

"Enjoy your money, Gus. Take care. And thank you. Let me know you've arrived safely."

"I will. The regular way," Gus said as he climbed into the truck.

Christophe opened the barn door and Emma waved as Gus pulled out into the night.

Christophe closed the barn door and turned to Emma. "Shall we go and have some wine and dinner?"

Emma shook her head. "We can't risk being seen together even now. Maybe next week. I will call you."

The next morning Emma drove her rental van to the Lyon self-storage facility she had rented six months earlier. She drove into the unit, unloaded the euros, and double-locked the door. She stopped by the rental office and paid for the unit in cash for the next two years, explaining in perfect French that she would be out of the country working on an exciting new job, but that she would be back to lovely Lyon just as soon as possible. After returning the rental van, Emma boarded a train back to Saint-Étienne. She did not call Christophe for dinner the following week. Or the week after that.

Christophe knew it was too dangerous to approach Emma at work, but he was undeterred in his quest. Without telling Emma—she had returned to her real job duties the day after the heist had been completed and was no longer monitoring the dispatch center—Christophe applied for a change in shift and was moved to daytime security at Terrenoire. That way he could see Emma on a daily basis ... even if she did not see him. He sold the Renault and rented a black Saab, so Emma wouldn't recognize his car. At night he sat outside her house.

Watching.

CHAPTER 19
SEPTEMBER 2000

About a week into his vigil, Christophe noticed that he was not the only one watching Emma's house. A black Peugeot also stayed until Emma turned out her lights each night. Two nights later, Christophe decided to watch from the bushes. The Peugeot returned, waited for the house lights to go out, then drove away.

The next day Christophe exchanged his Saab for a Fiat, and that night, when the Peugeot drove away, he followed. Twenty minutes later, the Peugeot pulled up in front of a small house and Giles got out of the car. Christophe assumed that the Le Clapier security guard was watching Emma because he wanted her, too, but he couldn't be sure. He knew Emma should know about the surveillance—Le Clapier had been one of her worst fears—but if he told her about Giles she would know that he had been spying on her, too, and that was not something he wanted to reveal. Instead, knowing that the best defense was a good offense, he called Emma the next day.

"Are you seeing the Security guard?" he asked.

"Who? Giles? No, Christophe. I'm not here to have fun. I'm working. What's up?"

"Nothing," Christophe said almost too quickly.

"Christophe, what the hell is going on?"

"I just have a bad feeling about that guy," Christophe said.

"Do you think he knows something about The Job?"

"No, nothing like that. About you and him," Christophe said.

Emma sighed. "There is no me and him. We have coffee

occasionally. It was part of The Job, if you'll remember. In fact, I'm giving up my office at Le Clapier—at all three of the warehouses—next week," Emma said.

"I think that is for the best," Christophe said.

"Is there something you're not telling me?"

"*Non.* Just want to make sure you are safe."

— € —

The next day Christophe took a trip to Lyon and obtained a high-powered listening device. He tested it from his car that night and heard Emma singing in the kitchen. He felt a bit guilty spying on her, but told himself he was trying to protect her.

A week later, Christophe was in his car watching Giles watching the house and listening to Emma alone in her home. She was talking to someone named JC, but no one was in the house. He knew that. He did not know that Emma was commenting aloud as she read the latest escapades of her new favorite Story: JCMI5, the English housewife living in France with the husband who was married to his job. JC had recently broken up with the adventurous René and was now cavorting with a twenty-five-year-old stud named Georges. Emma was so enthralled with their story that she didn't hear the knock at her front door. But Christophe heard it. He had seen Giles get out of his car and had instantly been on the alert.

Giles knocked twice more. Emma opened the door in her bathrobe. "Giles! What are you doing here?"

Christophe turned up the listening device volume.

"You didn't say good-bye," Giles said. "I wanted to thank you for the coffee and the cheesecake. I will miss those evenings with you."

"I'm sorry, I was so busy clearing out the office," Emma said. "I enjoyed those evenings, too."

Christophe tried to send a mental message. Don't ask him in. Don't ask him in.

"Please, come in." Emma opened the door wide.

Giles entered and closed the door behind him.

Christophe heard the chain lock engage. "Merde," he muttered. He gathered his equipment and walked quickly to the bushes just outside her door.

"This is a nice home," Giles said.

"Thanks, it suits me. Although I won't be here much longer," Emma said.

"Going back to the States?"

"Yes. My job is almost done here. I was making coffee, would you like some?"

"Your coffee? Always." Giles smiled and followed Emma into the kitchen.

"Giles ... What are you doing? No ..."

"I thought you would like?" Giles said.

"Giles, stop! You can't ..." Emma said.

Christophe slid a credit card into the door, prepared to pop the latch.

"Emma, please," Giles said. "I want to do for you. Is only small gift."

"A gift, for me?"

"To say good-bye."

Christophe returned the credit card to his pocket.

"Giles, this is really lovely. Thank you so much for stopping by." Emma said.

Christophe smiled. The Security Guard was not going to be invited to stay for anything more than a cup of coffee. Christophe was safely back in the Fiat when Emma's front door opened and Giles stepped out into the night.

The security guard waited until Emma closed the door behind him, and then he nonchalantly walked in the direction of his own car. When he was out of view, he quickly ducked and circled back to the driver's side of the Fiat, careful to keep out of view, and rapped sharply on the window. A startled Christophe looked back at him.

CHAPTER 20
OCTOBER 2000

Christophe didn't hesitate. He opened his door so quickly that Giles was knocked to the ground. Christophe was out of the car and had broken Giles's neck before the security guard knew what had hit him. Moving quickly, Christophe grabbed the security guard's car keys and moved the dead man's car behind his. As he worked, he constantly scanned the area. The last thing he needed was Emma seeing him disposing of Giles's body.

Christophe propped the security guard in the passenger seat of the Fiat, and slipped behind the wheel. He drove south from Saint-Étienne to a town called Tence. On the outside of town there was a cliff with a deep, water-filled quarry. You could smell the sulfur a mile away.

Christophe turned onto the dirt road leading to the quarry and stopped fifty feet from the edge. He took off his shoes and placed them on the side of the road. He drove the car to the quarry's edge, got out, and moved Giles into the driver's seat. He positioned the security guard's foot on the gas pedal, pressed down, and backed away quickly. As the car plunged into the sulfurous quarry depths, Christophe slipped back into his shoes, walked to a bar about a mile down the road, and ordered a beer.

— € —

The coffee had kicked in and, not sleepy, Emma went back to her laptop. JCMI5 must not have had coffee, because all was quiet on that email front. There was, however, a message from Coach, the first since Emma had left for France.

> **Dear MagicGirl—**
>
> **Haven't heard from you in quite some time. You must be busy with The Operation, and that is the way it should be. No news is good news, as they say. You are ready to be on your own. I will check every day, however, just in case.**
>
> **Be smart. Stay alert.**
>
> **Coach**

Emma started to reply when she heard a car approach.

It was late. This was unusual in her quiet neighborhood.

Thinking about Coach's words, Emma quickly closed her laptop to douse its light, and drew back the living room curtains slightly. The approaching car turned out to be a cab, and to Emma's surprise, Christophe got out, paid the driver, and headed not for her house, but for the Fiat that was parked down the road.

Emma let the curtain go quickly, her heart pounding. Where had Christophe come from? What was his car doing down the street from her house? Was he watching her? And, if so, why? First Giles and now Christophe. In the same night. What the hell was going on?

An hour later, with no answers, and no return appearance by Christophe, Emma fell asleep on the couch, clutching her laptop.

— € —

Two nights later, on a strange hunch she hadn't been able to shake off, Emma stopped by the Le Clapier warehouse and was unnerved to discover another watchman on duty.

"Where's Giles?" Emma said, flashing her badge.

"He has not been here for a few days, Miss. Don't know what's wrong. He hasn't called," the watchman said.

"That's not like him," Emma said.

The new guard shrugged. "I wouldn't know."

— € —

Two weeks later Emma received an email from Roger Coltman, informing selected individuals at the Bank that Giles Fougerouse had taken his own life. His car had been found in a quarry in a nearby town.

Emma shivered.

Something wasn't right, but she wasn't in a position to go poking around right now. She had to keep a low profile and get out of France as soon as possible.

She sent Coltman an email expressing her sincere regret, and then she began monitoring the facility manager's email. No matter what the email had said, Emma knew Coltman would not take Giles's death lightly, particularly since the security guard had been a favorite employee. After a week with no activity, Emma decided to pay Coltman a visit. He knew she'd often had coffee with Giles. It wouldn't seem untoward for her to inquire.

"Roger, do you have a minute?" Emma said, peeking through his office door.

"Certainly. Come in," Coltman said as he stood and came to greet her.

"It's not business really, I just wanted to talk about Giles," Emma said.

Roger closed the door and sat behind his desk.

Emma took a seat as well.

"What is it?" Coltman asked.

"Well, I guess I'd like to know what happened. I never noticed anything wrong," Emma said. "Nothing that would cause him to be suicidal, anyway."

"Neither did I, and that seems odd to me. But what did we really know about Giles?" Coltman said. "The police found a note in his home. I'm told it's typical in this type of situation."

Emma froze for a moment, remembering the night she saw Christophe outside her cottage. "Do you really think Giles committed suicide?" She said.

"I've decided that I didn't really know him."

"I suppose that's wise. I just can't help wondering what drove him to it," Emma said.

Coltman shook his head. "I suggest you stop wondering and move on. I hear you are doing that soon. What are your future plans?" Coltman asked.

Emma shrugged. "I don't have any at the moment, just some rest and relaxation. It will be nice after so much stress," she said.

"You've done well for us, Emma. Thank you."

"That's high praise from you, Roger. Thanks." Emma rose and shook his hand. She left his office and closed the door behind her. She leaned back against the wall and breathed a huge sigh of relief. Her fears had been unfounded. She was getting paranoid. She had not known Giles, either. Perhaps Christophe had known something she didn't and had been protecting her from something that night. She had not heard a word from him. When she got in her car, Emma called Christophe and asked him to meet her at a café in Lyon.

— € —

Christophe arrived first and ordered herbal tea instead of espresso. It was vile stuff, but he was already tense, and he needed to remain calm with Emma. She entered moments later and took a seat across from him.

"Christophe," Emma said, "it's time for you to give your two weeks' notice."

"What about you, Emma?" Christophe asked.

My contract runs for another three months, and I plan to stick it out. I need to stay in case they discover something," Emma said.

"I'll give my notice," Christophe said, "but I'll stay behind, too. I'm sure I can be of service in some way."

Emma looked at him sharply. "What kind of service might that be?"

Christophe shrugged. "Maybe you need a date for coffee now that the security guard is no longer here."

Emma gasped. "How do you know about Giles? Christophe ... did you have anything to do with it?"

"Why would you think that?"

"I saw you outside my house the night Giles came to say good-bye."

"He was trouble," Christophe said.

Emma's eyes widened. "He was not trouble. He was just a sweet man. What did you do?"

Christophe shrugged again. "I eliminated a threat."

"Oh, my God," Emma whispered. She stood to leave.

Christophe grabbed her wrist with too much force.

"Emma, wait. I need to see you," Christophe said through clenched teeth.

The couple at the next table stared. Emma smiled at them and then turned the smile on high, all showmanship now. "But my love, I'll see you soon enough."

God, what he'd give to hear her really mean those words.

"How soon, *ma chérie*?" Christophe said.

The couple went back to their cafés au lait.

"Look, Christophe," Emma sat back down at the table and whispered. "I don't know why you did what you did, why you thought you had to do what you did, but it makes me sick to my stomach, you make me sick to my stomach, and if it wasn't for Gus and for my mother, I'd turn your ass in right now, but this is still a critical time for the job, and I'm not going to let anything—and I mean *anything*—get in the way. But you need to get out—and stay out of my sight. I mean it, Christophe." She wrenched her hand from his grasp. "And now I'm leaving. Don't try to stop me or contact me. Give your notice tomorrow, and then get the hell out."

— € —

As she slid her key into the ignition, Emma's hand shook. Now that she knew what Christophe was capable of, she was terrified of him. She had to hide it, for now. Until it was time for her to leave France. And that date was going to have to get bumped up. Way up. Emma was in danger, she felt it. She would leave next week. She'd use her mother as the excuse, as her urgent need to return to the States. But she would not see her mother. Not for a long time. When she left France, Emma knew, she would have to leave without a trace. She wiped the tears from her face, and whispered to Giles: "I am so sorry."

— € —

When Emma got home, she pulled out her laptop and started typing:

> **Dear Coach–**
>
> **The Operation is done and could be considered a success. But something has happened. I'm scared Coach, scared of one of my cohorts. I need to disappear. Can you help me?**
>
> **MagicGirl**

She made coffee and sat on the living room couch in the dark, watching through a slit in the curtains for any sign of Christophe. An hour later, she checked her laptop and found a new draft in the inbox.

> **Dear MagicGirl,**
>
> **Assume you have the appropriate alias travel docs. Do not take your car to the airport. Take a form of public transportation. Pick an airport that is not known for international travel, make at least two connections and do not fly directly to your final destination. Take anonymous public transport as much as**

possible [bus or train]. Know your final destination before you embark, but travel around enough before you reach your destination that it won't be clear where you will end up. You should come see me where Scotty used to fish. I can protect you. Let me know when you have departed.

Coach

Emma felt a huge sense of relief. She had the Mallory Andrews documents she'd created while she was waiting for Coach to contact her the first time. At least she had thought of that. He wanted her to come to him and right now she wanted that more than anything, even if Emma didn't know who he or she was. The rest she could figure out.

She called The Bank and told them she was needed at home immediately and indefinitely. The Bank agreed that her job was basically done, and that she had fulfilled the duties and obligations of her contract. The process she had created to uphold the superior standards of the French euro printing was well in place and working efficiently. Emma didn't have to be there every day now to oversee it. They would be in touch with her landlord, no need to worry.

Emma packed quickly and lightly, and then she headed for her main facility office and its computer. She left the files and paperwork for the new process where they could be easily found, but cleaned her personal files and her secret exits and entrances to the company website off the mainframe. After she had intercepted the security dispatch schedule one last time, there was just one more thing Emma needed to take care of before she disappeared.

Two hours later, she pulled her car out of the parking garage and drove over the speed limit to Lyon. She carefully checked her rearview mirror and took an indirect route. She was certain she was not followed. She had thirty minutes before her train departed. She'd arranged for the BMW to be picked up at the station by the leasing agent later that morning. She arrived at the station and boarded her train, continually scanning the crowded platform. When the train pulled away fifteen minutes later, Emma closed her eyes and said a silent "thank you."

The 6 a.m. train was bound for Nice, where Emma would board the first of a series of planes bound for Montreal via Casablanca and then Boston. She was traveling as Mallory Andrews, with a new wig and a pair of glasses worn to match the passport photo. In the photo she sported light red hair and small tortoise shell frames. Just a name change to Mallory Emmett, she would be on to a new life.

— € —

At 10 a.m. Pierre Javilin, the head of warehouse security, summoned Christophe to his office.

"What's going on?" Christophe said.

"Nothing," Javilin said. "Just a random security check."

"I've never heard of this," Christophe said.

"I assure you it is standard protocol. Let's go."

The two men walked to the locker room.

"Please open your locker," Javilin said.

Christophe slowly dialed the combination lock and drew open the door. He stepped away. He wasn't worried, there was nothing in the locker, nothing anywhere anyone could find.

Javilin rifled through the clothes and toiletry kit Christophe stowed in his locker. He looked through Christophe's wallet.

"Where is your car?" Javilin asked.

"In the lot," Christophe said.

"Keys, please."

Christophe gave Javilin the keys to his Fiat and followed him to the parking lot. Javilin hit the unlock button and followed the electronic beep without waiting for Christophe. Javilin opened the trunk and found nothing in it.

"Travel light, ay Christophin?"

"I guess," Christophe said.

Javilin opened the back door on the passenger side and drew out a package that Christophe did not recognize.

"What's this?" Javilin said.

"I dunno."

Javilin tore open the brown paper and found a stack of newly minted fifty-euro notes. Christophe's mouth fell open.

"I've never seen that before," he said. "I don't know how that got in my car."

Javilin spoke into the microphone attached to his lapel. "Home base, we need the police here immediately." He turned to Christophe. "I think you're lucky, Christophin, that this money hasn't yet been issued. This is only a delit and not a crime. Still, you'll get 9 to 18 months."

"What are you talking about? I didn't take those," Christophe said.

"Then who did?" Javilin said.

Christophe contemplated running, but he had no chance. There was a police station nearby and he cursed himself for not plotting an escape route. He raised his hands in the air as it dawned on him who had planted the money in his car. He was certain Emma had betrayed him and she would pay, but not today.

Revenge was best served cold.

CHAPTER 21

NOVEMBER 2000

Mallory took the train from Boston to New Jersey. As she stood by her mother's bedside listening to her breathe, Mallory marveled at all that had happened during the past eight months. How much she and her life had changed. "You can officially have your name back, Emma," Mallory said softly. She reached for her mother's hand and squeezed. No response. Emma looked pale and drawn. Mallory didn't know when she would be able to return, but she vowed she would. "I love you, Mom," she whispered, and leaned down to kiss her on the cheek.

– € –

Mallory's father had made a semi-annual fishing pilgrimage to British Columbia to troll the Johnstone Strait. He'd often told her how beautiful it was, although he had never taken Mallory with him. He said he had a special fishing buddy there. When Coach had told her to come to that same tiny fishing village, Mallory realized he must have been her father's fishing buddy ... and his former partner in crime. Before her return to Montreal, Mallory drafted a message:

Dear Coach–

I made the trip safely, thank you for your help. I've just visited my mother in New Jersey and am now headed due north for a

bit of touring before I head for Roberts Creek. I feel the need to stretch my legs a bit, do some musing, and put some of the more unsavory events of the past eight months in my rearview mirror. When I do arrive, probably in a month or two, how will I get in touch with you?

MagicGirl

Dear MagicGirl–

Thank you for letting me know that you are OK. Take your time. I will be here. When you arrive, go to the local general store in town [you can't miss it] and ask if there is any real estate for sale. They will send you to me. Be safe.

Coach

The ocean had always calmed Mallory, so when she drove out of the car dealership in Montreal, she pointed her new Range Rover toward the nearest shore. She spent a month exploring Nova Scotia, Newfoundland, and Prince Edward Island. She bought a new camera and spent her solitary hours taking pictures of the coastal landscapes. She didn't stay anywhere long enough to get the film developed, and before long she had more than a hundred rolls of film piled in a box in the back seat. When the box couldn't hold another roll, Mallory turned the car around and headed due west for the Sunshine Coast and Roberts Creek.

The mid-section of Canada is big and desolate, particularly in winter, but Mallory didn't mind the privacy or the solitude. As she drove through the snow-covered country, Mallory let her mind wander back to a warm beach in the Caribbean. She remembered how Todd had described the Sunshine Coast, where the sun rarely shone. Mallory hadn't written to Todd in almost a year now, but it was comforting to know that she was headed to a place he loved.

Mallory drove into Horseshoe Bay on New Year's Eve, 2000.

The new euros would be distributed a year later, and Mallory would be a rich woman, although her share of the heist was tucked away in a little storage facility in Lyon. Someday she would go back and get it, but not anytime soon. For now, Mallory was living off of what was left of her trust fund. She figured, if she was careful, it would last another few years.

Mallory found a small Internet café in town and wrote a draft to Coach letting him know she would arrive the next day. She checked into a motel, had an early dinner in her room, and slept peacefully for the first time in eight months.

Early the next morning Mallory drove her Range Rover onto the first ferry of the New Year and cruised across the Bay. Enrobed in her winter gear from Syracuse, Mallory shot a roll of film as the ferry cut through the icy water.

Destination: Roberts Creek.

— € —

The tiny general store was dark and dank and smelled of something oddly familiar, something Mallory couldn't put her finger on.

"Can I help you miss?" said an old man, his chair leaned back against the wall.

"Yes, I was wondering if there's a real estate agent in town," Mallory said.

"Hah. Never had one of those," the old man said.

"So how do you sell property?" She said.

"Just put up a sign."

Mallory cocked her head at the old man. "And are there any signs up that you know of?"

"There's a place for sale down by the coast. Next to Rusty's. He's selling it for the past owner. Don't know what kind of shape it's in. Old man Rutter passed away just a few months ago, but there hadn't been a woman in the place for more than twenty years, can't imagine."

"Can you tell me how to get there?" Mallory said.

"Sure, it's just down the road to your right. For Sale sign in front. Rusty's house is just next door."

The store's smell was starting to make Mallory queasy, so she thanked the owner and headed back out to the fresh air.

She spotted the For Sale sign about two miles from the general store, on a gently curving road that teased her with occasional glimpses of the sea. She pulled into the driveway and quietly got out of the Range Rover, wanting to explore the property on her own a bit before she talked to this Rusty who lived next door. Mallory felt safe in taking this liberty because she couldn't see another home from the driveway.

The exterior of the house, more a cottage, was in disrepair. It was in desperate need of a paint job and several windows were missing shutters. It was a good size, she thought, not too big and not too small. It had a few interesting architectural features on both levels, so it wasn't the ubiquitous box-shaped cottage that seemed to be emblematic of this part of Canada. Mallory closed her eyes and imagined the house with a new paint job and flower beds lining the foundation. Yes, she could see it. Just beyond the house was a wonderful view of the sea. It had a dock and a boat, and Mallory could see a man working on the boat. He suddenly looked up in her direction, and Mallory looked for a place to duck out of sight, but it was too late. The man waved at her and headed up from the dock.

"Hello there," the man called out.

Mallory figured he was in his seventies, but he moved like a much younger man. As he got closer, she could see that his skin was weathered and wrinkled, although not as much as you might expect for man who appeared to pass his time outdoors. He had Robert Redford hair: soft reddish blond on top with white accents on the sides. He flashed a toothy grin; he still had great teeth. His smile was wide and turned up a little on the right side, making him appear as if he knew something Mallory did not. It intrigued her. She felt oddly drawn to this stranger and she could not figure out why. He stopped in front of her. "Can I help you?"

"Hi, sorry to disturb you, but the sign said 'For Sale,'" Mallory said.

"You're not disturbing me. I love company. Rusty Johnson." He extended his weathered hand.

"Mallory Emmett. Nice to meet you, Mr. Johnson."

"No need to stand on formality here. You can call me Coach," he said as he flashed Mallory the warmest smile she had ever seen.

Mallory's eyes widened.

Rusty nodded. "So how do you like our little town so far?"

Mallory gazed at her father's fishing buddy. "The general store is kind of creepy."

Rusty let out a hearty laugh. "I like a girl who speaks her mind. I've always wondered what that smell in there comes from. I shop at the IGA, only go in there to get my mail."

Mallory beamed at him. She felt a little stupid doing it, but she couldn't help herself.

"Would you like to go sailing?" Rusty said.

"Right now?" Mallory was surprised at how the offer excited her.

"We can talk out there ... about the house. Total privacy, no doubt."

Mallory jumped on the boat and cast off the stern line.

"You know your way around," Rusty said.

"My dad sailed."

"I know."

Mallory smiled. "Right."

Rusty turned the boat into the open water and Mallory hoisted the sails, obediently following Rusty's gentle instructions. Once they were well underway, he gestured for Mallory to join him in the cockpit.

Mallory was totally at ease with this man. He seemed familiar.

"Is everyone around here like you?" She asked.

"Odd question. I'd say I'm pretty unique."

"That's fair, stupid question," Mallory said.

"Not a stupid one, just odd. If what you're asking is, are folks here interesting? The answer is yes, but we're all um ... individuals." Rusty smiled.

"How did you come to know my dad?"

"Rusty Johnson is an alias."

Mallory smiled. "I've had a few of those myself lately."

Rusty nodded. "My real name is Robert," he said. "Robert Richards."

"Your last name is Richards?"

"That's the name I was born with," Rusty said.

"Me too."

"I know. Your father wasn't my friend. He was my son."

Mallory stared at him. "You're my grandfather?"

Rusty nodded. "I wanted to tell you when you first emailed, but I wasn't sure it was safe, for either of us."

"I thought you died in a fire."

"Your grandmother died in that fire and losing her almost killed me. I felt responsible because I wasn't there when it happened."

Mallory's eyes filled with tears. "I know how that feels. Where were you?"

"In Europe with your father. It was his first job and my last. After the fire, I just couldn't do it anymore. I came to Canada and started over here in Roberts Creek. Please don't be angry with me. This all happened before you were born."

Mallory looked at Rusty. She finally saw what had made him seem so familiar from the start; he had her father's eyes.

"Did my mother know about you?" she asked.

"She did, but we never met."

"Why didn't Dad tell me about you?"

"I asked him not to," Rusty said.

"I don't understand."

"Mallory, you have to know I love you. You are a gift to an old man. Please forgive me," Rusty said, his voice breaking. "I knew I could not visit you, be a part of your life. After my wife died, I didn't want to be a part of life anymore. Your dad came to see me twice a year. He brought photos and told me stories, so I've watched you grow. He also let me know that I might hear from you one day."

Mallory took a deep breath and looked directly into his eyes. "Thank you for telling me, Rusty—or should I say granddad."

"Rusty's fine. We good?"

Mallory nodded. "I have family again. It's nice not to be alone.

Rusty smiled. "Think you want to buy the house?" He said.

"Yes."

"The bank wants thirty thousand."

Mallory paused; it seemed awfully cheap. "I guess I'll need a boat."

"I'll throw in the boat."

"This boat?" Mallory said.

"Yeah, I'm getting too old to take it out by myself anyway."

"Rusty, you don't need to give me the boat."

"Just promise you'll take me out from time to time and it's yours," Rusty said.

Mallory paused, then smiled at her grandfather. "Okay. It's a deal."

"Good. You can stay there tonight if you want to. Still furniture in the house and all. Left the phone and electric turned on," he said. "Kind of feel responsible for you now."

"I don't want to be a burden," Mallory said, feeling an overwhelming sense of security nonetheless. It was a feeling she had not had since the accident.

"Can't help what you feel," Rusty said.

"Guess not."

They sailed back to the dock without speaking except for a few Captain-ly directions delivered by Rusty. Mallory loved being on the water. She didn't know if she could sail the boat alone, but she would try.

Back at the house, Rusty gave her the keys and his phone number in case she needed anything.

"Just make yourself at home. I'll stop by tomorrow to see about getting rid of anything you don't want," Rusty said.

"Thanks, Rusty. Is there someplace around here to get furniture and paint?" Mallory said.

"I'll take you on a tour tomorrow. That your car? Nice!" he said, pointing at the Range Rover.

"Yup. Other than a car, I need everything," Mallory said.

"I'll stop by around 10. We'll go shopping."

"Thanks."

"Mallory," Rusty said as he took her hands in his, "I'm glad you came." He turned and walked away but stopped to wave before he disappeared into the woods.

CHAPTER 22

MARCH 2001

Two months later, on a sparkling late winter's day, Mallory was lured by the sun from her work on the cottage interior to the great outdoors she had yet to explore. Rusty had pointed out a relatively remote hiking trail that he said wound its way up along a mountain stream to a beautiful waterfall, and that sounded perfect to Mallory.

The trail started out flat and even paved in some places, but after a mile there was only dirt, and the grade started to steadily increase. In another mile, the trail was infested with tree roots and no more than three feet wide. Mallory was looking down so as not to trip on the large roots when a rider came barreling down the trail on a mountain bike.

He spotted her just in time to swerve slightly and yell, "Look ouuu ..."

Mallory was thrown backwards and landed on her bum. The rider somersaulted over the handlebars but still managed to land on his feet. The bike was sprawled on top of Mallory. The rider ran over, lifted the bike, and placed it on the trail.

"Any more like you on their way down?" Mallory said, looking up.

"Nope, I travel alone. You OK?" He smiled, but looked concerned.

"Oh my God. Todd?" Mallory wasn't certain. He looked amazing—but not tanned. The sparkle was twinkling in his eyes.

"Mallory! Oh my God!"

Todd helped Mallory to her feet and wrapped her in a bear hug.

"Hey, easy there. I'm bruised."

Todd stepped back and looked at her. "Anything broken?"

"I don't think so," said Mallory. She did a mental inventory of what hurt: her back, her bum, her shoulder.

"I'm giving you a ride down," Todd said.

"Where's my camera?" She asked as she scanned the path. It had fallen a few feet from her, next to the path. She picked it up and unzipped the bag.

"Is it okay?" He came over and looked down with genuine concern.

She aimed and focused the lens. "Seems, okay. I can't go down yet. I haven't seen the falls." As she said this, Mallory realized she'd never make it down the path on her own, let alone go further up it. She was starting to feel dizzy.

Todd caught her just as her knees buckled.

"I'm taking you home," said Todd.

"Don't think I want to ride with such a reckless fellow," Mallory said. She started to lose her knees again.

"End of discussion," said Todd. "Glad, the camera's okay—was thinking I might have to give you back my most prized possession."

Mallory smiled. He treasured her gift.

Todd balanced the bike between his legs and boosted Mallory up onto the handlebars. They rode down the trail in silence, Todd steering the bike and keeping Mallory balanced at the same time, an impressive feat. Mallory's mind was racing. She was happy to see him, but now her cover was blown. Where had he been? How had he ended up here?

When they reached Mallory's Range Rover, they stood in silence for a minute, stealing glances at each other but mostly looking at the ground. When their eyes met, they looked away quickly, and then back just as quick.

"So how are you?" Todd finally said.

"I'm good, good," Mallory said. "But I think I need to sit down and soon. Do you want to come back to my place for coffee?"

"You're living here? In Roberts Creek?"

"Yup, have been for about a month now."

"Where?" Todd said.

"Old man Rutter's place."

"Really? Next to Rusty."

Mallory's cover was totally blown and now Rusty's was in danger, too. Her head spun. "I need to sit down," she said again.

Todd jumped. "Right, right. Sure, I'll have coffee. Throw the bike in the back?"

Mallory popped the hatch and Todd opened it. The bike fit easily into the roomy compartment.

"Would you drive?" Mallory asked.

"That bad?" Todd said.

"A bit."

They drove in silence for a few minutes and then Mallory turned to Todd, wanting to keep the focus on him for both her and Rusty's protection. She couldn't believe Todd was here! She knew she shouldn't be bringing him home, but she couldn't help but want to be with him. The attraction had not diminished for her. "How have you been?" she said.

"Okay."

"You sure?"

"Why?" Todd said.

She winced and rubbed her shoulder. "I don't know, just get a feeling."

"It's been a rough stretch for me, since uh ... we lost touch," he said.

"Care to share?" Mallory said.

"Been over it a lot ... tell me about you."

"I've had an interesting time myself. We can just leave it at that."

Todd said tentatively, "You look amazing."

"Thanks, so do you." Mallory blushed and looked away.

Todd pulled into the driveway and whistled appreciatively. "The house looks great. You've been busy."

Mallory smiled. "I'm pretty happy with it ... just a few more things I want to do. I need a shed built, probably over there." She pointed south. "Paint and flower beds, but that will have to wait until thaw."

"I can build a shed for you," Todd said.

"More hidden talents?"

"I think I'll let you discover them in time. Don't want to use all my ammunition on the first salvo."

Mallory chuckled. *He can still make me laugh*, she thought. They went inside and Mallory put on the coffee. Todd took a look around the place and settled into an overstuffed chair in the living room. Mallory sat across from him on the couch. He looked at her for a long while. She just looked back. After about five minutes she got up to fix the coffee and returned with two steaming mugs. Todd was still staring at her.

"What?" she said.

"Nothing. I'm just thinking about how stupid I was."

"Stupid?"

"To let you go," Todd said.

"Hope you still take it the same way." Mallory handed him a mug and smiled.

"You remember?"

"Light and sweet. I remember a lot about that week," Mallory said.

"I'm sorry I didn't respond to your emails," Todd said.

"It's alright. I'm not angry. It's not like you didn't warn me."

"You stopped writing."

"My life got very involved. Honestly until you mowed me down an hour ago, I'd almost forgotten about you," she lied.

"I need to explain."

"No, you don't." Mallory shrugged.

"Mallory, I need to."

"Right. Fine. Go ahead," Mallory said.

"I went to the Turks and Caicos club after Paradise Island. The manager of the village there wanted a good golf partner. I was also a bartender. The booze was free and the locals were happy to provide weed, blow, and whatever in the pharmaceutical department," Todd said.

"Hmmm, not a good environment?"

"Well, I thought it was great at the start, but after a few months I was really in trouble. I wasn't golfing because I wasn't waking up in time; I was even late for my late shifts. All I did was drink and party. I'm told one night I stole a motorbike and crashed it on the other side of the island. I got arrested and I don't remember any of it. They sent me home to Quebec the next day."

"Wow," Mallory said.

"I guess it was better than being in a Caribbean jail. But home meant living with my father again. He was already so disappointed in me and not shy about expressing it. I worked some at the local golf club. I hadn't given up drinking, but I didn't have much money so I could only indulge a little. When winter came, the only work I could get was as a bartender. Again, the booze was free and ultimately my father stuck me in rehab without the courtesy of an intervention."

"How did that go?" she said without a trace of judgment, only concern.

"It was tough, but it worked. When I got out, I didn't go back home. I came west, as far west as I could."

"Punishing dad?"

"Maybe a little," he agreed. "Maybe a lot. I stopped when I hit the coast and drove north. I always loved coming up here when I was in school. Stopped at a grocery store and saw a hand-lettered flyer looking for a bartender at the local golf club. Bartending probably wasn't a good idea, but I had experience. I applied, got the job, and they even gave me a room at the club as part of my pay."

"Great deal. No?"

"Not for long. I managed to not drink for the first few months. I had a good feeling about this place. Folks were friendly and spoke English. I played some golf and rode my mountain bike around the trails. When winter settled in, I started having hot toddies before I turned in. This place is dead in winter. When one of the local kids asked me if I wanted a joint one night that was it, I was back in my old rut," Todd said.

"I'm sorry to hear that," Mallory said. "So where are you now?"

"Been clean again for a few months. I've been getting back into exercise, burning up energy rather than burning myself out. It's been working so far. I think my reward might be running into you."

He smiled. "Literally." He took the last sip of his coffee and went into the small kitchen to wash out his cup. He stood at the sink for a moment and then he returned to the living room and said, "I should probably go."

Mallory stood, walked over to him, and stroked his face with her hand. Todd leaned into her hand and closed his eyes. "I've missed you," he said. He opened his eyes and gazed at Mallory. "I'm just now realizing how much."

Mallory smiled. "I will never understand men as long as I live."

"You mean it wasn't obvious?" Todd said.

"Nope," she said.

"It's getting dark—can I make you breakfast tomorrow?"

She raised her eyebrow. "Is the next line, Should I call you or nudge you?"

Todd shook his head. "Nope. Just breakfast."

"What time should I expect you?"

"Eight okay?"

"Sure," Mallory said. She walked him to the door and watched his familiar slight limp as he moved to the Range Rover. He lifted the bike from the back, turned to wave at Mallory, and then he pedaled down the long driveway.

Mallory liked watching him. A lot.

— ₠ —

Todd arrived on his bike the next morning with groceries in his backpack. He was hungry. He put four slices of bread into the toaster and hung over the glowing coils, urging the bread to pop.

"You are going to burn your eyebrows off," Mallory said.

Todd laughed and stepped back. "Man, I'm *ravenous,*" he said. "How about you? Want some toast?"

Mallory wasn't hungry, but sharing a meal with Todd, even a simple one like toasted bread, was irresistible. "Sure. I could eat."

He went through her cupboards retrieving plates, honey, molasses, and an unopened jar of blackberry preserves.

Mallory set the table, mostly as a way to watch Todd undetected.

"Todd," she said.

Todd was so busy stuffing toast in his mouth and re-loading the toaster that at first, he didn't respond.

"I want you to know how nice it is to see you again."

Todd swallowed and grinned. "Hold that thought," he said. "I gotta cook!" He pulled a carton of eggs and a package of bacon from his backpack and a skillet from the cupboard. Ten minutes later Mallory had a breakfast feast in front of her. "You can COOK!" she said.

"Another hidden talent," Todd said, reaching for his backpack. He pulled out a small photo portfolio. "Along with this one. Thought you might like to see what I did with your gift."

Mallory paged through the book, carefully studying each photo and asking Todd where each shot was taken. The last few pages of the book were photos of Mallory from Paradise Island. She smiled as she recalled how happy she had been when he was capturing her on film.

"You're good," Mallory said. "Show good."

Todd shrugged. "I have to go to Horseshoe Bay to get them developed, but I love it. Being good at it has kind of been my saving grace. At least I'm good at something. That kind of makes you my savior," he said.

"Hence the homage to Mallory at the end of the portfolio," she said.

"Those are the best portraits I have ever taken. They deserve to be in my book," he said.

"Wait here," Mallory said as she ran upstairs and fetched her box of film.

"Wow, that is going to cost a fortune to develop," Todd said.

"My grand tour of Canada!" Mallory said.

"I can't wait to see it."

"Maybe you can show me where to get it developed."

"We can make a day of it," he said.

"I'd like that."

"And I want to build that shed. Let's go get some wood."

"Do we have to? Today, I mean? Right now?" Mallory blushed. She was unaccustomed to being the aggressor.

Todd grinned. "Are you sure you're up for physical activity?"

"I'm tough," Mallory said.

Todd laughed and picked Mallory up and carried her upstairs to her bedroom. He tossed her playfully on the bed and jumped in after her. Mallory scrambled up and waved her finger at him.

"Not so fast, buddy," she said. "As I recall, you like to start with a little show."

Todd laughed and lay back on the bed, arms crossed behind his head. "I do."

Mallory slowly untied and pulled off his shoes, one by one. Then she slowly rolled down each sock, making a show of taking a sniff of each before tossing it aside.

Todd smiled. "I'm going need some help with this bra," he said and he arched his back.

"I don't recall you having a problem with bras," Mallory said, and she stripped off her top, revealing a bra with a convenient front clasp.

Todd raised an eyebrow. "Oh … a new-fangled one."

Mallory crawled onto the bed and Todd released the clasp with his teeth and nestled in between her breasts. She arched her back and raised her breast to his mouth. He moved just out of reach and blew on the nipple until she begged him to touch her. He touched her, licked her, and entered her. She gasped, quivered, and came and came and came. He did not build the shed that afternoon, but he got up the next morning and got started.

CHAPTER 23

MAY 2001

Todd built the shed, gave up his room at the club, moved in with Mallory, and started running the club's café. He was totally clean and happy for the first time in his adult life, and he and Mallory spent the winter tucked inside the cottage, getting reacquainted. Once spring hit, they moved outside and worked on the cottage exterior, making it look as happy and cared for as they felt as couple. Todd gave the cottage a new coat of yellow paint and painted the shutters forest green. He removed the woody overgrown shrubs that lined the edge of the cottage; their height had blocked most of the light that now streamed in through the windows, and Mallory planted flowers beds in their place. The flowers grew well in the loamy soil, but so did the weeds. Mallory considered weeding a constant struggle between good and evil. Diligent in her quest to create beauty in her life, Mallory regarded her time in the garden as a daily ritual, and her gardens were starting to flourish under her care.

The sailboat Rusty had given her, however, was in desperate need of an overhaul. One afternoon while Todd was at work, Mallory and Rusty sailed the boat to North Harbor in Vancouver.

"You're a natural sailor," Rusty said.

Mallory grinned at the high praise from her grandfather and shook her head. "I'm just good crew. Todd's the sailor," she said.

Her grandfather nodded and paused thoughtfully.

Mallory looked at him quizzically. "Rusty? What is it?"

Her grandfather shook his head. "Nothing. Sorry. Hey look over there." He pointed to an orca that was halfway out of the water and up on the shoreline with its mouth clenched around a seal's tail.

Mallory gasped as the seal screamed and the whale slipped back into the water and swam away from the shore, rhythmically breaking the water as it devoured the seal in methodical bites and gulps. It was a horrifying sight, a horrifying death for the young seal, but Mallory couldn't look away. "Oh my God!"

"Pretty amazing huh? That's why people up here don't have dogs."

"Dogs? I thought orca ate fish," she said.

"Sometimes they do, but they prefer mammals, like seals, wolves, bears, raccoons, and dogs," Rusty said.

"That's the stuff of nightmares."

Rusty nodded and they sailed on in silence until they were nearly at their destination.

"I'm glad we're taking this trip. I need to talk to you about something," said Mallory.

"I'm listening."

"I need an escape plan."

"From here? Why? And why now?" Rusty said.

"Because a person of concern might be looking for me," Mallory said.

"Why are you talking to me about this? You have Todd."

"Who may never need to know anything," she said. "Besides, you have special skills."

"Don't think it's a good idea to have secrets from your man?" Rusty said.

"That's not your choice. Will you help me?"

"You know I will. Against my better judgment."

"Duly noted," Mallory said.

"What do you need?" Rusty asked.

"I need to buy a powerboat and have you pretend that it's yours. I also need your help in mapping out an emergency plan."

"I don't need a boat. For God's sake, I just gave you this one," Rusty said.

"Don't you think a powerboat would be fun?"

"It's less work than a sailboat but somehow it seems like cheating."

"I thought we'd pick one out today. Drive it back," Mallory said.

"My reward for keeping my trap shut?" Rusty said.

"I didn't know a reward was required. But I'm prepared to let you pick it out. You and Todd can become fishing buddies like you and Dad."

Rusty gazed at his granddaughter for a long moment and then a light of understanding came into his eyes. "Mallory, you can't make a trip to New Jersey right now. It's not safe."

"I'm beginning to think you are psychic," she said.

"Not psychic, just understand human nature. He might know about her," Rusty said.

"No might about it. He does know. I told him—not everything, but probably enough. That's why I need to go. I need to make sure she's safe."

"Even if you get word that she's in distress, you can't go there as long as he's looking for you. It's what he wants you to do. It'd be like shooting fish in a barrel." He paused and put a hand on her shoulder. "And really, there's nothing you can do for her in her condition. She would want you to take care of yourself right now."

Mallory sighed. She knew her grandfather was right.

— € —

The sailboat would be in dry dock for most of the season; it hadn't been serviced in five years, so, albeit somewhat reluctantly, Rusty picked out a twenty-foot powerboat with two top-of-the-line Honda engines. The boat would be fast and stable enough to make it to Vancouver from Roberts Creek, her grandfather said, should the need arise.

— € —

A young woman was waiting for them on the dock when they returned.

"Sweetheart!" Rusty said. "When did you get back?"

"Today, Granddad. I came straight here to see you."

Rusty tossed the young woman a rope from the boat and she expertly tied them up.

"Hi," the young woman said as they climbed out of the boat. I'm Clara. You must be Mallory. Granddad has told me so much about you."

Mallory glanced at Rusty. "I wish I could say the same."

Rusty smiled. "This is my granddaughter, Clara. Actually, she's my step granddaughter, but that's too much of a mouthful."

"It's nice to meet you, Clara," said Mallory, wondering where this step-granddaughter had come from. Her father had been an only child ... hadn't he? Were there MORE secrets in Mallory's family closet? Not wanting to give up her cover, Mallory kept the question to herself. She would talk to Rusty later. She turned to Clara. "Where have you returned from?"

The young woman smiled. "I'm afraid I'm a fair-weather Roberts Creek fan. I went to Arizona for the winter, but I couldn't miss spring here."

Rusty looked from Mallory to Clara and back again, and shook his head. "You could be sisters. Amazing."

Mallory looked but didn't see it. Clara shrugged as well, indicating she didn't think so either. "Well Clara," Mallory said, "you'll have to come for dinner sometime soon. I'd love for you to meet Todd."

"Todd, the bartender at the club?"

"Yes," Mallory said. "Only not the bartender anymore. He runs the café."

"I know Todd. Oh no, you two are dating?"

"Actually, we're living together."

"Crap, there goes another one." Clara scowled.

"Now Clara," Rusty began, "I'm sure there's a man out there for you."

"Maybe out there ... way, way out there ... but not here in Roberts Creek. Todd was the last available man here, if you don't count old man Rutter before he died," Clara said. "Damn."

"Mallory, she doesn't mean anything by it," Rusty said.

"No worries, I don't offend easily," Mallory said gracefully. "You must come to dinner. Next week should be nice enough to barbeque."

"That's nice of you. Now I'm embarrassed." Clara blushed.

"Don't be. I've got to go. I'm sure Todd's wondering what happened to me. Nice meeting you Clara," she said as she scampered up the path.

"Hey, where have you been?" Todd said, greeting Mallory at the kitchen door.

"Went to Vancouver with Rusty. Took the sailboat to the marina for repairs. We probably won't get it back until the end of summer. Rusty bought a new boat," Mallory said.

"What kind?" He said.

"Power boat."

"Really? Well, that will be easier for him."

Mallory smiled. No questions asked. That had been easy.

"Mal," Todd said.

"What, Sweetie?" Mallory said.

"Marry me."

Mallory smiled. "Where is this coming from?"

"I'm happy ... so happy I want us to be committed and make a life together. The sooner the better."

Mallory paused and looked at Todd quizzically. "A quickie?"

He smiled. "We're good at them." He stood up from the table and got down on one knee. "You've made me the happiest man in the world the past few months. Please do me the honor of becoming my wife."

"You are more than a little sentimental today," Mallory said.

"And proud of it," Todd said.

Mallory smiled. "Yes. I would be honored to be your wife."

They were married two weeks later at the yacht club and soon settled into married life. Todd, sober and happy, slept like a baby every night, but Mallory often woke in the dark, afraid, as she watched her husband sleep, blissfully unaware of his new wife's old life, that her sins of the past were about to catch up with her.

CHAPTER 24

A YEAR LATER, JUNE 2002

Todd practically skipped to the dock to tie down the sails and clean up the boat. He was talking a lot about having a family these days. Mallory hadn't made any commitments, although she was hiding her birth control pills in the back of the silverware drawer. Almost two years since she had arrived in Roberts Creek and Mallory still wasn't sure she was completely safe.

Todd looked up at the cottage, saw Mallory in the kitchen doorway, and waved. Mallory smiled and waved back. She hated having secrets from him, past and present, but it was for his own safety.

Mallory sighed and headed out to work on her gardens. She adored the sound of that: her gardens. As though she had acres and acres of grounds. The small, two-bedroom cottage was on an acre of land, most of which was seacoast or woods. The flower beds, which Mallory had painstakingly planted and then parented throughout four Roberts Creek seasons, now flourished and surrounded the cottage.

As Mallory approached the shed, she noticed its door was slightly ajar. Although they didn't keep the shed locked, Mallory was always careful to shut and latch the door tightly. She was concerned about animals getting in and eating something they shouldn't. Her pulse quickening, Mallory edged the door open with one foot and scanned the small space. All the equipment appeared to be there. She stooped to examine the dirt floor and discovered a set of recent footprints that were too large to be hers and too small to be her husband's. The hairs on the back of Mallory's neck rose.

She methodically went over the rest of the shed and stopped when a speck of white in the black dirt caught her eye. Mallory dug with her fingers and pulled out a tiny cigarette butt. There was no brand name printed on the filter because there was no filter. The cigarette had been hand-rolled. Mallory lifted the charred paper to her nose. The tobacco smelled sweet. She raised an eyebrow at the familiar smell. Her heart raced as she looked out of the shed, searching the grass for any signs of where the intruder might have gone. The stone and shell driveway gave away no clues, nor did the woods or seacoast, so Mallory headed for the front gardens, trying to convince herself that she was overreacting. She knelt down in front of the living room window, gently parted the abundant flowers and there it was: the freshly imprinted proof that Mallory had had every right to be worried.

Whoever had stood in her garden—not too long ago—had been careful not to crush any flowers. But he hadn't bothered to cover his tracks. In the middle of the large print was a mirror image of the word Bexley. Mallory knew the French brand of boots well, and the sight of that image sent a chill up her spine. She also knew the chances of anyone who lived in Roberts Creek owning a pair were very slim. Mallory gingerly made her way through the flowers until she found a companion print. She stood and placed her own feet inside the footprints, and found she was staring into her living room window.

Sweating now, and slightly nauseous, Mallory walked directly to the exterior telephone connection line and examined it for a tap. She found none. "OK, relax," she told herself. "If it's him, you have a plan. You have Rusty." She went into the cottage through the kitchen door and splashed her face with cold water. She sat at the kitchen table for a moment, trying to regulate her breathing, but she couldn't sit still. She stood and grabbed the binoculars Todd kept by the kitchen window to watch birds, and focused on and followed the phone wires down to the dirt road. She didn't see a tap. If there was one, it had been well concealed. Even so, Mallory thought, if he had been here, if he were that close, he could have bugged the house. She had to assume he was listening.

CHAPTER 25

JUNE 2002

When Todd was called to the café that afternoon to cover for a sick employee, Mallory, for once, was happy to let him go.

"So much for the day off," Todd said. "But at least we got the sail in this morning."

When Mallory merely nodded, Todd looked at her with concern. "Still not feeling well?" he asked. He reached out and put his hand on her forehead. "No fever, but you're awfully pale, babe. Maybe you should see a doctor."

Mallory forced herself to smile through the fear. "I'm fine. Just still feeling a bit wobbly from the sea sickness."

Todd didn't look convinced.

"I'll be fine," Mallory said, standing to give him a kiss. "Go on, go to work."

"I'll try not to be too late," Todd said. "You get some rest, promise?"

Mallory nodded.

She watched from the doorway as Todd pulled his bicycle out of the shed and headed down the driveway, and when he had turned out of sight, Mallory grabbed the house keys, locked the door behind her and made a beeline for her grandfather's cottage.

Rusty was in his backyard manning the barbecue. His mop of white hair blew in the wind. He was humming in a deep baritone and swaying as if he were dancing. "Hey," he called out, seeing Mallory. "What a nice surprise! I saw you guys out sailing this morning." He greeted her with a hug. "Join me for lunch?"

Mallory shook her head. "Not hungry. We have a problem. Can you find out if anyone has seen a stranger around town recently?"

Rusty frowned. "Might have to implement the plan, eh?" He said.

"I hope not, but maybe." Mallory paced the grassy area.

"Easy there, I just got this grass to grow. Told him yet?"

Mallory shook her head. "Can't, don't know how," she said. "Soon though, there may be no choice."

— € —

Mallory was still wide awake when Todd returned well after midnight, but she pretended to be asleep until she knew, by his soft snore, that he was in dreamland. She opened her eyes and watched him sleep, smiling at his tranquility. Mallory cherished this bit of vicarious peace, because she could not find it herself. She tried to forget the afternoon's anxiety. She burrowed into the hollow of her husband's neck and kissed him softly. Todd wrapped his arms around her.

Mallory was almost asleep herself when she heard a small noise from downstairs. She gently extricated herself from Todd's arms, sat up in bed, and listened for a moment. She had almost convinced herself that it was nothing when she heard a louder sound. She swung her bare legs over the bed and grabbed her robe. Tightening the robe around her waist, she padded towards the doorway as the soft fabric silently brushed her legs. Careful to avoid the squeaky spots on the floorboards, which she had memorized the day she moved in, Mallory peeked furtively around the landing of the stairs.

A thin flashlight beam was dancing around the living room.

Mallory pulled back against the wall with a jerk and felt her pulse quicken.

Her first instinct was to flee, but she stopped herself from running back to the bedroom. She had to do this. Alone. When she peered around the corner again, the beam was still and pointed directly at one of Todd's portraits of Mallory. Her mind raced with disturbing possibilities. The light went off. Mallory looked toward the source of the light and what she saw confirmed the worst.

It had been more than a year since she had last seen him, and her plan had been never to see him again. The figure disappeared into the darkness, but Mallory knew he would be back. Christophe had found her, and this Mallory knew for certain: someone was going to die.

The only question was who.

— € —

The light of day dawned harshly and Mallory begged off her morning run with Todd, claiming she was feeling a little tired. She watched him trot down the driveway and turn left on their regular route, and then the second he was out of sight, Mallory went into the bathroom to begin to implement The Plan.

She cut her hair close, and a box of Miss Clairol number 37 transformed her from a redhead into a mousy brunette. After a quick blow dry, Mallory pulled a wig that resembled her former hair over her newly shorn head and took off for the house next door.

Rusty's granddaughter was sitting at the kitchen table. Mallory and Clara had become friends, despite the fact that Clara had cursed her for snagging Todd. "I can't thank you enough for being willing to help me," Mallory said as they embraced.

"Don't worry about that, you need help. It's not a problem. I'm thrilled to spend the night in Horseshoe Bay," Clara assured her. She grinned at Mallory. "Maybe I'll meet my Prince Charming. Since you got the only one in Roberts Creek."

Clara would not have been Mallory's first choice for this assignment. She was a little dim and way too chatty, but Roberts Creek was not exactly replete with candidates. Rusty had actually suggested Clara for the assignment if it ever were necessary, because she and Mallory were approximately the same age and body type.

Clara pulled on the jeans and black turtleneck Mallory had brought for her.

"Clara," Mallory said as the girl finished changing. "Please don't talk to anyone about this, even if they seem nice. You can talk about the weather, about life, about politics, but not about this. Understand?"

"You're such a worrier," sang Clara as she walked out the door.

Rusty poured a cup of coffee for Mallory and sat down next to her. "Mallory, I'm worried about *you*. I feel like I should be going with you. Doing more. I don't even know your whole plan. Just the basics."

"I appreciate that, but please don't be. I know what I'm doing and I'll be fine. Just follow The Plan," she said firmly.

"When are you going to tell Todd?"

"When I know for certain," she said with a finality that stopped the conversation. "We need to leave."

Rusty nodded his head and moved to the door.

On the way to the ferry Mallory finally broke the silence. "I'm sorry I snapped at you, Rusty. I have a lot on my mind. This is serious and I need to be focused. I can't afford to be afraid. Trust me, I know what I'm doing. I really appreciate all of your help, but the less you know the better. I'm just the girl who lives next door," Mallory said.

"Mallory, I love you," Rusty said. "And—"

"Rusty, this is dangerous. The more you know, the greater the risk," Mallory shot back with panic in her voice.

"Honey, I'm an old man, what's the worst that could happen? I think I could help. I'm gonna die sooner or later anyway," Rusty said.

Shocked by the emphatic response, Mallory said softly, "I'd rather it be later, much later. Please, Rusty, don't push. I'm just the girl who lives next door, okay?"

He nodded his head.

As they pulled into the parking lot, Mallory gave her grandfather a tight hug. "I'll be back on the 1:10 ferry," she whispered and she got out of the car.

She scanned the parking lot and spotted Clara's car. As she walked away, she waved to Rusty. "See you tomorrow."

He waved and drove off.

— € —

Shortly after Mallory boarded the ferry, a dark blue Chevy pulled into the parking lot and a small man in dark clothing and Bexley boots hurried to the ticket window. He grumbled to himself about having to track her on the water, but really, Christophe relished the challenge. However, it was early and he was a grumpy morning person.

He had been following her for three days.

After seeing her picture in the cottage, Christophe was certain that, whoever she was claiming to be now, she used to be Emma Scott. The fact that she was living with someone infuriated him, and his first instinct had been to kill the guy on the spot, but he knew he needed a better plan. He didn't think Emma knew he was here yet, thought he had a few days before any action was required, and he wanted her to suffer. She had underestimated him when she'd planted those euros in his car and she was about to see how much. No one else had known him or cared what happened to him. She'd had access to the money and had known his car. Christophe swore softly. He should not have trusted her. His heart had betrayed him. He would not make that mistake again. Ticket in hand, he took a final drag of his hand-rolled cigarette and then tossed it into the water before boarding the ferry.

— € —

Upon his release from prison, Christophe hadn't bothered to look for Emma in France. He had known she would leave the country; she had told him that much. Her trail in France would have only led him to some international departure point. He knew she spoke only English and French fluently, so that would have deterred her from choosing Italy, Spain, or Germany as a departing point. He had checked only England and France. Although it had been almost two years, it hadn't been all that difficult to pick up her trail: through his mastery of the Internet, Christophe had gotten access to the flight departure manifests from both countries. He had determined that since she'd been new to disappearing, she would have tried to get out of the country as soon as possible, after his arrest, so he'd limited his search to the days immediately following.

It had been a bit more difficult to figure out what name she'd traveled under. It certainly would not have been Emma Scott. Christophe had grinned to himself, remembering how clever Emma had believed her father was when he'd created the cover names for him and Gus, but that had been Christophe's most valuable clue to picking up her trail. He had searched for variations on Emma, Scott, and Andrew. Being that they were all relatively common names, the process had been more tedious than he had hoped, but after checking 236 flight itineraries, he had found it: a female named Mallory Andrews had flown from Nice to Casablanca, Morocco, at 4 p.m. the day after his arrest. Not definitive in itself, but the next morning, Mallory Andrews had flown to Boston, Massachusetts, and then on to Montreal, Canada. It was the oddness of the connections, flying that far south to just go north and then east the next morning that had caught Christophe's trained eye. Trusting his well-honed instincts, Christophe had booked a flight to Montreal. It had taken two weeks for his contact to secure a passport for Gilbert Christophe, as well as a set of police credentials in the same name declaring him a member of the force of a small hamlet in Quebec. He had a new name, a new job, and a mission.

Figuring Canada had been relatively easy, but by the time he'd arrived in Montreal, Emma's trail had been cold for a year and a half. He could find no record of a rental car or airport car transport. It seemed she'd been pretty attached to her new name, Mallory Andrews, because she hadn't changed it on her final connecting flight to Montreal. Still, Christophe knew: a name was just a name. Emma had probably changed her appearance, perhaps more than once, along the way.

She was, after all, her father's daughter.

In Montreal, Christophe had checked into a hotel and had spent the next few days using his computer to create a "sketch" of Emma as he remembered her. Armed with the sketch, he had hit the train station, the bus depot, the rental car agencies, and then, deciding that Emma must have purchased a vehicle, which meant she must have had plans to stay in the country, Christophe had moved onto Montreal's myriad car dealerships. He'd started with inexpensive, reliable cars, but after a week wasted on Hondas and Toyotas, he had switched his focus to luxury car dealers and, less than a week later, he had a hit.

"Bonjour. Parlez-vous Anglais?"

"Of course, Sir. We are, after all, a British company," the Land Rover salesman had said with a broad grin.

Christophe had smiled. "Very good. I am Inspector Andre from St. Georges Police Department." With a quick flash of his fake credentials, the salesman's smile had faded.

"Yes, Inspector, what can I do for you?"

Christophe held up the computer sketch of Emma. "I'm looking for this woman."

The salesman had given the photo a good look and nodded. "Yeah, I think she was in here last year." He pointed at the sketch, "But she had shorter hair, it was brown, not red. Bought a loaded Range Rover. Forest green. Paid cash. I remember that. Doesn't happen very often. She had briefcase loaded. $55,000 US. It took an hour to count it. Nice commission for me. That what this is about? She a bank robber or something?"

"You still have the paperwork, right? I need her name."

"We should, let me check."

Christophe smiled unconsciously. She had made mistakes.

"Let's see," the salesman had said as he'd scanned the items in the folder. "Her name is Emmett, Mallory Emmett." The salesman handed him the folder. "I can make you a copy if you like, but we really need to keep the original paperwork here."

Christophe read quickly. She had purchased a nationwide warrantee for the Range Rover, because, the salesman had noted, she'd said she planned to travel throughout Canada. "Oh, and I gave her a list of preferred Land Rover service centers. You'll probably want that."

"Yes. Do you have the model she purchased on the floor?"

"Sure."

"Great. I'll check it out while you're making my copies."

It had been a bit of a search, but as Christophe ran his hand along the smooth leather-appointed interior of a white Range Rover, he had imagined Emma cruising along a Canadian highway, feeling safe in the knowledge that she would not be found.

"Surprise, *ma chérie,*" he'd said softly.

The salesman had returned with the file folder and a Post-it note. "I also found a local address Miss Emmett used while she was waiting for us to add a few special features to her Rover. It's a hotel just a few miles from here."

Christophe had been over the moon. It had gotten almost too easy. "Thank you," he'd said to the Land Rover salesman. "You've been most helpful."

The salesman beamed. "Hope you catch her, whatever she's done."

"Oh, I will catch her. You can be sure of that."

He had checked into her hotel that day and had chatted up the staff for a few days before he started asking about Mallory Emmett. And then one day, in the hotel bar, he had hit pay dirt.

"What can I get you?" asked the bartender, who's employee tag indicated her name was Joan.

"Just coffee, black."

"Nice accent, but not French Canadian, I think."

"No, the real thing. France," he'd said.

"Oh, what part?"

"The mountains."

"The Alps?" The pretty bartender sighed. "They sound so beautiful, never been there. There was someone here a few months ago who told me all about France. She had just gotten back."

"No kidding?" He said, "what was her name?"

"Mallory something," she said.

"Right, listen, what time do you get off of work?"

"My shift ends in fifteen minutes."

"Would you like to get some coffee?"

“More coffee for you?” she’d said with a warm smile. “Sure, there’s a place down the block.”

At The Second Cup, they sank into the café’s comfy chairs. The café was dimly lit and, even by the window, they had been masked in shadows. Christophe ordered another coffee black; Joan, a mochaccino and a Nanaimo bar.

“What is a Nanaimo bar?” he asked when the strange dessert arrived.

“They’re the brownies of Canada.” She pointed at the bar. “It’s got chocolate cake, coconut, nuts, and sweet cream. My mom used to make these.” She took a bite and offered him one. He declined.

“Does ‘Nanaimo’ mean something?”

“It’s a city on Vancouver Island, in the west.”

“Is that where they invented it?”

“I guess. You know I’m not sure why they call it that. It’s just something I grew up with.”

“So how well did you know Mallory?”

“Well enough. She used to sit for hours in the hotel bar reading Canada travel books.”

“Any place in particular she was interested in?”

“Mostly the coasts, Nova Scotia and BC.”

“BC?” Christophe said.

“British Columbia, it’s the province on the West Coast.”

“Have you been there?”

“Nope, never been out of Montreal,” Joan said.

“Did you know she was leaving?” Christophe said.

“Who?”

“Mallory Emmett.”

“Look, what is this, the third degree on Mallory? I thought this was a date, and all you want to talk about is her. Hey, how do you know her last name? I don’t remember telling you that. In fact, I don’t think I ever KNEW her last name.” The pretty bartender’s eyes narrowed and she stood. “What is this anyway? Who are you?”

Christophe took one last gulp of coffee, put money on the table and stood up.

"Joan, it's been a pleasure. I'll never forget the Nanaimo bars."
He was gone before she had a chance to respond.

– € –

Back in his hotel room, Christophe had hacked into the Land Rover Canada service network. He located four women named Mallory who owned one-year-old dark green Range Rovers. Two had been serviced out of the Vancouver Service Centre: Mallory Robinson in Vancouver and Mallory Matthews in Roberts Creek. Christophe stared at the screen and decided that Mallory Matthews was his girl. Her car had higher mileage and the vehicle had not been purchased at that dealership. He booked an e-ticket to Vancouver for the next day and started to pack. He had pushed the bartender too far too fast with his questions, and that had raised suspicion and drawn attention to himself. It was time to get out of town and on with his mission.

– € –

When he'd arrived in Vancouver, Christophe had headed straight for 1730 Burrard Street, the Land Rover Dealership.

He walked into the Service Manager's office, looking serious and as official as possible without a uniform. The manager was speaking to a man in grease-stained overalls. It was not at all what Christophe expected in a Land Rover dealership.

The manager glared at him. "Is there something I can help you with?"

"Yes." Christophe flashed his badge. "I'm Inspector Andre, from the St. Georges Police Department."

"And?" The service manager said.

"I'm looking for a woman who purchased a Range Rover in Montreal. We believe she has settled near here. This is a likeness." He displayed the sketch.

"She doesn't look familiar," the manager said, eyes narrowing.

"Hey boss. Remember? That's Mrs. Matthews. Beautiful blue eyes, a redhead, great smile. You tried to ask her out," the man in the overalls said.

The manager shifted his glare to his employee. The man in the overalls turned and walked quickly into the service area.

"That sounds like the woman I'm looking for."

"Can I see that badge again?" the service manager said suspiciously.

Christophe displayed the badge. The manager inspected it carefully and finally said, "It might be a customer."

"I'd like to see her paperwork," Christophe said.

"I don't like this," the manager said. "This is not Quebec."

"I can get a warrant. If you'd prefer?"

"No, no. I'll be right back."

"I'll take a copy too, please."

The manager scowled and went into the main office. Christophe wondered why the man had been so uncooperative. He suspected that Emma had flirted with the manager and he was feeling protective. He was beginning to think that people from Quebec were not well liked in this province.

The manager had taken a long time to find the paperwork.

Too long.

When the Vancouver police cruiser pulled up to the front of the dealership, Christophe had already gone out the side door. He had what he needed. He could not risk being detained. Again.

CHAPTER 26

JUNE 2002

Mallory stood by the rail on the second deck, trying not to look around too much. It wasn't easy because she desperately wanted to get a glimpse of him. She tried to concentrate on the familiar smell of the sea air. The ferry's horn blasted, and Mallory was practically knocked over by the blast. She regained her composure and moved a bit to the left as the ferry pulled out into the bay. The wind blew with fierce force and Mallory was thankful for the kerchief she wore. Her wig certainly would have blown off without it. Her newly shorn hair felt itchy under the wig. Mallory had been in such a rush that morning that she hadn't taken the time to wash the cut remnants from her neck and she realized now that had been a mistake. She headed to the ladies' room to try to reduce the itching, and was swiping the back of her neck with a damp paper towel when Clara came into the bathroom.

Without words, they efficiently exchanged clothes, careful not to let a bare foot land on the unsanitary floor. Clara donned Mallory's sunglasses and wig, and Mallory handed her an envelope and instructed her to go to the main deck and, upon departure, to make a trip to the bank, make the deposit, and then check into the Horseshoe Bay Motel, which was just a few blocks from the ferry dock. She also handed Clara her instructions for the next day, along with a credit card and some cash and told her to enjoy her day in Horseshoe Bay. They exchanged a quick hug and then Mallory hustled Clara out of the bathroom.

Clara was now dressed in the lively printed sundress and sweater that Mallory had worn when she'd boarded the ferry. In the sunglasses and wig, Clara looked exactly like the Mallory who had recently stood on the ferry's bow. Mallory sat, fully clothed, on a toilet in the ladies' room stall, until the ship's horn, muffled by the outside wall, sounded a few minutes later.

At the sound of the horn, Mallory made her way casually to the upper deck and stood at the rail. She spied Clara in her "Mallory" disguise standing at the rail on the main deck, and she scanned the deck for Christophe. She spotted him and gave an involuntary gasp.

The ferry docked, and Clara was the first off. Christophe was next, at a respectable distance, but he certainly appeared to be following her. As Mallory watched, Clara set about the circuitous route to the bank. The sound of a camera shutter click startled her, and a slow chill crept up Mallory's spine as she turned and spotted a camera lens pointed first at Christophe and then at Clara. As Mallory watched, the man with the camera ducked into his car and drove off the ferry.

A few minutes later, through her binoculars, Mallory saw Christophe standing outside of the CIBC bank. As she watched, the man with the camera pulled up across the street from the bank.

"Damn, this is worse than I thought," Mallory whispered.

Who was this man, and why was he following Christophe? It had been a while since Mallory had checked the email activity at The Bank of France, and she wondered, suddenly, if the euro theft had been discovered. She tried to discount the thought—it was too soon and they had been so careful—but it was the only probable explanation for the tail on Christophe.

Mallory lowered her binoculars. She had thought her biggest problem was going to be how to tell Todd she had to leave Canada. Now that thought had some major competition. The ferry's horn sounded for the return trip to Roberts Creek and Mallory was tempted to go inside, away from the biting wind, but she bore it for one last look back with the binoculars. Christophe and the strange photographer were both still outside the bank, and poor, unsuspecting Clara was inside.

Mallory sighed and mentally crossed her fingers.

The less Clara knew, the more innocent and safer she would be.

— € —

Horseshoe Bay was the anchor of Roberts Creek and its ferry was a lifeline for the tiny hamlet that Mallory had come to think of as home. With those waiting to board the ferry and those disembarking, the small Horseshoe Bay harbor bustled with activity all day. At night however, the town of Horseshoe Bay slept. There was almost nothing open after 9 p.m.; even the local bar closed down. The majority of the townspeople either worked on the ferry or in a service business that counted on the ferry for survival. There was nothing to do in town, not even a laundry or grocery store; people had to drive five miles to find those. Tourists never stayed in Horseshoe Bay for more than one night, and were only too happy to catch the first ferry out the next morning.

The tiny motel where Clara was spending the night was the same place Mallory had stayed the previous year. The dated motel, with its TV with manual dial, rotary phone, and linoleum floors, had charmed Mallory, though she was fairly certain the flimsy locks on the rooms' doors wouldn't keep out anyone bent on entry. As Mallory stood on the ferry deck and watched the town of Horseshoe Bay get smaller and smaller, she hoped Clara would lock and chain hers just the same.

— € —

Rusty was waiting at the Roberts Creek dock when the ferry arrived. When Mallory climbed into his car, he was shocked by her appearance. Mallory's beautiful red hair had been cut short like Clara's and dyed Clara's same mousy brown.

"If I didn't know better, I'd swear you were my granddaughter," Rusty said. "And so?"

"It's him. He's here. I have to leave first thing tomorrow morning. I'll have to take the boat. I'll make sure it gets serviced, and you can pick it up in Vancouver next week."

"I don't give a damn about the boat. I want you to be safe," Rusty said.

"Rusty, promise me that you won't try to find this man. He's dangerous. It won't help me."

Rusty set his jaw. Mallory knew this look; her grandfather wasn't subtle. "Rusty, please. He will break into my house. Don't stop him. Promise me. I need you to promise."

He hesitated. "I promise."

– € –

The ferry photographer had been tracking Christophe—whom he knew as Christophin—for months, all across Canada to this wee little town on the BC coast. Silent stalking was not the photographer's style. He preferred more action. But the case would be very lucrative, he thought confidently, once he found the money. He sat in his car and snapped a photo of Christophin outside the bank, and then one of the women in sunglasses who had just exited.

– € –

After checking into the tiny motel, as directed, Clara, bored and hoping to run into someone fun, wandered around Horseshoe Bay. The photographer watched and followed as Christophe watched and followed her.

She had dinner at The Boathouse on the Bay. Christophe sat in the bar, which the photographer discovered when he went to use the head. After dinner, Clara took another stroll around the town and, finding nothing fun, returned to the motel alone.

Christophe settled into a booth at The Second Cup coffee shop across the street from the motel, and the photographer settled into his car. His prey was roused several times by the coffee shop's night shift, and each time he ordered more coffee, obviously trying to stay awake. The photographer sat in his car, without the luxury of caffeine, and kept his own vigil. He hated the waiting. He'd spent far too much time on this assignment, biding his time and waiting for the right moment. But this would be his last job, The Big One. Once he'd nailed this one, he would be able to retire, sit on a beach Down Under and watch the girls go by. No worries. Well, he wouldn't just watch them go by, he'd chase them. A lot more fun than sitting in this puny town in Canada watching this man drink cup after cup of coffee.

"Do something," the photographer willed Christophin. "Do something."

CHAPTER 27

JUNE 2002

Rusty dropped Mallory off at the end of her driveway. She watched him drive away and fought back tears. On the ferry trip back to Roberts Creek, Mallory had been concentrating so hard on what she was going to have to do to leave safely that she had not allowed herself to realize all that she would be leaving, everything and everyone she had come to love.

She trudged slowly to the house and walked around it twice, soaking up the beauty of the gardens in the early afternoon sun. She never expected to see them again. The sun wouldn't set until midnight tonight, but there was already a different glow from the sea.

Mallory went inside, poured herself a glass of wine, took it out onto the patio, and sat watching the changing light patterns dappling her lawn, one of her favorite pastimes. The deep forest to the south did not seem as impenetrable as in the morning; small beams of light danced in its spaces, opening it to the possibility of exploration. The garden shed cast a long shadow that almost reached the forest. The remnants of the aroma from Rusty's lunch barbecue reached her nose and Mallory tried to determine what it was. Chicken, she thought. Or maybe fish, or was that just the sea breeze? The sea was starting to change color: less green, more red. It was almost a muted purple now. The boat tied to the dock was reflecting a slightly orange hue. It bobbed a little more furiously as a cold gust of wind caused Mallory to wrap her arms around her body. She shivered. *Damn him,* she thought, *why couldn't he let me be?* Mallory knew why—Christophe was obsessed—but she did not understand why. She had done nothing to encourage him, well, after that first time. She shook her head and stood. She had things to do before Todd got home from work. She went inside and upstairs to the second bedroom, pulled down the attic stairs and climbed them quickly. They'd always seemed too rickety to hold anyone's weight, but somehow, they did. Mallory located the key, hidden under an old wooden birdcage next to the small, clouded window, and inserted it into a trunk tucked away in a dark back section of the attic. The trunk was neatly filled with backpacks, maps, equipment, and a gun. Mallory filled two backpacks quickly and efficiently. One she would take with her, and one would either go with Todd or be left behind. Mallory knew she had to face the reality that she might be traveling alone. This made her pause. Mallory pushed the thought away and finished her task. She went back down the rickety steps, folded them back up into the attic, and headed for the shower.

As the soothing warm water pelted her face, Mallory calculated the odds that Todd would go with her. She gave it 60/40. She had not lied to her husband, but it had been a pretty big sin of omission. Mallory knew Todd loved her in a way she'd never thought she would be loved, but considering what she was facing, would love be enough?

She dressed and packed two more backpacks with clothes and toiletries, one for her and one for Todd. If he wasn't willing to go, she had to be ready to go without him, and she would have to leave immediately. Once Christophe realized that she had given him the slip, Mallory knew, her former partner in crime would be out for blood. Mallory prayed that Todd would go with her, for his sake if not for hers. She sighed. At least she knew, for tonight, they were safe and would be together. She also knew tonight might be their last.

Mallory stowed the backpacks in the spare room and had just closed the door when Todd came in from work. He took one look at Mallory and stopped in his tracks.

"Hell Mal, what happened to your hair?"

"It changes my look, don't you think?" she said, pretending to be happy with it. "Something exciting and new."

Todd frowned. "I liked the old look. What's going on?"

"I thought you might like sleeping with a stranger," she said.

Todd frowned again. "Bobby saw you get off the ferry."

Mallory walked up to her husband and stroked his cheek, "Sweetie, we need to talk."

Todd nodded. "It's about time."

Although he'd known she'd been hiding something from him since they'd re-met, Todd had also known that pushing his wife to reveal her secret would not have made it happen any sooner. Mallory was not a woman to be pushed. She had her own timetable.

"I need coffee," Mallory said. "And then we'll talk."

They went into kitchen and Todd sat at the table, silent, until Mallory placed a mug in front of him and took the seat opposite. She set her mug down, untouched, and looked up at her husband. "Todd, do you have any idea how much I love you?"

"Yup, but don't let that stop you," he said with a glance and a smile.

Mallory smiled sadly back.

"What's going on?"

"I have something to tell you." She paused and looked in his eyes. "Can't start," she said.

He took her hand. "Hey. It can't be that bad, spill it."

"I ... have to leave Roberts Creek."

Todd's mouth dropped open. "What? Why?"

"Tomorrow morning."

He took a deep breath and said stoically, "I said why, not when."

"And I want you to come with me."

"Why do you have to leave?" His voice was taking on a higher pitch.

"I have been running from something that happened a year ago. Someone from that time in my life has found me. He's dangerous and I can't stay here."

"Don't be ridiculous," Todd said. "I'm here now. You have me. I will protect you." He rose quickly and pulled Mallory gently up from her chair. He wrapped his arms around her. She briefly returned his embrace, then broke away and walked a few paces before turning around.

"I know you want to, but you can't. I'm more afraid for you than me."

"I can take care of myself," Todd said, obviously wounded that his wife didn't believe this.

"Todd, I know this man. He has killed in cold blood at least once. And I know he won't hesitate to take another life to get what he wants."

"What does he want?"

Mallory didn't speak.

"You?"

She nodded her head. "Yes."

Todd looked at his wife for a long moment. "Are you just running from this man, or is there something else? This thing that happened?"

Mallory nodded. "There's more, but I don't want to get into it now. I promise I will tell you everything if you come with me," Mallory said. "If you don't, the less you know, the safer you will be."

Todd stared at her for several moments.

"Come with me," she said.

"How do you know he's here?" Todd said.

"He was looking in our living room window last night."

"What! How do you know? Why didn't you tell me?"

"I was hoping it wasn't true," she said.

"Is he in love with you?"

"He thinks he is. There was never anything there. He doesn't know me," Mallory said.

After a long pause Todd said, "Do I?"

When Mallory didn't respond, her husband left the kitchen silently, went upstairs, changed into running clothes, and walked out the front door without a word.

"Todd … please talk to me," Mallory yelled after him.

But he kept going.

– € –

For as long as he could remember, Todd had been a runner. When he was five, he used to run alongside his father in the mornings before school. Even with his small stature, he had kept up with his dad. Todd's father had expected his son to be a professional football player. He'd certainly had the talent. What Todd hadn't had was the drive to practice. In recent years Todd had hated running even more, but he had done it anyway, because his wife loved it, and in time, it had become a habit. For the past year, he and Mallory had started their mornings together with a run. Except for today, he remembered suddenly. This morning, Mallory had begged off. And now he had left without her. Now, for the second time in one day, he was running without her. The thought made Todd grimace. He felt like someone had clipped him. What was happening to his lovely little life with his lovely wife? How could he leave his life, his sobriety, and his happiness in Roberts Creek and just run off with her? Then again, how lovely would his life be without her? Todd ran and ran and ran. As he placed one foot in front of the other, he thought, at least with physical pain you can take something for it. This heart pain was something new. He remembered the torturous months of emotional pain before Mallory had reentered his life; pain that he had deadened with painkillers and booze. He wanted that release now. He briefly thought about getting it. And that thought literally stopped him in his tracks. In the past year he hadn't thought about attaining an altered state once, and that was due to Mallory. Todd needed her. No matter what she had done, no matter what had happened, he could not imagine his life without her. He turned and headed back for the cottage at a full sprint.

He found Mallory sitting on their bed, staring at the wall. "I'm in," he said. He sat down on the bed and took his wife his arms. "When do we leave?"

"First thing in the morning," she said.

"Well, then we have tonight for you to fill me in and prepare. What's the plan?"

"We'll take the boat to Vancouver."

"Isn't that pretty obvious? A big city. An airport exit route? Why not go north where we would be more remote?" Todd said.

"I would go north if I was going to be alone, but the two of us will attract too much attention. There are hardly any people up north, and you're pretty memorable. Don't worry: one night in Vancouver will be fine. It's a big enough city, he won't have time to find us."

"Isn't Rusty going to be pissed about his boat?"

Mallory shook her head. "He knows. And it's not his boat. It's my boat. He'll pick it up in Vancouver."

Todd blinked. "Rusty knows? And I don't?"

"He only knew that I needed a plan. No one knows more than you."

"Except the mystery man," Todd said.

"His name is Christophe Rabat."

"So ... spill."

Mallory sighed. "There's so much to tell, I don't really know where to start."

Todd smiled. "At the beginning."

Mallory smiled, too. "Thank you," she said. "I love you."

And then she launched into the story.

— € —

The next morning, Mallory rose at five, made coffee, filled a thermos, and packed a few energy bars. At 5:30 she shook Todd awake. "We have to go."

"Can I shower?" Todd said.

She shook her head. "You'll have time once we get to Vancouver."

Mallory was grateful that, having heard the story, Todd had gotten on board and wasn't pressing her for more details.

"Do you have a Harbor chart?" Todd asked.

Mallory nodded and they headed down the path for Rusty's dock.

The path was heavily wooded and darker than she'd expected. An icy wind tore through her jacket and Mallory wished she had worn heavier slacks. As they approached the forest's edge, Mallory looked up and saw the steel-cold gray sky.

Todd stopped abruptly before they stepped onto the dock.

"This isn't a good omen," he said.

"You can stay," Mallory said. "I wouldn't love you any less. This is my mess."

Todd took her hand and led her onto the boat. "We're married. It's OUR mess."

The waves tossed the boat like it was a toy. In all of her time in Roberts Creek Mallory had never seen the sea so restless. It wasn't going to be an easy ride. The sky darkened and began to pelt them with frigid rain. A large swell breached the side of the boat. Mallory and Todd's eyes met in a mutual look of concern.

"We have to go," she said.

"And we will," Todd said as he started the engine. "Do you have a patch?" Mallory nodded.

They donned their life preservers. Although it was unlikely they would survive for long in the icy water should they get dumped into it, this routine safety procedure seemed like the right thing to do. Their wind jackets were cinched tightly around their already numbing faces as they settled in for the rocky ride. As they started out, a pod of orcas flanked the boat, like an armed guard escort. "Now that's my kind of omen," Mallory whispered.

For the next four hours the raging sea challenged their intestinal fortitude as an occasional wave broke over the side of the boat. At one point Mallory thought the killer whales were accompanying them because they sensed prey would soon be in the water, but her earlier thought of escort was rewarded when they finally spotted Vancouver Harbor. As they pulled into port, the sea suddenly calmed, and the sun's rays broke through the clouds.

The first part of their journey was complete.

CHAPTER 28

JUNE 2002

It took all of Todd's considerable skill as a seaman to negotiate North Harbor Marina. Because of the uncharacteristically beautiful weather, the pleasure craft were out in force, all going in the opposite direction. When they finally docked, Todd and Mallory left the boat keys with a mechanic, told him the boat was scheduled to be serviced, and that someone would be back in a few days to pick it up.

– € –

Clara slept so soundly and woke feeling so good that she almost flung open the window drapes, but stopped herself just in time. Of course, she hadn't slept in her disguise, and it would not be good to be seen in front of the window without it. She checked the clock on her hotel room nightstand and realized she didn't have time to shower if she was to make the early ferry that Mallory had instructed her to catch. She started to pack her things, and then decided she just wasn't ready to leave yet. She wanted to have a nice breakfast and then get a manicure, and neither was possible in Roberts Creek. "What could it hurt?" she said to herself, and she made an executive decision to live a little and take the 3:20 afternoon ferry instead. She donned her disguise, dropped the key with the desk clerk, and headed around the corner to Nancy's Cut and Curl.

– € –

Christophe, watching from the lobby and assuming his prey was headed for the morning ferry, followed Clara out of the motel and was surprised to see her walk into the hair salon. He ducked into the deli next door and headed for the men's room. It had been a long night of coffee drinking and it took Christophe some time to relieve himself. When he emerged from the loo, he came face to face—or rather face to chest, since Christophe was about a head and a half shorter—with a man he thought he'd seen around Roberts Creek.

The photographer smiled at Christophe and moved quickly past.

– € –

Finished with her beauty treatments—she had indulged herself with a pedicure and facial, as well the manicure—Clara rushed to catch the ferry.

– € –

Christophe was happy to finally be on the way back to the smaller town of Roberts Creek where tracking his prey was easier. He headed for the top deck of the ferry and spotted her on the deck below. When she left the deck, he didn't fret. There was only one way off the boat.

– € –

As the ferry approached Roberts Creek, Clara dumped the wig and the clothes in the ladies' room trash. She donned the jeans and leather jacket she had stuffed into her backpack. Standing in front of the mirror, she fluffed what little hair she had and smiled at her reflection. She was glad to feel herself again, all mani-ed and pedi-ed and facial-ed and five hundred dollars richer for this little jaunt on behalf of Mallory. Feeling good, she strode out of the bathroom confidently and smacked into the photographer.

"Whoops. I'm so sorry. I wasn't paying attention," she said.

"No, no worries. I'm sure it was my fault," he said.

"What a delicious accent you have. British?"

"Australian actually, originally I'm from the Mauritius Islands," the photographer said as he looked up and down her length.

Clara was appraising him, too, with approval. "Haven't I seen you in Roberts Creek?"

"That's possible, I've been staying there the past few days."

"Why?" she said incredulously.

"I think it's a lovely place. Very peaceful. I'm doing some research for a book."

"Are you going to be there long?"

"I don't know. But if you'd like to give me your number, I'll give you a call. Perhaps we could share a meal?" He extended a hand. "I'm Joe."

"Clara," she said, shaking his hand. "And I'd like that." She fumbled in her purse for a pen and a scrap of paper, wrote down her number, and handed it to him.

"Ladies and gentlemen who drove aboard, please return to your cars," the loudspeaker boomed.

"Excuse me, I have to tend to my auto. Lovely meeting you."

Clara smiled. Roberts Creek had just gotten infinitely more interesting. She was one of the first off the ferry, and she headed quickly for her car. Mallory had told her that this would be the most dangerous part of her mission. Well, Mallory hadn't called it a mission, but Clara had liked to think of it as one. She was supposed to get out of the area as soon as possible without being noticed. She reached her car and took off down one of the back roads to Roberts Creek.

— ₠ —

Mallory and Todd strolled casually through Stanley Park among the tourists and Vancouverites out to enjoy a rare bit of sunshine. Mallory was enjoying the sun, too, and the brief moment of respite, but eventually she realized they could not afford to ignore reality any longer. When they had walked about a mile, Mallory hailed a cab.

"1277 Robson please," she told the driver.

"What now?" Todd said.

"Just give me a little more time," Mallory said.

"Just want to know what's next."

"Try to think of it as a surprise date that I've planned for you, my love." Mallory wrapped her arms around her husband's waist and nestled into his chest.

"You're very persuasive," he said kissing the top of her head.

They sat in silence for the 20-minute ride. The taxi pulled up in front of a 16-story hotel in a quiet part of downtown. Mallory paid the driver and added a conservative tip. She was normally an excessive tipper, but she didn't want to be remembered. She paused just inside the door as they entered the hotel. "Wait here," she said. Todd nodded and set their backpacks down. One of them hit the floor with a metallic clunk. Curious, Todd kneeled to open the pack, and when he saw what was in it, he blanched. He quickly re-zipped the backpack, but Mallory knew from the look on his face that he had seen the gun. She turned and walked quickly to the front desk and checked them in as Matthew and Jessica Todd. The room was guaranteed with a MasterCard in that name. She told the desk attendant that they would be staying only one night and would be leaving early in the morning. She said she would leave the key in the room, and she instructed the attendant to mail the receipt to a fictitious billing address.

"Come on honey, we're on ten," Mallory said, linking her arm with Todd's.

In the elevator, Todd turned to his wife, his faced drained of color. "Mal, what's going on? I thought I had broken something when I set down the backpack ... but then I saw ..."

"I know," Mallory said. "Hang on. We're almost there."

As the elevator carried them to the 10th floor, Todd turned to his wife. "A gun, Mallory?"

Mallory sighed. "Look, this is a new world we're in. There are rules. First rule, you can't call me Mallory anymore. I'm Jessica and you are Matthew. We're Jess and Matt." She smiled. "We're on an adventure."

"BUT A GUN?"

"I told you he's dangerous. Did you think I was kidding?"

"No. But I thought we were running, not shooting."

The elevator stopped on the 4th floor and an elderly couple stepped in. There was stony silence as the elevator clicked up to 8th floor observation deck, where the couple departed.

As the doors closed, Mallory said, "I don't want to shoot anyone. I never have, but we have to be prepared. Can you fire a gun?"

Todd sighed. "I know how. I mean, I'm a hunter, but there's a big difference between shooting a deer and shooting a person. Another human being. I don't know," he said with exasperation.

"Hopefully, it won't be necessary," Mallory said.

Inside their room, she was all business. "We need to get started. We don't have a lot of time."

"We need to get started on what?" Todd asked.

"I'll brief you on the plan, and then I need to run across the street to the Internet café."

Todd pulled off his jacket and sat on the bed. "Can I just say one thing first?"

"Sure," said Mallory.

"I realize that I'm just along for the ride here, but I'm here because I love you. I want to help you, and I feel pretty damn helpless right now. I think I've been more than patient with this whole thing, so cut me a little slack. This was just an adventure until I saw that gun. So now I know that this is really serious and that you," he paused, "WE are in trouble. Whatever you need, I'm here for you. When we have the time, you can tell me everything. I just don't want you to worry about me right now. I'm all in."

Mallory threw her arms around him and kissed him deeply. "I love you."

"Me too," he said. "So, what's next."

"These are your papers," Mallory said, handing Todd a passport, two credit cards, and a driver's license.

"Matthew Todd," he said, "not a bad choice. You can call me Todd."

"Why do you think I picked it? But you cannot call me Mallory."

He smiled. "Okay, Jessica. I'll do my best."

Mallory handed Todd a black-and-white photograph. "This is Christophe. The photo is about five years old, but he hasn't changed much. He's about my height, but he usually wears boots that put him up another inch or two. It's very important that you can recognize him. Christophe knows what you look like, and you need to know him."

"Do you think he knows yet that we know he has found you?"

"Probably. I had Clara impersonate me in Horseshoe Bay yesterday to give us some time and hopefully throw him off our trail. But I'm sure by now he knows I've given him the slip." Mallory thought for a beat. "Yes. I'm sure he knows and I know that he is pissed as hell. But it was the only way. We needed time."

Todd nodded. "Good call."

"There's another problem," Mallory said.

"Another one?"

"Yes. Someone is following Christophe."

"Couldn't that be a good thing?"

"It might have been if this man hadn't known Christophe was following Clara. She was disguised as me. If this person had what he wanted, he wouldn't be following Christophe. I think he is working for The Bank of France," she said.

"And that's a bad thing?"

"Yes, it's a bad thing. I need to get on the Internet to find out how bad. Let's go."

They left the hotel and walked across the street to the café.

"Why are we getting on the Internet?" Todd said.

"I need to see The Bank's files, to see if I can find out who is following Christophe," Mallory said.

"You can do that?" Todd said, astonished.

"Yes, I used to work there and I'm actually a damned good hacker."

"I've never even seen you use a computer," Todd said.

"I had hoped to have given it up for good," Mallory said with a sad smile.

They entered the Internet café, and Mallory headed straight for the best computer in the place. Todd ordered some food and arranged for payment with his new credit card. He had to pause before signing for it and he wished he had thought to practice his new signature before he left the hotel. Thankfully the cashier didn't even look at the back of his card. It was unsigned. He made a note to take care of that.

Mallory was already through The Bank's firewall and scanning their email files when Todd arrived. She swiped some code from her favorite search engine, Google, and modified the engine to search each word in all of The Bank's email since they had completed the euro job. She typed in: *Robbery, Theft, Thieves,* and *Investigation,* and when nothing hit, in desperation, Mallory typed in the word *Missing.* When that word yielded 28,453 hits, Mallory realized it was a waste of time to peruse them all.

"I can't think of another word to use." She sat slumped with her head on her hands.

"Tell me what happened. No, wait, just tell me what's missing," Todd said.

"Euros," Mallory said. "Millions of them. They were stolen during the printing process, before they were distributed. It would be embarrassing for The Bank to have discovered this only now. Not only that, it would shake the member governments' confidence in their ability to manage the currency. Quiet recovery would be their goal," she said.

"Try Recovery," Todd said.

Mallory typed in "Recovery" and got forty instant hits. The first one was an email from Roger Coltman. The subject was: Operation Recovery. She turned to her husband and caressed his cheek. "Score! You are a genius," she said.

Todd shrugged and smiled.

A quick scan of Coltman's email let Mallory know that the smart warehouse manager had sent a Request For Proposal for

Operation Recovery, but the attachment describing the proposal requirements was encrypted. Mallory could usually break encryption easily, but this was more sophisticated than she'd encountered before, and she didn't have the time to try to break it. But the biggest shock to Mallory was that the email was dated one week before she had left France and she had never seen it.

"I can't believe it," she murmured. She cursed herself for being careless.

"Sir," said the café cashier to Todd, "your food is ready."

"Can you make that to go?" Mallory asked.

While they waited for their food to be packed, Mallory paged through the other 39 RECOVERY hits and finally landed on another one of interest. The email had been sent to Roger Coltman from a Joe Templin. In it, Templin had accepted the terms of the Recovery Operation and had responded that he would begin immediately. The last thread of the email made Mallory shiver. It was from Templin, and dated two weeks ago, reporting that he had identified one target and was following him.

"Oh my God," she blurted.

"What, what is it?" Todd asked, as he read the email over her shoulder. "There's no mention of a female being followed. That's good, no?"

Mallory shook her head. "It just means he's being careful and doesn't want to get them excited about nothing. The fact that he has focused in on Christophe is bad, it means he's sure. Come on, we're not done yet," she said.

"Hold on, what's this guy's name again?" Todd asked.

"Joe Templin," Mallory read.

"Mal ... er Jessica, I think he's the Brit who's been in town the past few days. He's been in the club for dinner most every night. Said his name was Joe."

Mallory typed for a more few minutes before her eyes suddenly widened in fear. "Todd, this is bad. Joe Templin is ex-MI5."

"MI5, what's that?" Todd said.

"British Intelligence, like James Bond," she said.

"Oh, come on," Todd said.

"Of course, Bond is fictional, but this is much worse than being tracked by some ex-cop or private investigator. Leave it to Roger Coltman," Mallory said.

"Roger Coltman?"

"The anal Brit who ran one of the warehouses we robbed."

"WE ROBBED?" Todd said.

"Never mind," Mallory said.

She logged out, erased the search history, and shut down the computer. Todd grabbed the food from the cashier and followed her out the door. He had to sprint to keep up with her.

Mallory didn't slow down until they were back in their room. She headed straight for the red backpack and pulled out some papers. Todd sat on the bed and pulled out one of the sandwiches. He took a large bite and offered it to Mallory. She declined.

"Come on, we haven't eaten in hours and you need your strength. It will help your brain power."

Mallory took the sandwich and took a bite. She hadn't realized how hungry she was and she took another.

"Don't worry, there's another one," Todd said, grinning.

Mallory smiled as she paced and ate. She knew she was very lucky to have him with her. She gobbled up her sandwich. "Okay," she said to Todd, tossing the paper wrapper into the trash. "It's time for you to know the plan."

Todd was more excited than upset now. He felt like Mallory was starting to treat him like a partner instead of an employee, and he gave Mallory his rapt attention.

"Tomorrow morning we will go to the train yard. It's east of the city. We will hop a freight train on track 37 headed for Banff and then Calgary," Mallory said.

"Hop a freight train? Isn't that dangerous?" Todd said.

Mallory raised her eyebrow.

"Sorry, I lost my head," he said.

"It won't be moving when we get on. We just have to watch for workmen."

"Have you done this before?"

"No, but I've researched it."

"No doubt!" he said.

"Come on, I'm serious."

"I know." He tried to put his arms around his wife, but Mallory got up and went into the bathroom.

"Where's that picture of Christophe?" She called out.

"On the desk," Todd said.

"Bring it to me."

Mallory took the photo from Todd and dropped it into the bathroom sink. She tossed the plans she had outlined, and dropped that piece of paper into the sink, too, and then she lit a match and set it to the papers.

"Isn't that a bit of overkill?" Todd asked. "How could he find us here?"

"Sweetie, I didn't think he could find me in Roberts Creek. From now on our motto is: Take No Chances.'"

Mallory came out from the bathroom and flopped down on the bed.

Todd flopped down next to her and pulled her close to him. His hand fell next to the pillow and it hit something metal. "Jesus Christ, Mallory. Is this necessary?" Todd roared as he pulled the gun from under the pillow.

"Yes," she said in a quiet cold tone. "It is."

Todd knew there wasn't any use arguing. He got up off the bed, went into the bathroom, and shut the door. He wanted to wash his face, but the papers were still burning in the sink. He ran water on them to extinguish the fire and put the wet mess into the waste can. He turned back to the sink, made the water so cold that it stung, but it served the purpose. When he went back to bed, he turned his back on his wife and tried to sleep. Mallory pressed herself against his back and tried to wrap her arms around him, but he would not lift his body to accommodate her. She had to settle for stroking his hair and draping her arm over his waist. Todd did not respond.

Mallory sighed, got up, and went into the bathroom. She found the partially burned papers in the trash and held them up to the light. She used the complimentary hairdryer on the wet sheets and held them up again.

It should still work, she thought.

She stuffed the papers back into the trash can.

When Mallory returned to bed, Todd's breathing had settled into sleep, but she was too keyed up and could not close her eyes. She sat on his side of the bed, looking at his beautiful face, which didn't look quite so peaceful tonight.

That's my fault, she thought.

"Maybe I should have gone without you. You don't deserve to live like this," Mallory said softly.

Todd's eyes opened and he grabbed her hand. "Don't say that. Don't ever say that. If you left me, I would have died. This isn't easy for either of us, but we are a team, there is not one without the other. I won't leave you and I won't let you go. Understood?" Todd said.

Mallory smiled. "Understood."

CHAPTER 29
JUNE 2002

Christophe had started to sweat when he didn't see her in the first crowd of people off the ferry. He scanned the parking lot for the car that had dropped her off, or her car, or Todd's. When he saw none of them, he cursed in French and headed for the ferry's ladies' room. After knocking and calling, he entered, checked the stalls, and then flipped the lid on the trashcan. He cursed again as he pulled out the wig, sunglasses, and dress. He stopped and contemplated for a moment. Emma had known he was here and she had given him the slip. He rushed off the ferry, planning his next move. He was a master tracker, particularly when he knew the target as well as he knew this one. She might have given him the slip this morning, and only because he hadn't known she was on to him, but it wouldn't happen again.

Christophe's face was flushed with anger as he drove back to Roberts Creek. He went directly to Mallory's cottage. He was certain that the house would be empty, but when he arrived, he noted that both cars were in the driveway. Still, he knew the house would be empty. Emma wouldn't have taken the cars; she was smarter than that. What had she and Todd taken, and where were they now?

Christophe opened the back door as easily as if he had a key. The house was neat, as though its occupants were coming back soon. "Oh, she's good," Christophe thought. He headed for the bathroom, because all that coffee was kicking in again, and as he scanned the décor, he thought it was not Emma's taste. As soon as the thought entered his head, he recognized how foolish it was. Did he really know Emma or Mallory or whoever she was? He went into the bedroom. It was not neat. The bed was a mess. The sheets were freshly rumpled.

"Emma, you bitch!" he screamed at a volume that overwhelmed him.

Christophe crumpled to his knees. This messy bed had been intentional. She was sending him a message. He threw the comforter roughly over the sheets to cover what had recently happened there, and sat down in an overstuffed chair across from the bed. His eyes narrowed and his brain scanned over every detail of their brief time together in France.

He rose from the chair with renewed commitment and walked the rest of the second story, stopping in the spare bedroom. He grabbed a small backpack on the floor. He saw a cord hanging from the ceiling, pulled it, and scrambled up the stairs to the attic. There was an open trunk but it was empty. He took the backpack back down to the master bedroom to inspect its contents.

Christophe felt as though he were drawing power from this bedroom. THEIR bedroom. It was feeding his anger. He briefly regretted relieving himself earlier because he had the sudden urge to mark the territory. Childish, he thought. So primal. He sat down in the overstuffed chair again and opened backpack. There was a single small envelope inside.

Christophe opened the envelope and pulled out a map of British Columbia and Alaska marked with a red pen. The red mark stopped in Juneau. He shook his head. "She wouldn't stop there. It's too obvious." He examined the map. The number of islands and possible places they could have gone was overwhelming. He reached into the backpack again and pulled out two other items: A passport for a Mary Todd with Emma's photo and a Visa card, also in the name Mary Todd.

Christophe smiled. She hadn't been sure Todd would go with her. He smiled again. That meant she hadn't told him about The Job. She was keeping secrets from her husband, and that could work in Christophe's favor. He took out his cell phone and dialed the club.

"Todd, please," he said.

A woman replied: "I'm sorry, he's not here."

"Will he be in tomorrow?"

"No, he'll be gone at least a week. Can I help you?"

Christophe frowned and disconnected the call. Damn. He'd gone with her. He got up from the chair and paced the floor to relieve some tension. Emma had left him, but she hadn't left Todd, not even when she knew she was in trouble. Christophe steamed, he cogitated, the anger brewed in his gut, not just at her, but also at his replacement. But where had they gone? He studied the map again, and realized, with company, Emma wouldn't have tried to hide out on one of the small islands. They must have headed south for Vancouver and the anonymity of the big city.

Christophe left the house, drove like a maniac, and reached the ferry terminal just before 8:20, but the ferry gates were closed to cars; in fact, they had turned several away before him. Christophe tried to board as a foot passenger, but they'd just closed the gates. He knew there was no chance of getting to Vancouver by ferry. He called a local man he had contacted shortly after his arrival.

"I need to get to Vancouver now."

"Sorry, can't fly now, it's almost dark and there is quite a fog rolling in," his contact replied.

"I'll give you $1,000 U.S., cash, if we go now."

"That's a tempting offer, but I won't enjoy it if I'm not alive. I'll take you at first light tomorrow morning."

"What time is that?"

"About 5:30 a.m. That should get you into Vancouver about 6:45."

"I'll be there," he confirmed.

With nothing but time and his building rage on his hands, Christophe returned to Emma's cottage. He searched through her drawers, not entirely certain what he was looking for. Something was driving him to search. He found nothing of interest, nothing that looked familiar. There was no sign that he had ever been a part of her life.

Christophe plugged his computer into the phone line and logged onto the Internet, trying to analyze the plan that Emma had left behind. It was reasonable to assume that the plan they were now following had some elements in common with the one he had found. Emma had chosen mid-sized hotels in each of the false destinations. There were probably about a hundred hotels that fit into that category in Vancouver, but if he limited his initial search to the downtown area, which he presumed to be busier and therefore less noticeable, there were probably only about twenty. Christophe logged into a Vancouver lodging site and shortly was into the underlying reservation systems for the mid-sized downtown hotels. He found it on the fifth try: Matthew and Jessica Todd had checked into room 1014 at the Pacific Palisades Hotel at one that afternoon.

Christophe smiled with satisfaction and toyed with how he could taunt her. Yes, he did love the chase. He would send flowers. Torment her a little and let her know she couldn't hide from him. After finding a florist in Vancouver with evening hours, he dialed his cellular. He paid a large premium and included a tip to have the flowers delivered at six the next morning. Perhaps their trail would be cold when he arrived, but he thought not. Emma had left France over a year ahead of him and still he had caught up with her. One more day was no problem.

Behind the bathroom door Christophe found a bathrobe. It was white cotton with little whales and dolphins on it. It seemed very un-Emma, but it had her smell. He held it to his face and inhaled deeply. He sat down at her dressing table. He carefully opened every bottle and jar and examined the contents of each. In the very back of the drawer he discovered a small dark blue jar that contained a white powder. He dipped a finger into the powder, tasted it, and it numbed his tongue. Christophe took a long slow sniff of the jar's contents, and knew what he'd found. He knew this jar could not possibly have been filled by Emma. He knew her well enough to know this. Christophe smiled. So Emma wasn't the only one keeping secrets in the marriage. He closed the jar and slipped it into the pocket of his jacket. It was late and Christophe gave into his fatigue. He walked over to their bed, pulled back the comforter and climbed in. He set his cell phone alarm for 4:00 a.m. and smiled as he fell asleep.

Tomorrow would be a long and fruitful day.

– € –

The alarm rang at four and again at five. Christophe was accustomed to waking before the alarm and was a little disturbed that he hadn't this morning. He wasn't aware that he'd hit the snooze button three times. It was the deepest sleep he'd had in weeks and still he did not want to wake. He lolled for just a moment, breathing in the scent of Emma on the bed sheets, and then he remembered the mission at hand and shot up out of bed. He looked at the bedside clock and cursed in French. He had to leave now. Still fully dressed, he headed for the car and he drove full tilt to the tiny Roberts Creek airfield twenty-five minutes away.

– € –

Joe Templin was waiting at the airport before Christophe was out of bed, doing his pre-flight check.

He'd monitored Christophe's cell call arranging the flight the night before.

"G'day," Joe said to the private pilot who had just entered the small hangar, "I need to go to Vancouver this morning. Is there a private craft airport in Vancouver?"

"Mornin'," John Hamilton said sleepily. "No, you would think there would be, but everything goes into Vancouver International. You need to call for clearance, but this hour of the day you shouldn't have a problem. I was just about to call in my flight plan. I'm headed there this morning, just waiting for my passenger. I'll get you a slot, too."

"Much obliged," said Joe as he waited for the call. He smiled at his finesse. Not many people could follow someone by going ahead of them.

"All set," said John, "your clearance number is 74 and mine is 75. Maybe I'll see you there."

"Thanks. Have a great flight." Joe waved and climbed into the cockpit of his small plane.

— € —

Joe was in the air, headed for Vancouver Airport, about an hour's flight away. His next stop would be the Pacific Palisades Hotel. Just in case, he would wait in a taxi until he saw Christophe leave the airport and then follow at a reasonable distance. He was starting to get impatient, and he knew that wasn't good. These things could not be forced. He had to let Christophe lead him to the money.

Christophe saw a plane taking off as he arrived at the airfield. "Damn!" He said, and then he remembered he had chartered the plane and it wouldn't leave without him. He cursed himself again for having slept so long; for still being so fuzzy. He needed his wits about him today. John Hamilton was in the cockpit, warming up the plane, when Christophe arrived. As he climbed into the charter, he realized his laptop was still in Emma's kitchen. *Merde,* he thought, *I needed that computer. What is wrong with me?* He had to leave it. He had no choice; if they didn't leave now, he would probably miss Emma altogether. He chastised himself for getting emotional again. Sleeping in her bed had made him late, and sending the flowers had assured that she would run from the hotel as soon as she got them. Christophe shook his head and vowed not to let his emotions get the best of him again.

CHAPTER 30

JUNE 2002

Mallory emerged from the shower at 6:05, just as there was a knock at the door. Todd checked the peephole. "Looks like a bellboy," he said.

"What is it?" Mallory said.

"What is it?" Todd echoed.

"Flowers for Jessica Todd," the bellboy said.

Mallory walked out of the bathroom wrapped in a towel. "You?" she asked Todd.

He shook his head. "Nope, and 6:00 a.m. is kind of an odd time to deliver flowers," he said apprehensively.

Mallory walked to the door and called out: "Just leave them, please. We're not dressed yet."

Todd watched through the peep hole as the bellboy set the elaborate arrangement down outside the door and walked away.

"Mistake?" he said, seeing that Mallory was dressing quickly.

"Big one. Open the door and let me see the card," she said in the directive voice that she had used most of the day yesterday. "And get dressed. Fast."

Mallory knew it was Christophe; it couldn't be anyone else. He'd found the envelope she had left in the guest room backpack, her trail of breadcrumbs. They had to get out now. She just hoped Christophe had missed the last ferry the night before. But she knew Christophe, and knew it was conceivable that he had spent the night in the next room. "He's found us," she said.

Todd opened the card, and handed it to her.

There was no message. Just one letter: C.

"Him?" Todd asked.

Mallory nodded, pulled on her jacket and gathered the backpacks while Todd finished dressing. She opened their door and scanned the hallway. Empty. "No elevator," Mallory whispered, and they quietly rushed to the stairway and took it two steps at a time. Both fine athletes, they were at the bottom floor fire door in record time. They stopped and listened.

Mallory cracked the door to see where it put them. It opened onto a deserted street in back of the hotel. They sprinted across the street and ran down an alley to a Ramada Inn three blocks away. Pretending to be Ramada customers departing early, they hailed a cab in front of the hotel and directed its driver to the Marina. Several blocks from the hotel, Mallory changed their destination and directed the driver to a small diner near the train yard in East Vancouver.

The driver shrugged, happy for the extra money he would gain from the detour, and Mallory and Todd sat back in the cab. Their hearts were pounding from the exercise and the close call they'd just had. Their heavy breathing caused the cabby to look back at them curiously. Mallory didn't want the driver to be able to remember their faces if asked, so she turned to Todd and started kissing him. "Newlyweds," Todd grinned, picking up on Mallory's ruse, and they continued necking, their faces blocked from the driver, for the half hour it took to get to the diner. Todd paid the driver, included a healthy tip, and they slipped into the diner and found a table in the back.

"Do you think we lost him?" Todd asked.

"I don't know. We just need to get on that train," Mallory said.

"What'll you have, folks?" the waitress barked.

"Pancakes ... do you have banana pancakes?" Mallory said.

"Yup! Coffee?"

"Yes, and bacon," she said.

"Same here," said Todd. "And can you make sandwiches to go?"

"Sure."

"Four turkey and Swiss on rolls, mustard, no mayo," he said.

The waitress left to fill their order and Mallory allowed herself a smile. "You catch on quick. We're going to need food later."

Todd smiled. "Glad to do my part."

— € —

Christophe hopped a cab from the airport and was at the hotel at 7:05 a.m. He handed the cabby $100 U.S. and told him to wait. "There is more where that came from," he said.

Christophe took the elevator directly to the tenth floor and found room 1014. When he saw a lone flower petal in front of the door, he was fairly certain they had gone. Regardless, he knocked on the door: no response. Christophe jimmied the door with ease, went in, and scanned the room. The impressive flower arrangement was standing on the desk. He checked the sheets for signs of sex and found none. This made him smile. It annoyed him that he still wanted her. That was dangerous.

The flowers may have been a fatal mistake, Christophe thought, as he turned toward the bathroom. The waste can contained pieces of burned paper, some heavier than others. Christophe took the trashcan to the desk, turned on the lamp and tried to reassemble the heavier pieces of charred paper. It became clear very quickly what Emma had burned. It was an old photo of Christophe. "She kept a photo of me," he whispered. "Todd knows what I look like." The previous night Christophe had searched Emma's home for some remnant of him, an indication that she still thought of him. The photo comforted him; he was still in her thoughts. But that didn't help in the current dilemma. He needed to know where they had gone. The lighter pieces of paper were burned more severely; still, Christophe could make out some fragments.

1) ific des 47 obson, —he decided that was the name and address of the hotel.
2) 9 a.m. Yard— argo ain anff.

Christophe pondered the charred pieces for a moment.

He held the fragments up to the light and could make out a bit more.

9 a.m. Van Tr Yard—Cargo ain to anff.

"Think!" He said. "Think!" He looked at his watch: 7:20 a.m. "Damn, the computer would really help now." He took a deep breath and studied the fragments again.

9 a.m. Van Tr Yard—Cargo ain to anff. "Vancouver Train Yard."

He dropped the fragments, and phoned the front desk. "Where's the Vancouver Train Yard?"

"Hold on please, Sir," the receptionist said. She returned a few seconds later. "It's in East Vancouver."

"How far is that from here?"

"About a thirty-minute taxi ride, but Sir, it is only freight trains."

"Thank you, you've been helpful." Christophe hung up. They were taking a freight train somewhere. He smiled in appreciation. Emma was very good; he would never have thought of that.

— € —

"Vancouver Train Yard," Christophe instructed his cab driver.

"Okay, man," the driver said. "But its only freight trains there. No passengers."

"I am aware of that, thank you. Just drive."

"Okay, man," the driver said again. "But I hope you're not thinking about hopping one. That's dangerous stuff. A hopper lost his legs doing that last year."

"Nah," Christophe said. "I'm meeting someone who is working the train to Anff."

"You mean Banff?" the driver said.

"Right. Where is Banff?" Christophe tried to ask casually.

"I guess you're not from around here," the driver laughed as he spoke. "It's in the mountains to the east." The driver continued to drone on about the mountains and skiing, but Christophe wasn't listening.

When they arrived at the train yard, the shack near the entrance was unoccupied. However, there was a chalkboard with the day's freight train schedule scrawled on it:

7:30 a.m. Jasper—Track 27—estimated arrival 11 a.m. next day
8 a.m. Kamloops—Track 18—estimated arrival 4 p.m.
8:30 a.m. Revelstoke—Track 11—estimated arrival 1 a.m. next day
9 a.m. Banff/Calgary—Track 37—estimated arrival Banff 6 a.m. next day.

Mallory and Todd ran the length of track 37 looking for an empty boxcar. It was not as easy as Mallory had thought it would be. Most trains were devoid of boxcars anymore. They had newfangled cars that were just like a shelf that held much of what the boxcars used to hold. They finally found a row of three empty or almost empty cars and decided on the middle one. It was 8:45 a.m. when they climbed into the car and settled in, Mallory silently reprimanding herself for not having realized that boxcars were small enclosed spaces. If the door was shut, she would not do well. She moved over to the side of the car opposite the door and tried to quell her anxiety.

A few minutes later, the train slowly pulled out of yard.

Mallory breathed deeply. The door was still open.

As the train gathered speed, Mallory opened one of the backpacks and pulled out two small, strange looking tanks with chest straps and tubes.

"What the heck are those?" Todd asked.

"Oxygen," said Mallory. "For the spiral tunnels."

"We need oxygen for train tunnels?"

"For these tunnels, we do," Mallory said. "We'll spend almost half an hour in them. There's very little oxygen in the tunnels and with the diesel fumes from the train, it gets pretty toxic. Mallory pulled a map from her coat pocket." We won't hit them for hours yet, but when we do, we'll need the tanks." She pointed to the map.

"That's almost to Banff. Why do we need them now?" Todd said.

"Because I want you to be safe no matter what," Mallory said, kissing him. She pulled up his shirt and strapped the tank to his side. She snaked the tube up his chest, and attached the small hook to the collar of his T-shirt. "You put this in your mouth and suck on it when you need a breath. Try not to use it until you start to feel a little dizzy. The tanks only last 20 minutes. Don't breathe through your nose. Here, help me with mine."

When he was done, Todd settled back against the wall and let out a sigh. "Okay, I think it's time."

"Time for what?" Mallory said.

"We've got almost a whole day to kill. Tell me the story."

– ₠ –

Christophe chose the boxcar just behind them. He wasn't yet sure what his plan was, but he felt a moving train was the ideal place for a confrontation. Even though he paced up and down, he wasn't concerned. He had time to figure it out.

– ₠ –

Joe Templin's cab pulled into the train yard just in time for Joe to see Christophe sprinting towards track 37. He watched his prey climb into an open boxcar and couldn't help but smile. "Now, this is getting interesting," the photographer said softly. He briefly contemplated jumping onto the bandwagon, but decided against it. He knew the train was headed for Banff, and there were faster and more comfortable ways to get there.

CHAPTER 31

JUNE 2002

Mallory rose and stretched as she finished the story. She looked out the wide door at the beautiful Canadian scenery zipping by. She wanted to stop and look and walk and smell the flowers like she did in Roberts Creek, but she was running again. The train rumbled over an old bridge that crossed two rivers. One river was very brown and rich with silt; the other was clear and blue. Mallory could see where the waters combined and melded with each other. Ultimately, the clear blue water was overtaken by the silt, cloudy and murky, racing towards the sea. Her fresh start in Roberts Creek with Todd had made her feel clear, clean, and blue again, after all that had transpired since her parents' car accident almost two years ago. Now it seemed muddy brown waters were threatening to drown her. Mallory shook her head to try to clear it, with no luck. The boxcar door was wide open, but Mallory still felt like it was closing in on her.

"Lovely view isn't it?"

Mallory wheeled around. "Christophe."

The gun trained on her drew her eyes away from his face.

Christophe smiled. "Get on the floor next to your husband, my dear Emma. Actually, I don't know what to call you. Emma? Mallory? Jessica? You've been busy since you set me up."

"What are you talking about?" Mallory asked.

"Don't play games with me. I know you planted those euros in my car. Your father would be ashamed. You should not have given me up," Christophe said.

Mallory started to respond, but Christophe put up his hand. He took a roll of duct tape out of his coat pocket and tossed it to her. "Wrap his ankles and wrists," he said, pointing the gun at Todd.

Mallory obeyed, keeping the tape as loose as possible without being obvious.

"Now do your ankles and tear off a piece for your wrists," Christophe said.

Todd started to get up, but Mallory put her hand out to stop him. When Mallory was finished, Christophe placed the gun in the waistband of his pants and quickly bent to wrap her wrists.

"You've lost her," Todd said to Christophe. "We're married. She's with me. Give up."

Mallory shot a warning look at Todd and shook her head.

Christophe laughed. "Is that what she told you? That I'm in love with her? My friend, make sure you know your wife. She had me thrown in jail after I killed for her. Fine gratitude."

"I'd have been crazy to have you arrested. I didn't do that," Mallory said.

"You're a liar."

"I'm telling you the truth, Christophe. Think about it, why would I set you up? I didn't want you to follow me. I wanted to disappear forever, not just for a year, forever. Setting you up would assure that you would come after me," Mallory said. "I just wanted it all behind me."

"Shut up!"

"What do you want?" Mallory said.

Christophe shrugged. "I want to see you suffer in prison for a little while. Like I did. So let's get started." He pulled the little blue jar from his pocket. "I found this at your house. It's good stuff, one little sniff last night and I almost missed this train. Nodded right out." He held up the jar. "I'm guessing this is yours, Todd. I heard about your problems from your friends at the club in Roberts Creek."

Mallory looked at Todd.

"I can explain," Todd said.

She shook her head tightly, signaling "Not now."

Christophe opened the jar and waved it under Todd's nose. He smiled as Todd moaned. "Starting to waver already, I see. This will be easier than I thought. Here, have a taste." Christophe knelt and put his knee to Todd's stomach, pinning him against the wall of the car. Covering Todd's mouth tightly with his hand he held a pinch of the powder under one of Todd's nostrils and held the other closed. Todd tried not to breathe, but eventually he drew the powder in and the effects were almost immediate. Christophe watched and then smiled. "Good boy." He patted Todd's cheek. Todd looked up and spat at him.

Mallory gasped.

Christophe wiped the spittle off his face. "At least you're not a total wimp. But it's not very smart to aggravate your captor." He turned to Mallory. "Your turn, *ma chérie*."

Mallory shook her head violently, but Christophe managed to subdue her and she was soon feeling the effects of the drug as well. It was euphoric and her head was spinning. Mallory thought she was hallucinating when she heard Christophe say to Todd, "Enjoy that for a bit, young man. Once we are through this tunnel you will have the pleasure of watching me make love to your wife." He turned back to Mallory. "Are you ready for that, Emma? It's been so long."

Christophe grabbed her face, gave her a hard kiss, and then pushed her away.

— € —

When Mallory came to, it was pitch black outside the boxcar. She struggled to clear her head, listening to see if she could determine where Christophe was, but all she heard was train noise. How much time had passed? Was it night, or were they in the tunnels? If so, she had to get the oxygen tube in her mouth. Mallory bit at the collar of her shirt, desperately feeling for the tube. Her lips clasped around it. She took a short silent breath and inched closer to Todd. Next to him, she leaned to his ear and whispered "Oxygen." There was a loud thump in the darkness, followed by gasping. Mallory pressed into Todd, trying to figure out if he was breathing. Taking small silent breaths from her oxygen tube, Mallory willed Todd to do the same.

The sudden appearance of light blinded her.

The mountains sparkled in the afternoon sunshine.

Mallory breathed in the pure fresh mountain air.

Across the car, Christophe was sprawled on the floor.

"Todd, can you hear me?" Mallory whispered.

Her husband nodded.

"Put your wrists up to my mouth," Mallory said, and when he did, she tore at the tape at his wrists with her teeth.

With his wrists free, Todd removed the tape from hers, and they undid their ankles on their own.

Todd looked over at Christophe. "Is he?"

Mallory crawled over to Christophe and checked his pulse at his wrist.

There was none.

Mallory tried again at his neck.

There was none.

"He's dead."

"Are you sure?"

"Yes. The spiral tunnels. He had no oxygen."

Todd stood and took a deep breath. "I'm glad. Bastard."

Mallory sighed. "It worked."

"What worked?" Todd said.

"My plan," Mallory said.

"You planned to kill him?"

"I didn't kill him. The tunnels did. I just had to get him into the tunnels."

"Why?"

"Because we would never have been safe while he was alive and I couldn't kill him."

Todd rubbed his wrists. "So now we go home."

"Not yet, but we need to get out of here," Mallory said.

"What do you mean get out of here?"

"A man died in the tunnels in this boxcar. We can't be here on arrival. Not still alive anyway. We've got to go. Now."

Todd looked at her. "You mean jump?"

Mallory smiled. "We can do it. The train will slow down when we get near Lake Louise." She spread out the map.

Todd walked over to Christophe, pulled the gun from his waistband, wiped it off, and tossed it into the Canadian woods that were flashing by at 60 miles per hour. He patted Christophe down for other weapons and found the blue jar in Christophe's jacket pocket. He held the jar up to the bright light. "Once upon a time, I thought I couldn't live without this stuff." He looked at Mallory. "I kept some, just in case. But I never touched it, I swear. All I needed was you." He turned and threw the jar out of the boxcar. "All I still need is you."

CHAPTER 32

JUNE 2002

When the train slowed down, Todd and Mallory gathered their backpacks and prepared to jump. Todd tossed the packs out first. An aggressive jump was necessary to clear the train tracks and the wheels. They held hands and leapt hard, fell into soft, mossy ground and rolled, briefly losing touch. A bit bruised, they scrambled quickly to their feet and walked back down the tracks to find their backpacks. A few hundred feet into the woods, they crossed a raggedy trail with a marker indicating the way to town. They paused for a moment to recover from the landing. Mallory sat on a log and checked her body for damage. "You alright?" Mallory asked.

Todd checked, too. "Nothing broken, but I think ... ooh, yeah." He raised his shirt to reveal a nasty bruise. "You?"

"Just my upper arm. I'll live. But, Sweetie, that looks bad." She patted the rock next to her.

Todd sat down and Mallory pulled some arnica, a natural healing balm, out of the backpack. She smoothed it on the burgeoning bruise. Todd winced, but bore it. He pulled his shirt down and offered his hand to his wife. "Let's get out of here."

They had covered a few miles when Todd stopped dead.

Mallory ran into the back of him. "What's the problem?" She peered around him.

Todd pointed.

Standing in the middle of the path was a male elk with a full rack of antlers staring right at them. The elk was taller than Todd, which made him at least seven feet. He was making a low, growling noise, kind of a grunt, and then he slowly began to paw the ground.

"Back into the woods slowly," Todd whispered. "Don't turn around."

Mallory didn't move.

"GO!" Todd hissed, and he continued to stand his ground and hold eye contact with the angry animal while Mallory slowly backed away. When she was safely twenty feet from the path, Todd also began to slowly back away. He inched toward a large tree, and when he reached it, he signaled to Mallory to join him behind it. As they watched, the elk, confused, stopped grunting and pawing, and without another look their way, turned and trotted past them up the path. An elk calf was waiting, and as the couple walked off together into the sunset, Mallory giggled and whispered, "The path to true love ..."

Todd didn't laugh. "That was close. We need to be more alert."

"I need a bath," Mallory said.

It took an hour of fairly easy trails to make it down to the Lake Louise Post Hotel, a lovely little inn with detached cottages and wonderful food. Their romantic cottage came with a king-sized bed, fireplace and very big bathtub. They made good use of the tub, and though they had the best of intentions afterward, the day's events quickly overtook them and they fell asleep in each other's arms.

CHAPTER 33

JULY 2002

Joe Templin was waiting for the freight train when it arrived in Banff. He waited to see who, if anyone, would leave the train. No one did. He waited until the train yard was quiet, and then he searched the car he had seen Christophin leap into back in Vancouver. It was empty. In the car next door, however, the former MI5 operative found what he was looking for. Templin knelt down and took Christophin's pulse. Nothing. He sighed, rose, exited the boxcar, and walked to the pay phone near the office. He dialed the local police, filed an anonymous sighting of a dead body on the freight train; he'd had a job to do, yes, but this was a dead man, and someone somewhere, he thought, would need to know. He hung up the phone and drove his rental car back to the Banff airport, trying to figure out what to do next.

– € –

In the end, Templin thought it best to retrace his steps, so he flew his plane back to Roberts Creek, and after a brief stop at his hotel room, he headed for Todd and Mallory's cottage. He pulled on latex gloves before he tried the door and was surprised to find the house unlocked. A laptop sat on the kitchen table. He pressed a key and a desktop in French appeared. He opened word documents and prowled the directory for the most recently used files. He found nothing of note and cursed his lack of computer skills. He carefully inspected the rest of the kitchen and moved on to the other rooms, finishing in the attic. Nothing. His prey was dead in a boxcar in Banff, and so was his trail. He couldn't go back to the bank empty-handed, or he would wind up in the same boat. He had to know what had happened to Christophin, and more importantly, what had happened to the stolen euros. Christophin was no longer going to be any help, and the woman—and her husband—Christophin had been chasing were obviously long gone.

Templin had only one still-live trail, and he followed it.

— € —

Clara was filling in for Todd when Joe Templin walked into the Roberts Creek club during the lunch rush.

Clara greeted him with a sparkling smile. "Hey! I thought you had gone."

Joe smiled. "When such a beautiful woman is here? I doubt that very much."

Clara giggled and blushed.

"Would you like to have dinner with me tonight?"

"Sure."

"What time do you get off work?"

"Six."

"I'll be here. I look forward to it."

"Me too," Clara said.

Templin smiled and left the café. He didn't care in the least about this woman. He needed information about the OTHER woman and her husband, and their whereabouts. The young woman worked with the husband, so it stood to reason she must know something about them, hopefully where they were now. He headed back to his hotel, took a quick nap, and then woke and took a quick shower, splashed on his favorite cologne and dressed in his most flattering outfit: black from head to toe.

In his MI5 days Joe Templin had cut quite the dashing figure, but the small gut that had developed the past few years disconcerted him. The only thing that would camouflage it now was a dark color. The black clothing also set off his caramel skin and made his green eyes pop. He examined himself with vain approval in the mirror and caught sight of the clothing-strewn room. He tidied up, thinking that if things went well tonight, he would be back here with Clara. During his MI5 days, Joe had found that pillow talk was a very effective method for extracting information, and Clara seemed more than a little bit interested.

— C —

When Joe arrived intentionally a few minutes late, Clara was pacing outside the club café door.

"Oh, I thought you might not come," she said.

"Not come? I'm looking forward to spending the evening with you, luv."

Clara flushed. "So, where are we going?"

"How about Molly's Café? I hear it's quite good."

"Oh, I love Molly's!"

Clara was particularly happy about his choice because Roberts Creek's biggest gossip worked at Molly's. Gabby would see Clara with Joe tonight, and tomorrow the news would be all over town. It had been so long since Clara had had a date, and she had started to fear people in town were thinking she might be a lesbian. She wasn't, of course, but there weren't very many eligible men in Roberts Creek to prove her wrong. In fact, there were none. Clara had often thought about staying in Arizona year-round, but she really loved Roberts Creek, and her granddad was getting old, and he was the only family she had left.

It was an easy evening. Clara was happy to talk about herself and Joe was an avid listener. She prattled on and on, pleased to have an audience, until both her story and dinner were finished. In the ensuing silence as they waited for coffee, Clara asked: "So, Joe, what about you? What brings you to Roberts Creek?"

"I just needed a break. It is a very quiet place."

"That it is. What do you do for a living?"

"I'm a writer."

"Oh right. I remember you told me that when we first met. Anything I've read?"

"Probably not. Just a lot of dry non-fiction stuff about British Intelligence."

"Like James Bond?"

"Nothing that exciting," Joe replied. "What do you say we skip the coffee and make some of our own excitement?"

Clara smiled. "What did you have in mind?"

"A moonlight walk along the water?"

"Sounds lovely."

The walk, of course, led back to Joe's hotel room. He found Clara to be an enthusiastic partner, and they made love until almost three in the morning, after which Clara fell into a satisfied sleep.

"So much for women wanting conversation after sex," Joe chortled.

He got up, opened a window and smoked a cigarette while breathing in the crisp night air. Clara stirred, struggling for covers in the chill. Joe watched her in amusement; it was all he could do not to laugh out loud. Unlike most men, Joe found the chill excited him and he crawled into bed to wake Clara again. She obliged him, half awake, and rolled over to sleep again when he was finished. The sex was okay, but the night was not accomplishing Joe's information objective, and that thought kept him awake.

Around seven Clara opened her eyes and wrapped her arms around him.

"Sleep well?" she said.

"Not at all really."

"Too cold?"

"No, just not quite dozy," said Joe. "Do you have to work today?"

"Oh gosh, let me use the phone." Clara dialed and spoke urgently, "Hi, I'm kind of indisposed today. Can you work for Todd?" She listened. "That's great. Thanks Pop." She hung up carefully.

"All set?" Joe asked.

Clara nodded. "Pop's filling in today, and Todd's coming back tomorrow, so I'm free for two whole days. What would you like to do first?" She cuddled up next to him. "Me?"

Joe smiled. "Todd hasn't been around?"

Clara kissed his shoulder. "No. He and Mallory are off on some adventure. You know Todd?"

"I met him a few times at the club, good golf game. Nice bloke. Didn't know he was attached."

Clara sighed. He wasn't until Mallory showed up. "She's a quiet sort, but she managed to take the last eligible guy in these parts. She and Todd got married a year ago. Hey, I know ... let's go to Vancouver! I've got two days and I'd love to get out of this tiny town and see the city. I'll show you the sights!"

"Can't, Sweets. Got to do some writing today," Joe motioned to his computer. "But maybe I could swing a stroll down by the sea later."

Clara snuggled against his bare back. "Let's go to the club and have some breakfast. I want to show you off."

"Sounds good. I'm famished."

After a quick bite of breakfast, Joe bid Clara good day with the promise of dinner and more that night. He returned to his club room and broke out his laptop. He logged on to the Internet and searched for Mallory Matthews. At first, he felt lucky that there were only 4,210 matches. Mallory was an unusual name, so that helped, but nothing matched up. He didn't like to resort to his other source, but it seemed he had no choice. He typed in the address of the MI5 database and entered his security code. He wasn't sure it would still work, but it did. He breathed a sigh of relief and wondered how much longer his luck would hold. He entered *Name: Mallory Matthews. Current Address: Roberts Creek, British Columbia, Canada.* One entry was returned. Mallory Matthews married Todd Matthews, February 17, 2001. Maiden Name: Emmett. Joe smiled and warmed to his task. He entered *Name: Mallory Emmett* and got a hit that she'd purchased a car in Montreal in February of the previous year.

The timing is right, thought Joe.

He requested a copy of all female passport scans at the time, ages 20 to 30. He back tracked the purchase, and after a few hours of tedious scanning, a picture he recognized flashed on the screen.

Her name was Mallory Andrews.

She had arrived from Casablanca, Morocco, connecting from Nice.

France.

In the right place at the right time, and now on the run.

Templin smiled. Bingo. He smiled again and nodded as he composed a carefully phrased and encoded email to Roger Coltman.

— € —

In the ferry parking lot, Rusty paced in front of his car. He wasn't nervous; he was just the type of man who had trouble sitting still. He'd been retired forever, but Rusty was always doing something. He loved getting up early and working at the club every day and was planning to ask Todd if he could continue. He didn't even care to get paid; he just loved the social activity that whirled around the place.

Rusty spotted Todd towering over the rest of the disembarking ferry crowd. He spotted Mallory next, and gave the young couple a grin and a broad wave. Mallory came bounding over with her arms spread wide.

"Rusty, we missed you," Mallory whispered into his ear.

"Hey, you're smothering me. It hasn't been that long," Rusty said.

"It's seemed like forever," said Mallory.

Todd nodded in agreement.

"How's the club?" Todd said.

"No problems," Rusty said. "Clara and I handled it just fine."

"Let's go," Mallory said. "I want to get home."

— € —

As they drove along the winding roads, Mallory, in the backseat, took in the beauty of the peninsula. It was so natural, almost untouched. Mallory felt like she was being born again in the wilds of Canada.

Rusty dropped them off at the end of their drive, and when Mallory saw her cottage in the distance, she drew a quick breath.

"What's wrong?" Todd said.

"Nothing. Nothing at all. I just never thought I would be here again. I'm just happy."

Todd embraced her. "Me too, Pumpkin. Me, too."

Mallory broke into a run, leaving Todd with the backpacks.

She just wanted to be home again.

Christophe was dead.

She and Todd were relatively safe.

The door opened without a key, and Mallory stopped and turned to Todd.

"I know I locked it when we left."

"Wait here. I'm going first," Todd said protectively. He pulled the gun out of the backpack and stepped over the threshold. He scanned the living room and moved into the kitchen. There was a laptop computer open on the kitchen table. Todd touched a key and the screen flashed up in French.

"Mal, it's OK. It was Christophe. He left his laptop."

Mallory came into the kitchen, sat down at Christophe's computer, and started navigating.

"What are you doing?" Todd asked.

"It might come in handy," Mallory said.

Todd sighed. "So even though he's dead, we're not done."

"I don't know. There's still the photographer, the guy following Christophe. We don't know if he's done or not."

Mallory shut off the computer. She went upstairs to their bedroom and found it a mess. All of her dresser drawers were open, and clothing was scattered everywhere. Her dirty laundry was spread on the unmade bed. Mallory scrambled to straighten it up, but Todd entered the room almost immediately.

"He was up here, too," Todd said.

Mallory nodded.

"Well, he's gone now for good," Todd said, and with one motion he cleared the laundry from the bed and boosted Mallory up onto it.

CHAPTER 34

JULY 2002

Invigorated after their morning run, Mallory set about her gardening. Stepping into the garden shed made her shiver with déjà vu. She vividly recalled the last time she had been there. The footprints were still on the dirt floor. Mallory grabbed a broom and swept them away, but they were still indelibly etched on her brain. She left the shed and headed out to water the front garden.

Minutes later, a car pulled into the driveway.

As Mallory watched, Clara and the photographer climbed out of the car. Mallory took a deep breath, turned off the hose, wiped the dirt from her hands and waved to Clara. "So good to see you," she said and she hugged Clara tightly. "You have a handsome companion," she whispered in Clara's ear. "Who is he?"

"Isn't he dreamy?" Clara whispered back. "Wait till you hear him talk!"

Mallory turned to Clara's dreamy companion with a raised eyebrow.

He extended a hand. "Joe Templin, Ma'am."

Mallory shook his hand. "Pleased to meet you." She smiled. "But ma'am is a bit formal for these parts."

"Sorry, it's the Brit in me. We call everyone ma'am. I'm not used to the Canadian idioms yet."

"So you're living here."

"No, Ma'am."

"Mallory, please."

He smiled. "Right. Mallory. No, not living here. Just staying for a bit. I'm a writer and I needed some peace and quiet."

Mallory smiled back. "Roberts Creek is an ideal place for peace and quiet. Is your home in a big city?"

"London."

"Oh, my. This IS quite a change," Mallory said.

"You've been to London?"

"Yes. It's a little damp for my tastes."

Templin laughed. He actually liked this woman. She seemed warm and friendly and altogether NOT a criminal. He wondered if she was smart enough to pull off the euro heist.

"We recently returned from a trip," Mallory said, "so I don't have any food to offer you. But perhaps a cup of coffee?"

"We'd love it," Clara said.

As Mallory opened the door she said, "Sorry, the place is still a bit of a mess. Unpacking and all."

"It's a brilliant location," Templin said.

Mallory brewed some coffee, and while she and Clara made small talk, Templin took the opportunity to excuse himself to use the bathroom.

Mallory pointed out the downstairs loo, and when the door had closed, she turned to Clara. "He seems quite lovely. Wherever did you meet him?"

"On the ferry, after my night in Horseshoe Bay. Isn't he dreamy?" Clara said.

"Yup, he's a fox," Mallory said.

The front door opened and Todd sang, "Hi, honey, I'm home!"

Mallory met him in the living room. "Joe Templin is here," she whispered. "With Clara."

Todd sighed and nodded. "Here we go."

"Just be cool for now," Mallory said.

Templin came out of loo, spied Todd, and smiled. "Todd, I didn't realize you had such a lovely and charming wife."

Todd grinned. "I got lucky. Didn't see you today at the café. I thought maybe you had left while Mallory and I were out of town."

"Nope," Templin said, as he put his arms around Clara. "Just been a little busy with my Sweets."

Clara blushed. "We should be going, seeing you've just gotten back and all. I just wanted to stop by and say I'm glad you're back and safe."

Mallory smiled. "Thanks Clara." She turned to Templin. "Nice to meet you, Joe."

Mallory and Todd stood at the front door of their cottage and watched Clara and Templin walk to Clara's car. When they were gone, Mallory shut the door and leaned heavily against it.

"What are we going to do?" Todd asked.

"I have to check The Bank of France email again," Mallory said. "And then we can make a plan."

– € –

It was handy to have Christophe's computer, complete with Internet service and a modem. Mallory could log in without having to make a trip to Horseshoe Bay. She accessed The Bank of France, scanned Roger Coltman's email file, and found a message from Joe Templin, dated the day before.

The message was brief and to the point: Still tracking Target One. Target Two deceased.

"Good God," Mallory said.

Todd leaned forward. "What?"

"I'm Target One. Templin hasn't been tracking Christophe. He's been tracking me. Christophe was a lucky find." Mallory ran her hands through her hair. "This is impossible. There is no way he could have connected me to the euro heist. It's been almost two years."

Todd sighed. Would this ever be over? "So this means we have to get rid of him, too?"

Mallory's sigh echoed her husband's. "I've run out of plans."

"We're off again?" Todd said.

"I want to live here with you in peace," Mallory said. "I need this to be over."

Todd shrugged. "Unfortunately, that is not an option. What now?"

"I need to find out what he wants. If it's me ... or the money."

Todd went into action mode. "Do we still have the gun?"

"He's Ex-MI5, Todd. A professional. Not sure a gun will help us."

"Still, I'd feel better," Todd said.

"It's in the attic."

"Uh-huh." Todd started for the stairs.

Mallory put her hand on his arm. "I think we should wait."

"Wait?"

"Yeah, wait. Don't push it and don't confront him. It's possible that he really likes Clara."

Todd raised an eyebrow. "Wishful thinking."

Mallory sighed. "We can only hope."

— € —

For the next week Mallory and Todd went about their ordinary daily business. Todd saw Templin every morning at the club café, and sometimes in the afternoon for lunch. The Ex-MI5 was always casual and friendly, and Todd started to think that Mallory's fears had been unfounded. Mallory, on the other hand, was still certain they were just waiting for the other shoe to drop. By the end of the week, Todd's optimism had begun to wear Mallory down and she had just begun to let her guard down and get back to her gardening when the kitchen phone rang.

"Mallory, this is Joe Templin, Clara's friend. I was wondering if I might speak with you this afternoon."

Mallory insides turned to ice. "About?"

"It's a personal matter that's important to you," he said.

"Fine. When?"

"In an hour?"

Mallory stood in the kitchen for a long time with the phone in her hand. Her mind was racing with the alternatives. If Templin were going to arrest her, he wouldn't have made an appointment.

He would just arrest her. She didn't think he had that power. Still, she dialed Todd.

"You have to come home right away," Mallory said.

"What? Why? Are you alright?" Todd said.

"Templin called; he's coming over here in an hour to discuss a personal matter."

There was no response.

"Todd, are you there?"

He wasn't.

Seven minutes later, Todd's car pulled into the driveway.

"What is this personal matter?" Todd said.

Mallory shook her head. "Don't know."

"And?"

"We'll have to see. I don't think we have an alternative," Mallory said.

"The gun?"

Mallory lifted a living room couch cushion, pulled out the gun, and handed it to Todd.

He tucked the gun in his waistband and sat in a living room chair. He looked up at her. "Do you have anything that looks like maternity clothing that you could change into?"

Mallory shook her head. "Why?"

"You should look pregnant."

Mallory smiled. "Nice try. But really, I don't think that will work."

Todd shrugged. "Humor me."

With a new respect for her husband's take charge attitude, Mallory trudged upstairs and put on an oversized shirt. She puffed her flat stomach out as much as she could, and shook her head. Todd was going crazy and she was going right along with him. She heard a car pull up, looked out the window, and saw Templin coming up the walk. She pooched her stomach out as far as it would go, and headed down the stairs.

"Todd. I wasn't expecting to see you," Templin said.

"Home for lunch. What are you doing here?"

"I have an appointment with your wife."

"Mr. Templin," Mallory said, as she descended the stairs, trying to lumber a bit. "You're early."

Templin smiled. "One of my faults. I hope it's not too inconvenient."

"No, I'd like my husband to hear what you have to say," Mallory said.

Templin nodded. "Your call."

He took the seat in the overstuffed chair offered by Mallory.

She and Todd sat together on the couch.

Templin looked at Mallory and began. "I know that you are responsible for Olivier Christophin's death, although I'm fairly certain that wasn't his real name."

"Who?" Mallory said.

"Huh. We're going to play games?" Templin asked.

Mallory gave him a deadpan look. "I have no idea what or who you are talking about."

Templin sighed. "I saw the three of you board the same freight train. You two are still alive. He is quite deceased."

"I don't know WHO he is," Mallory said.

"That's your story and you're sticking to it?"

"I'm afraid I don't know the man you are referring to."

"Olivier Christophin. I was following him. He was my link to completing a very lucrative contract. And now I'm at a dead end."

"That's unfortunate," Mallory said.

"More for you than me. Because now YOU are my link," Templin said.

Mallory feigned ignorance. "I'm afraid you've lost me."

"I was hired by an official at The Bank of France to find the perpetrators of the theft of a large amount of European currency. When I've found said perpetrators, I will receive twenty percent of the amount recovered."

"And this Christophin fellow was involved?"

Templin frowned. "Cut the crap. I know that you two gave him the slip in Horseshoe Bay and I watched him follow you onto that train. I don't give a shit about the two of you, or why you offed him. I just want the money."

Mallory looked at Todd and the two of them burst out laughing. It was funny, really. This man's agenda had nothing to do with Mallory and her part in the heist, and everything to do with what Templin suspected was CHRISTOPHE's thievery, not hers. The way Templin was seeing it, Mallory was just a means to an end of the trail.

This was a relief.

And a way out.

"Sorry," interrupted Templin, "I fail to see the humor."

"Joe," said Todd, "that guy was tracking us because he was obsessed with Mallory."

"So why did you run and why did you just tell me you didn't know him?" Templin said.

"He's killed before," Mallory said. "He was a hired killer. And don't ask me how I know because I won't tell you. All I will say is that we ran because I couldn't risk the chance that he would kill Todd."

Todd smiled. "She's gotten attached to me since we were married last year. And he was a bit jealous."

Templin shook his head. "Your wife is lovely, for sure, but I don't buy the tortured lover thing." He turned to Mallory. "I know that you worked for The Bank of France during the euro printing, and that you left France soon after the heist occurred. You've changed your name, more than once, but I've done my research and I recognize your face. You were there. And Christophin was a guard at the warehouse. And then you were gone. And then Christophin went to jail, and when he was released, he headed after you. There's more to this story. Maybe I should return to France and show your photo around the warehouse and see?"

Mallory smiled through her fear. "What do you want?"

"Tired of the cat and mouse?" Templin said.

"What do you want?"

Templin nodded. "My investigation points to three culprits. Is that correct?"

"I won't tell you who else was involved."

Templin ignored her. "I have a reputation to maintain and must deliver at least some portion of the proceeds back to the Bank. But I've spent the better part of three months working on this investigation and I'm tired. I'd like to retire and I would like to do so comfortably." He smiled. "You and your husband seem to have a nice life here, you seem like a nice young couple, and the one true bad guy is dead, thanks to the two of you ..."

Mallory frowned. "Is this line of thought going somewhere? If so, out with it."

Templin nodded. "I'm offering you a deal. I'm thinking that you were the brains behind this operation—now that I've seen you in action—and that Christophin and your unnamed third partner were the muscle, and I'm thinking it would be a shame to waste all that brainpower of yours. I've always fancied myself good at delegating, so I'm going to let you do the rest of my work for me."

"I'm not following you," Mallory said.

Templin nodded again. "Okay, let me make it simple. I want Christophin's share of the euro heist take ... and yours. If I get the money, I'll leave you and your husband alone to live in sweet domesticity here in Roberts Creek. If not, I'll set Interpol on you."

Mallory could not have imagined this scenario, and it stunned her.

Todd started to reach for the gun, but a look from Mallory stopped him.

Templin smiled at Mallory's wise restraint. "Oh, and so you don't get any foolish ideas. In the event of my untimely demise, I've arranged that you will get your just desserts."

Mallory nodded. "You can have my share. I never wanted it, anyway. But I don't know where Christophe's money is."

Templin nodded in return. "Well, that's a bit of a problem. Because we've got no deal until I have both takes. But you're a smart girl, I'm sure you'll figure it out. You have one month to deliver."

"I can't deliver my share; it would be impossible to get it across the border. But I can tell you where it is and give you access."

Templin shook his head. "Both shares. One month." He reached into his pocket, pulled out a cell phone, and handed it to Mallory.

"While you search for Christophin's share, you will call my computer every day by ten in the evening, Roberts Creek time, and stay on the phone for five minutes. The calls will tell me where you are. If you fail to call, I will slap your hand by punishing your friends, Rusty and Clara, before I turn you in to Interpol." He smiled. "Please, call. I really abhor violence." He stood. "The clock is ticking now. Call me every day. You have one month. G'day."

— € —

"What are we going to do?" said Todd aloud, not to Mallory, but to the air.

"We find Christophe's share," Mallory said, getting up from the couch and going into the kitchen. She pulled Christophe's laptop out of the cabinet and turned it on. She had already discovered his password: Emma Scott. She searched the dead man's computer file by file. After an hour, she gave up. "There isn't anything about the money on this computer," she said.

Todd sighed. "So what do we do now?"

"We need to get the clothes Christophe was wearing when he died."

"Huh?" Todd said.

"What he was wearing on the train. It's a long shot, but it's the only one we have. Gustavo used to keep his most important information in the soles of his Bexleys. His boots. Christophe idolized the guy. That's why he started wearing Bexleys. I think the information we need might be there."

"How the hell do we get to his clothes?" Todd asked. "The man is dead ... and buried by now."

"I will prepare some identification that says you are Matthew Christophe, and you will go to Calgary as Christophe's brother. If no family member came to claim him, they would have kept his belongings, just in case."

Todd sighed. "Mal, the odds are a million to one that Christophe kept the location of his take in his boots."

Mallory looked up at her husband. “The odds are four million to one against us if we don’t find out.”

— € —

When Todd woke at eight the next morning, Mallory was already on the phone.

“Thanks, we’ll be there in a few hours,” she said, and hung up. “I’ve got your ID set up. We need to go to Vancouver this morning.”

“Just let me call Rusty and ask him to fill in,” Todd said sleepily. “Aren’t you tired?”

Mallory shook her head. “No time.”

— € —

The trip to Vancouver went smoothly. Mallory created and secured a fake French Passport for Todd with his photo and signature under the name Matthew Christophe, birthplace: Meribel, France. They checked into a hotel and called in to Templin’s phone at 8 p.m.

The next morning, Todd left on the early West Jet flight for Calgary, and Mallory returned to Roberts Creek.

CHAPTER 35
AUGUST 2002

Mallory knocked on Templin's door.

"Mallory." He smiled. "Come in. Please, have a seat."

Mallory evaluated the enemy for a moment and stepped inside. She was taken aback by his warm smile. She didn't feel like smiling at him. Templin was blackmailing her. "I won't be staying. I just wanted to tell you that Todd is in Calgary today and I'm here, so a phone call won't help you keep track of us. This is my 'phone call.' A personal appearance."

Templin nodded. "Well played. And I appreciate the personal effort."

Mallory shrugged. "My hands are effectively tied."

Templin nodded again. "So they are. Tell me, Mallory, however did you get mixed up in a bank robbery at your young age?"

"It wasn't a bank robbery. That sounds cheap."

Templin laughed out loud at her audacity. "Oh, excuse me. I apologize if I've offended your delicate sensibilities, but it was, at core, a bank job. You and your cohorts robbed The Bank of France—even if the euros had not yet been officially issued—of millions. The money, though hidden for two years, is still viable currency. Like a female Jesse James, no?"

Mallory gave Templin a contemptuous glare. "Look, I may have to submit to your blackmail, but don't try to analyze me. You're no good at it." She stood. "This is my daily check in, and that's all it is. You will hear from us tomorrow."

— C —

Todd entered the morgue in Calgary with a knot in the pit of his stomach. He wasn't very good at lying, and his French had fallen off a bit during his time out west. He was pretty sure he wouldn't find anyone fluent in French in Calgary, so he would have to put on bad English.

"Bonjour," Todd said to the morgue desk clerk.

"Hi," the clerk responded. "Don't speak French."

"Oh, sorry. My English is not the so good. My brother, he is the here."

The clerk nodded. "Name."

"Olivier Christophe. He was brought to you the week ago."

The clerk checked his computer files. "Yeah, here it is. Sorry, he's been buried. You shoulda called."

"I did not the know until yesterday. How can we be certain it is mon frere? My brother."

"We have his clothes and his passport."

"May I see them?"

"I need some ID."

Todd nodded. "But of course." He pulled out his fake passport.

The clerk half-heartedly inspected the passport and nodded. "Ok, follow me." He led Todd down a hallway and into a room that smelled vaguely of formaldehyde. The gray walls and gray metal furniture blended together. "Wait here," the clerk said.

Todd did as he was told, but it wasn't long before the smell of death started to gnaw at the knot in his stomach. He was relieved when the clerk returned with a sealed plastic bag.

"Take your time," said the clerk, handing the bag to Todd. "I'll be at the desk when you're done."

Todd nodded and waited for the clerk to leave the room. He stared at the bag in his hands, not excited about opening it, but hoping it contained what he and Mallory needed. He took a deep breath, unzipped the bag, and pulled out the clothing and Bexley boots Christophe had been wearing when he'd tried to kill Todd and Mallory on the freight train. He set the clothes and the left

Bexley down on the gray couch, and, as instructed by Mallory, wedged a finger under the insole of the right boot. The sole was tight and impossible to pull loose. Todd felt inside the boot: nothing. He removed a small flashlight from his back pack and peered into every corner of the boot: no writing, no paper, nothing was there. He set down the right Bexley, picked up the left, and started the process all over again. The left boot was even more difficult to access than the right had been, and when he finally managed, the result was the same: no paper and no writing. Todd sighed. This had been a waste of time. His heart sank. Mallory had been wrong. What were they going to do now?

Todd stuffed the clothing and boots back into the plastic bag, thanked the clerk, and returned to his hotel room. He thought about calling Mallory, but decided against it. He'd give her one more night of restful sleep.

The next morning, Todd boarded a plane back to Vancouver.

Mallory was waiting at the airport.

She ran into his arms.

"I've missed you," she said.

"Me too," he said. "Mallory, um."

"It wasn't there."

He shook his head.

Todd kissed her forehead as she buried herself in his chest.

"Come on." He pulled her hand. "I'll drive."

They were very quiet on the way to the ferry.

Once underway, they went up to the top deck.

"I was thinking this morning," Mallory said. "Why would a private investigator be looking for the missing euros when Interpol could—and should—be involved?"

Todd nodded. "Good question."

"Because Roger Coltman didn't want Interpol involved."

"Coltman's the warehouse guy?"

Mallory nodded. "There's been no news coverage of the heist. I think that's odd since it seems, according to Templin, that the robbery has been discovered."

Todd nodded. "Go on."

"Interpol typically uses the news media to help in international cases because there is so much ground to cover," Mallory said.

"Don't want to know why you know that," Todd said.

Mallory smiled. "From the emails I tapped into between Templin and Coltman. It looks to me like Roger didn't tell his superiors about his discovery of the missing euros, which makes sense; he would want to cover the whole thing up. It happened on his watch, which would bring him disgrace and possible firing, so he hires Templin to get the money back, promising him a percentage. After all, no one but Coltman knows any euros are missing. He just wants the bulk of the money back, so the heist will never be discovered. The other warehouses probably haven't discovered that any euros are missing. Coltman knows only about HIS warehouse, and he wants it kept quiet to save face."

A light went on in Todd's eyes. "Ah. Templin is only looking for the ten million that you took from Coltman's warehouse. He doesn't know about the other two."

Mallory nodded. "That's what I believe, although I will have to confirm this, and I can't get the information from Templin."

"So how can we get confirmation?"

"We go to France," Mallory said.

Todd's eyes widened. "Why? That's where all the trouble is."

Mallory sighed. "Because that's where Christophe's money will be. If we don't go, Templin will be suspicious."

"When do we go?"

"Soon. But first, I've got to make some plans," Mallory said. "And get some supplies." She looked up at her husband. "I'm going to have to become Emma Scott again for a bit. That's the only way I'm going to confirm that Templin only knows about Coltman's warehouse."

Todd grinned. "And who does that make me?"

Mallory smiled. "Emma Scott's wonderful new husband."

— € —

That afternoon Todd and Mallory went supply shopping. They started at a local drug store, where they picked up more hair coloring in Emma Scott's mousy brown. At an optical store, Mallory had a pair of glasses made for her and a pair for Todd. Finally, they hit a high-end department store for several Emma Scott-esque outfits and some very un-hip, business-like clothes for Todd. At the end of the day Todd's head was spinning. He lifted the shopping bags into the air and said, "You're good at this."

Mallory shook her head. "If I were really good at this, we wouldn't be doing it now."

— € —

They slept for most of the Toronto to Paris leg of their trip, except for Mallory's brief requisite call to Templin from the plane's bathroom. They passed wearily through customs in Paris. They rented a car for the drive to Saint-Étienne, and arrived near sunset.

"There it is," Mallory said, as they neared their hotel. It was small and nestled into a hillside. The ivy that crept up and around the small inn almost engulfed it, but a window peeked out from behind the vivid green.

"It's beautiful," Todd said, as he pulled in front of the hotel. He marveled at his wife's new look as he unloaded the suitcases from the trunk. "You look great, Mal."

Mallory, who had started into the hotel, turned suddenly. "You can't call me Mal anymore. Or Mallory. It's Emma or honey from now on."

Todd nodded and thought, if there wasn't so much at stake, he might actually grow to like this role-playing stuff. The bellman relieved Todd of their bags and Todd walked up behind his wife and wrapped his arms around her, playing the role of a newly married American. "Got the room yet, Em? I can't wait to get you upstairs, Mrs. Scott."

His wife smiled. "Just about."

The woman at the desk gave Todd an appreciative look and handed Mallory two keys. "Have a delightful stay."

"Merci," said Mallory. She headed to the elevator, pulling Todd along. When the elevator doors closed, Mallory turned to Todd and kissed him. "I'd forgotten the effect you have on women. I probably should have thought of a way to disguise that, but I don't think there is one."

Todd grinned. "If you're trying to ply me with flattery, Mrs. Scott, it's working."

Mallory turned the key in the lock, walked into their room and pulled off her dress.

Todd tackled his wife on the bed.

"Wait!" Mallory yelped. "We have to call Templin." She jumped up and dialed the cellular phone. Todd slumped on the bed. Mallory connected with the computer and completed their nightly check-in. Once the message had been sent, she turned back to her husband and straddled him. "Where were we?"

Todd sighed. "Maybe we should be ..."

"Doing this," Mallory whispered. "We're newlyweds, after all."

Todd smiled. "That we are."

The next morning Todd woke to the sound of his wife singing in the shower.

"Hey," he shouted, smiling. "What are you so happy about?"

"I love France and I LOVE YOU!" Mallory said as she exited the shower. She wrapped herself in a towel, skipped over to their bed, and kissed her husband on the nose.

Todd pulled at the towel. "So, what's on the agenda today?"

Mallory stepped back, wrapped herself in more tightly, and headed back to the bathroom to get ready for her morning meeting. "I'm going to Le Clapier, Coltman's warehouse. I'm going to drop in on him. But I have to go alone. He would never tell me anything with you there."

Todd nodded, but was disappointed.

"I thought I'd ask Roger and his wife to join us for dinner," Mallory continued. "I definitely need you to meet him. I want your take on the kind of person he is. Whether or not you think he would keep something like the robbery of his warehouse quiet."

Todd nodded again. "That's a good idea. We can do some male bonding over dinner. Just make sure we go to a place with man food."

Mallory smiled. "Like steak and potatoes or … barbecue? For heaven's sake, Todd, we're in France. We have to eat French food."

"Says who?" Todd yelled.

Mallory was trying to get her short hair to behave. "Says me!" She yelled back.

A few minutes later, Mallory exited the bathroom. "So how do I look?"

Todd propped himself on one elbow. "Like a completely different person and that's really turning me on." He tossed off the covers and started to climb out of bed, but Mallory grinned and held up one hand. "Relax, lady killer. I'll be back before you know it."

CHAPTER 36

AUGUST 2002

Mallory, now Emma once again, arrived at Le Clapier and was greeted by a security guard. "Hello, Mademoiselle Scott. It's nice to see you again."

Mallory smiled. "Jacques! How is your wife?"

"She's fine, pregnant again."

"Congratulations!"

The security guard blushed. "Thank you. You are looking very well."

Mallory smiled again and held up her left hand. "I'm married. And very happy."

The security guard beamed. "He is a lucky man."

Mallory beamed right back. "I'm the lucky one."

Jacques nodded. "What is your business here today?"

"I'm back with my husband on a belated honeymoon, and I thought I would pop in for a visit with Mr. Coltman. I don't have an appointment."

"Let me call up and make sure he is here. Don't want to make you go through the search process for nothing."

Mallory nodded and waited patiently while Jacques called up for authorization.

"No problem, Mademoiselle Scott. Sorry, MADAME now. Like Americans, you have kept your maiden name, I see."

Mallory nodded.

"You can see him in ten minutes, but I'm sorry I have to do the search and pat down. The security has gotten even more strict, if that is possible, since you left."

"Why?" Mallory asked. "The euros are out now."

Jacques shrugged. "No one knows. We think it might have to do with the death of Giles."

Mallory squelched a wince, turned her back to Jacques, and spread her arms and legs.

Jacques ran the metal detector up and down Mallory's body. He started to touch her, but stopped. "That's good enough."

Mallory turned. "Thank you."

The guard nodded. "Congratulations on your marriage, Madame. Enjoy your belated honeymoon. No better place for lovers than France." And with that he buzzed her through the security door.

As she headed for Coltman's office, the wince Mallory had squelched in front of the security guard came back full force. She was sad that Giles was not there, not only because she'd played a part, no matter how removed or innocent, in his death, but also because she knew that Giles would have told her about the beefed-up security measures at the warehouse over a cup of coffee. She knew Coltman would have confided in Giles, and Giles would have confided in her. She felt a large pang of guilt at the demise of her friend, but pushed the thoughts away as she knocked on Coltman's office door. He rose, smiling as she entered. "Emma, so lovely to see you. You look brilliant."

"Thanks Roger, I feel pretty good." Mallory said.

"Obviously haven't missed us a bit."

Mallory shook her head. "That's not true. I was just thinking about Giles on the way to your office," she said honestly.

"Yes, he was a good man. I do miss him. Don't know who to trust anymore."

Mallory nodded. "Jacques told me about the increased security. Problems?"

Coltman shrugged. "Nothing unmanageable."

Mallory nodded again. "Still, you look a little stressed. Is everything all right at home? How's Julia?"

Coltman smiled. "She's well. Love to see you, I imagine."

Mallory smiled, too. "I was hoping we might have dinner tonight. My husband is here with me ..."

Coltman glanced down at her left hand. "Husband? When did that happen? Nice ring."

"About a year ago. And thanks. But *he's* the real gem."

Coltman laughed. "Well, we must celebrate. Where are you staying?"

"Le Petit Hotel. Under Emma Scott. Kept my maiden name."

Coltman laughed again. "Ever the independent American girl, eh? Brilliant. This is the best news I've had in months."

Mallory frowned. "Months? That doesn't sound good. So what's the bad news?"

Coltman sat down in his desk chair and indicated to the one across from him. "We've had some problems. Giles's death was just the beginning. I have been struggling with a few things this past year, but I'm confident they are about to be resolved." He smiled. "Can't share with you now that you're no longer with us, confidential you know."

"Of course. But you DO look stressed. You need to take care of yourself."

"You sound like my wife."

"Maybe you should listen to her."

Coltman smiled. "Point taken. Now tell me about this gem of a husband of yours."

Mallory launched into an animated retelling of Todd literally knocking her off her feet.

"Great story."

She grinned. "Isn't it? Who knew? We're very happy." She stood. "I should let you get back to work. Let me know about dinner. I'd love for you to meet my husband and I'd love to see Julia again. Mind if I say hello to a few more people on my way out?"

"I'm sure they'd love it. I'll call about dinner, but plan on tonight."

"I look forward to it."

— € —

Coltman's personal assistant worked in a small office next to her boss. It was Mallory's next stop.

"Veronique!"

"Emma! C'est fantastique!"

"English please, my French is so rusty," Mallory said.

"You sound like Roger. How are you?"

"Great, thanks. I got married."

"No! When?" Veronique asked.

"A year ago."

"Where is he?"

"He's at our hotel at the moment, but I have a picture." Mallory showed Veronique the picture of Todd holding the wheel on *The Barbecue.* His eyes were twinkling and his hair was blown by the wind. He was flashing the special smile he saved just for Mallory.

"Wow, he's TRES gorgeous. You are lucky, mon amie."

Mallory smiled. "He's a great guy. And you're right. So what's new here? Jacques told me about the heightened security measures. Is something up, or has Roger finally gone over the edge?"

"He has his reasons, trust me." Veronique said.

"I'm sorry to hear that. I was hoping he was just being overly careful as usual."

"Well, that too. I'm afraid that is all I can say to you now."

Mallory nodded. "I understand. I should run. So nice to see you, Veronique." She hugged the French assistant, and waved good-bye. She said hello to a few other employees, then left Le Clapier with a farewell and best wishes to Jacques.

She drove back to the hotel quickly and burst into their room. "Todd?" There was no answer and no note. Mallory called the front desk and asked about her husband. After she gave a brief description of Todd, the girl giggled and said, "Oh yes, Monsieur went for a run not long ago and said he would be back within the hour." Mallory smiled as she hung up the phone. They had to get out of Roberts Creek more often. She loved being reminded how gorgeous her husband was. She was, indeed, a lucky girl.

— € —

The door slamming shut woke Mallory with a start.

"Sorry, honey," Todd said. "I didn't know you were back. How did it go?"

Mallory yawned widely. "That's okay. It was okay. How was your run?"

"Great. You're right. There is something in the air here."

Mallory grinned. "Do you think we can bottle it?"

"I wish. Now, tell me, really. How was your morning?"

Mallory sighed. "I don't have direct confirmation yet, but signs point to YES."

"You sound like a magic eight ball. What does that mean?"

"Security is on high alert and Coltman made reference to some concerns, but wasn't specific, as did the security guard and Coltman's assistant. Something is going on."

"Are we having dinner with the Coltmans?" Todd asked.

"That's the plan, but he is going to call to confirm."

"Good, we've got some time. Let's go for a drive. I want to see all the places you've told me about."

— € —

They returned from their drive to find a message from Coltman waiting for them at the front desk. They were to meet at the Bistro Noir, a few blocks from the hotel, at eight. Mallory glanced at her watch. It was six. "Good. I'll have time to look fantastic."

"You already look fantastic."

Mallory pushed him away.

"That's because you think I'm someone else. You're cheating on me!"

"Never," Todd said.

— € —

The dimly lit bistro was less formal than Mallory had expected. She had always taken Roger Coltman for a man to whom appearance was everything, but this place was quiet and casually charming. There were tattered red-and-white checked cloths on the tables, and old wine bottles with candles burning in them served as the lighting. Roger and Julia Coltman were already there when Mallory and Todd arrived, seated at a table in the back.

Julia's eyes brightened when she saw them approach. She jumped from her chair. "My dear, you look marvelous! Marriage obviously agrees with you." Julia hugged her tightly, and said with a wink, "And I can see why."

Mallory smiled and stepped back from the hug. "Julie, Roger, this is my husband, Todd."

"So pleased to meet you," Julia said as she extended her hand. Todd awkwardly shook the hand even though it was clear Julia had intended for him to kiss it.

"Lovely to meet you, Old Man," Coltman extended his hand and Todd shook it firmly.

"Emma's told me about all you folks. It's nice to finally meet you," Todd said.

"We took the liberty of ordering some wine," Coltman said. He poured half a glass of a hearty burgundy into three of the glasses, until he got to Todd, who put his hand over the wine glass.

"I'll stick with sparking water, thanks."

The waiter was there almost before he finished his sentence with a bottle of Perrier.

"To old acquaintances and new ones." Roger raised his glass. There were clinks all around.

"So, Todd, where are you from?" Julia asked.

"Canada, originally Quebec," Todd said automatically. Mallory lightly grabbed his leg under the table. He flinched and clammed up.

"Where are you two living now?" Coltman asked.

"We're in the west. Very rustic," Mallory said quickly.

Coltman's eyebrows raised. "Emma, I thought you were from the States."

"We met while I was sightseeing in Canada—I took some time off after I left France to do some traveling—and well, once I caught sight of Todd," Mallory said, looking at her husband, "I decided to stay."

The Coltmans laughed appreciatively.

Julia smiled. "How could you not?"

The moment had passed.

"Any children on the horizon?" Julia asked.

"If I have any say there will be soon," Todd replied.

Mallory gave him a "well played" smile, and turned to Coltman. "So what's on the horizon for you two? Are you planning to stay with The Bank of France?"

Coltman shook his head. "Retirement. Actually, my second retirement."

"I'm already retired," Julia said.

"What did you do?" Todd said.

"I was MI5; so was Roger," Julia said.

"MI5?" Mallory asked.

"I thought you knew," Coltman said.

"No idea. I thought you said you were in the British Service."

"MI5 is THE British Service," he said.

"Sounds exciting. Why did you leave?" Todd asked.

Julia answered for them: "We were getting a little long in the tooth for the physical stuff. The average MI5 agent retires at thirty-five. We were in our forties, lucky to last that long."

"You must have had fascinating lives," Mallory said.

Coltman nodded. "It was interesting, but we can't talk about any of it. MI5 makes you sign a non-disclosure agreement, and they take it seriously, vigorously ... for life."

Julia laughed. "Darling, don't be so dark. Let's order dinner. I'm famished!"

— € —

The foursome got along famously; they joked and laughed and ate and drank, and at the end of the evening, after promising they would do it again before they left for home, Todd and Mallory walked hand in hand back to the hotel. They made love, slowly and leisurely, and slept in the next morning. After an even more leisurely breakfast, Mallory took Todd to the storage facility where her euros were hidden. After checking to see that no one was around, Mallory opened the two locks and lifted the facility door. They slipped into the room and Todd closed the door behind them. She turned on a flashlight.

Todd's mouth dropped open at the sight. "Wow. This is real money. LOTS of real money."

"What did you think? I made it up?"

"It was a pretty unbelievable story."

"It looks like it's all here," Mallory said.

Todd suddenly shivered, the reality of his wife's prior life finally sinking in. "Let's go. This place gives me the creeps." He turned and raised the garage door and found himself staring into the back of a large cargo van.

It was the last thing he saw before everything went black.

"Hello Emma," greeted Roger Coltman as he held the square of chloroform to Todd's nose.

Julia Coltman stood, holding a revolver trained on Mallory's head. "Hands up, dear," she instructed, and she signaled for her husband to frisk Mallory.

Mallory slowly raised her hands in the air and squirmed with discomfort at Coltman's thorough search. He found her flashlight, but let her keep it. "You're going to need that later," he said.

"Later?" Mallory asked.

"All in good time, my dear, all in good time. Right now, you're going to help me load the van."

Coltman gently shoved Mallory toward the stacked euro palettes. They lifted the packets of money together as Julia supervised with a steady hand on the gun.

"Why did you hire Joe Templin?" Mallory asked. "Why didn't you turn me in to Interpol?"

"I couldn't leave Le Clapier, and I had no desire to turn you into Interpol, my dear. I wanted Templin to smoke you out and send you back here to me ... and to your share of the take."

"How did you know it was me?"

"I didn't, for sure, until you showed up yesterday. Returning to the scene of the crime is a little cliché, Emma Scott, or whomever you are, but clichés become clichés for a reason."

Mallory stopped working. "What about Templin?"

"I'm afraid he's your problem now."

"You're not going to call him off?"

"Why would I do that? Then he'd be after us. Templin's a former colleague; he's best quality, he's relentless, although somewhat ... how shall I say, Julia?"

"Disorganized. It's his downfall," Julia said.

"He's going to have me arrested ... or worse," Mallory said.

Coltman nodded. "Believe it or not, I regret that. But all is not totally lost yet. You're resourceful, Emma. I've seen that for myself. I'm sure you'll figure something out. Come on, let's move."

They loaded the rest of the euros into the van in silence.

When they had finished, Coltman closed the cargo van door and turned to Mallory. "You might want to sit down. It will be more comfortable when you wake up."

"How kind of you," she said.

Coltman nodded. And then he smiled. "I do have to thank you, Emma. You and your cohorts did an extraordinary job of hiding the theft. No one in the bank has any idea there is any money missing. They could use you in MI5."

"How did you find it?"

"I personally checked each currency delivery. The punctilious part of me, as you so aptly used to put it."

"So you knew right away?" Mallory said.

"Yes. I was watching the drivers. YOUR drivers, as it turns out. Ustinov left quickly and I could not locate him, so I planted the euros in Christophin's car. He was easy to keep track of in jail, and I needed some time to pass before I could implement my plan. I just had to be patient. When he was released, I hired Templin to follow him, hoping it would flush out the brains of the operation, namely you, and it did."

Mallory slowly shook her head, letting it all digest. "So I was Target One?"

Coltman nodded. "Of course, the brains would be Target One. I didn't know it was you, but I'm not surprised. You are a smart girl." He picked up the chloroform bottle and soaked a cloth in the liquid.

"Are you going to kill us?" Mallory asked.

Coltman shook his head. "No, my dear, I am no killer, unlike you and Christophin. He killed Giles; I know you did not. And you killed him. It was his just desserts. No, I am not going to kill you or your handsome young husband. This is just chloroform. It will knock you out for a while. No need to dirty my hands. You have enough on your hands with my former colleague. Unlike me, he has no qualms about killing to get what he wants. Like Julia said, Templin's ... disorganized. It gets him in trouble. Now, close your eyes and we'll get this over with." He placed the cloth over Mallory's mouth and nose. She tried to take shallow breaths, but eventually lost consciousness.

Her next memory was Todd shaking her awake.

At least she thought it was Todd.

It was dark, and Mallory couldn't see.

"Mallory, are you ok?"

"Yeah, stop shaking me. Oh, my head."

"Mine too. What was that?" Todd said.

"Chloroform."

"Do you have your flashlight?"

Mallory felt in her pocket, took it out and turned it on.

The storage facility was empty.

"The money?" Todd asked.

Mallory shook her head. "They took it. All of it."

"Christ! Coltman?"

"Yeah, who knew? I don't care. It's over. Let's just get out of here."

Todd tried the door. "I can't lift it."

"What time is it?"

Todd checked his watch. "Nine."

"Do you have Templin's check-in cell phone?"

"Right here." He opened it, but there was no signal.

Mallory had taped the peephole of her storage facility so no one would be able to see the euros stashed inside. She stood up, removed the tape, and peered out into the darkness. "Help, Help!" she screamed, pounding on the door. Todd joined her and they yelled and pounded in tandem until it became clear to them both that the storage facility was deserted, shut down tight for the night.

Mallory held the cell phone up to the peephole to see if she could get a signal, without luck. She shook her head in resignation. "I guess we're here for the night."

Todd shook his head. "What are we going to do?"

"Sleep if you can. I'll probably just pace," Mallory said.

"I mean once we get out."

"We could try to find the Coltmans, but even if we did, what would we say? Give me back my stolen money? He'd have Interpol on our asses in a heartbeat. He may already."

"And Templin?" Todd asked. "Now that there's no money, is he still a problem?"

Mallory nodded. "Yes, he's still our problem. Coltman told me that before he knocked me out. But I'd rather not think about Templin right now, my head already hurts."

Todd opened his arms. "Come here, baby."

Mallory went to him. "I'm sorry," she said. "For everything."

Todd wrapped his arms around her. "We'll work it out. You and me."

CHAPTER 37

AUGUST 2002

Mallory woke at six the next morning, still feeling a little foggy from the chloroform. Todd was starting to stir.

"Awake?" she said.

"Almost."

"We've got about an hour before the place opens," Mallory said.

Todd sat up and shook his head to clear it. "You know, France is losing some of its luster."

Mallory stood and looked out the storage door peephole. "Oh, I see someone. Come on, get up, we need to make some noise."

After a few minutes of kicking and door pounding, the man Mallory had seen through the peephole heard the ruckus and came to the door. He peered through the peephole and jumped back when Mallory peeped back at him. "*Mon Dieu!* What are you doing in there?"

"We're locked in," Mallory said in English.

The man slid the latch back and opened the door.

"*Merci.*" Mallory flashed him a big smile.

"*De rien.* Not allowed to sleep here, you know," the man said.

"Sorry, it was an accident," Mallory said.

"Don't let it happen again," the man said.

"No Sir," she said.

They walked quickly to their car, which was parked by the office. As Mallory drove, Todd dialed Templin's check-in cell phone. The computer did not answer the call. This was not a good sign. They were eight hours late checking in. He tried twice more with the same result.

When they returned to their hotel, Mallory called Rusty in Canada while Todd tried Templin's phone again. There was no answer at either end. "I don't like this," Mallory said.

"You don't think—" Todd said.

"That was his threat," Mallory said, as she dialed Clara's home phone. "He said he'd go after Rusty and Clara if we missed a call."

After the third ring the line connected. "Hello?" said a timid female voice.

"Clara?"

"Mallory?"

"Yes. Hi. How are you? I'm trying to reach Rusty, but he's not answering the phone. Do you know where he is?"

"He's at the clinic. I'm on my way there now. The police called me."

"The police? Is he okay? What happened?"

Todd gave Mallory a questioning look. She waved him off.

"I don't know," Clara said. "He called the police and they found him unconscious. They did CPR and took him to the clinic. I'll know more when I see him. I'm so glad you called! I knew you would want to know, and I had no idea how to reach you."

"What were his symptoms?"

"They only gave me brief details. He told them he'd had a sudden blinding headache, couldn't breathe, and was very confused. I need to go. I need to stop by his house and get some things for him, and then get to the clinic. Give me your number and I'll call you after I've talked to the doctor. They say he's okay, but they're going to keep him overnight."

Mallory's eyes widened. "DON'T GO TO THE HOUSE, CLARA."

"Why not? What's wrong, Mallory?"

"I don't know if anything's wrong, but just to be safe, don't go to the house. Trust me on this. And don't let Rusty go back there, either. If they release him from the clinic before we get back, take him to your place, or to ours. You know where the extra key is. Todd and I will be back tomorrow and we'll check on the house when we get there."

"Mallory?"

"I've got to go, Clara. Just, please, trust me. And give Rusty a hug for me. We'll see you soon."

"What happened?" said Todd.

"Rusty's at the clinic. He called the police in distress and they found him unconscious, but they revived him, thank God."

Todd frowned. "It sounds like carbon monoxide poisoning. Might be Templin sending us a message."

"How do you know that?"

"Happened to my uncle. The exhaust hose to his furnace came loose. Those old cottage furnaces."

"What should we do?"

"We could run."

"I don't want to run. Then he might hurt someone else, like Clara, or your parents, or kill Rusty next time. We can't risk that," Mallory said. "I won't be responsible for that."

"Should we try to find Coltman?" Todd asked.

"A waste of time."

"How much time do we have left to get the money to Templin?"

"Two weeks."

"What do you want to do?"

"Go home, take care of Rusty, and come up with a new plan. If we're not too late. Try Templin's cell again."

Todd and Mallory caught the next flight home, dropped their bags at their house, and went directly to Rusty's cottage. Mallory carried the carbon monoxide detector from their cottage. It started beeping before they went in the door. "Leave the door open," Todd ordered, "and cover your mouth and nose. I'll check the furnace, you check the kitchen vents, and make it quick."

Covering their mouths and noses, they entered the house. Todd headed for the basement to check the furnace. Mallory went to the kitchen to check the vents. She opened the kitchen doors and windows and called down to Todd in the basement, "Everything is all right up here, you OK?"

"I'm coming up. Go outside. NOW!"

Mallory heard the urgency in his voice and ran out the kitchen door. Todd appeared a minute later. They went back to their cottage, where Todd called a repairman to fix the broken furnace. "I turned it off, but you'll probably need a few hours to let it clear." He hung up the phone. "I know what we're getting Rusty for his birthday this year," Todd said.

"Share."

"A carbon monoxide detector."

"Todd, seriously, tell me," Mallory said.

"The exhaust pipe was disconnected."

"Intentional?"

"Looks that way. From what I could see that furnace hasn't been worked on in years. The pipe was unscrewed. The screws were missing, not on the floor anywhere."

"Templin?" Mallory said.

"That'd be my guess," Todd said.

Mallory's eyes filled with tears. "I need to see Rusty."

— € —

It was disturbing, but not surprising, to see Templin standing with Clara at Rusty's bedside when they arrived at the clinic. Mallory glared at Templin as she hugged Rusty. She could feel his weakness, and he was still on oxygen.

"You okay?" Mallory asked.

"Well, I've been better. Still have a bit of a headache. Can't wait to go home," Rusty said.

"It will be a few days before you can do that. We just checked and the house is full of carbon monoxide. The furnace malfunctioned," Todd said.

"Don't use the furnace in the summer," Rusty said.

"It was on, so we turned it off, opened all the windows and called the plumber. Should be okay in a day or two," Todd said.

"You can stay with us," Mallory said.

Rusty nodded. Mallory could see he was feeling worse than he let on. "We're going to go now. I don't want to tire you out. We'll be back tomorrow."

"I'll stay with him tonight," Clara said. "I want to."

"Sorry your trip had to be cut short," Templin said with mock sincerity.

"I'll bet," Todd said tightly and Mallory saw his fists clench at his sides.

She took him by the arm. "Let's go. Rusty needs his rest."

"Thanks for coming, honey," Rusty croaked as he closed his eyes.

Mallory stroked his hand for a moment before she turned to leave.

– € –

Two days later, Mallory arrived at the clinic to bring Rusty home.

He was waiting for her, dressed and looking like himself again, and Mallory embraced him for a long time.

"Hey, now. What's wrong?" Rusty said.

"I thought I was going to lose you, too."

Her grandfather chuckled. "Not me, honey. I'm tough."

He was forced to take a wheelchair ride out of the hospital, but he waved Mallory off when she tried to help him into her car. As Mallory pulled out of the clinic parking lot, Rusty turned to her. "Spill it."

Mallory shook her head. "When we get home and get you settled in."

They rode home in silence, not the comfortable one they usually shared, but an uncomfortable one that neither of them wanted to break.

Todd was waiting for them at Rusty's cottage. "The house has been given the all clear, and a new furnace is being installed this weekend."

Rusty turned to Mallory. "NOW SPILL IT."

"I've made coffee," said Todd.

They sat at the kitchen table.

"You look better. Less red," Mallory said.

Rusty chuckled. "I hope not a lot less, I want to keep my nickname. Now quit stalling."

"Joe Templin did it. The furnace. He disconnected the exhaust, turned it on, and left you to die," Mallory said.

Rusty's eyebrows raised. "Why would he do that? He's in love with Clara."

Mallory shook her head.

Rusty sighed. "So much for my hopes for her."

"He's after me," Mallory said. "Well, not me. He's after my ten million euro."

Rusty smiled. "Ah yes ... my little chip off the old block. I had almost forgotten."

Mallory sighed. "I wish I were a chip off the old block. First time out, I got caught red-handed. You and Dad never did. And now I've almost gotten you killed and put all of us in danger."

"It's harder nowadays. So much sophisticated stuff. I'm old school, couldn't do it now," Rusty said. "What do you mean, danger? What kind of danger? Is Clara in danger?"

Mallory nodded. "I'm afraid so. We're all in danger unless I get him the money. The problem is that I don't have it anymore. It was stolen. Happened while Todd and I were in France. We went there to get the money for him and someone beat us to it. So now we have two choices: Disappear or kill Templin," Mallory said.

Rusty nodded. "Which way are you leaning?"

"I don't want to disappear. I love it here. I love my life here. And I really don't want to make you and Clara leave, either. But as long as he knows where we are, we aren't safe."

"So? We must do what we must do, I'm thinking."

"The thing is," said Todd, "Templin warned us that if something happens to him, the authorities will be notified and we'll be arrested. He was MI5. He's retired, but he has connections with Interpol."

Rusty smiled. "Well, he's a crook now, no matter who he once worked for, and he's not telling anyone anything that might attract attention to him, trust me. He's flying under the radar. And solo. Let me do it."

Mallory set down her coffee. "What?"

"The son of a bitch tried to kill me."

"Rusty, I know, but ..."

"Honey, I can handle this."

"With my help," Todd said.

Rusty nodded.

"And mine," said Mallory.

Rusty shook his head. "I think Todd would like a chance to take care of you for a change, as would I. You've been the lead operative for quite a while now. You've earned a rest. You're going to have to sit this one out, my dear, okay?"

Mallory smiled at him and nodded.

— € —

Two days later, Templin picked up his hotel room phone on the second ring.

"Joe, it's Rusty. It's a beautiful summer day, rare in this part of the world, and I'm feeling a bit itchy after my clinic stay. Care to take a boat ride with an old man? Maybe do some deep-sea fishing? Mallory and Todd are off on another adventure, and Clara's at work. Always nice to have company on the boat, and I thought of you. I'd like to thank you personally for all you did for me and Clara when I was laid up."

Templin smiled at the thought of Mallory and Todd out hunting up his money. Their daily check-in call had come in two hours ago and he had nothing to do for the next 24 hours but wait for the next. Templin wasn't all that good at waiting. Never had been. Patience wasn't one of his virtues. Come to think of it, he really didn't have any virtues, and it WAS a beautiful day. Might as well get out and enjoy it. "Sure, why not?" He said. "Can I bring anything?"

"How about a six pack of beer and some ice?" Rusty said.

— € —

When Templin arrived at Rusty's cottage, the old man was already aboard the boat.

"Come on out," Rusty shouted.

Templin waved and carried the ice and beer down to the dock. "Permission to come aboard, Sir," he said, setting the ice down and giving Rusty a salute.

"That kind of formality is a bit out of place here in the Great White North." Rusty extended his hand and helped his would-be assassin aboard. He started the engine and cast off the dock. "You fish?"

"Never much had the stomach for it," Templin said.

"Okay. We'll go sightseeing instead. Maybe see some whales."

He headed the boat away from the shore and turned north.

"Whales?"

"Yeah, killer whales. Orca. They run in the straights this time of year. How long have you been here again?" Rusty asked.

"A month or so."

"Must've had your head in the sand not to have heard about the whales."

"Guess so," Templin said.

Rusty pointed out the sights until land eventually faded from view and they were surrounded by open water. He reached for a beer, tossed it to Templin, and then cracked one open for himself. He took a long swig, and wiped his chin with the back of his hand. "So, what are your intentions with my Clara?"

"Intentions?" Templin asked, as he opened his beer.

"You've been seeing a lot of each other. She seems kind of attached," Rusty said.

Templin sipped his beer. "I'm temporary here," he said. He took a long swallow and lowered the can. "She knows that."

"Does she?"

"I'll make it clear," Templin said.

"I'd appreciate that."

They rode in silence until they were in deep water with no other boats in sight. Rusty threw the engine into idle, pulled out a pair of binoculars and handed them to Templin.

"Scan the surface for a fin or a puff of smoke," Rusty said.

"A puff of smoke?" Templin asked, raising the binoculars.

"How they breathe," Rusty said. "Gotta come up for air."

"Ah, right." Templin said, scanning the water. "Hey, I think I see something ..."

Rusty took him down fast.

Templin's head landed hard on the deck of the boat. He was woozy but not unconscious. *The old man is quick,* he thought. Templin lost consciousness shortly after his nose and mouth were covered with a cloth. His last thought:

Chloroform.

— € —

Mallory and Todd watched Templin board Rusty's boat through their kitchen window.

"Here we go," said Todd.

Mallory walked her husband out to the deck.

Todd focused his binoculars on the boat until it was out of sight. "That's my cue."

Mallory kissed him. "I want to go with you."

"Nope, sorry. I'm taking care of you this time, remember?"

"First Rusty, now you. I'm beginning to feel like a helpless female."

"Mallory, you are the least helpless female I know. I'll be back in a few hours."

"Good luck."

"Hopefully I won't need it."

— € —

Todd hoped Templin had made the first part of his job easy and had adopted the Roberts Creek tradition of leaving his car keys in the ignition. Nobody stole cars here, so why bother removing the keys? "Bingo," he whispered as he peered through the car window. He put on latex gloves, got into the car, and drove off, headed for Templin's hotel. He parked close to the entrance, and put on a fedora—Templin's signature topper—before he left the car. He stooped a bit as he walked, just in case anyone was watching; tall as he was, he was easily recognizable, but again, luck was on his side. The town was deserted, and the hotel front desk clerk, per usual, was across the street, lunching at the local diner.

He had an hour.

Once inside Templin's room, which was locked, but an easy old lock to jimmy, Todd worked efficiently. Locating a suitcase, he filled it with the contents of the dresser drawers. He loaded Templin's toiletries and books into a plastic shopping bag, and loaded it all into the car's trunk. He went back for Templin's papers and his computer, straightened up a bit, turned off the lights and left the door slightly ajar.

Mallory was waiting outside when Todd pulled up in Templin's car. She took Templin's computer and papers into the kitchen, which was beginning to look more like an office than a kitchen, and sat down at the table, hoping this would all be over soon. She scanned the loose papers, found nothing of interest, and turned her attention to Templin's laptop. It was not password protected, but Mallory's first attempts at hacking into his email were unsuccessful. Mallory didn't know Templin well enough to try to guess his password. "Clara" didn't work, "Coltman" didn't work, and "Aussie" didn't work. She even tried MI5, and it did not work. Mallory suddenly remembered another MI5 email account. The one she had found in France: JCMI5. She took a deep breath. In retrospect, she was sure JC had been Julia Coltman. She crossed her fingers, and logged into JCMI5's email account. She canned the "sent" and "saved" emails to be sure the incriminating stuff was still there. It was. Mallory smiled. And began to type.

TO: Roger Coltman
FROM: JCMI5@hotmail.com
Date: August 7, 2002
Subject: Your Wife

Dear Roger,

Just wanted to send you a little something to thank you for cleaning out my storage cube. This email account belongs to your wife—I thought you might be particularly interested in the sent and saved emails. Ironically her password is "Roger."

Enjoy.

Emma.

Mallory hit send and sat back and nodded. She might not have her money, but now, even with her ten million euros, Coltman would never have another day of peace. That made her feel better.

– € –

While Mallory took her small bit of revenge on the Coltmans, Todd drove Templin's rental car to the ferry terminal. He boarded the ferry and stayed in the car for the entire trip. After disembarking in Horseshoe Bay, he drove to the north side of Vancouver and found a drugstore with a large dumpster located in back. He tossed the plastic bag with Templin's books and toiletries into the dumpster, then moved down the block to a Goodwill depository where he dumped the clothing from Templin's suitcase. The suitcase itself was a more difficult matter. It was soft-sided, so Todd started tearing it with a fishing knife. It didn't need to be completely ruined, just in bad enough shape that no one would rescue it from the trash. When it was sufficiently tattered, Todd found a tumbledown apartment building and deposited the bag in an empty dumpster. He drove to a gas station in Vancouver proper, filled the tank, drove to the airport, left the car at the rental agency's quick drop, and grabbed a cab to the Pacific Palisades Hotel. He walked across the street to the Cactus Café, had a sandwich, and then he grabbed another cab to the Horseshoe Bay Ferry.

– € –

Rusty maneuvered the boat closer to the shore. Orcas tended to favor mammals as food, and they had better luck near the coastline. He was trying to find a pod, so the body would be completely destroyed. No evidence. No doubt. He spotted his prey, turned the wheel, and guided the boat toward the fins that were knifing through the water. He stopped in the midst of the pod and dragged the limp body to the prow of the boat. Smelling the blood that oozed from Templin's head, the orca circled the boat. Rusty slipped a rope around Templin's torso and under his arms, edged the body over the side of the boat, and stepped back fast. When Templin's body hit the water, the pod instantly turned as one. Rusty pulled the rope to simulate a struggling animal, but it was hardly necessary. Within a few seconds the whales were striking. Rusty released the rope and Templin disappeared into the roiling waters, now streaked with red. Rusty watched until the cloud of blood was no longer visible, then he quickly put the boat into gear. He made several small circles around the kill spot just to be sure the blood had dissipated. He nodded. "That's the end of you then. Good riddance to bad rubbish." He turned the boat and motored at top speed back to Roberts Creek.

— ₠ —

Mallory came out to meet him.

"How'd it go?"

"Found a big pod. He's gone. Todd get off okay?"

"Yeah, the keys were in the ignition."

"Got his computer?"

"Yup, nothing. Where's Clara?"

"She's in Vancouver, as planned, probably buying a new dress for a date she will never have now." He shook his head sadly. "My sweet girl has never had good taste in men."

— ₠ —

Todd saw Clara standing on the upper deck of the ferry and waved. Clara smiled and waved back. Todd took the stairs two at a time and joined her. They stood off to port to avoid a direct hit from the horn. There was a warm breeze uncharacteristic for this time of year.

"What were you doing on this side of the bay?" Clara asked.

"Needed to go to the bank. You?"

"Needed a dress. Big date tonight. Could be a pop-the-question date! Do you need a ride home? I'll have time."

Todd shook his head. He felt sorry for Clara. "Mallory is picking me up. Thanks."

He paused. "I know you're crazy about Joe, Clara, and that you've got your hopes up, and I really hate to say this, but he just doesn't strike me as the type that would stay in Roberts Creek."

"Do I?" Clara said.

"Well, you've been here for a long time."

"Maybe too long." She shrugged. "Even if he does leave, he might take me with him."

They stood silent for a bit.

"Has he said something to you?" she said.

"Huh?"

"Like he's leaving town?" Clara said with a note of desperation in her voice.

Todd felt very uncomfortable. He knew what he was about to say would hurt Clara, but that was unavoidable. Now or later, she was going to get hurt. Todd nodded. "At the Club. He said he was heading out soon. Said he was getting itchy for some new scenery."

"When was that?" Clara asked sharply.

"Two days ago."

Todd could see tears forming in her eyes. He put his arm around her. "Come on, now. I'm sure he wouldn't leave without saying good-bye." Another lie, he thought. What a tangled web.

"I think maybe he would," Clara said.

"Maybe you should ask him."

"Maybe I will," she said.

As the ferry pulled into port, Todd spotted Mallory's Range Rover idling by the foot passenger exit.

He gave Clara a hug. "Good luck tonight."

"Thanks, Todd. A girl can hope, can't she?"

— € —

Todd slid into the passenger seat and leaned over to kiss his wife.

"How did it go?" Mallory asked.

Todd sighed. "According to plan, no glitches ... until I ran into Clara on the ferry."

"Oh, no. Rusty said she'd gone to Vancouver this morning. What did you say?"

"I told her I'd heard Joe talking about leaving town the other day at the club."

"That's good," Mallory said.

"Too good. I don't want to be good at this. How about Rusty? How did the voyage go?"

"According to plan. Templin's gone."

"You okay?"

Mallory nodded. "I guess. Self-defense, right?"

Todd nodded, too. "Yep. Did you get a look at his computer yet?"

"Tried, no luck," she said.

Todd smiled. "Try, try again," he said. "You'll find it. No doubt."

— € —

Two hours later, Templin's useless computer had been set aside and Christophe's laptop was now powered up on the kitchen table. Mallory poured a cup of coffee, breathed in the aroma, sighed, and sat down at the table. She stared at the photo displayed on the screen. It was a small chalet with two people holding skis standing out front. Mallory zoomed in on the front door. There was writing above it: "Chalet Les Elfes." *House of the Short People.* Mallory zoomed in on the faces of the short people. One was definitely a young Christophe, probably around 15. The other, a petite older woman, looked like him, probably his mother. Mallory's eyes widened. She set down her coffee cup. "Oh my God, Todd," she whispered. "I can't believe I didn't see it before. That's where his money is."

"I don't get the connection."

"Christophe told me his mother's name when I first met him. He said he told me so I would trust him. I thought he was nuts, but it makes sense now. He was telling me where he was going to hide his money. I can't believe it took me this long to figure it out."

"Where's the house?" Todd asked. "And why would he tell you where he was going to hide his money?

"In the French Alps somewhere."

"Can you narrow it down more than that?"

"Maybe," Mallory said. "Can you refill my coffee?"

Todd smiled. "Sure. Glad to be of simple service for a change."

While Todd refilled her coffee and made some sandwiches for sustenance, Mallory started searching phone directories in the provinces that covered the Alps region of France. She found what she was looking for in a small town called Les Allues.

The name: Laurence Front.

The address: Chalet Les Elfes.

"That's it." She showed the screen to Todd.

He smiled. "Have you booked our tickets?"

CHAPTER 38

AUGUST 2002

Mallory and Todd, traveling as themselves for a change—at Todd's request—deplaned in Paris and took the Train à Grande Vitesse to Lyon. Mallory had learned on their first trip not to subject her lanky husband to long road journeys in tiny French rental cars, so they rented a van in Lyon, which would make the ride to the mountains more comfortable. They arrived in Méribel shortly before dark and checked into the Club Med. The town of Les Allues was just up the mountain from Méribel, so Club Med was a perfect home base, as well as a nice trip down memory lane for the newlyweds. They enjoyed a long romantic dinner and spent the night in each other's arms, recreating the day they first met.

The next morning, before sunrise, they headed up the mountain to Les Allues.

They drove through the dark, winding streets until they located the tiny Chalet Les Elfes. As the sun rose over the mountain, illuminating the chalet, Mallory gasped in delight. "Look at her gardens, Todd. Oh, they're so beautiful. That's our way in. She's got to work on them every day."

"So?" Todd asked.

"We'll go back to town, leave the car there, wait till the sun is all the way up, and then we'll hike up to the chalet and strike up a conversation with her while she's gardening. She'll ask us in for coffee."

"Just like that?"

Mallory nodded. "It's a tiny town, like Roberts Creek. People are friendly. They aren't suspicious. Trust me. We're in."

— € —

Two hours later, as predicted, Christophe's mother, the tiny Laurence Front, was on her knees in her front yard when Mallory and Todd "happened by" on their hike.

"Bonjour!" Mallory called out in perfect French. "You have such beautiful gardens. Just lovely!"

"*Merci, merci.* Would you like a tour?" Laurence waved them over.

"We would love one," Mallory replied.

"Come over, come over," Laurence beckoned.

Todd looked at Mallory and whispered, "Oh, you're good."

Mallory silenced him with a look, and took his arm. "We are so grateful to you. These gardens are so beautiful!"

Christophe's mother proudly showed the young couple around the small but lush grounds, lovingly explaining where she had gotten each cherished flower and why she had planted some together and some apart. "They are like my babies. I'm only sorry the season is so short. Please come in, I'll give you coffee," Laurence said. "And a sweet."

Mallory smiled. "That would be lovely. It was a long hike."

They headed inside and Laurence went directly into the kitchen, instructing Mallory and Todd to make themselves at home. Mallory walked over to the living room fireplace mantle and gazed at the photos there. Front and center was Christophe's laptop screen saver.

"Is this your son?" Mallory asked.

"Yes."

"He's quite handsome. Is he a good skier?"

"Excellent, it's like walking for him. He skied with the French army, a very elite group."

"You sound very proud."

"I am. I just wish I knew where he was," Laurence said.

"You don't?"

"No, his work takes him away for long periods."

"What does he do?" Mallory asked.

"I don't know ... something with security systems."

"I'm sure you have a good one here."

Laurence chuckled. "No, we don't need security systems here. It's a little mountain town. I know everyone, we don't even lock our doors."

"Wow," Mallory said, "even in Canada we lock our doors. May I use your W.C.?"

"Of course, up the stairs to the right. Canada! So that's why you speak French so fluently."

Mallory shook her head. "Only me. I studied it in college." She pointed to Todd and said in French: "He's hopeless!"

Laurence laughed and took Todd with her into the kitchen while Mallory went up the stairs to the bathroom. To the left was a small bedroom. There were trophies on the shelves and several hockey sticks in the corner. To the right there was a thick wooden door with a small, high window in the center. There was a dial next to the door indicating the temperature in Celsius. Mallory opened the sauna door and saw what she was looking for: euros.

Millions of them.

She went into the bathroom, hands shaking, and flushed the toilet and ran the sink. She calmed herself, taking deep breaths, and then she went back downstairs and back to the mantel. This time her eye was drawn to a photo of a group, including Laurence, dressed in quaint costumes. She reached for the photo and went into the kitchen.

"Is this you?"

"*Oui, oui.* That is my folk dancing group."

"Looks like fun. Is this a local festival?" Mallory asked.

"No. Just a dance meeting. We always wear the costumes. Two nights a week."

"How fun! When is your next meeting?"

"Tomorrow night at eight."

"Can people watch?" Mallory said.

"No. If you come, you must dance."

"What a shame," Mallory said. "I would love to have seen you dance."

The threesome chatted over coffee and pastry, and then Todd and Mallory thanked Laurence for the garden tour and treats and said good-bye.

"Come again soon!" Laurence called out, waving. "I love the company!"

Mallory waved back. "If we can!" she called back. And then to Todd: "I found it!"

"Where?"

"Upstairs. There's a small sauna. The euros all still in their wrappers. She obviously doesn't know the money is there. She must not use the sauna. Her age, probably. Christophe must have known that. The door handle was dusty and the door was swollen shut, hard for me to open, probably impossible for her. We can get in and out with the money tomorrow while she's dancing."

Todd shook his head. "Mallory, do you really want to do this? We killed her son."

"We did not kill her son. He was in a dangerous place."

"You don't believe that."

Mallory nodded. "I do. I have to believe it. It's the only way I can get through this. Let me be. It's done, there isn't anything we can do to undo it. The money is just sitting there. She doesn't need it. Not all of it. We do. I need it for my mother. For Rusty. For our future. It's ours for the taking. I took it once, for sport. That wasn't right. This time I'm going to take it and put it to good use. No one even knows it's missing. And now they never will."

EPILOGUE

SEPTEMBER 2002

When Todd and Mallory deplaned at Kennedy Airport, a driver from Babe's Taxi Service was waiting outside the terminal to ferry them to Fort Lee, New Jersey.

Mallory stood inside her childhood kitchen and she knew instantly that it was no longer home. Nothing and no one she cared about was here any longer. Her home now was with the lanky man from Roberts Creek who was making coffee. Mallory smiled at Todd, blew him a kiss, sat down at the kitchen table, and powered up her laptop. Within seconds she was logging in to a Swiss bank account.

"Checking already?" Todd asked, handing her a cup of steaming java.

"Surprised?"

Todd smiled and shook his head.

Mallory sipped her coffee and watched as the account opened on the screen. She smiled as she read the recent activity log. There was a deposit on August 15, 2002, for $9,816,050 U.S. dollars, followed by a $10,000 currency conversion finance charge.

Todd looked over her shoulder, saw the finance charge, and let out a long, low whistle. "Damn, keeping secrets is expensive."

Mallory nodded. "Switzerland is the only European country that would allow this kind of transaction. Without them we'd have to be living in Europe right now to cash in. Who'd have thought using cash would be such a problem? But with the new terrorism laws and such, it's not easy."

"This is a great house," Todd said, looking around. "Are you sure you want to sell it?"

Mallory smiled. "No doubt."

— € —

That afternoon, Todd went with Mallory to visit her mother.

While Mallory talked to the doctor, Todd sat in Emma's room, held his mother-in-law's motionless hand and told her how wonderful her daughter was and how much he loved her. He was hoping against hope that he would get some kind of response, a squeeze, a twitch, a smile, something to give his wife hope, but it had been almost three years since the accident, and all hope, it seemed, was gone. Emma Scott looked gaunt and lifeless, save for the slow mechanical inhale and exhale spurred by the respirator, which seemed to Todd rather violent, and no way to live.

Mallory came in and kissed her mom. "Has he been talking your ear off? Not sure you can believe anything he says." She kissed Todd. "Anything?"

Todd shook his head.

Mallory nodded and blinked back tears.

"What did the doctor say?"

"Nothing has changed, and nothing will."

— € —

Mallory and Todd spent the next two weeks clearing out the New Jersey house. They donated the bulk of the family's furniture and possessions to Goodwill and shipped the few things Mallory chose to keep, including some things she thought Rusty might like to have, to Roberts Creek. In the evenings, while Todd cooked dinner, Mallory poured through her parents' personal files. There were a lot of them, particularly in her mother's office; she'd saved every article she'd ever read on printing. Mallory kept those and kept looking, while Todd read his father-in-law's journals, learning about his wife's parents, who he would never know.

On the last night of her paper chase, Mallory came across a document in her father's office that made her heart skip a beat. "Todd!" She cried with an urgency that made him drop the journal he was reading and leap from his seat.

"What is it?"

"Look at this—am I reading it correctly?"

Todd scanned the document. It was signed and notarized. He nodded. "It's a living will, your parents both signed it."

"Why didn't their lawyer know about it?"

"Who knows, maybe they didn't do it with him. Looks like maybe it came from the Internet. You'd know better about that than me."

"My dad, on the Internet?" Mallory asked.

"He was emailing with Rusty."

Mallory nodded. "This means I can let her go. She can be with Dad." She started weeping softly.

Todd took her in his arms and stroked her hair. "I didn't know them, but I think it's where she would want to be."

— € —

The next morning, Mallory called Gus in Italy.

"Mallory."

"Hi, Gus."

"Uh oh. What's wrong."

"Christophe is gone. He's dead. I didn't do it. But I led him to it. I had to."

"He came after you after the job?"

"How did you know?"

"It was what I warned you about. My friend could be obsessive and dangerous," Gus said. "I suspect there was no choice."

"There wasn't."

"People make their own beds."

Mallory sighed. "I really didn't have the stomach for this business."

"I know, *Tesoro,* I know."

"I have another problem," Mallory said.

"Dimmi."

"Mom isn't getting better, she isn't going to get better, and last night I found a living will signed by her and dad both."

"So you know her wishes."

"Yes," Mallory said.

"And the problem is?"

"I'm not sure I can do it."

"You don't have to, you can have the doctor—"

"I know, but he won't do it if I don't tell him to. It is still me making the decision—"

"No, *Cara,* it is your mother's decision. It is what she wishes. Do not take responsibility that is not yours to take. Let her go, *Cara.* And get on with your life. YOUR life, *Cara.* Not your father's life. Not your mother's life. But one of your own making. It's time."

Mallory swiped at a tear. "Thank you, Gus."

"Take care, *Cara mia.*"

"I will Gus, you too. *Ciao.*"

Todd was waiting in the kitchen when Mallory came in for coffee. "What did he say?"

"He told me to live my own life."

"Wise man."

"Yes, he is." Mallory looked at Todd. "I just need a little more time. I'm not ready to say good-bye just yet ..."

Todd nodded. "I understand. And I have an idea."

Mallory raised an eyebrow.

"Are you up for another adventure?" Todd asked.

"What kind of adventure?"

"I've been thinking about *Le Barque,*" Todd said. "It's the only thing left in the house to dispose of. And I have a plan."

Mallory smiled. "I've created a monster. Do tell."

"I was thinking we could put it back."

Mallory's eyes widened. "PUT it back? Why not just send it back? Anonymously, of course."

"We could, but then we wouldn't have your mother's masterpiece."

"You want to steal my mother's painting?"

Todd nodded. "I do. It would be kind of like restoring the criminal balance in the universe, you know? And we'd have your mother's *Le Barque* to hang in our home in her memory."

Mallory's eyes filled with tears. She was certainly getting soft these days. "It's a fabulous idea, Honey. And I love you for it. But do you think we could pull it off? Look what happened to my one and only attempt as a professional thief. Abysmal failure. Do you have a plan?"

Todd shook his head. "No. But Andrew Scott did." He held up her father's journal. It's all here, every step. The perfect plan. He pulled it off. And so can we, with him as our guide."

"But he had Christophe," Mallory said. "And Gus. Especially Gus."

Todd nodded. "And you have me. AND Rusty." He grinned. "I think he would love it. One more time back in the saddle."

Mallory laughed.

"What do you say?"

"Let's do it," Mallory said. "IF Rusty agrees to help us."

— € —

Three days later their plan was set, Rusty was in, and Mallory went to say good-bye to her mother.

She sat with Emma for almost an hour, telling her softly about the last three years and what they were planning to do with *Le Barque*. When she was finished, Mallory knew it was time to reunite her parents, and she finally felt right about it. She kissed her mother good-bye, squeezed her hand, and then she got up and left the long-term care facility with Todd.

The doctor who had cared for her mother for the past three years would do for her what Mallory could not. Emma Richards buried next to her beloved husband. There was nothing more for Mallory to do. There was nothing more she could do. Instead, she would head to Paris with her husband and her grandfather and bring back her mother's masterpiece. The faux *Le Barque* hanging in her home in Roberts Creek would give Mallory a living, breathing testimony to her mother's artistic brilliance and her father's love of adventure forever.

— € —

Following the detailed description in Andrew's journal, Mallory and Todd hid the original *Le Barque* in a large carpet purchased new for the occasion. They packed it, and shipped it to a mail center near the small Paris flat Todd had rented close to the musée. It wasn't the same flat Mallory's parents had stayed in many years before, but it was in the same neighborhood, and Mallory loved her husband for taking such care with each detail.

Mallory and Todd flew into Charles De Gaulle Airport and took a cab to their rented flat.

As planned, Rusty arrived the following day.

Rusty and Todd spent a few weeks getting to know the museum. They watched the security guards. It appeared the schedule hadn't changed much since Andrew's job, and judging from the age of the guards, some were still the same, as well.

Like her mother before her, Mallory became a regular at the museum, sitting day after day in the basement on a bench, sketching the copy of *Le Barque*.

To Rusty's surprise, the alarm system hadn't been updated. There still were no motion detectors or sensors on the paintings. The windows and entrances were wired, in the same way Andrew had described in his journal, so a small piece of aluminum foil strategically placed would again keep the circuit in the window of the men's room complete while they entered the building. When Rusty checked, the latch on the window was still on backwards, to appear as if the latch were locked in place, when in fact it was open.

Unlike Mallory, her father had never been caught, and his handiwork was still in place, which was a boon to the new threesome.

— € —

On a beautiful warm Paris night, at the stroke of midnight, Mallory, Todd, and Rusty, dressed in black, left the small flat and made their way to the small museum. Mallory's tall, lanky husband quietly raised the window and boosted Mallory into the men's washroom, then passed the rolled and carpeted original painting to her. Rusty gave Todd a boost in through the window, and remained outside to keep watch.

Todd and Mallory, as Andrew and Emma Scott in reverse, moved to the basement staircase without a light. The small, windowless gallery made Mallory break out in a sweat, but she had gotten used to breathing her way through the panic as she had sketched.

"Okay?" whispered Todd.

Mallory nodded. She took a large sheet from her backpack, unpacked it, and laid it on the floor. She held the flashlight while Todd removed *La Barque* from the wall, laying it face down on the sheet. Todd took the flashlight and lit the way while Mallory removed the hammer from her backpack and knelt down to pull the old nails that attached Emma's canvas to the stretcher bars. She was careful to place each nail in the ramekin that had been packed for just this purpose, per Andrew's journal instructions. When all the nails were removed, Todd lifted the support and leaned it against the wall. They rolled the fake painting in the sheet and tied it tightly. Todd then unrolled the original *Le Barque* and laid it down on the floor. Mallory repeated the hammer and nail process and took the flashlight as Todd put *Le Barque* back where it belonged, after more than twenty years away. He was just finishing hanging the painting when Mallory's cell phone vibrated.

It was a text from Rusty:

GET OUT!

Mallory held the phone up for Todd to read. He nodded, and they packed up quickly and hurried upstairs. "Todd," Mallory whispered as they entered the men's room. "I forgot the hammer. It's under the bench. Damn! I've got to go back." She moved to the door just as the lights went on.

"No, you have to go now!" Todd said, reaching for her. He hoisted Mallory up and out the window, tossed the faux painting out to Rusty, and then shimmied up and out and closed the window. They hurried to a parallel alley, waiting for the sound of sirens, but none came. "It must have been a light sensor," Rusty whispered as they made their way to the flat. "Not an alarm. Sorry."

When they got back to the flat, they unrolled the Persian rug in which they had shipped the original Monet back to France, and rolled up the copy. They re-wrapped it in plastic and brown paper, and the next morning, Rusty shipped the rug to the post office in Roberts Creek.

That afternoon, they returned to the museum. Mallory found her hammer under the bench in front of *Le Barque,* and slipped it, undetected by the sleepy old security guard, into her bag.

They sat on the bench for a few minutes, looking at the original Monet.

"Balance has been restored," Todd whispered.

Rusty nodded. "The family has come full circle."

Mallory smiled, too. "Now we can go home."

— ₠ —

Yes, Mallory thought, *this is home.*

She smiled and sipped her coffee.

She was sitting in bed, propped on a pillow, watching Todd sleep—one of her favorite pastimes. He wasn't going to be up for a while, and after what she'd put him through, he needed rest, so Mallory set her coffee on the bedside table and opened her laptop.

She set up a Google alert for the Musée Marmottan.

"What are you doing?" Todd asked.

"Nothing. Go back to sleep."

"When you pull out that computer, I get nervous."

Mallory smiled. "One last thing I have to do." She turned to the keyboard and started typing.

"What are you up to?" Todd said, sitting up.

Mallory smiled again and turned the screen toward him. "It's an email. To our Swiss banker." The email directed their account manager to send an anonymous money order for five thousand euros to Laurence Front, Chalet Les Elves, Les Allues, France, on the first of every month for the duration of the occupant's natural life. With a dramatic stroke, Mallory hit the enter key. "NOW balance has been restored," she said. "Well, it will have been once I set up the same for Giles's family."

Todd grinned. "I like it." He kissed her. "Now, what about OUR family?"

Mallory laughed. "That's a HUGE adventure," she said. "And one that I know now I am ready for ... next year. For now, it's a beautiful morning and my work here is done. Let's have coffee on the deck."

As they stepped out into the sun, Rusty came up from the dock, holding up his morning's catch on a string. "LUNCH!" he called. "Barbecue. My place! Clara is bringing the beer and her new beau!"

They waved, smiled, and nodded.

"Perfect balance," Mallory said.

"No doubt," Todd said.

He reached for his wife's hand and, as the young couple sat in quiet contentment watching the morning light glint on the gentle waves, a sated pod of orcas sliced through the water on their way north.

The End

ACKNOWLEDGMENTS

Much of the inspiration for this novel comes from my life. They say "write what you know," so I did. Well, sort of.

I got the idea for the heist at a business meeting discussing the implementation of the euro. Because of the very euro-savvy Marion Blanchard, I was armed with enough information to be dangerous. That was in 1998. When I started writing, this was about current events; it has become historical.

My 42 vacations at Club Med provided the source material for Mallory's trip to Paradise Island and a plethora of characters and character names—the rest is fiction. Thanks to Florent Fourgerouse, Joe Templin, Sam Salant, Gustavo Latanzia, the Coltmans, Todd Allen, and Sherry Whalen.

The details for Canada and France sprouted from vacations there. They are real places and I have actually been in the spiral tunnels (in an enclosed railcar). I attended Syracuse University and lived in Fort Lee, NJ, for almost twenty years; some of my experiences there are reflected in the novel. I worked in technology for the last forty years, I love solving puzzles, and I am an artist. Although I imbued Mallory with some of those skills, make no mistake, I am not Mallory, despite the fact that we share a hair color (hers being natural).

No Doubt got its start in online workshops at The New School for Social Research and Gotham Writer's Workshops. Who knew when it finally got published we'd all be in online school due to a pandemic? To be honest, I took the online classes because reading your work to the class was standard procedure back then, and there was no way I was going to do that.

This book would not be on paper without the support of friends, pets, and family, many of whom were readers (excepting the pets). I can't remember them all (it has been over twenty years) but I want to call out a few.

Graciously, Scott Coulter wins the prize for reading the most drafts, which makes sense as he is the most voracious reader I know, and he consistently gave me actionable feedback that made the book more enjoyable and readable.

The incredibly talented Cindy Whitman served as my Development and Copy Editor. She encouraged and supported me throughout the second and final attempt to complete this. Always careful to retain my voice, her suggestions, edits, and vision made this novel immeasurably better. For that, I am grateful.

Apologies to the cats I have ignored at times because of this project. Folly, my honey-colored Persian, who was with me at the start, sat patiently on my lap during the initial drafts. My sweet Bengal kittens Mojo and Gijo did their best to distract me from my keyboard, often by sitting on it.

I have a great family filled with strong women—Alice, Edith, Jean, Virginia, Elizabeth, Marcia, Cindy, and Mikhaila, to name just a few. My stepdad Ralph Teller is the best step anyone could ask for; we were lucky mom was Membership Chairman at Parents Without Partners. She snagged you before anyone else could, Ralph.

Finally, I want to thank my Accountant, Terry Malaghan, for encouraging me to use my Company or close it down. Publishing this book is my answer to that.

ABOUT THE AUTHOR

Barbara Seith creates and performs one-woman musical comedy shows in NYC Cabarets including "Web Site Story" and "Magical Thinking." She is an accomplished watercolorist with paintings in collections across the globe. She studied fiction writing at Gotham Writer's workshops and the New School for Social Research. This is her first novel. She has an MBA, an MS in Information Systems, and worked in the Investment and Information Technology fields for over 30 years. She is widely traveled and draws from her destinations in her writing. Barbara lives in Westerly Rhode Island with her Bengal cat, Gijo, who tries to assist by sitting on her keyboard—unfortunately, he needs serious editing.